THE PEN

PENDRAGON

BOOK FOUR IN THE PENDRAGON CYCLE

STEPHEN R. LAWHEAD

AVONOVA

AVON BOOKS • NEW YORK

PENDRAGON is an original publication of Avon Books. This work is a novel. Any similarity to actual persons or events is purely coincidental.

AVON BOOKS
A division of
The Hearst Corporation
1350 Avenue of the Americas
New York, New York 10019

Copyright ©1994 by Stephen R. Lawhead
Cover illustration by Mike Posen
Published by arrangement with the author
Library of Congress Catalog Card Number: 94-19258
ISBN: 0-380-71757-3

First AvoNova Printing: September 1995
First Morrow/AvoNova Hardcover Printing: October 1994

AVONOVA TRADEMARK REG. U.S. PAT. OFF. AND IN OTHER COUNTRIES, MARCA REGISTRADA, HECHO EN U.S.A.

Printed in the U.S.A.

RA 10 9 8 7 6 5 4 3 2 1

For
Bruce

PENDRAGON
PRONUNCIATION GUIDE

While many of the old British names may look odd to modern readers, they are not as difficult to pronounce as they seem at first glance. A little effort, and the following guide will help you enjoy the sound of these ancient words.

Consonants—as in English, but with a few exceptions:

c: hard, as in *c*at (never soft as in *c*ent)
ch: hard, as in Scottish Lo*ch*, or Ba*ch* (never soft, as in *ch*urch)
dd: *th* as in *th*en (never as in *th*istle)
f: v, as in of
ff: f, as if off
g: hard, as in *g*irl (never *g*em)
ll: a Welsh distinctive, sounded as "tl" or "hl" on the sides of the tongue
r: trilled, lightly
rh: as if hr, heavy on the "h" sound
s: always as in *s*ir (never hi*s*)
th: as in *th*istle (never *th*en)

Vowels—as in English, but with the general lightness of short vowel sounds

a: as in father
e: as in m*e*t (when long, as in l*a*te)
i: as in p*i*n (long, as in *ea*t)
o: as in not
u: as in p*i*n (long, as in *ea*t)
w: as "double-u," as in vacuum or tool; but becomes a consonant before vowels, as in the name G*w*en
y: as in p*i*n; or sometimes as "u" in but (long as in *ea*t)

(As you can see, there is not much difference in i, u, and y— they are virtually identical to the beginner.)

Accent—normally is on the next to last syllable, as in Di-gan-hwy

Dipthongs—each vowel is pronounced individually, so Taliesin=Tally-essin

Atlantean—Ch=kh, so Charis is Khar-iss

Prologue

  WHAT IS THERE TO SAY OF ARTHUR after all these years?

His birth you know, and something of his end. You know his battles and his triumphs—those, at least, which the story-makers tell. And Aneirin's book is open to all who care to read it. Poor Aneirin, he labored so hard at his black book. Yet even Aneirin caught but the slightest glimpse of the man he meant to honor. It brought him misery in the end.

Arthur's fame, his very presence, like bright sunlight on clear water, obscured more than it revealed. So, you hear tales and think you know the man. You hear a part and think you know the whole. You hear one of a thousand speculations spun out by dim and dreary dreamers and think you have grasped the truth.

But do you know the highest achievement of Arthur's life? Do you know his sorest trial, when he stood alone on the battle plain and all Britain hung in the balance? Do you know how he labored to save the Kingdom of Summer from its deadliest foe? No?

Well, I am not surprised. In this ill-born age, much is forgotten that would best be remembered. Men always give over the best of their birthright for the small comfort of the moment; the treasures of the previous age are sold cheap, its wealth trampled underfoot. Alas, this is ever the way of things. And where Arthur is concerned much that should be known remains hidden. Because Arthur himself was hidden in those troubled early years.

But I, Myrddin Emrys, know all the lost and hidden tales, for I was with him from the beginning. And I stood beside him on his darkest day. A day unlike any other in the long history of our race—a day of deceit, and dread, and, oh, great glory. Yes! Great the glory. For on that day Arthur won the name he treasured above all others: Pendragon.

That is a tale worthy of its telling. Lost and forgotten it may be, but if you would hear such a tale, if you would learn the measure of a man whose name will outlast this sorry age, listen then. Listen and remember. For I tell you the truth, you do not know Arthur until you know the Forgotten War.

BOOK ONE

HIDDEN
TALES

1

 THEY SAY MERLIN IS A MAGICIAN, an enchanter, a druid of dark lore. If I were and if I were, I would conjure better men than rule this island now!
I would bring back those whose very names are charms of power: Cai, Bedwyr, Pelleas, Gwalchavad, Llenlleawg, Gwalcmai, Bors, Rhys, Cador, and others: Gwenhwyvar, Charis, Ygerna. Men and women who made this sea-girt rock the Island of the Mighty.

I need no Seeing Bowl, no black oak water, or fiery embers by which to perceive them. They are ever with me. They are not dead—they only sleep. Hear me! I have but to speak their names aloud and they will awake and arise. Great Light, how long must I wait?

I climb the green hills of the Glass Isle alone, and I wear a different name. Oh, I have so many names: Myrddin Emrys among the Cymry, and Merlin Embries to those in the south; I am Merlinus Ambrosius to the Latin speakers: Merlin the Immortal. I am Ken-ti-Gern to the small, dark Hill Folk of the empty north. But the name I wear now is a name of my own choosing, a simple name, of no consequence to anyone. Thus I guard and protect my power. That is as it should be. One day those who sleep will awaken, and those who guard their slumbers will be revealed. And on that day, the Pendragon will reclaim his long-abandoned throne. So be it!

Oh, I am impatient! It is the curse of my kind. But time will not be hurried. I must content myself with the work given to me: keeping Arthur's sovereignty alive until he returns to take it up once more. Believe me, in this day of fools and thieves that is no easy task.

Not that it ever was. From the very beginning, it took my every skill to preserve the Sovereignty of Britain for the one whose hand was made to hold it. Indeed, in those early years it was no small chore to preserve that small *hand* as well. The petty kings would have roasted the lad alive and served him up on a platter if they had known.

Why? Well you may ask, for the thing has become muddled with time. Hear me then, if you would know: Arthur was Aurelius' son, and Uther's nephew; his mother, Ygerna, was queen to both men. And while Britain had not yet succumbed to the practice of passing kingship father-to-son, like the Saecsenkind, more and more men had begun to choose their lords from the kin of previous kings, be they sons or nephews—all the more if that lord were well liked, fortunate in his dealings, and favored in battle. Thus, Aurelius and Uther, between them, had bestowed a prodigious legacy on the babe. For never was a sovereign better loved than Aurelius, and never one more battle-lucky than Uther.

So Arthur, yet a babe in arms, required protection from the power-mad dogs who would see in him a threat to their ambitions. I did not know Arthur would be Pendragon then. The way men tell it, I knew from the beginning. But no; I did not fully appreciate what had been given me. Men seldom do, I find. My own deeds and doings occupied me more than his small life, and that is the way of it.

Still, I recall the first faint glimmerings of the splendor that would be. Though it was a long time coming, when it finally broke, that glory blazed with a light so bright I believe it will shine forever.

Hear me now:

The nobles of Britain had been called to council in Londinium upon Uther Pendragon's death to decide who should be High King—and there were plenty who thought to take his place. When it became clear no agreement could be reached—

and rather than see a hissing toad like Dunaut or a viper like Morcant seize the throne—I thrust the Sword of Britain into the keystone of the unfinished arch standing in the churchyard.

"You ask for a sign," I shouted, my voice a roar of fury. "Here it is: whosoever raises the sword from this stone shall be the trueborn king of all Britain. Until that day, the land will endure such strife as never known in the Island of the Mighty to this time, and Britain shall have no king."

Then Pelleas and I fled the city in disgust. I could no longer abide the scheming duplicity of the small kings, so quit the council and rode with all haste to find Arthur. There was an urgency to my purpose, certainly. But even then I did not fully comprehend what drove me. I did not think him the future king, only a babe requiring protection—all the more since the High Kingship remained unresolved. Even so, I felt an almost overpowering desire to see the child. The bard's *awen* was on me, and I could but follow where it led.

Later, yes. Understanding would come in its own good time. But when I bade faithful Pelleas saddle the horses that day, I simply said, "Come, Pelleas, I want to see the child."

And so we flew from Londinium as if pursued by all those angry lords we had left behind. It was somewhere on the road to Caer Myrddin that I began to wonder if there was more to our speed than a simple wish to see Arthur.

Indeed, something in me had changed. Perhaps it was the strain of contending with the small kings. Or perhaps it happened when I joined the Sword of Britain to the stone. However it was, this I know: the Merlin who had ridden into Londinium so full of hope and anticipation was not the same Merlin who rode out. I felt in my soul that the course of my life had taken an unexpected turn, and that I must now steel myself for a far more subtle warfare than any I had known.

Alia jacta est, said old Caesar, a man who knew a thing or two about power and its perversities. For good or ill, the die was cast. So be it!

Leaving Londinium and the yapping of the petty kings behind us, Pelleas and I rode directly to Caer Myrddin. We traveled amicably; the road was good to us, and the journey pleasant. It does not need saying that our arrival on that wind-swept, wintry morning was a surprise. Loyal Tewdrig, who had faithfully shielded the child at my bidding, was still at the Council of Kings, and we were not expected.

Upon reaching Caer Myrddin we were met by the spectacle of young Arthur and the spitting cats. I saw the child clutching those two half-grown cats, one in each fist, and it seemed to me a sign. "Behold the Bear of Britain!" I declared, gazing at the chubby child. "A wayward cub, look at him. Still, he must be taught like any young beast. Our work is before us, Pelleas."

As we climbed down from our horses, Tewdrig's men came running to welcome us. Caer Myrddin—Maridunum in an elder time—seemed bursting with wealth, and I was pleased to see my old settlement so prosperous. Above the noise of our greeting, the clang of an iron hammer reached my ears and I remarked on it.

"Lord Tewdrig has found a smith," explained one of the men taking the reins from my hand. "And all day long we are kept running for him."

"Better that than running from the Sea Wolves!" declared another.

With their words in my ears, I stared at the child Arthur and listened to the ring of new-made steel in the air. I peered with my golden eyes beyond the thin veil of this worlds-realm into the Otherworld and I saw the shape of a man there, straight and tall, a big man, born to walk the earth as a king. Truly, this was my first premonition of Arthur's future. Believe it!

Presently, I came back to myself, and turned to greet Llawr Eilerw, battlechief and advisor to Lord Tewdrig, who held the caer in his lord's absence.

"Welcome, Myrddin Emrys! Welcome, Pelleas!" Llawr gripped us by the arms in greeting. "Ah, and good it is to see you both."

Just then we heard a shriek and turned. A young woman had appeared and was standing over Arthur, scolding him. She slapped his hands to make him release the cats, and the child cried out—in anger, not in pain—and reluctantly let them go. The woman stooped and gathered up the child, saw us watching, blushed, and turned hurriedly away.

"She has the care of the child?" I inquired.

"She has, Lord Emrys."

"What happened to Enid—the woman I brought?"

Llawr regarded me with a frankly puzzled look. "That *is* Enid—the very same you brought here. There has been no one else."

"Remarkable," I confessed, much surprised. "I would not have known her. She has changed, and much for the better."

"I will summon her, if you wish."

"Later, perhaps," I replied. "It is not necessary now."

"Of course," said Llawr, "forgive me. You have ridden far today and you are thirsty. We will raise the welcome bowl between us."

The beer was dark and frothy good. Tewdrig's hall was warm. The jar went around several times and we talked idly with Llawr and some of the men who had met us. Typically, no one would ask us outright why we had come; that was unthinkable. Although they knew we had attended the council, and must have been near to bursting with curiosity—*Who is the new High King? Who has been chosen? What has happened?* . . . Nevertheless, they respectfully allowed us to come to it in our own time.

"It has been quiet all year," Llawr said. "And now that winter is here, we need not worry. The snow will keep the Sea Wolves home."

"Indeed!" replied the man sitting next to him. "We have had more snow than last year. The cattle do not like it, though. It is not easy for them."

"But favorable for the crops," put in another.

"If this year's harvest is as plentiful as the last," observed Llawr, "we will have surplus grain to trade—even with our new storehouses."

"I noticed those," I remarked. "Four new granaries. Why? Is the caer growing so big?"

"We are growing, it is true," said one of the men, Ruel by name. "But Lord Tewdrig wants to begin storing more grain. 'The more we save now,' says he, 'the less we will want later.' So he tells us."

"And I agree with him," said Llawr sharply. "Times are uncertain enough. We can no longer live from one harvest to the next and be content. We must have a care for the future."

"There is wisdom in it," I told them. "In these evil days only a fool would trust past benefits to continue."

The men regarded me warily. Llawr forced a smile and attempted to lighten the mood. "Evil days? Surely, Emrys, things are not so bad as that. The Saecsens are gone, and the Irish have not raided all year. We have peace and plenty enough— any more and we will become soft and lazy." The others nodded agreement with their chief.

"Enjoy your peace and plenty, my friends. It is the last you will know in this life."

The smile faded from Llawr's face. The others looked on aghast. I was to have this effect on men more and more as the years went by.

But it is not possible for the Cymry to remain downcast any great length of time. The mood quickly lightened once more, and I, too, brightened as the talk turned to other matters. When the beer was gone, the others took their leave and we were alone with Llawr.

"Were Lord Tewdrig here," he said, "no doubt he would command a feast for you. But"—he spread his hands help-lessly—"I do not know when he will return."

This was Llawr Eilerw's attempt at guiding the conversation toward the reason for our visit. Now that we were alone, I was happy to oblige. "I think your lord will not be far behind us," I told him. "As you have no doubt guessed, we left the council before the others."

Llawr only nodded sympathetically—as if he knew all about the contrariness of kings, which no doubt he did.

"I might as well tell you," I continued, "since you will learn of it soon enough, and it is no secret in any event: there will be no new High King. The council was deadlocked. Agreement was impossible; no one was chosen."

"I feared such," sighed Llawr. "Evil days, you said. Aye! You were right." He considered this for a moment, and then asked, "What will happen now?"

"That remains to be seen," I replied.

Llawr might have asked, *And have you seen it?* But if the question was in his mind, he refrained. "Well," he said stolidly, "we have lived this long and longer without a High King, we will go back to the way we were before."

To this, I shook my head gently. "Nothing," I whispered, looking past Llawr and out through the doorway—as if into the very heart of the future itself—"*nothing* will be as it was before."

That night we ate simply and went early to our beds. After breaking fast the next morning, I summoned Enid to me. We waited for her in Tewdrig's chamber, talking softly. "It is good that we have come here," I told Pelleas. "This morning I am content, as I have not been for a long time."

"I am glad to hear it," Pelleas replied.

In a moment the young woman Enid appeared. She had brought Arthur with her and stood shyly on the threshold. She held the child close, as if afraid we would steal the infant away from her.

"Closer, Enid," I coaxed her gently. "Let me look at the two of you."

Deer-like, she moved cautiously forward, but only a step or two. I smiled and beckoned her. I can be persuasive when I choose to be: am I not of the Fair Folk, after all? Enid returned my smile and I saw the line of her shoulders relax slightly.

"When I saw you yesterday, I did not recognize you. You are grown a very pretty young woman, Enid," I told her. She inclined her head shyly. "And I am pleased to see that you have cared well for the child."

She nodded, but did not raise her eyes.

"What would you say if I told you he must go away?"

Enid's head snapped up and her eyes sparked fierce fire. "No! You must not! He belongs here." She held the child more tightly. Arthur struggled in her embrace. "I am . . . this is his home. He would not be happy somewhere else."

"You love the child so much then?"

"This is his home," Enid pleaded—as if this were the thing closest to her heart. "You must not take him away."

"He has enemies, Enid," I explained softly. "Or he soon will have—when they remember him. And they will not now be slow in remembering. He will not be safe here any longer. The more cunning among them will look for me and hope to find him."

Enid bent head and said nothing. She held Arthur's cheek against her own. The child tangled a small hand in her soft brown hair.

"I did not bid you here to frighten you," I said, rising. "I only wanted to ask after the child." I stepped close to her and the child reached out a hand to me, taking hold of the edge of my cloak. "Sit, please; we will speak no more of leaving just now."

We sat down together and Enid placed Arthur between her feet. The child toddled to Pelleas and stood gazing up at him. Pelleas smiled, reached down to take his hand, and, on a sudden inspiration, thought to test the child. Allowing Arthur to hold two fingers of either hand, Pelleas slowly raised his hands, pulling Arthur off his feet to dangle above the floor. The infant liked this game and squealed to show his pleasure.

Holding him off the ground, Pelleas started to swing the boy gently from side to side—Arthur did not let go, but started to laugh. Pelleas swung him faster, and Arthur began to giggle. Faster and faster, and Arthur roared with delight. Deliberately, Pelleas pulled one of his hands free. The child held on the more tightly with his remaining hand and laughed the harder. Though we had seen him with the cats the day before, and should have been prepared, still the lad's grip surprised me.

The strength in those pudgy little fingers was considerable.

At last, Pelleas lowered Arthur to the floor, to his loud protest: the babe wanted to play the game again! Kneeling before the child, I took one tiny hand in my own, opened it and looked into it as if I were gazing into a Seeing Bowl.

"That hand was made to hold a sword," Pelleas murmured.

I gazed long into the child's wide, innocent face and merry blue eyes, then turned again to my talk with Enid.

That was all. The briefest of instants, but from that moment, Pelleas never again spoke of Arthur as "the child," but used his proper name, or some form of it.

"I mean to discuss this with Tewdrig when he comes," I continued, turning my attention once more to Enid. "Meanwhile, do not worry over it. I may be mistaken. Who knows? As it is, there is no danger at present." I offered a smile by way of reassurance. "You may go now, Enid."

The young woman rose, caught Arthur up, as he clung to her knees, and walked to the door. "Enid," I said, rising and taking a step toward her as she stood half-turned in the doorway, "you have nothing to fear from me. I will not take Arthur from you. Nor will I allow any harm to come to either of you."

Enid inclined her head in solemn assent, then turned and hurried away. "I hope Tewdrig returns soon," Pelleas said. "I think he will have something to tell us."

"You are curious to know what happened at the council after our departure," I replied.

"In truth, I am," he admitted with a grin. "But my curiosity is more than idle, Emrys."

"Did I suggest otherwise?"

We did not have long to wait. Tewdrig arrived the next day. He was pleased to find us waiting for him, and wasted not a moment summoning his counselors to his chambers. "I want my advisors and I want my cup. I have ridden from one end of this island to the other and I am thirsty." He bade me attend him and went directly to his chamber at the far end of the hall.

Meurig, who had been in Londinium with his father, ordered beer to be brought. The young man muttered, "You would have thought his hall was afire! We have been in the saddle since before sunrise, Myrddin. I have eaten nothing from that time to this."

Just then Tewdrig's voice sounded from behind the curtain at the end of the hall. "Meurig! I am waiting!"

The young man sighed again, and made to hurry away. "Pelleas will see to the beer," I told him, sending my companion away with a glance. "Let us attend Lord Tewdrig."

"I tell you, Myrddin, you have stuck a sharp stick into the hive this time," Tewdrig said when he saw me. "Coledac was so angry he could not speak. Dunaut's face went black with bile, and Morcant—well, I thought the old snake would swell up and burst." He laughed mirthlessly. "What I would have given to see that!"

"I have never seen such anger that did not find release in swordblows." Meurig kneaded the back of his neck with his hand. "But you had vanished, Myrddin Emrys. What could they do?"

"I tell you the truth," said Tewdrig in solemn tones, "had you not left when you did, you would be a dead man now. I swear on Dafyd's altar, your head would be hanging above the gates of Londinium. Dunaut would have insisted."

"Do they know where I have gone?" I asked.

Tewdrig shook his head. "I do not see how anyone could know: I did not."

"Then we still have time," I replied, mostly to myself, for Pelleas appeared just then with cups and jars.

Meurig clapped his hands sharply. "Ah, here's the beer. Good! Fill the cups, Pelleas, and do not stop filling them until I call enough!"

"Time for what?" wondered Tewdrig as the cups were passed.

"For disappearing."

Tewdrig eyed me curiously. "A wise plan, no doubt. Where will you go?"

"To Goddeu in Celyddon. Arthur will be safer with Custennin."

"So," replied Tewdrig slowly. "You still believe the child a danger to himself."

"What can Custennin provide that we cannot?" demanded Meurig, wiping foam from his mustache. "Let them come. If there is any safe place in all the Island of the Mighty, it is Caer Myrddin. We can protect our own."

"No," I told him. "It cannot be that way."

"When will you go?" asked Tewdrig.

"Soon—depending upon what took place at the council," I answered.

Tewdrig raised his cup and gazed at me in disbelief. "Hmph!" he snorted. "That you know as well as I!"

"I mean," I explained, "will they abide the challenge of the sword?"

"Well, it was difficult. You did not make it easy for us." The chieftain drew a hand through his hair. "But in the end it was agreed that we would meet your challenge." Tewdrig shook his head slowly. "Oh, you were shrewd, Myrddin. I think Dunaut and Morcant and the others believed that they would win the sword through strength alone. The fools should have known it would not be as easy as that."

Tewdrig drank deep from his cup. When he lowered it again he laughed, saying, "You should have seen them! They might sooner uproot high Yr Wyddfa as budge that sword. It is planted fast—and I know: I tried my own hand. Twice!"

Meurig smiled ruefully and said, "I confess, Myrddin, I tried mine too. But had I been the giant Ricca himself, there was no removing that sword."

"You said they would abide the test—are you certain?"

"What else can they do?" said Tewdrig. "At first, they expected that one of them should obtain the sword and settle the thing for once and all. By the time they realized their mistake it was too late—we had all vowed to honor the decision of the sword. None of them guessed it would be so difficult, or they would not have sworn so. To back down now would be to admit defeat. Men like Dunaut would rather die than prove you right, Myrddin. So the thing stands."

"When no one succeeded," put in Meurig, "Bishop Urbanus declared that the lords should come together at the Christ Mass to try the sword again."

Yes, that was Urbanus: eager for whatever crust the kings would toss him. Well, if it brought them back to the church, so be it. I wanted nothing more to do with them; I saw a different path stretching before me now, and I grew eager to see where it would lead.

"Will they go, do you think?" asked Pelleas.

Tewdrig shrugged. "Who can say? It is a long time until next midwinter—much can happen. They may forget all about the sword in the stone." He laughed sharply again. "But, by the God who made me, Myrddin Emrys, they will not forget *you*!"

2

 As it happened, we stayed with Tewdrig through that spring, and would have stayed longer had not Bleddyn ap Cynfal, of Caer Tryfan in the north, come to visit. The Lords of Rheged maintained close alliance with the Lords of Dyfed in the south for mutual protection. Tewdrig and Bleddyn were kinsmen; they visited one another often to trade and discuss matters between them.

I did not know Bleddyn, but he knew me. "Greetings, Lord Emrys," Bleddyn said; he paid me the compliment of touching the back of his hand to his forehead out of respect. "I have long wanted to meet you. Indeed, I hope one day to show you the generosity of my hearth."

"Your offer is most kind, Lord Bleddyn," I replied. "Be assured that if I ever have need of a friend in the north, I will call on you."

"We are both kinsmen and friends," Tewdrig said. "Trust Bleddyn as you would trust me."

Bleddyn accepted Tewdrig's compliment with easy deference. "It may be, Lord Emrys, that you will require a northern friend sooner than you think."

I heard the subtle warning in his words. "How so?"

"They say Dunaut and Morcant are turning over every stone in their search for Uther's bastard. They say they are looking for the boy to protect him from all harm—though if you believe that, you are more fool than Urbanus."

"So, it begins at last. It has taken them longer than I expected to remember Arthur."

"As to that," Bleddyn replied, "Uther's queen has just given birth to a daughter. No doubt they merely waited to be certain which way to jump. Of course, it is nothing to me one way or the other. But if the child is Uther's, then it would shame us to allow either of those two to get his hands on the boy. It would be, I think, a brief fostering. Too brief, perhaps, for your liking—or the boy's."

In those days, many noble houses still observed the custom of fosterage where the young were raised in households of trusted kinsmen. The benefits of this practice were many—chief among them the strengthening and increase of bonds of kinship. Indeed, Bleddyn had brought his young son Bedwyr, a boy of four or five summers, to receive his first brief fostering at Caer Myrddin.

I considered his words carefully, and before I could reply, he said, "Come, Lord Emrys. Return with us when we go back to our lands. You will be welcome there."

"It is long since I sojourned in the north," I told him, making up my mind at once. "Very well, we will return with you. Let Morcant find us if he can."

Thus, when Bleddyn returned to Caer Tryfan, four more rode with him: Pelleas, Enid and Arthur, and I. We made camp along the way, avoiding as much as possible any contact with those whose lands we passed through, especially the strongholds of lords and chieftains. We might have received warmth and welcome, to be sure, but it was best that no one knew my movements.

Caer Tryfan proved a good place for us. If I had searched every glen in the north, I could not have chosen one better: protected by high crags of rock, sheltered both from the fierce northern winds and from the prying eyes of proud southern lords. Bleddyn made us welcome and showed himself the openhanded lord of a frank and generous people.

We settled there and made our home among them. Autumn, winter, spring, summer . . . the seasons progressed uneventfully. Enid continued to look after Arthur, and seemed well-pleased with her new home; in time she even married and began another family of her own. Arthur grew hale and healthy, going from strength to strength as he mastered the small tasks of childhood. Soon, it seemed, Bleddyn's youngest son returned and found a ready friend in young Arthur. Bedwyr—a slim, graceful boy, dark as Arthur was fair—bold shadow to Arthur's bright sun—took young Arthur under his care.

The two became constant friends, inseparable: golden mead and dark wine poured into the same cup, as they say. It was joy itself to see them at play. The fervor of their purpose was not the less for the fact that their swords were wooden. Oh, they were ferocious as mountain cats and just as wild. Each day they returned from their weapons practice trailing clouds of glory.

On account of the boys' friendship, Bleddyn delayed sending Bedwyr to his second fostering. But the day could not be held off forever. Sooner or later, Bedwyr and Arthur must be separated. For Arthur's sake, I dreaded the day. Then, just after harvest time in Arthur's seventh year, we took the boys to the Warriors' Gathering.

Once a year, the northern lords assembled their warbands for a few days to feast and hold games of skill at arms. It was for sport, of course, but it produced a considerable benefit in allowing the younger men a chance to try their skills against more experienced warriors, to test their mettle before actual battle—albeit in a sometimes painful way. Better a bruise from a friend, however, than a bloodletting at the hands of the foe. And the Saecsen kind were not known to leave off at a cry of "I yield!"

Bedwyr and Arthur had heard of the Gathering and began badgering me about it. "Please, let us go, Emrys," Bedwyr pleaded. "We will stay out of the way. You will not know we are there, and neither will anyone else. Say yes, Myrddin."

The Gathering was for warriors who had already joined a warband. Boys were not normally allowed to attend, and they both knew this. I was about to say them no on this account.

"It would be good for us to go," insisted Arthur seriously. "It would help with our training."

I could not argue with this logic; it was in nowise a bad notion. Still, it was not the tradition, and I was doubtful. "I will ask Bleddyn," I told them, "if you promise to abide by his decision."

Bedwyr's face fell. "Then we will be staying here *another* year. My father will never let us go."

"Another year?" I asked. "I do not recall you asking to go last year."

The young prince shrugged. "I wanted to ask, but Arthur said no. He said we were still too young, and it would do us no good to go. So, we waited to ask this year."

I turned to Arthur. "You have been waiting all year?"

He nodded. "It seemed better to me."

Later that night, I argued their case before Bleddyn. "Such thinking shows wisdom, and should be rewarded. Undoubtedly, they would learn much. I say they should be allowed to go."

Bleddyn considered this for a moment, and asked, "Assuming I allowed it, what would they do at the Gathering?"

"I honestly cannot say." I laughed. "But I do not think it would matter overmuch to them if all they did was stand aside and watch. And Arthur is right: it would help with their training."

"Next year, perhaps; they may be ready for it," Bleddyn allowed. "They are too young yet."

"So I told them, but Bedwyr informed me they have already waited a year." Bleddyn raised his eyebrows in surprise, so I explained quickly. "It is the truth. They wanted to go last year, but Arthur decided they would have a better chance if they put off asking until this year, when they were a little older. So they waited."

"Remarkable," mused Bleddyn. "Such patience and forethought is indeed rare in one so young. You are right, Myrddin, it should be rewarded. Very well, I will allow it. But you and Pelleas will have to look after them and keep them out of trouble. I have business with the northern lords."

So it was that Pelleas and I became shepherd to two young boys on shaggy ponies at the Warriors' Gathering.

Bleddyn's warband, the largest among the northern clans, numbered over a hundred, but the five lords who owed Bleddyn fealty each boasted warbands almost as large. Thus, with several hundred warriors in attendance, the Celyddon Gathering was by no means an insignificant affair. In later years, the Gatherings would draw whole settlements, clans, and chiefdoms to the spectacle. But at this time it was for noblemen and their warbands alone—*and* two young would-be warriors who had the king's let to attend.

Within Celyddon forest itself there was no clearing large enough to hold a gathering of any good size. But north of Celyddon, where the forest gave way once more to high, windswept moors, there were many broad valleys well suited for such a venture.

One bright autumn day, soon after the harvest was completed and secured for the winter, Bleddyn mounted his warband, and we started for the hills. For two days we rode through the forest, hunting in Celyddon's game-tracks along the way.

The warriors' spirits were high; there was much good-natured jostling and jesting. The forest echoed with the sound of laughter and song. At night the men built great fires and clamored for a tale of valor; I summoned my harp from Pelleas and sang to the throng. Bedwyr and Arthur were foremost among them, of course, bright-eyed and eager to the last, lingering note.

Early on the fifth day we reached the forest's end, and by dusk arrived at the gathering place: a wide valley formed at the meeting of two rivers. The sun had already dropped behind the high shoulder of the hill, but the sky was illumined with the soft, golden light peculiar to the northern country.

Suffused in this honeyed light, we crested a long ridge and

paused to look down into the valley. Three or four warbands were already there, and the smoke from their cooking fires hung silver in the still evening air.

At the sight of the fires below, blazing like new-fallen stars, the boys halted. "I never imagined there would be so *many*," Bedwyr gasped. "There must be ten thousand!"

"Not as many as that," I assured him. "But it is more than have gathered in many years."

"Why?" asked Arthur.

"Because the lords are increasing the warbands each year. We need more warriors to fight the Saecsens."

"Then it is good Bedwyr and I have come," he replied thoughtfully.

Bedwyr put the lash to his pony and rode ahead to join the first of the warriors making their way down to the valley. "Arthur!" Bedwyr shouted. "Come on! Hurry!"

The two boys slapped their horses to respectable speed and flew down the hillside, whooping like the *bhean sidhe*. "I hope we have not made a mistake," Pelleas said, watching the two boys streaking away. When Pelleas and I finally caught them again, they were sitting by a fire listening to a harper sing the Battle of the Trees. Since there could be no stirring them until the song was over, we settled down beside them cross-legged on the ground to wait.

The harper belonged to the household of one of Bleddyn's kinsmen, a man with a Roman name: Ectorius. This Ectorius held lands a little north and east of Celyddon on the sea, a difficult region to protect, since the Saecsens and their minions—Frisians, Angles, Jutes, and others—often sought landing there in one of the innumerable, nameless rock bays, coves, and inlets.

He was a big man with a fiery red beard and a head of frizzled, copper-colored hair which he wore bound at the nape of his neck. Though not tall, he stood on sturdy legs like oak stumps, and was reputed to have once crushed a cask by squeezing it in his thick-set arms. If his feats of strength were storied, his skill at arms was legendary. One swift stroke of his sword could part the purple from the head of a thistle, or as easily split a man in half.

Ectorius was as jovial as he was fearless. Never a man laughed but Ectorius laughed louder and longer. And no man enjoyed a good song more, nor beer, nor meat. If his taste was not particularly discriminating, at least it entertained the widest possible latitude of acceptance.

No harper, however mediocre, was ever turned from Ectorius' hearth. As long as the wretch could warble a tale to its conclusion, his patron was in bliss. In consequence, his generosity to bards was well known and he rarely wanted for a night's entertainment. The better bards vied for the opportunity of singing for him.

Thus, it was Ectorius' fire which had drawn the boys. There they were made welcome, and were not unnecessarily reminded of their youth.

The harper knew his tale, and he sang with fervor, if in a peculiarly tuneless voice. Still, no one seemed to mind—least of all Arthur and Bedwyr, whose faces glowed with pleasure in the light of the fire.

When, at last, the tale was finished, a cheer went up. The harper accepted his acclaim, bowing modestly to his listeners. Ectorius elbowed his way forward and clapped the singer on the back, praising him loudly. "Well done! Well done, Tegfan. The Battle of the Trees. . . . Splendid!"

Then the lord's eye lit on the boys, as we rose to return to our camp. "Och!" he called. "Hold, men! What have we here?"

"Lord Ectorius," I said, "allow me to present King Bleddyn's son Bedwyr, and his swordbrother, Arthur."

Both Arthur and Bedwyr saluted the lord, touching the backs of their hands to their foreheads in the age-old sign of respect.

Beaming broadly, he placed a big hand on each boy's shoulder and squeezed. "Stout lads. I give you good greeting! May you fare well while you are among us."

Bedwyr and Arthur shared a secret glance, and Arthur spoke up boldly, "We are not to take part, Lord Ectorius."

"We are not deemed old enough to try our skill," Bedwyr explained, throwing a dark look at me—as if *I* were the cause of all his worldly problems.

"Well, is that so?" replied Ectorius, beaming even more broadly. "Then perhaps we must change that. Come to me tomorrow and I will see what can be done."

The boys thanked him and then dashed away, willing to be abed now in order to awaken all the sooner next morning. Just before closing their eyes, both boys thanked me again for letting them attend the Gathering.

"I am glad we are here," yawned Bedwyr happily. "This will be a Gathering to remember. You wait and see, Artos."

"I am certain I shall never forget it," Arthur assured him solemnly.

To be sure, I do not think he ever did.

3

  IN THE DAYS THAT FOLLOWED, I saw nothing of Bleddyn. He was about business of his own with the other lords of the Gathering, as I was about mine. Seeing that no one took any interest in Arthur— to the northern chieftains he was just another young boy—I left the boys in Pelleas' care and rode alone into the hills. There, I sought out those whose eyes were keener than my own, and whose advice would be well worth the effort to obtain. Impossible for anyone else, it took me several days to raise so much as a trace of the Little Dark Ones.

Searching among the empty, windswept hills for the tracks I knew were there, I came upon a faint trail at dusk the second day. I made camp there so that I would not lose it again, and the next day followed the near-invisible trail along the ridge-tops to a Hill Folk settlement: the low humps of earth-covered dwellings, or raths, nestled in a secret fold of a secluded glen. But the settlement appeared deserted.

The day was far spent, so I made camp. Picketing my horse outside one of the dwellings, I went for water to the nearby stream at the bottom of the glen. I drank my fill, and then replenished my waterskin, and returned to camp—to discover my mount surrounded by seven diminutive men on shaggy ponies. I had neither heard nor seen them approach; they might have sprung from the heather banks around us. Bows and arrows in hand, they regarded me coldly, deep distrust in their dark eyes.

I raised my hands in greeting. *"Sámhneach, breáthairi,"* I called to them in their own tongue. "Peace, brothers." I touched my fingers to the faded blue fhain-mark on my cheek. *"Amsarahd Fhain,"* I told them. "Hawk Fhain."

They gazed at me and then at one another in amazement. Who was this tallfolk stranger who spoke their tongue and claimed to be a clan member? One of the men, no larger than a boy of twelve summers, slipped from his mount and advanced to meet me. *"Vrandubh Fhain,"* he said, touching his fhain-mark. "Raven Fhain."

"Lugh-sun be good to you," I responded. "I am Myrddin."

His eyes went wide and he turned to his brothers. "Ken-ti-Gern!" he shouted. "Ken-ti-Gern has come!"

At this the men threw themselves from their ponies and out from the raths streamed women and children. In the space of three heartbeats, I was surrounded by Hill Folk, all of them reaching with eager hands, touching me, patting me.

The she-chief of the clan appeared, a young woman dressed in soft deerskin with raven feathers stuck in her tightly plaited black hair. "Greetings, Ken-ti-Gern," she said, smiling with pleasure. Her teeth were fine and white against the hue of her tawny skin. "I, Rina, welcome you. Sit with us," she invited. "Share our meat this night."

"I will sit with you, Rina," I told her. "I will share your meat."

With much clamor and ceremony, I was conducted to the largest of the three dwellings. Inside, presiding over a peat fire, sat an old woman with long white hair and a face so wrinkled I wondered that she could see out from among the puckers. But she tilted her head and regarded me with a clear black eye as I knelt before her.

"Ken-ti-Gern has come to share meat," Rina told the woman, who nodded silently—as if she knew I would one day appear at her hearth.

"Greetings, Gern-y-fhain. Lugh-sun be good to you," I said, and reaching into the pouch at my belt, produced a small gold bracelet I had brought with me for such an occasion.

"Take this, Gern-y-fhain. May it bring you good trade."

The Wise Woman smiled regally, and accepted the gift with a slow bow of her head. Then, turning to Rina beside me, I produced a small bronze dagger with a stag-horn handle. Rina's eyes lit with innocent delight at the sight of the knife. "Take this, Rina," I said, placing the prize in her outstretched palm. "May it serve you well."

Rina's fingers closed over the dagger and she raised it before her sparkling eyes, clearly overwhelmed by her good fortune. In truth it was nothing—a bit of bronze and bone. A steel knife would have served her far better, but the Prytani fear iron and distrust steel; these rust, which suggests disease and decay to them.

Gern-y-fhain clapped her hands twice sharply, and one of the women brought a bowl filled with a pungent foaming liquid. The Wise Woman drank and then passed the bowl to me. I took the bowl between my hands and drank deeply, savoring the bittersweet bite of heather beer. The taste brought tears to my eyes as memory flooded through me; I remembered the last time I drank that fine heady brew: the night of my leave-taking from Hawk Fhain.

I drank as if partaking of my former life, gulping down the rich memory, and only reluctantly passed the bowl to Rina. When the ceremony of the welcome bowl had been properly observed, the clansmen who had been crowding at the entrance came tumbling into the rath. Children, small and brown, lithe as fawns, appeared in our midst. Young women, cradling tiny fuzzy-headed babies, crept in and settled behind the clan Wise Woman. By this, I understood I was being granted a glimpse of the fhain's treasure—their *eurn*, their child-wealth—a high honor for a tallfolk stranger.

The men began preparing our meal, cutting strips of meat from the haunch of a small deer. The strips were wound on wooden skewers, and the skewers stuck in the earth around the peat fire to be turned idly from time to time. While the meat cooked, we began talking about the year.

Winter had been wet, but not too cold, they said. And spring likewise. Summer was dryer, and warmer, and the sheep had fattened nicely. Raven Fhain had expected the Gathering to take place, and knew how many were in attendance and whence the participants had come. The Hill Folk did not seem to mind the warriors' presence. "They do not raid like the Seaxmen," Rina explained.

"Those of the Long Knife steal our sheep and kill our children," Gern-y-fhain added bitterly. "Soon our Parents will take us home."

"Have you seen the Long Knife?" I asked.

The Wise Woman made a small motion of her head. "Not this season," she said. "But they will return soon."

One of the men spoke up. "We have seen Picti boats flying north and east over the sea. The Cran-Tara has gone out, and the Seaxmen will come."

This was said without bitterness or rancor, but I could feel the weight of sorrow in the words. The Small Dark Ones could see their world changing, diminishing before their eyes. They believed, however, that their Parents—the Earth Goddess and her consort Lugh-sun—would summon them to their proper homeland: a paradise in the western sea. After all, they were the Firstborn of the Mother's child-wealth, were they not? They had a special place in her great loving heart; and she had prepared a homeland for them far, far away from the bedeviled tallfolk. They yearned for that day, which, considering the ever-increasing predations they endured, could not be long in coming.

I listened to the recitation of their troubles, and wished I could aid them in some way. But the only thing that would help would be a long season of peace and stability in the land, and that was something I had no power to give.

Pelleas watched over Arthur and Bedwyr while I was gone. Rising early to begin the day, and resisting sleep to the last possible moment to prolong their participation, the two greedy cubs roamed the Gathering: young wolves out to devour as much of warrior life as they could clamp jaws to.

They watched the trials of skill and strength with great eagerness and enthusiasm—mostly in the company of Lord Ectorius, who welcomed them as lords and sword brothers. Their high-pitched yelps of pleasure could be heard above even Ectorius' roar of acclaim whenever a skillful blow was struck or a fine maneuver accomplished. They never missed an opportunity to view the trials, and when there were none, they practiced on their own, imitating all they had seen.

The weather held good all the while, and as the Gathering drew to an end, I returned to camp and lingered near the boys—but out of their notice.

"What is it, master? Are you troubled?" Pelleas asked me once when he saw me alone. The boys were watching a trial of accuracy with the spear on the back of a galloping horse.

My eyes never left the scene before me. "No," I replied, shaking my head slightly, "I am not troubled. I am wishing there was a way for them to remain together." I gestured toward the two boys across the way.

"It would be well for them to remain together," Pelleas agreed. "They are very fond of one another."

"But it is not to be."

"No?"

"No. When the Gathering is over Bedwyr will go to Ennion in Rheged, and we must return to Caer Tryfan."

"Perhaps Arthur would rather go with Ectorius," Pelleas suggested lightly. He had been thinking about this, I could tell.

"It could be arranged," I mused. Bleddyn would have no objection, I thought, and judging from what I had seen of Ectorius, the boy Arthur would be welcome at his hearth.

"But that is not what kept you from camp these last days," Pelleas said, turning patient eyes on me.

"You are right, Pelleas," I told him. "The Picti and Scoti have sent out the Cran-Tara—the summons to war. In the spring they will amass their forces in the camps and then turn south to raid."

"Is it something you have seen?"

"It is something the First Children have seen." I told him

where I had been for the last few days: wandering among the hollow hills in search of the Little Dark People. "I was hoping to find some of them up here this summer, and I succeeded—rather, they allowed me to find them."

"Hawk Fhain?"

"No, another: Raven Fhain. But they recognized my fhain-mark." I touched the small blue spiral on my cheek—the reminder of my time with the Hill Folk—and could not help but smile. "They knew me, Pelleas; they remembered. Kenti-Gern—that is how I am known among them now. It means Wise Leader of the Tallfolk."

"They told you about the Cran-Tara? It is certain?"

"Their gern, the fhain's Wise Woman, told me, 'We have seen the ships flying east to Ierneland, and west to Saecsland—flying like gulls, like smoke disappearing over the wide water. We have heard the blood oaths spoken on the wind. We have seen the sun rise black in the north.' " I paused. "Yes, it is certain."

"But, master," Pelleas said, "I do not understand why this should prevent the boys from remaining together."

"What they must learn they will learn best alone," I explained. "Together, they would only hinder one another. Their friendship is a high and holy thing and it must be carefully conserved. Britain will need its strength in the years to come."

Pelleas accepted this. He was used to my reasons. "Would you have me tell them?"

"Thank you, Pelleas, but no. I will tell them." I turned. "But that will keep until tomorrow, I think. Come, we are to go and speak to Bleddyn and his lords; they are waiting."

Bleddyn received us in his tent, and offered us wine and barley cakes. After exchanging observations about the Gathering, Bleddyn introduced us to one of the lords with him, a nobleman named Hywel, who, after he had greeted us, said, "I bring a word which may be of value to you."

"Then you have my complete attention," I replied, settling myself to listen.

Hywel leaned forward. "We have seen barbarian encampments in Druim, and along the Cait coast. Five altogether—some of them large enough for three hundred men. We came upon them abandoned, though not long so. They appear to have been in use early this summer."

"The Cran-Tara," I said, nodding at this confirmation of the Gern-y-fhain's words.

"You know this already?" Bleddyn wondered.

"Only that the war summons has gone out. It remains to be seen if any will answer it."

Hywel regarded me for a moment. "I thought to be of service to you, but it seems that you are better informed than I."

"There is yet something you can do, if you are willing."

"You have only name it, Lord Emrys."

"Set watch in the spring and bring word to Caer Edyn if anything follows from the Cran-Tara."

"It will be done, Lord Emrys."

"Why Caer Edyn?" Bleddyn asked when we were alone once more.

"Because that is where I will be," I replied. Bleddyn expressed surprise, so I explained. "The time for Bedwyr's fostering is here, and Arthur must begin his own. I cannot praise your generosity highly enough, nor properly thank you for all you have done for Arthur."

"I mean to foster the lad," protested Bleddyn.

"And you would serve him well—of that I have no doubt," I told him. "These last years have been good ones, but we must not grow complacent. I think we must move on now."

Bleddyn accepted this, but was saddened nonetheless. "My loss will be Ector's gain," he said. "I feared this day would come. I had hoped to hold it off a little longer."

"I wish it could be otherwise," I replied. "But the world will not wait. We must move with it, or we will be left behind."

"I am sorry to see you go." The king regarded me sadly.

"You know the way to Caer Edyn," I told him. "You have but to saddle a horse and you are there. Though it would be best if you forgot you ever heard of Arthur—at least for a while longer."

The next day—the last day of the Gathering—I went to our tent at dusk as the boys sat eating their supper together before a small fire Pelleas had made. Arthur welcomed me warmly, and when I had settled down beside him on the ground, he said, "You have been scarce as boar feathers, Myrddin. And you have missed most of the trials. I watched for you. Where have you been?"

I put my arm around Arthur's shoulders. "I have been searching here and there, and learning the condition of the Island of the Mighty. Of spears and swords and mounted drills, I have had enough."

"Had enough?" wondered Bedwyr. "You never ride with the warriors, Myrddin."

I shook my head slowly. "You are right; I have not ridden with the warband for many years. But I did once."

Bedwyr's look of astonishment did not go unnoticed. "Is that so hard to believe?" I countered. "Then I will tell you something more difficult still: once I *led* the warband of Dyfed."

"Is that so?" Bedwyr was dumbfounded.

"I believe him," said Arthur staunchly.

"Well, I did not come to talk about *my* time as a warrior, but about yours." The boys leaned forward in anticipation. "Tomorrow the Gathering will end, and everyone will return to their homes—everyone except the four of us."

This was news. The boys glanced nervously at one another, and at Pelleas. What is this? What does it mean?

"A prince must receive fostering in a king's house." I stated the thing squarely. "Is this not true?"

"It is," replied Bedwyr, giving a sharp nod of assent.

"From time past remembering, brother lords have trained one another's sons. This is how it should be. You two are of an age to begin your training. Therefore, your fostering has been arranged."

The initial excitement created by this pronouncement faded

rapidly as the implications began to sink in. Bedwyr voiced his apprehension. "We will not be together, will we?"

Again, I shook my head slowly. "No. That would not be for the best."

How quickly the moods of the young can change. Black gloom settled over the boys. It was as if they had been told that they must choose between them which one to sell into Saecsen slavery.

Though it hurt me to do it, I let them live with their sadness for a moment before offering solace.

Then, speaking softly, I said, "You will be great lords, each of you. I have seen this. What is more, you will live out your days in one another's company. This have I seen as well.

"Therefore, take heart. Apply yourselves to the tasks set before you and the time will pass more quickly. Soon enough you will ride together: true sword brothers. And the world will tremble at your passing."

This pleased them enormously. Arthur jumped to his feet, and, lacking a sword, raised his fist in the air. "Hail, brother! Let us go gladly to our new homes, since it is for our benefit."

Bedwyr, on his feet now, too, echoed this sentiment. "Remember," Arthur continued, "we will meet again at next year's Gathering."

"And the next after that!" cried Bedwyr. If they were pleased before, they were delighted now. "Hail, Arthur!" they cried noisily, fists in the air. "Hail, Bedwyr!"

I rose to my feet. "Well said," I told them. "Each year at the Gathering you shall come together to ride and feast—until the day when you will no longer be separated."

The next morning when the arrangements were formally explained, the boys accepted their elders' decisions with good grace. As the camp was being struck and the first warbands began their homeward journeys, the boys lingered with one another, pledging and repledging their friendship until Bedwyr was summoned to leave.

"I must go," said Bedwyr, his voice trembling slightly. "I will miss you, Artos."

"And I will miss you, Bedwyr."

"Lord Ectorius has a good warband. You will do well."

"And Lord Ennion's warband is second to none other. Take care to learn all you can." Arthur clapped a hand on Bedwyr's back.

Bedwyr's lower lip quivered and he threw his arms around Arthur. The two boys hugged one another for a moment, before remembering their dignity. "Fare well, Arthur," Bedwyr said, sniffing back a tear.

"Fare well, brother," returned Arthur. "Until next year!"

"Until next year!"

Ennion departed soon after. Arthur rode to the crest of the hill that he might watch them out of sight. In a little while, I went to fetch him and found him there, watching still, although Ennion and his warband, and Bedwyr, were gone.

"It is time, Arthur. Lord Ectorius is taking his leave now." He made no reply. "The year will pass quickly," I told him, mistaking his silence. "You will see Bedwyr again before you know it."

He turned to me, his blue eyes solemn and dark as slate. "I did not realize until just now that you and Pelleas would not be going, too. Somehow, I thought we would be together always. . . ."

"But we will be together," I replied. "At least much of the time."

He brightened at my words. "You mean it, Myrddin? Really? What of Pelleas? Will he join us, too?"

"Of course."

Arthur became suddenly thoughtful. "You said we would be lords. Did you mean me, too?"

The uncertainty of his birth lurked behind his words: he did not know his father.

"You have been with Myrddin a long time, lad. Have you ever known me to speak a false prophecy, or to jest in such matters?"

My answer delighted him. Beaming, he slapped the reins across his mount's withers and rode back down the hill, eager to begin his new life in Ectorius' stronghold by the sea.

I rode back, but more slowly, ashamed of myself for dodging his innocent question. As I had spoken the words they seemed true. But why did I hesitate now? Why not tell him of my dreams for his future? Why not lay the vision before him and let him see the possibilities for himself?

The temptation was strong, but no. No. The time was not come. He was too young yet, too young to shoulder such a burden. Once he took it up, he would carry it to the grave. Let him live free a little longer.

4

  CAER EDYN SAT ON A BLUFF OVER-looking a broad expanse of shining water called Muir Giudan, an east-ward-looking bay that opens onto what had come to be known as the Saecsen Sea. Lord Ectorius ruled his realm with a steady hand. Fair, generous, as ready for a feast as a fight, Ectorius was descended from a long line of Roman officers—centurions mostly, and a tribune or two as well—who had served the coastal garrisons of the eastern shores.

Ectorius was carrying on his family's ancestral trade: watching the sea for the dark, knife-shaped hulls of enemy ships.

Bluff Ector served a king, however, rather than a legate; his service was for life, not the twenty years of the Roman army; and instead of Mithras of the legionaries, he worshiped the Christ of the British saints. Apart from these minor distinctions, life for Ectorius was little different from the life his Roman forefathers would have known.

His stone-walled stronghold lay three days' journey from the place of Gathering. It was a fine ride through the Eildon hills north and east to the sea. Arthur stayed near me all the way; not from any apprehension, I think. He merely seemed glad of familiar company. We talked about the things we had seen at the Gathering: the warriors, their skill with the various weapons, the differences in styles of fighting.

Arthur had an eye for subtlety—a quality not usually associated with him in later times. But he could tell the difference between a squared bit and a round one in a horse's mouth by the way the animal behaved as its rider maneuvered on the field. Or from which kind of wood a spear shaft was made by the way it sounded when struck on a shield.

Talking to Arthur was not like talking to another boy his age. At eight, he had already acquired a wide and practical knowledge of many subjects. He could read and write good Latin, and speak it well enough to make himself understood by even the most demanding cleric.

He also knew the craft and lore of wood and field: the various trees and shrubs and their uses; the proper herbs for simple medicines and potions; the edible wild plants and where they might be found; all the birds and animals and their habits . . . and much else besides.

I was responsible for this, yes. From our earliest days with him, Pelleas and I had schooled the boy in lore of every kind, filling his head with the wonders of the world around him. And Arthur, little Arthur, took to it as he took to everything else: with a fever of passion and determination.

In this, his breeding told. He had inherited all of Aurelius' ardor and intensity, and Ygerna's quick intelligence. He also had a generous portion of Uther's dauntless tenacity—which sometimes showed itself as courage, and otherwise as blunt bullheadedness.

He also possessed Aurelius' curious innocence in battle: the fearless forgetting which led him to attempt and to achieve the impossible. This would, of course, come to be noticed much later. But even now he could be seen to exhibit a certain disregard for his own safety. I recognized it well, and knew its source, for I had ridden with Aurelius.

In anyone else it would have been called carelessness. Or foolishness, more like. But it was never that. Arthur simply did not feel *afraid*. Daring, bravery, boldness, valor—these are qualities of overcoming fear.

What is it, then, when there *is* no fear?

As I say, we talked of the Gathering and of the year to come. I could see that Arthur was determined to make the best of his necessary exile. He liked Ectorius, and respected him as a ruler and warrior; he was eager to learn the skills Ectorius could teach him.

At dusk on the third day, we came upon Caer Edyn, approaching from the west along a wide, winding glen. At the end of the valley we began the ascent to the bluff. The fortress stood on the bare hump of an enormous rock, overlooking the better part of the bay far below.

Rock walls topped by a timber palisade and ringed by a great, deep ditch bore testimony to the fact that Caer Edyn had seen more than its share of Saecsen fighting—and survived.

In the golden light of a fiery northern sunset, the stone and timber shone as bronze; solid, invincible. And although the land around the fortress appeared comfortable enough—sheltered as it was behind the high sea bluffs—I knew the northern realm climes could be harsh and unforgiving.

Circling seabirds and the uncluttered view of the wide, empty sea made Caer Edyn appear a lonely place. Arthur felt it, too, withdrawing into himself as we climbed the narrow hill track leading to the stronghold. But any melancholy was instantly dispelled upon reaching the summit.

"Myrddin!" Arthur motioned me to him. "Look!"

I rode to him and we sat gazing over the long, curving swath of blue water that formed Muir Giudan. Across the bay, wooded hills, steep and dark, came down to the water's edge. Away to the north we could see smoke from a small shoreside settlement threading into the air.

"Peanfahel," one of the warriors told us. He had stopped beside us to take in the view. "And beyond it there," he said, pointing farther north and west, "that is Manau Gododdin. The Saecsen always want to settle there. We have fought in Gododdin many times, and will again."

The man continued on his way to the caer. Other warriors were hurrying by. "What do you think of your new home, Arthur?" I asked.

"It suits me, I think. It is more open than Caer Tryfan— more like Caer Myrddin." He turned in the saddle to face me.

"And here I am not so far from Bedwyr. Perhaps we might see each other sometimes."

"Perhaps," I allowed. "But travel to and from Rheged is still very difficult."

"Well, sometime . . . maybe . . . " He looked out across the bay and at the dark hills on the other side, as if he were looking at the Orcady Islands and wondering how to get there. Presently, he lifted the reins, coaxing his pony forward, and we continued on to the caer.

Ectorius was waiting for us as we entered the stone-paved yard. "Welcome, my friends!" he called, his voice ringing off the stone. "Welcome to Caer Edyn, the last outpost of the Empire!"

So began our long sojourn in the north.

That first night in Caer Edyn Arthur missed Bedwyr sorely. It had been years since either of them had been without the other. He slept poorly, and woke early, finding his way to the stables to see his pony. Satisfied that all was in order, he returned and with slow steps made his way to the hall where Ectorius waited with a surprise.

"My son, Caius!" announced Lord Ectorius with noticeable pride as he presented a sturdy, stocky youth a few years older than Arthur. The boy scowled, uncertain whether to trust us. "This is Arthur," Ectorius told his son. "He will be living here from now on. Make him welcome, son."

"W-welcome, A-A-Arth-thur," muttered Caius. Then he turned and hobbled off quickly, all but dragging his right leg behind him.

"As a babe, the lad fell from a rock and broke his leg," explained Ectorius gently. "The bone set poorly, so Caius has limped ever since." His father did not mention the stutter— an affliction noticeable only when he became excited, frustrated, or, as now, anxious.

Clearly, Ectorius hoped for the best between the boys. "It is lonely for the lad," he explained. "They will learn a liking for one another, I think. Yes."

I, too, wondered how Arthur would get on with the surly Caius. But since there is no force in all the world that can make friends of two boys who do not want to be friends, I let the thing rest.

As it happened, the matter was settled quickly enough. For later that same day, Arthur induced a most reticent Caius to show him something of the land round about the caer.

They rode to the little shoreside settlement at Peanfahel, and on the way, Arthur learned a remarkable thing about his reluctant new friend: the boy could ride like a young god, or like the *bhean sidhe* of the hollow hills, whose horses were descended from the steeds of the Everliving on the Glass Isle in the Western Sea.

Caius had more than made up for his infirmity by learning to ride with such skill and grace that, once in the saddle, he became a wholly different person—one of those half-man–half-horse beings of the Latin books. He could coax miracles from any horse he happened to light upon; even the sorriest beast somehow performed better than its best with Caius on its back.

As the day was warm, the two stopped in the settlement to water their horses at the ford above the shore. Some children from the place were playing nearby and when the boys rode up they gathered around and, consequently, noticed Caius' crippled leg.

That was all it took. Instantly, they began to taunt and jeer. "Cripple! Cripple!" they called, mocking his halting gait. They laughed loud and Caius lowered his head.

Arthur watched for a moment, appalled. Never had he witnessed such calculated cruelty. The jeering was bad enough, but when the older boys began throwing rocks at Caius, Arthur decided the thing had gone too far.

Balling his fists, he loosed a wild whoop and charged head down at the biggest ruffian, striking him squarely in the stomach. The startled youth fell on his back, legs kicking, with Arthur on his chest. Though the boy had three years' advantage, Arthur's size all but evened the contest.

It was a short scuffle, all told. The breath driven from his lungs—and Arthur sitting on his chest so that he could not draw another—the youth, fainting, lost consciousness for a moment.

The mocking stopped. The children looked on in astonishment. Arthur rose slowly to his feet, and, glowering with rage, demanded to know if anyone else had anything to say. No one did. The rascal came to and ran away; the rest quickly scattered. Caius and Arthur remounted and continued along the shore.

By the time they returned to the caer later in the day they were the best of friends, and Arthur had given Caius' name a Celtic cast. He was to be Cai ever after.

I suppose because he openly admired Cai's prowess as a horseman, it never occurred to Arthur to make fun of the way he walked or spoke—something too many others did, and with disheartening regularity.

But never Arthur. And for this, Arthur was rewarded with Cai's undying loyalty and devotion.

Cai, God bless him! He of the flame-bright hair and red-hot temper; whose pale blue eyes could darken as quickly as the summer sky above Caer Edyn with the storm's sharp fury; whose rare smile, when he gave it, could warm the coldest heart; whose brassy voice carried like a hunting horn through the glens as it would one day rally men on the field of battle . . . Cai, the dauntless; Cai, the dogged, willing to strive and go on striving long after another would have given up the fight for lost.

We spent those first bright days of autumn discovering Caer Edyn and surrounding lands. Arthur made a game of it: seeing how far he could ride out of sight of the Rock, as he called it, before attempting to find his way back. Pelleas and I rode with him sometimes; more often, Cai went.

It was, he quickly learned, a strange land, full of surprises. The first was the large number of people living in the narrow, creased valleys that seamed the rugged hills. There were hundreds of these glens, each with its own small holding or settlement. We soon came to expect them: a few rock-and-turf houses; long streamside fields for rye, oats, and barley; a pen for cattle and sheep; the round hump of a stone granary; an oven or two burning wood or pungent peat. Little clumps of people were sown all through the land, separated one from the other by the high, bleak hills.

There were woodlands aplenty, as well, and the hunting was good: boar and bear, hart, deer, wild sheep and hare, and various kinds of fowl—some, like the grouse, not found in the southlands. Eagles and hawks abounded, and there were fish of endless variety from river, lake, and sea.

In short, Arthur very soon came to view Caer Edyn and its lands as something of a paradise—and certainly less a place of exile than he first expected. It would have been perfect, but for the unspeakable winter.

However we weathered it and revelled in the short, brilliant spring. In all, Caer Edyn provided a splendid home for a boy. At my prodding, Ectorius sought and secured the services of a tutor for Arthur and Cai—one of the brothers from the new-built abbey at Abercurnig. Thus the Latin resumed, as well as reading and writing, under the indulgent rule of Melumpus.

Added to this, Ectorius began instructing Arthur in king-craft: all the skills necessary to the sustaining of a kingdom and the effective leadership of men. Weapons practice continued, growing ever more demanding as the lads' skill increased.

Thus life settled into an easy rhythm of leisure and learning, work and play. The seasons passed and Arthur ceased longing for Bedwyr. He applied himself to his various lessons with diligence, if not fervor, becoming an able scholar.

In all, it should have been a good time for me. But I was not content. Thoughts of the Cran-Tara gnawed at me, and I could not shake them. As winter closed on us, I began to feel trapped on the rock of Caer Edyn. There were, I imagined, events taking place in the wider world—events of which I knew nothing. After years of activity, my enforced seclusion chafed me now. Day by day, I receded into myself, keeping my own counsel. And on the cold, gray days of wind and rain

I paced the hall before the hearth, my mood, I fear, as cheerless as the day.

At last, it came into my mind that the small kings, led by Dunaut and Morcant, had discovered our hiding place and were even now moving against us. Although I knew Ector would receive ample warning of any enemy moving along the borders of his realm, I worried over this, and fear—irrational, yes, but potent all the same—coiled around my heart.

Pelleas watched me and worried. "Master, what is it?" he asked at last, unable to bear my stormy restlessness any longer. "Will you not speak?"

"I an suffocating here, Pelleas," I told him bluntly.

"But Ectorius is a most generous lord, he—"

"That is not my meaning," I snapped. "I am troubled and can get no peace. I fear, Pelleas, we have made a mistake in coming here."

He did not doubt me; neither did he understand. "We have had no word of any disturbance in the south. I might have thought that would cheer you."

"Far from it!" I cried. "It has only made me suspicious. Make no mistake, Dunaut and his ilk never rest. Even now they are scheming how to seize the throne—I can feel it." I struck my chest with my fist. "I feel it and it fills me with *fear*."

The fire fluttered as the wind gusted under the door. A hound beside the hearth lifted his head and looked around slowly, then lay his muzzle back on his big paws.

A chance occurrence, signifying nothing; I do not believe in omens. Still, I felt a chill touch my spine, and it seemed as if the light in the hall dimmed.

"What will you do?" Pelleas asked after a moment.

A long silence stretched between us. The wind moaned and the fire cracked, but the strange feeling did not return. An ocean wave flung upon a rock, it had receded once more.

When I made no answer, Pelleas said, "What is your fear: that the petty lords will find us here, or that they no longer care to search?"

Staring into the fire, I saw the flame-shapes shifting and

colliding and it seemed to me that forces were gathering, power was massing somewhere and I must find it to direct it aright. "Both, Pelleas. And I cannot say which disturbs me more."

His solution was simple: "Then we must go and see how matters stand in the south. I will ready horses and provisions. We will leave at daybreak."

I shook my head slowly, and forced a smile. "How well you know me, Pelleas. But I will go alone. Your place is here. Arthur needs you."

"Far less than he needs you," he replied tartly. "Ectorius is most competent and able. He will discharge his duties toward Arthur with all honor—whether we remain or no."

In truth, I did not actually care to spend a winter in the wild alone, so I relented. "Have it your way, Pelleas. We go! And may God go with us."

5

  WE LEFT CAER EDYN AS SOON AS Pelleas had satisfied himself with his preparations. Ector advised us to wait until the trails had thawed once more, but spring always comes late to the north, and I dared not wait until the snows and rains had stopped. Arthur asked to go, but was not disappointed to stay behind.

The day of leaving dawned cold and gray, and did not improve. We camped in the lee of the hill that night, rose early and continued on our way. The sky did not clear, and the wind grew biting, but the snow held off and we were able to press on, wending our slow way through the glens and over the smooth, cold hills—if more slowly than I would have liked.

Prudence demanded discretion; Arthur's continued safety depended on my ability to keep his identity and whereabouts hidden. Secrecy was my most potent ally, but since we could not shun every settlement and holding, nor avoid every other traveler, I made myself as invisible as possible. Thus began what was to become my custom when moving about the land: I would adopt various guises to ease my passage among men: now an old man, now a youth, now a shepherd, now a beggar, now a hermit.

I would embrace humility and wear it like a cloak. Among unsuspecting men, I would hold commerce with the humble things of the world, and so pass unseen and unmarked through the Island of the Mighty. For men seldom heed the humble things that surround them; and what they do not heed, they do not hinder. In this way, we passed through the north country and into the southlands below the Wall, striking an old Roman road just south of Caer Lial. The road was still in good condition and Pelleas marveled that this should be so. "Why?" I asked him. "Did you think these paving stones would vanish with the Legions? Or that the Emperor would roll up his roads and take them back to Rome?"

"Behold!" Pelleas cried, raising a hand to the much-encroached-upon track stretching straight and narrow before us. "Our path is made smooth for us; the way is clear in the wilderness." I smiled at his allusion. "This suits our purpose perfectly, Emrys. We will travel more quickly, and our passing will not be marked."

It was true, the stone-paved track remained smooth and unbroken as ever; and though shrubs, small trees, and thickets of all kinds now crowded so close as to hide it from view, the undergrowth had not obscured the road. And if other men had long ago forsaken the old roads, preferring more open trails, this same close-grown vegetation would allow us freedom in our movements. We would travel without being seen—appearing here and there when we chose, or when need arose, then disappearing once more . . . only to reappear somewhere else.

I had to agree, the old Roman roads seemed heaven-made for us, and I praised the Great Light for it. Often I have noticed that when a way is needed, a way appears. This is not to be wondered at, neither is it to be ignored.

We journeyed then with lighter hearts, though deprived of other human company for the most part, since we stayed away from settlements and the hearths of men, camping alone, sleeping under the naked sky at night. Occasionally, we ventured into a settlement along the way for provisions. Everywhere I listened to what men said and I weighed their words carefully, sifting all I heard for any hint of the trouble I feared.

By the time we reached the southlands, warmer weather betokened an early spring, and soon soft air soughed in new-budded trees; blossoms quickly appeared, seeding the drifting currents with sweet, heady fragrance. Water ran high; river, lake and stream swelled to overflowing. In a little while, the hillsides blushed shocking color: yellow, crimson and blue. The sun wheeled through dappled, cloud-crowded skies, and the moon steered her bright course through star-filled night.

Peace seemed to have claimed the land, but I drew no comfort from this. Indeed, the farther south we rode, the greater my anxiety grew.

"I am yet uneasy, Pelleas," I confessed one night over the fire. "I mislike what I sense here."

"That is no surprise," he told me. "We would not have come this far otherwise. Perhaps it means we are nearing the end of our search."

"Perhaps," I allowed. "Morcant's lands are nearby. I would give my harp to know what he is about."

"There will be a settlement close, no doubt. Perhaps someone will tell us something."

The next day we set out for the nearest settlement, and found one of goodly size straddling the ford of a swift-running river. A muddy track linked the two halves, whose houses were mud-and-twig thatched with reed, poorly made; but the two large cattle enclosures boasted goodly wealth.

Wearing the guise of a wandering priest—a long, shapeless robe of undyed wool which Pelleas had purchased for me at an abbey along the way, my hair in disarray, my face smudged with dirt and soot—I surveyed the place from the side of an overlooking hill. "This will do. The people here are trading cattle; they will know what is happening in the world hereabouts."

As I approached the holding, the skin at the nape of my neck prickled to danger. I leaned close to Pelleas to tell him of my fear, but he waved me to silence and reined his horse to a halt. Rising in the saddle, he called out in a loud voice, "Is anyone here?"

We waited. No sound came from any of the dwellings. Presently, Pelleas called again. "We are waiting, and will not leave until we have watered our horses."

I imagined sly whispers behind the mud walls around us: insinuations, quick and sharp, flung like knives at our backs.

"Perhaps we should go elsewhere," Pelleas suggested under his breath.

"No," I replied firmly. "We have come here in good faith, and I will not be put off."

We waited. The horses snorted and chafed the ground impatiently.

At last, when I thought we must move on, a thick-necked man with an oaken club appeared. Stepping from the low doorway of the center house, he straightened and strode forth with a swagger.

"Greetings," he said, more threat in the word than welcome. "We do not see many of your kind hereabouts. Travel is difficult these days."

"Agreed," I answered. "If need were not great, we would not trouble you for hospitality."

"Hospitality?" The word obviously had no meaning for him. His heavy-lidded eyes narrowed with suspicion.

Pelleas feigned indifference to the man's rudeness and swung himself down from his saddle. "We ask a little water for the animals, and for ourselves. Then we will continue on our way."

The man bristled. "Water is all you get, mind."

"God's precious gift—we ask nothing else," I replied, smiling loftily.

"Huh." The man turned abruptly. "This way." Pelleas gave me a dark look and fell into step behind him. I gathered the reins and led the horses. We were shown a stone trough filled by a trickle from a hillside spring through an ancient clay conduit.

Pelleas drank first, cupping water into his hands. When he finished, I bent down and drank. "Sweet the blessings of God," I said, drying my hands on the front of my robe. "Thank you for your kindness."

The man grunted and swung the club against his leg.

"We have been in the north," I said, as Pelleas started watering the horses. "Whose lands are these?"

"King Madoc's," the man spat.

"And is he a good king?"

"There's some as would say that—though some would say otherwise."

"And what would *you* say?"

The brute before us spat again, and I thought he would not answer. But he was merely warming to his tale. "I say Madoc is a fool and a coward!"

"The man who calls his brother fool stands in danger of God's wrath," I reminded him. "Surely, you must have good reason for such harsh judgment."

"Good reason right enough," snorted the man. "I call him fool who lets another steal his lands and lifts not a hand to stop the thief! I call him coward who stands by and sees his son slaughtered and does not demand the blood price."

"This is a serious matter. Land stolen, a prince killed: who has done these things?"

The man grimaced in disgust for my ignorance. "Who else?" he sneered. "Morcant of Belgarum, of course! Two summers ago it began, and since then it's every holding must defend itself, for we can expect no protection from Madoc."

I shook my head sadly. "It grieves me to hear this."

"Ha!" barked the man scornfully. "Let your grief defend you! I mean to hold what I have." His lips curled in an ugly sneer. "You've had your water, now get you gone from here. We have no use for priests."

"I could give you a blessing—"

The man hefted the club in reply.

"So be it." I shrugged and took the reins from Pelleas' hand. We mounted and rode back the way we had come. Once out of sight of the place, we stopped to consider what we had learned.

"So Morcant makes war on his brother kings," I mused.

"For what purpose? A little land, a little plunder? It makes no sense."

"Will you go to Madoc?"

"No, I can do nothing there. Morcant has set strife among his neighbors, and I would know why. As I am a priest today, we will do the priestly thing, and seek guidance from a higher power."

The Belgae are an ancient tribe whose seat is Caer Uintan. Making peace with Rome allowed the Belgae to establish themselves in the region; old Uintan Caestir prospered and grew large serving the Legions. But the Legions were long gone now, and the city shrank in upon itself—like an overripe apple withering where it had fallen.

Like Londinium to the southeast, Caer Uintan maintained a wall of stone around its perimeter. But Caer Uintan's *vallum* was never as high as Londinium's because it was never as needed; it served as a reminder of the Belgae strength, rather than as a real defense.

So Pelleas and I were both amazed coming upon the city at dusk: the wall of Caer Uintan had grown tall indeed. And a deep ditch had been dug below the wall to make it higher still. The city of Caer Uintan was now a fortress.

The gates were already closed and barred for the night, although the sky was still light. We halted on the narrow causeway before the gates and called to the gatesmen. We were made to wait, and then answered rudely.

The surly gatesmen were loath to admit us, but as I claimed business with the church—the church Aurelius had built for the city—they grudgingly, and with much cursing, unbound the gate and let us in, lest they fall foul of Bishop Uflwys, whose sharp wit, and sharper tongue, was renowned in the region.

"Shall we go to the church at once?" Pelleas asked as soon as we passed through the gate. The streets of the city were dark with shadows and smoke from the hearth fires beginning to glimmer behind the thick glass of narrow windows. Caer Uintan was a wealthy city still; those of its people who could maintain life in the old Roman style lived well.

"Yes, I would speak with the bishop," I replied. "Uflwys may have a word for us."

Bishop Uflwys was a tall, stern man of deep thoughts and hard-won convictions. It was said that those who came to Uflwys seeking God's forgiveness for their sins and crimes left his presence much chastened, but much forgiven also. As bishop he feared neither kings on earth nor demons in hell, and he treated all men the same—that is to say: bluntly.

He had come to Caer Uintan to help build the church and stayed to guide it with a strong hand. The church, like its leader, stood aloof from the world, unadorned, bespeaking a firm and steadfast faith. I was interested in what he would say of Morcant.

The bishop received us cordially; he still held some small respect for me, it seemed, for he had loved Aurelius. Indeed, Uflwys appeared genuinely glad to see us. "Merlinus! Dear brother, I hardly know you!" He rose as we were announced and came to us holding out his arms. I met him and gripped his arms in the old Celtic greeting. "Come, come, sit with me. Are you hungry? We will eat. I have often wondered where you had gone. God bless the sight of you! Why are you dressed like a beggar?"

"Glad I am to see you, Uflwys. In truth, I did not think to come here. But now that I see you, I believe that my steps have been directed here from the first."

"Where the good Lord leads, his servants must follow, eh? And from the look of you, I would say you were led a merry chase. What are you about, Merlinus?" Uflwys indicated my clothing. "Not taken holy vows at last?"

Before I could explain, Uflwys held up his hands. "No, say nothing yet. We will eat first. You are both tired from your journey. Break a crust with me, yes? There will be time enough for talk later."

Bishop Uflwys' table was as spare as the bishop himself:

simple fare—bread, beer, meat, cheese—but good. Pelleas sat
with us at the board and we were served by two young monks
from the nearby monastery. Our table talk touched on the
ordinary observations of traveling: the weather, planting, commerce, news gathered along the way. When we had finished,
the bishop rose from his chair. "We will take some mead in
my chamber," he told the monks. "Bring a jar and cups."

We settled in Uflwys' bare chamber—a white-washed cell
with one narrow unglazed window and tramped-earth floor,
and a short ledge on which rested the pallet of clean straw that
was his bed. But he was accustomed to receiving guests in his
cell, and in deference to them the room was furnished with
four big, handsome chairs and boasted a small hearth.

No sooner were we seated than the monks appeared; one
of them carrying a wooden tray with jar and cups on it, the
other bearing a small three-legged table on which to put the
tray. These were placed beside Bishop Uflwys's chair and, after
pouring the mead and lighting the fire, the monks departed
without a word.

Uflwys handed around the cups, saying, "God's health to
you!" We sipped the sweet, heather-scented liquid for a moment in silence. "Well now, my friends. Will you not tell me
why I have the pleasure of your company tonight."

I put aside my cup and leaned forward. "We have heard that
Morcant raises war against his neighbor Madoc. I would hear
what you can tell me about how the matter stands."

The holy man's face grew grave. "Morcant at war? You
must believe me when I say that, until you spoke the hateful
word, I heard nothing of it." He looked from me to Pelleas
and back again. "Nothing."

"Then I will tell you what little I know," I replied. I related
what Pelleas and I had learned, and explained how we had
come by our information.

Uflwys stood and paced fretfully before the fire. "Yes,"
he said when I had finished, "I am certain what you say is
true, for it explains much. Morcant has no doubt taken
pains to keep this from me, but no longer." He turned sud-

denly towards the door. "Come, we will confront the king with this foul sin. I will not sleep until I have laid the crime at his feet. He must not think the church will remain indifferent to this outrage."

6

AN IMPORTANT *CIVITAS* UNDER the Romans, Venta Bulgarum had been the Belgae lords' stronghold before the Legions came; Morcant never let anyone forget that his line boasted long and lucrative cooperation with Caesar, and that the lords of the Belgae were proud of their past. Though the forum and basilica had been claimed for private use, King Morcant maintained them worthily. Indeed, for all his talk of Britain, he still styled himself a provincial governor.

The doors were shut and bolted for the night, but Morcant received us. Bishop Uflwys was too imposing a figure in Caer Uintan to treat lightly, or disgracefully. I doubt that I would have been likewise welcomed. Nevertheless, we were conducted to a chamber hung with woven rugs on the walls, and lit with rushlights.

"It is late for a priest, is it not?" Morcant asked, smiling as if receiving the bishop in the dead of night was a most natural thing to him. "I understood a monk rose and slept with the sun."

"As our Lord the Christ is always about his business, so must his servants stand ready to serve when need arises," the bishop answered him, "whether day or night."

"And Merlin—" said Morcant, deigning to recognize me at last. Though I had put off my priestly garb, I was still dressed humbly. "I *am* surprised to see you. I had thought you dead."

No doubt that was his dearest hope. "Lord Morcant," I

replied coolly, "you cannot think I would leave Britain without a word of farewell. When I go, the whole world will know it."

The answer was given lightly enough; but the words held an ominous cast, and they were received with awkward silence.

"Well," offered Morcant, allowing himself a sly, satisfied smile, "at least we may presume to enjoy your presence a goodly time yet. Now then, will you take some wine with me? Or does your lord's business require more sober attention?" The king folded his hands and made no move to summon the wine. Rather, eyeing each of us in turn, he returned to his chair and sat awaiting whatever should happen next.

Bishop Uflwys lost no time. "Save your refreshment," he said flatly. "It would be a waste to pour good wine tonight. Merlinus brings me word of this war you pursue. What is the truth of it?"

Morcant stared innocently at us. Oh, he had studied his reactions carefully. "War?" he said, as if uttering an unknown word. "There must be some error here. I know nothing of any war. Why, we are at peace. The Saecsen devils have—"

"Spare me talk of Saecsens," snapped Uflwys. "It is being voiced in the settlements hereabouts that you have attacked King Madoc, taken some of his lands, and killed his son. Is this true?"

Morcant contrived a pained expression. "Did Madoc set you to this?" He sighed and slapped the arms of his chair with his hands in apparent exasperation. "Why is he saying these things against me?"

But Bishop Uflwys was not deterred so easily. "I ask you again and demand an answer, Morcant: is the accusation true? I would caution you to bethink yourself before answering, for you put your soul in peril with a lie."

If this worried Morcant, he did not show it. He arranged his features in a grave, hurt expression. "You cannot believe I would do these things."

"That is the trouble, Morcant; I *do* believe it," Uflwys insisted. "And I have yet to hear you say otherwise."

Feeling the impossibility of his position, Morcant attacked. *"You!"* He bounded from his chair and thrust a finger in my face. "This is your doing! You have inspired Madoc to contrive these rumors against me!"

But I answered him firmly. "No, Morcant. I did not."

"Then it is all Madoc's doing," Morcant replied petulantly. "Oh, I see it clearly now."

"You have not answered the accusation, Morcant," declared the bishop, rising from his chair. "I take your silence as proof of your guilt. I will remain here no longer, lest you do further violence to your soul." He stepped toward the door, where he paused and turned. "I will pray for you, false lord, that you quickly come to your senses and repent before it is too late."

Morcant made no move to stop him, but stood firm, glowering belligerently. The good bishop had him trussed and tied. There was nothing he could do but worry the knots, and tighten them at every twist.

Pelleas and I followed Uflwys from the palace and across the yard. "I had hoped better from him," sighed the bishop.

"But you are not surprised?"

"No, I know Morcant too well for that. I am not surprised. Still, I hope always for the best. As I said, his silence damns him. He did the deed." Uflwys stopped and turned to me. "What is to be done now?"

"That we will see. If Madoc will suffer his hurt in silence, it may end there. If not . . . " I raised my eyes to the night-dark sky. "The war will continue, and others will be pulled into it. Which, I suppose, is Morcant's intent."

We made our way back to the church, but no more was said until the next morning, when we came before the bishop to take our leave. "Will you try to stop the war from going any further?" asked Uflwys hopefully.

"Yes. They must be made to see that when it comes to fighting among ourselves, no one can win but the Saecsens: they will stand aside and watch while we slaughter one another and then swoop in to carve up the leavings."

"Then I commend you to your task," Bishop Uflwys said.
"I will do what I can here, of course, and I will pray for a swift
and satisfactory resolution." He raised his right hand in blessing. "Go with God, my friends, and may our Lord uphold you
in all grace."

To the west of Caer Uintan the land is all bold hills and
hidden valleys. The woodlands are less dense, the settlements
more numerous and more prosperous than in the north. The
Summerlands lie to the west; and but a little farther, Ynys
Witrin, the Glass Isle of old, now called Ynys Avallach: home
of Avallach, the Fisher King, and his daughter, Charis, my
mother.

Taliesin's people were gone from the Summerlands—as the
region between Belgarum and Ynys Avallach was known—
and the realm was held by a man named Bedegran. As a young
man, Bedegran had fought alongside Aurelius, and I remembered him as a fair and forthright lord.

The next day we came to Bedegran's stronghold at Sorvym.
His was a large realm, and as it was open to the sea by way of
the Afen River—whereby the Sea Wolves often sought landfall—he had learned the value of vigilance.

Bedegran was out with part of his warband when we arrived.
His steward assured us of our welcome, and bade us stay until
his master returned. Being so close to Ynys Avallach, I was of
half a mind to continue on, but agreed to wait if there was a
chance of learning anything from Bedegran.

We were given a meal while we waited, and I slept a little.
Pelleas meanwhile passed the time with Bedegran's steward,
who said much that his master later confirmed: Morcant had
been threatening their lands for some time, trying to provoke
a war between them.

As yet, it was nothing but nuisance and vexation—a few
cattle missing, fields trampled, and other such like. Bedegran
had thus far succeeded in keeping his head and avoiding open
confrontation which was, I reckoned, Morcant's desire.

Still, this uneasy peace could not survive much longer, for

when Bedegran returned at dusk he wore his rage like a cloak aflame.

"I tell you I have suffered Morcant's insults long enough!" Bedegran complained as he stormed into his chamber. "I have avoided bloodshed and battle by turning a blind eye. But when he begins forcing my people from their settlements, I can no longer look away!"

He stopped fuming long enough to acknowledge our presence. "Greetings, Merlin Embries. Pelleas. Greetings and welcome. It is good to see you again. Forgive my anger just now. I did not know I entertained guests at my hearth."

I dismissed the apology with a flick of my hand. "We are aware of Morcant's treachery," I told him. "Your anger is justified."

"He wants war," Bedegran explained flatly. "I have held it off this long, but keeping the peace needs two. If it is war, then I will fight—though loath am I to say it." He began pacing back and forth before us. "But this—this outrage! Merlin, I cannot stand aside. My people must be protected. Do not think to persuade me otherwise."

"Protect them as you see fit," I replied. "I have not come to teach you your affairs."

"Listen to me rant! Such tutelage as yours, I would endure. You are the one man above all others I would heed." Bedegran smiled for the first time since entering. "So? I am listening. Speak."

"I have little enough to say. Nevertheless, I will tell you what I know: Morcant is raiding in Dobuni. Some of Madoc's lands have been seized, and Madoc's son has been killed, they say. But, as yet, Madoc has refused to fight."

"Madoc is getting old. He knows he cannot win against Morcant. All the more, since Dunaut is hard by his other flank. Agh! Worse than vipers, the two of them."

"Are they together in this?"

Bedegran shook his head. "If they are I have not heard of it. But then, I had not heard about Madoc until now." He paused. "I am sorry about his son."

"A hateful waste," I mused, and it seemed that a young man's form instantly appeared before me, stretching out a hand as if beseeching aid. But it was not Madoc's son; this boy was younger—Arthur's age, no more. "The son . . . the *son* . . . I had not considered the son. . . ."

Bedegran raised his eyebrows. "Merlin?"

"Does Morcant have a son?"

"He does," Bedegran replied. "A young lad. I think his name is Cerdic. Yes, Cerdic. Why?"

Understanding broke over me. I knew what Madoc's herdsmen meant by collecting the blood debt. How stupid of me! Morcant was actively ridding himself of rivals, and making the path clear for his son. At least Arthur was safely out of sight in the north. I had been right to move him.

We talked of other matters then, and soon it was time for supper. Over meat, Bedegran asked, "What will you do, Merlin Embries?"

"Whatever I can. For now, I mean to prevent war from devouring the south. Have I your pledge to keep the peace?"

"That you have, Merlin," Bedegran answered, but added: "If you can but keep Morcant and that snake, Dunaut, on their own lands all will be well."

Later, when we were alone in our chamber, I told Pelleas, "This is as bad as I feared. Fortunately, however, we have not come too late. This is for me alone, Pelleas. Who else can move with impunity from king to king? I stand between Britain and disaster."

Oh, I was drunk with it! And I believed what I said—just as I believed that peace could be mediated between these yapping hounds who called themselves noblemen. I rested well that night, and the next day rode out full of confidence and high-minded intentions to save Britain from becoming enmired in a war which would benefit only the Saecsen in the end.

Madoc—sullen, frightened, and grief-struck over the loss of his son—received us with as good a grace as he could command in the circumstance. He was in pain, and I hoped I might speak some consolation.

"Well?" he demanded, when the formalities of the greeting had been observed. "What does the exalted Ambrosius of Britain require of this old man?"

Since he was prepared to be blunt, I answered him in kind. "Do not allow Morcant to draw you into war."

His chin came up sharply. "Draw me into war? I have no intention of going to war with him, but if you think to talk me out of collecting the blood debt he owes me, save your breath. I mean to have satisfaction."

"That is precisely what Morcant is counting on. He only waits for you to give him reason enough to strike openly."

"What is that to you, great Ambrosius? Eh?" the aging king growled. "What makes this affair your concern?"

"The safety of Britain is the concern of all right-thinking men. I mean to do what I can to preserve the peace."

"Then take yourself away to the Saecsen-brood!" he shouted. "Go talk to them of peace. Leave me alone!"

There was no reasoning with him, so I departed, saying, "You cannot win against Morcant; and Dunaut is likely with him in this. Do not think to make Bedegran your ally; I have spoken to him already, and he will not support you."

"I need no help from *anyone*! Do you hear?"

Pelleas and I rode next to Dunaut, to tax him with his duplicity. Like Morcant, he proffered a cordial, if false, welcome. He sat in his big chair and smiled like a cream-stealing cat, but would answer none of my questions seriously. Finally, I lost all patience. "Deny that you and Morcant are riding together," I challenged. "Deny that you are raising war against your neighbor kings."

Shrewd Dunaut pursed his lips and appeared distracted. "I do not understand you, Merlin," he answered. "We have these past years upheld your absurd trial. Even now, the Sword of Britain stands in the stone waiting to be claimed. Are you content with that? No! You attack us with accusations of war.

You flit here and there raising suspicion and anger." He paused, appearing hurt and distressed. "Go back to your Glass Isle—go back to Celyddon, or wherever you abide. We do not need you here, meddler!"

Since I could get no more from him, I shook the dust from my feet and left the viper in his nest. Morcant and Dunaut were intent on war, that much was plain to me. Blind with ambition, and stupid with greed, they would conspire to Britain's fall.

God help us! It is ever the same with the small kings. As soon as the Saecsens give them breathing space, they begin hacking one another to pieces. The hopelessness of it!

"It grieves me, Pelleas. I am sick at heart," I confessed to him once we were away. We rode on, turning the matter over in our minds.

"What of Tewdrig?" Pelleas wondered after a while. "Surely he is more than a match for the likes of Morcant. Perhaps," he suggested, "you should let Tewdrig settle it for once and all."

I considered this, but only for a moment. "No, the cost is too great. We are not strong enough to war among ourselves and fend off the Saecsen as well." That much was obvious to me; less evident was how to bring about peace and enforce it among those who did not desire it for themselves. "We must make them understand, Pelleas."

We spent the whole summer in a desperate attempt to make the petty lords of the south understand that warring among themselves weakened Britain and doomed us all. "How long do you think the Saecsens will wait to seize the land you leave unprotected? How long do you think they will strive with the lords of the north when a weakened south beckons them?"

My questions, like my accusations, went unheeded and unanswered. I spoke words of truth and received lies in return. I persuaded and cajoled, threatened and charmed, pleaded, begged, coaxed and prodded. Morganwg snubbed me, Coledac grew haughty, and the others . . . Madoc, Ogrvan, Rhain,

Owen Vinddu and all the rest feigned innocence or indifference and plotted treachery in their hearts. All my efforts came to nothing.

Exhausted in body and spirit, I turned at last to Ynys Avallach. It had been too long since I sojourned in that blessed realm. I ached to see Avallach and Charis again, and hoped to find solace and sympathy. In truth, I desperately needed a balm to heal my troubled spirit.

The Fisher King's palace remained unchanged as ever. The green mound of the tor rose above the quiet lake, its image reflected in the still waters. Apple trees graced the steep slopes, rising to the high, graceful walls. Peace and calm wreathed the isle like the mist upon the reed-fringed lake, and breathed an air of tranquility soft as the light upon its shaded paths. Westering sun struck the soaring ramparts and towers, causing the pale stone to blush like fire-shot gold. The quality of this radiance suffused the very air so that it seemed to tingle on the skin—living light, transmuting all baser elements to finer, purer stuff.

Avallach, regal and dark, his beard curled and oiled, welcomed Pelleas and me gladly, and made much over us. Charis, Lady of the Lake, fairly glowed with love for me; her green eyes shone and her long golden hair gleamed as she led me, arm in arm, among the apple trees she tended with such care. We strolled the deep-shaded groves, or rowed the boat on the glassy lake in the evenings and went to our sleep with the song of nightingales on the night air.

Still and all, I ate and slept ill. I fretted. Even fishing in the lake below the tor with the Fisher King, I could not rest. Nor could I unburden myself to my mother. Charis, whose sympathy knew no restraint, comforted me as best she could. But I would not be comforted. In truth, it was not succor I needed, but a vision. And that I lacked.

I ask you, O Soul of Wisdom, tell me if you can: what remedy for the lack of a vision?

Day by day, my spirit grew colder. I felt as if I were freezing from the inside, as if my heart were hardening within me. I felt my very soul growing numb and heavy like a dead limb. Charis saw it. How could I hide it from the one who knew me better than any other?

One night, I sat at the table with my plate untouched before me, and listened to Charis explain the work of the good brothers in the nearby abbey; there were, she told me, plans for a place of healing. "It is only fitting," she said. "Taliesin saw the Summer Realm as a place where disease and infirmity were banished forever. And many come here seeking aid for their afflictions. The abbot has brought monks from Gaul and elsewhere—men who know much of healing and medicines."

I was only half listening to her. "Of course."

She stopped, put her hand on my arm. "Merlin, what is wrong?"

"It is nothing." I sighed. I tried to smile, but found even that small effort too much. "I am sorry. The abbey? You were saying—"

"Only that the healing work continues to flourish hereabout," she replied quickly. "But we are talking about you now. You are unhappy. I think it was a mistake for you to come here."

"A sojourn in the Summer Kingdom is never a mistake," I replied. "I am simply overtired. God knows, I have reason enough—what with riding on one errand after another all summer."

She leaned forward and took my hand in hers. "It may be that you are needed elsewhere," she continued, brushing aside my objection.

"I am not needed at all!" I shouted, and regretted it at once. "I am sorry, Mother. Forgive me."

She pressed my hand more tightly. "Arthur needs you," Charis said simply. "Go back to Celyddon. If all you say is true, that is where the future lies."

"Unless the southern lords turn from their warring ways, there is no future," I concluded gloomily. I paused, remembering Uther's fiery temper. "We need another Pendragon."

"Go, my Hawk," she said. "Return when you have found him."

I slept poorly that night, and woke before dawn, restless. "Ready the horses, Pelleas," I told him curtly. "We will leave as soon as we have broken fast."

"Are we going to Londinium?"

"No, we have finished here; the south must fend for itself. We are going home."

7

IT IS A LONG WAY TO CAER EDYN, and a long time in which to contemplate the folly of self-important men. Despair embraced me to its bony breast; misery settled in my soul. The road took us east before turning north, passing close to the old Cantii lands of the coast. This south-eastern region is the Saecsen Shore, so called by the Romans for the linked system of beacons and outposts erected against the fierce seaborne invader. A tribe of Sea Wolves under a war leader named Aelle had taken over several of the abandoned fortresses on the south-east coast between the Wash and the Thamesis.

It was along this same stretch of southern coast that Vortigern settled Hengist and Horsa and their tribes in the vain hope of ending the incessant raiding that was slowly bleeding Britain dry. And it was from this coast that the barbarians spilled out to flood the surrounding land, until Aurelius contained and then defeated and banished them.

Now they were back, taking once more the land Hengist had overrun . . . the Saecsen Shore—its name would remain, but for a different reason. Unlike their fathers, these invaders meant to stay.

I thought of this and felt the sudden rush of the *awen* as it passed through me. I stopped and turned my horse to look back at the lands sloping away behind us. I saw the land fading as into a twilight haze, and it came into my mind that despite my best efforts, the night had already claimed the south. Now

would begin a dark time; this I saw most clearly: despite rav-
enous Sea Wolves crowding his borders, Morcant would continue to press his idiotic war; Madoc, Bedegran and others
would be forced to increase their warbands, and there would
be much senseless bloodshed.

I had cried for a vision and now I had one. Oh, but it was
bleak indeed. Great Light, have mercy on your servant!

Turning away from that grim prospect, I proceeded once
more along the bramble-choked path, as if along the future's
tangled pathways. There was little hope in what I saw, little
comfort to hold against the gathering gloom. The darkness
must have its season, and the land must endure its travail. That
is the way of it!

Putting the south to our backs at last, Pelleas and I pressed
on our way through the long, wide valleys which gave way
eventually to deep green glens and cold-running streams and
wild, wind-mumbled heights. The world was growing colder,
I thought and it was more than idle speculation, for we woke
several times to snow in the night, though Samhain had not
yet passed.

At length, we arrived at Ector's Rock weary and disheart-
ened, the futility of our long sojourn clinging to us like our
own sodden cloaks. Ector, who had been riding the circuit of
his lands with Cai and Arthur, found us a little way from Caer
Edyn.

Arthur gave a loud whoop and raced to meet me. "Myrddin!
Pelleas! You have returned." He threw himself from his horse
and ran to me. "I thought you would never come back. I am
glad to see you. I missed you both."

Before I could reply, Ectorius rode up, shouting, "Hail, Emrys! Hail, Pelleas! If you had sent word, we would have met
you on the road. Welcome!"

"Hail, Ector! I give you good greeting," I replied. My gaze
fell upon young Arthur, standing at the head of my horse. He
fairly danced in place, hopping first on one foot, then the other,
as he held the reins of our horses. "I have missed you, lad," I
told him.

"Things are well in the south?" Ector asked.

"The south is lost," I answered. "Folly reigns. All day long the petty kings give themselves to treachery and war. What they do not destroy, the Saecsen stand ready to steal."

Ectorius, the smile still playing on his face, glanced from one to the other of us, as if struggling to believe. Indeed, the rain had ended, the sun shone brightly, and hopeless words held no force against it. He cocked an eye toward the dazzling sky. "Well"—Ector shrugged his shoulders lightly—"you have had a long and difficult journey, to be sure. Perhaps you will find yourselves in a different mind after you have washed the road from your throats. Come, there is ale aplenty for that purpose."

He turned and called to Cai and Arthur. "What? Do you still linger here, young sluggards? Get you into your saddles and take the news home. Our friends have found their way back to us; we must celebrate their return. Tell the kitchens to prepare the best we have at hand. Ectorius demands a feast, tell them. Hie! Away!"

Arthur was in the saddle and off before Lord Ectorius had finished speaking. And he was waiting at the gate when we arrived at the fortress, grinning, calling out our names. "Myrddin! Pelleas! Here I am!"

Just seeing the enthusiasm burning bright in the boy's face made me laugh—and I had not laughed in a very long time. In this way, Arthur, just being Arthur, cheered the Soul of Britain—a deed unsung yet no less worthy than any lauded by the bards.

Yet the trouble I sensed was not in the imagining only. The oppression, the darkness, was real enough, and as cogent as I believed it to be. Did I not intimately know its source?

That day of homecoming, it was only the boy Arthur lifting our hearts with his boundless joy at our return.

"I was wrong to leave him, Pelleas," I confessed. "All our roaming accomplished nothing. Instead, I have no doubt made matters worse for my ill-conceived interference." I paused, watching Arthur run toward us.

"Myrddin! Pelleas! You were gone so long—almost a year!

I missed you! Do you want to see me throw a spear?" He had spent the long summer hours perfecting his throwing arm, and was proud of his growing proficiency.

I quickly dismounted. "I have missed you, too, Arthur," I said, pulling him to me.

"It is Earth and Sky to see you! Oh, Myrddin, I am so happy you have returned!" He threw his arms around my waist.

"And it is joy itself to see you, Arthur," I whispered. "I am sorry to have been gone so long. It could not be helped."

"You missed Lugnasadh," Arthur said, pulling away. "Still, you are just in time for the autumn hunt! I was afraid you would miss it. Lord Ector says Cai and I can ride this year. I want to ride with you, Mryddin, so you can watch me. Some of the northern lords are coming, and Lord Ector says that we can—"

"Peace, Arthur! What of the Gathering?" I asked. Had we missed that, too?

Arthur's fleeting frown gave the answer. "There was no Gathering this year," he replied. "Because of some trouble somewhere, Custennin said the Gathering could not take place."

"Oh," I said, nodding. "That is too bad."

"But," continued Arthur, brightening immediately, "Ectorius says that next year we will have an even bigger Gathering—twice as big! That makes it almost worth the wait." He turned and darted off. "Come on, I will show you how well I throw a spear! I have been practicing all summer!"

He was gone in an instant.

"Well?" I turned to Pelleas. "It appears that we are to witness a throwing trial. Ectorius' good ale must wait a little, I think. This is more important. Send the lord our regrets; tell him a matter of some urgency has arisen, and that we will join him as soon as may be."

Pelleas hastened to do as I bade him, and returned to find Arthur and me on the field behind the boys' house. There we watched Arthur display his considerable ability as time after time he struck the mark—a feat made more remarkable by the fact that he threw the longer, warrior-sized shaft, and not the shorter practice length used by the boys.

The dying day stretched our shadows long on the field and we stood together watching Arthur tirelessly throwing and retrieving his spear, his face ruddy with the flush of pride in his new-mastered skill. We cheered his successes and praised his prowess while the flame-struck sun sank lower behind us.

A last "Well done" and I gathered the boy beneath my arm. We started back to the hall where the feast was being prepared. "You have a champion's touch."

"Do you think so? I can do better—I know I can."

"I believe you." I stopped and placed both hands on Arthur's shoulders. "I will make a king of you, Arthur."

The boy shrugged off the promise. "So you say. I just want to fight Saecsens!"

"Oh, you will fight the Saecsen, son," I assured him. "You will be a warrior—the greatest warrior the world has seen! And much else besides."

Arthur was happy with this prophecy. But then, he would have been just as pleased with a new spear or a sword of his own. He hurried off to return his spear to the armory, and came back on the run a few moments later.

I waited for him, and watched as he ran. "Look at him, Pelleas. He knows nothing of the powers arrayed against us. And even if he knew, I think it would matter as little to him as the dust beneath his feet."

It is a strange and subtle thing, but I believe now that I *had* to fail—to understand that all my pains at peacemaking amounted to nothing—before I could recognize the reality standing bold as life before me. In order to welcome redemption, one must first embrace the utter hopelessness of failure. For how can a man look for rescue unless he knows he is truly lost? It was there before—it was there all along!—but I could not see it. I saw it now for what it was, and, oh, for all it would become. Yes! I remember the moment well. Truly, that golden afternoon with Arthur so happy beside me remains one of the most glorious of my memory. For in that brief time I beheld the shape of our salvation. Great Light, to think I might have missed it!

Sadly, its glory proved short-lived. Bad news awaited us. Ector glanced up, frowning, as we entered his chamber. He was sitting in his favorite place—a chair made from the interlaced antlers of red deer and boar tusks. "Here you are!" he snapped, and thrust a parchment roll into our faces as we came to stand before him. "Read it out!" He spoke as if whatever was written there was all my doing.

I took the roll and opened it, scanning the cramped script slowly before passing the parchment to Pelleas. He read quickly and handed it back to Ector.

"That," Ectorius growled, "was waiting for me when I returned—from Lot. Saecsen war bands have been seen in the north. There are women and children with them." Each word carried a weight of dread. "They are settling. The Picti have welcomed them; Lot believes they have formed an alliance, and so it appears."

"Where is the man who brought the letter?" I asked.

"Gone," answered Ectorius. "He and the men with him rested but a day before returning. We missed them by that much." He held up his thumb and forefinger to show how narrowly.

"Saecsens settling in the north," I muttered darkly. "So, it begins again. The turmoil we have feared is upon us."

Ectorius, hoping for some solace from me, now sought to soften the blow himself. "Well, things might be worse. A few settlers. That is all. Surely, they can do no—" he began halfheartedly.

But I cut him off. "It is *not* just a few settlers, as you well know!"

Ectorius glowered; his jaw bulged dangerously but he held his tongue.

"Think, man! As in the north, so in the south: the first of

the mighty waves that henceforth shall wash over this island have broken on our shores, and with them the first of the great battlelords who will lay claim to Britain."

"You are mad to speak so!" Ectorius leaped from his chair. "You do not know this."

"It is true, Ector. The Saecsen Shore has fallen. The barbarians even now establish strongholds in which to gather their warbands, and from these they will spread like plague to ravage the land.

"And then," I concluded grimly, "when they have stolen enough to sustain them, they will seek to put all Britain beneath their heathen rule."

Ectorius, his worst fears confirmed, scowled at the parchment for a moment and then threw it to the floor.

"You do not leave a man much for courage," he said gruffly. "Yet, it is no less than my own heart has been telling me. Though I had hoped Aurelius and Uther had taken the fight out of them."

"They did, but only a fool would think it could last forever. As it is, we have had some measure of peace these last years. Still, if we are very fortunate, they may content themselves with establishing their settlements for a time before the raiding commences."

"Let them begin when they will," Lord Ectorius declared. "By the God who made me, Emrys, I mean to hold my own. I will not be driven from my land."

"Bravely said," I replied. "But strength alone will not prevail this time."

"How then? What else can we do?"

"Pray, good Ector," I intoned softly. "Pray God is for us. Pray for the strength of right and the valor of justice. For I tell you plainly: without these we will not hold Britain even a day longer than is granted."

Ectorius, grim-faced, shook his head slowly as the truth of these words found their mark within him. "This is a bitter draught, Emrys. I do say it, and it cheers me not at all."

"Let this be your hope then, my friend. There is one under your care even now who carries within him all that will be required in the day of travail. One whose life was kindled in this worlds-realm for no other purpose."

Ectorius stared. "He is but a boy."

"This very day I have seen the future, Ector," I assured him. "And it shone in the glad welcome on that boy's face."

8

 THE NEXT DAYS WERE GIVEN TO preparation for the autumn hunt. Horses were reshod, spears sharpened, dogs groomed. Everyone in the stronghold was busy. From early morning to far into the night Caer Edyn resounded with shouts, songs, and laughter. It was a celebration of sorts—though a most serious celebration with a starkly earnest purpose: we hunted for the smokehouse and the winter table. We needed the meat to see us through the cold days and nights ahead.

Every detail was seen to with most exacting care, for a spoiled hunt made a lean winter. Above the Wall, a lean winter is a killing winter.

The morning of the hunt, Arthur rose before daylight and made certain that Pelleas and I were awake, too. We washed and dressed, and hurried to the hall, where some of Ectorius' guests and men were already gathered, waiting for the food to be served. This morning we would break fast on hot pork stew, black barley bread, and beer, for we would be in the saddle all day.

Arthur scarcely touched a bite. He kept leaping up from his place beside me on the bench, wanting to dash off to see to his horse, or his tack, or his spears.

"Eat, lad," Pelleas told him once and again. "There will be nothing more for you until supper."

"I cannot eat, Pelleas," Arthur complained. "I must see to my horse."

"Your horse can wait. Now, eat what is before you."

"Look! There is Cai! I must speak to him!" He was up and away before either of us could stop him.

"Let him go, Pelleas," I advised. "You are trying to hold back the tide with a broom."

After eating, we assembled in the foreyard, where the horses were ready and waiting. The day had dawned gray and chill, the mist thick and damp—a raw foretaste of the long bleak winter ahead. The hound handlers—six men, each with four dogs straining to the leash—strove to calm their animals and keep them from getting tangled with the others. The yard stank of wet dog and horse. Everything boiled in a fine, convivial confusion, excitement heightened by keen anticipation.

The horses stamped and snorted impatiently as the hunters lashed their spears into place. The younger boys darted here and there, teasing the dogs and setting them barking. And the women, who had come to see husbands and sweethearts away, challenged their menfolk with good-natured taunts to bring home the biggest boar or stag, or failing that, a hare for the pot.

Pelleas and I were to ride with Ectorius, and we found him near the gate, conferring with his master huntsman—a bald crag of a man called Ruddlyn, who, it was said, could scent a stag before the stag could scent him—no mean feat, surely, for even I could smell him quite plainly. The huntsman wore a coarse leather tunic through which two great bare hairy arms were thrust; his legs were stout as stumps in tall, hair-covered boots. Ruddlyn and Ectorius were talking about the weather.

"Na, na," Ruddlyn was saying, "this *liath* will clear before long. This be just a piddling; pay it no mind. The valley runs will be clearing by the time we reach them. The mist will not last, I tell ye."

"Then sound the horn, man," Ectorius told him, making up his mind at once. "It is a sin to keep the hounds back any longer."

"Aye," agreed Ruddlyn, who lumbered off, unslinging the horn from around his neck.

Our horses were before us, so up we mounted. Ectorius, grinning, his face wet from the misting rain, saluted the eager hunters. "My friends! We are assured of a fine day. We have had a good summer, so the runs are full of game. The day is before you. I give you a good hunt."

Just then the master huntsman sounded his horn—a long, low, braying note that set the hounds bawling in reply. The gate swung open and we all surged out onto the track.

Lord Ectorius' hunting runs lay hard by Caer Edyn to the northwest, for there the forest crowded close. Beginning in the glen of the Carun River, the runs followed the stream into the forest for a goodly way before dividing.

On the right hand, the trails continued a slow easy ascent into the hills and bluffs above the Fiorthe and Muir Giudan to the east; the left-hand trails bent westward, rising sharply to meet a steep and treacherous rock ridge that marked the beginning of the harsh and lonely region known as Manau Gododdin.

The deep-folded land was dense with oak and ash, the undergrowth thorny briar; the uplands and hilltops were gorse and heather clinging to bare stone: a rough land. But the hunting was unmatched.

We rode to the glen, allowing the more eager parties to speed on ahead. At the entrance to the run the first pack was loosed, and the baying hounds dashed away, slavering, the scent already burning in their nostrils; the first group of hunters raced after them.

"Let them fly! Let them fly," shouted Ectorius. "Myrddin, Pelleas! Stay close to Ruddlyn and he will find us a rare prize. You have my word on it."

We continued on, the glen ringing with the sound of hounds and hunters. Cai and Arthur passed us, whooping like the *bhean sidhe* as they plunged headlong through the Carun and galloped into the forest.

"I used to ride like that," remarked Ectorius, shaking his head and laughing, "but stare at an empty board once or twice and you soon learn to rein in your high spirits. Oh," he chuckled again, "but it was great fun."

Ruddlyn arrived just then, dismounted, and, taking the leashes of the five dogs he had with him—big, black, square-muzzled brutes all—he wrapped all five leather straps around his hand, saying, "I have seen a fair-sized stag further on. It would be worth saving the hounds for him."

With that he was off, running with the dogs, his stout legs carrying him with surprising speed through the brush-choked trails. Curiously, the dogs did not yelp, but trotted stiffly, heads down, tails straight.

Ectorius saw my wondering glance, and explained, "He has them trained to silence. They never give voice until the animal is sighted. We get much closer that way." He lashed his horse and started after the huntsman and his hounds.

Pelleas followed and I came after, leaning close to our mounts' necks and shoulders to avoid low-hanging branches. The trail was dark and damp; mist seeped along the still air. Gradually, the sound of the other hunting parties receded, muffled and muted by the dense forest growth.

Ruddlyn, moving with the quickness of his dogs, soon disappeared into the murk of the dim, tunnel-like trail ahead. We rode after him, slashing through the pungent bracken that clung to us as if to hold us back. In no time, our horses were streaming water from the withers down and our clothing was soaked through.

The trail veered always to the left, and I soon understood that we were following one of the western runs into the craggy hills of Manau Gododdin. On we chased, the sound of our passing muted by the heavy, damp air.

We caught Ruddlyn in a clearing where he had halted to wait for us. Hardly winded, he stood with his dogs around him, face to the low, leaden clouds above. "It will clear," he announced.

"What have you found?" asked Ectorius. "Is it the stag?"

"Aye."

"Will we see it soon?"

"Right soon, lord."

With that, he turned and strode away once more. The ground, I noticed, began to rise and in a little while the forest began to thin somewhat. We were beginning the climb to higher ground; the trail became more uneven.

The pace was not fast, but I kept my eyes on the trail, alert to any obstacle there. In the chase, even small dangers—a jagged stone, a fallen branch, a hole in the ground—can mean disaster if unheeded.

I had been lulled by the running rhythm of Ruddlyn's ground-eating pace when I was jolted by the sudden sharp sounding of the hounds. I jerked my head up and, just ahead, saw Ruddlyn pointing into the brush, the dogs straining at the leather, snouts raised to heaven.

I looked where he pointed and saw the reddish blur of a disappearing deer. An instant later, the dogs were loosed and flying to the chase, Ruddlyn with them.

"Hie!" cried Ectorius. "God bless us, we have a fight on our hands! Did you see him?"

"A very lord of his kind," shouted Pelleas, snapping the reins. His horse leaped after the dogs.

I followed, exulting in the chase, the wet wind on my face, the spirited baying of the hounds in my ears. The forest thinned. Trees flashed by. The horse and I moved as one, leaping felled logs and rocks, surging through the brake.

Once and again I glimpsed one or another ahead—now Pelleas, now Ectorius—as the forest sped by in a gray, mottled haze. The trail rose more steeply now. There were stones and turf-covered hillocks all around. We fairly flew over these, rising all the while.

All at once we broke cover; the forest fell away behind us. Ahead rose the steep, many-shadowed slopes of the rock ridge. In the selfsame moment, the clouds shifted and, standing in the center of a single shaft of shimmering light, head high, regarding us casually . . . a magnificent stag—enormous, perhaps the largest I have ever seen. A dozen or more points on his antlers, his mane thick and dark across heavy shoulders, his sides solid and his hindquarters well muscled—a true Forest Lord.

Ectorius gave a shout. Pelleas hailed the creature with an exclamation of delight. The hounds, seeing their quarry near, howled with renewed vigor. Ruddlyn raised the horn to his lips and sounded a long rising note.

The stag swung his head around, lifted his legs, and leaped away, floating up the slope as lightly as the shadow of a cloud. The hounds, ears flat to their heads, dashed after the wonderful beast, their master right behind.

We galloped straight up the slope. Upon gaining the crest, I discovered it to be but a shoulder of a higher hill, the upper portions of which were still mist-wrapped and obscure. The stag turned and began running easily along this wide, grassy shoulder, which itself rose as it climbed to meet the ridge to the west.

As I wheeled my mount to follow the others, I saw a movement at the forest's edge below. I glanced back to the lowlands we had just quitted. Two figures on horseback and a dog had cleared the trees and were driving up the slope for all they were worth. I had no need to look a second time; I knew them for Arthur and Cai, a single hound between them. I paused to allow them to join us.

"He is ours!" cried Arthur when he caught me up.

"We saw him first!" Cai informed me. "We have been on the scent since fording the river."

Both boys glared at me as if I had conspired to steal their manhood. The dog circled us, yapping, impatient, the scent of the stag rich and heavy in his nostrils.

"Peace, brothers," I told them. "No doubt you crossed his scent some way back. But it appears we have sighted him before you."

"Unfair!" hollered Cai. "He is ours!"

"As to that," I told him, "the prize belongs to the man who makes the kill. And that prize is making good his escape while we stand here flapping our tongues at one another."

"Truly!" cried Arthur, whirling in the saddle to view the

track ahead. His eyes followed the shoulder of the slope, then traveled up the scree-strewn rise on the right. "This way!" he shouted, lashing his horse to speed once more.

Cai threw a menacing glance at me and bounded after Arthur. "Wrong way!" I called after them, but they were already beyond hearing. I watched them for a moment and then set about catching Pelleas and Ectorius.

I found them a short while later in a sheltered upland cove filled with gorse and briar. I could not see Ruddlyn, although I could hear the dogs baying close by. "The beast has vanished," declared Ectorius as I reined in. "Took my eyes from him for a blink and he is gone."

"The hounds will raise the scent again," Pelleas offered. "He cannot have gone far."

"Na, we cannot have lost him," Ectorius said. "We will have the kill."

"Not if Arthur and Cai have their way," I replied.

"How so?" Ectorius wondered in surprise.

"I met them on the trail back there. They have been tracking the stag as well. They claim they saw him first."

Ectorius laughed and shook his head. "God love them, the whole forest to hunt and they strike upon our beast. Well, they will have to kill it if they hope to claim it."

"That is what I told them," I replied.

"Where have they gone?" asked Pelleas, looking behind me.

"Arthur led them up the slope to higher ground."

"It is all rocks and brambles," Ectorius pointed out. "There is no cover at all up there. The rascals should know better."

Ruddlyn returned to us on the run, his broad face sweaty. He had leashed the dogs once more and they pulled at the close-held traces. "Stag was not in there," he puffed, indicating the gorse-filled hollow behind, "though he has been. There is scent everywhere, we could get no clear mark."

"He must have jumped off the track at the bend," said Ectorius.

"Oh, aye, could be that," agreed the huntsman. "A canny

creature, he is. We must backtrack as we can go no farther
from here."

We rode back along the trail, keeping the dogs on a short
leash until they could raise a fresh scent. And at the place Ectorius suggested, we crossed the stag's path once more. The
dogs began howling and strained to the trail; it was all Ruddlyn
could do to keep them from scrambling up the sheer sides of
the hill.

"Is this the way Arthur and Cai went?" asked Ectorius.

"Yes," I told him, "but I met them back there a little, where
it is not so steep."

"That makes three canny creatures," observed Pelleas.

"It seems we will have to follow the lads," replied Ectorius.
"God knows we cannot climb this. We will but break our
bones in trying."

"Show us the place," Ruddlyn called, already retreating
down the shoulder trail. I wheeled my horse and rode to the
spot where I had last seen Arthur and Cai.

"They started the climb here!" I called and, turning my
mount off the trail, began the ascent. It was hard riding to gain
the top, and once up the way did not become easier. It was,
as Ectorius had said, all rock and briar thickets. The sheer stone
cliffs of the ridge loomed above, and loose scree lay all around,
making riding difficult. I dismounted and waited for the others.

"We will have to go on foot from here," Ectorius observed,
swinging down from the saddle. "We dare not risk the horses."

"Which way did they go?" wondered Pelleas. He scanned
the high crags above us, all black and shining slick with the
mist that seeped and spread around them. There was no sign
of the boys.

Just then, one of the dogs gave voice and started jerking on
its lead, haunches straining, head low over the track. "This
way!" shouted Ruddlyn. With a sharp whistle, he gathered the
hounds before him and they trotted away once more.

We each snatched two spears from behind our saddles and
hurried away. The ground was indeed rough with rock, the
rubble made slippery by the mist and rain. I tucked the spears

under my arm and jogged along as quickly as possible over the treacherous terrain.

The hounds led us into a narrow defile leading between two humps of stone like misshapen pillars. This passage opened onto a narrow gorge that rose at its end to meet the ridge above. I glanced toward the far end of the gorge and saw, galloping up the scree-covered slope, Cai and Arthur—the stag in full flight just ahead. Even as I watched, the stag cleared the crest and disappeared from view over the top.

Ectorius and Ruddlyn saw them in the same instant. Ectorius shouted for the boys to wait for us, but they were too far away and could not hear him. "The young fools will kill themselves!" shouted Ectorius. "And the horses, too!"

There was nothing to be done but press on as quickly as possible, and that we did.

The slope at the end of the gorge was much steeper than it appeared from a distance. Climbing it on foot was difficult enough. I do not know how Arthur and Cai managed it on horseback.

The ridge formed a natural causeway between the steep rock slopes falling away on either hand, running east to west. In the lowlands behind us, the forest appeared a dark, rumpled pelt with Caer Edyn rising a little above it some distance away.

The mist was heavier here, the clouds more dense. Water formed on my brow and ran down the sides of my neck. Despite the chill air of the heights, I was sweating and my clothes were wet; only my feet were dry.

The hounds led us east along the ridgeway, and we followed—our pace slower now as fatigue began to gnaw at us. Even Ruddlyn's ground-eating strides became slower, though he pushed on relentlessly.

The ridgeway snaked along—as uneven and perilous a killing field as I have seen. We ran. The track lifted slightly beneath our feet and ahead loomed a bare granite mound, lifting like a shattered head, blocking the ridgeway. To the right rose a cracked and fissured curtain of stone; to the left, a sheer plunge to a broken ledge below. Directly ahead were Arthur and Cai and the stag.

This is what I saw:

Arthur sits tense in the saddle, head down, shoulders square, spine rigid. The spear is gripped in his right hand. Well I know the strength of that grip! Cai beside him a few paces away, spear leveled. Both are staring at the stag, breathing hard.

The stag—what a champion! He is even larger than I first thought—fully as large as a horse. Cornered, he has turned at last to meet his pursuers, and stands facing them, head erect, his sleek sides heaving. Blood-flecked foam streams from his muzzle. The rack of his antlers spreads like the branches of a weathered oak—eighteen points if one.

Oh, he is a prize!

Cai's black hound is circling, barking savagely. The dog seizes an opening and attacks. The stag wheels and lowers its head. The dog yelps and tries to jump away, but is caught and speared by the antlers, and is tossed lightly aside to die on the rocks.

At this we begin running forward. We approach, but Ruddlyn halts us. "Stop!" he calls. "Let the hounds do their work!"

He is thinking that it is too dangerous. If we rush in the stag may charge one or the other of the boys and they could be killed. Instead, he will loose the hounds and they will surround the stag, harry it, and wear down its strength.

Then, when they have wearied the beast and taken some of the fight out of him, we will close in with our spears to make the kill. It is brutal, yes. But this is how it is done with a cornered beast. Any other way is deadly dangerous.

Loosed, the dogs raise a rattling yelp as they fly.

But the stag is an old warrior. The wily creature does not wait to be set upon by hounds. He lowers his head and charges!

I see the head tilt down . . . the feet planted . . . shoulders bunching . . . flanks tightening . . . hindquarters lowering as the back legs begin churning, driving the animal forward.

The lethal rack slices the air as it sweeps toward Arthur.

Cai shouts.

And Arthur . . .

Arthur cradles the spear. He holds it like a fragile reed now. His eyes are hard and level. He is as unflinching as the death hurtling toward him.

But his mount is not. The animal shies, wheeling at the last instant. Arthur jerks the reins hard to bring the animal round, but it is too late.

The stag throws his head low, the points of the antlers rake the ground . . . then up! . . . Up like a Saecsen blade thrust deep into the horse's belly.

The wounded animal screams in agony and terror. The stag is shaking his head. His antlers are caught. The horse is scrambling to keep its legs. Arthur's knee is pinned against the side of his mount. He cannot leap free of the saddle.

Blood is everywhere.

The dogs race to the kill, but they are too far away. They will not come in time.

The horse falls. It is rolling over, its eyes wide and nostrils flared, its legs churning, hoofs lashing wildly at the air. Oh, Arthur! Arthur is stuck there. Help him!

The stag pulls free. He rears back, forehoofs raking in the air. The head angles down to plunge those deadly tines into the enemy struggling on the ground.

Arthur's spear is wedged beneath the horse's flank.

I am running to him. I gasp for breath. I cry out because I cannot run fast enough to save him.

The stag towers over Arthur . . . seems to hang there poised. The stag lunges.

The sky cracks wide open and sunlight suddenly spills onto the causeway in a brilliant flood. The light is dazzling. I blink.

I look again to see Arthur's body pierced by the stag's antlers . . .

But no. His arm flashes up. He has a knife. The sunlight strikes the blade and it flares like a firebrand in his hand. The stag veers, plunging its rack into the hindquarters of the helpless horse.

Arthur swings his arm, aiming for the stag's throat. He cannot reach it. The blow goes wide and strikes the beast's shoulder as it worries the wound deeper into the feebly thrashing horse.

The stag pulls back to strike the killing blow. Cai heaves his spear, but it falls short and glances off the deer's rump.

Arthur twists on the ground and kicks free of his helpless mount. We are screaming now to distract the stag. We are shouting to burst our lungs. The first of the dogs reaches the stag.

The stag turns on the hounds, scattering them. Arthur struggles to his knees, Cai's spear in his hand. The stag turns on Arthur.

I see them: stag and boy, regarding one another across the distance of a few paces; a short spear throw separates them, no more. The dogs nip at the stag's flanks. He turns and catches one of the hounds and flings it aside, then gathers himself for the last attack.

Arthur braces himself. His spear does not waver.

Desperate, Ectorius launches a spear. It falls heartbreakingly short, iron tip striking sparks as it skids away across the rocks. He readies another. We are almost within range.

The dogs surround the stag, but the Forest Lord has fixed his eye on Arthur.

"Run!" Pelleas cries. "Arthur! Run!"

The stag gathers his legs beneath him and charges, the powerful hind legs churning, driving toward Arthur.

"Run!" we shout. But it is too late. The stag is already hurtling straight at Arthur once again. The boy cannot turn to run or he will be impaled upon the antlers.

Arthur stands his ground, crouching, fearless, spear ready.

The stag closes swiftly—he is so fast!

Now! I throw my spear with all my strength and watch it slide uselessly under the legs of the onrushing deer. Ectorius lofts his one remaining spear.

In the same moment the stag simply lifts his hoofs and sails lightly over the crouching Arthur, and runs to the edge of the cliff. Arthur is already racing after the beast.

The Forest Lord pauses on the edge of the precipice, gathers its legs and leaps. What a wonder! It leaps over the cliff and we all dart to the place, thinking to see the proud animal battered as it plunges to its death on the rocks below.

Arthur turns wide eyes toward us as we run to him. He thrusts out a finger and I look where he is pointing.

I see the stag—sliding, leaping, running, flying down the cliff face to the ledge below. The beast tumbles sprawling onto the ledge, rolls to his feet and then, head held high, trots away to safety without so much as a backward glance. He is free.

It comes to us slowly what has happened.

"Arthur, are you hurt?" I demand, taking the boy by the shoulders and gazing at him intently.

Arthur shakes his head. He is disappointed rather than frightened. "I could have taken him," he says. "I was ready."

"Son, he would have killed you," Ectorius says in a small, awed voice. "It is a true miracle that you are alive." He shakes his head in amazement at Arthur's still-unshaken courage.

Cai frowns. He is angry that the stag has escaped. "The dogs ruined it. We had him."

Ruddlyn has gathered the dogs and is hurrying to us. "He had *ye*, young buck!" the huntsman snorts, showing his contempt for Cai's assessment. "Never think otherwise. That King o' the Glen was your master from the start. It is a wonder the both of you still tread the land of the living."

At this, Arthur bows his head. Is he crying?

No. When he raises his eyes once more they are clear and dry. "I am sorry, Lord Ectorius. I have lost the horse you gave me."

"Fret not the loss of the horse, lad. It is only a horse, God love you." Ectorius shakes his head again.

"I will do better next time," vows Arthur. The steel in his voice could shear hard leather.

"You will," I promise him, "but not this day. The hunt is over for you."

Arthur opens his mouth to protest, but I will not hear it. "Return to the caer and contemplate the gift you have been given this day. Go now—you and Cai together."

They do not like it, but they do as they are told. They mount Cai's horse and ride off. While Ruddlyn buries the two dead dogs, we unsaddle Arthur's dead mount and, lugging the extra tack, return to our horses. No one says a word; even the dogs are quiet.

None of us, not even Ruddlyn, is certain what to make of what we have witnessed. It seems best not to speak, so we hold our tongues. But there is wonder in our souls. It is no doubt that we have seen a marvel—more perhaps, a sign.

Its fulfilling would follow in due season. I did not know what it meant at the time, but I know now. It was God's saining witness to Arthur's sovereignty, and a portent of the trial to come. For one day I would see that same young man make the same desperate stand against a great and terrible adversary wielding swift and certain death. And on that day Arthur would become immortal.

BOOK TWO

THE BLACK BOAR

1

THE DAYS DRAW DOWN; THEY dwindle and run away. See how swiftly they scatter! But not a single day passes that I do not recall with pleasure the kingmaking of Arthur ap Aurelius. And because he *was* Aurelius' son—despite whatever ignorant slanderers may say—I strove to give him the same crowntaking as his father.

You will excuse me if I say nothing of that long season of strife we endured at the hands of certain southern lords and lordlings, or the fierce battles with the Saecsen that followed. More than enough has been written about those war-wasted years—even small children know the tales by heart. I will say only that after seven years of incessant fighting, Arthur broke the back of the barbarian host at Baedun Hill: a fearsome battle, lasting three days and costing lives in the very thousands. This, and Arthur not yet king!

I was there, yes. I saw it all, and still I saw nothing: I was blind from my encounter with Morgian. Some little time before Baedun, you will recall, I had left the war host and traveled south, determined to break the power of the Queen of Air and Darkness for once and all. Dread Morgian was at that time beginning to take an interest in Arthur's deeds and I could not stand by and watch her spinning her evil schemes around the future High King of Britain.

I went alone, telling no one. Pelleas, following me, was

lost and never returned—may the Gifting God grant him
mercy. I know Morgian killed him. She all but killed me
as well. Bedwyr and Gwalcmai found me in Llyonesse,
and brought me back: blind, but unbeaten, having cleared
the way for Arthur's sovereignty. And that day was not far
off.

After the bloodbath of Baedun, as terrible in necessity as in
execution, we retreated to nearby Mailros Abbey to rest and
give thanks for the victory we had won. Though the abbey
was yet little more than a ruin, the good brothers had returned
and were even then beginning repairs. As it was nearest Baedun—indeed, within sight of that blood-drenched, double-
humped hill—Arthur chose it as the place to offer his prayers
of thanksgiving.

We stayed two days and then, having bound our wounds,
continued up the Vale of Twide to Caer Edyn, where Lord
Ectorius, his great heart bursting with pride, hosted a feast such
as few men ever enjoy. For three days and three nights we sat
at table, eating and drinking, healing our battle-bruised hearts
and souls in the company of true men.

Good Ector, last of his noble breed, lavished his best on us,
giving all without stint. Of good bread and roast meat there
was no end; freely flowed the ale and rich honey mead—no
sooner was one bowl emptied than another appeared, filled
from the huge ale tub Ector had established in his hall. White
foam and sparkling amber filling the cups and bowls of the
Lords of Britain! Sweet as the kiss of a maiden, sweet as peace
between noble men!

"I do not understand it, Myrddin," Ector whispered, pulling
me aside the evening of the third day. "The ale vats are not
empty."

"No? Well, it is not for lack of exertion, I assure you," I
replied.

"But that is what I am saying," he insisted.

"You are saying nothing, my friend," I chided gently.
"Speak plainly, Ector."

"The ale should have run out by now. I had not so much in store."

"You must have mistaken yourself. And a happy mistake, too."

"But the ale does not diminish," he insisted. "As many times as I send to it, the vat remains full."

"No doubt in all this merrymaking the servants have become confused. Or maybe we have not drunk as much as you think."

"Do I not know my own brewhouse, man?" Ectorius countered. "Look at them, Wise Emrys, and tell me again I am mistaken."

"It is for *you* to look, Ector," I replied, touching the bandage on my eyes. "Tell me what you see."

"I did not mean—" he blustered. "Oh, you know what I mean."

"Be easy, Ector," I soothed. "I believe you."

"I know! I will tell Dyfrig—he will know what to do."

"Yes," I agreed, "send for the good bishop. He will be my eyes."

Ectorius departed at once. Meanwhile, the feasting continued unabated; the circling of the cups did not cease. Soon, the bottom of the tub began showing through the foam once more, and a cry went up for the serving lads to fill it again. This time, I went with them. "Lead me to the alehouse," I ordered the oldest boy, placing my hand on his shoulder.

He led me out from the hall and across the foreyard to one of the stout outbuildings of Ector's holding. Inside were three great oaken barrels—two for ale, and one for mead. "Bring the brew master," I told my guide as the other boys set about replenishing their buckets. "I will speak to him here."

Making my way to the nearest container, I put my hands on it and felt the wooden staves; I rapped the side with my knuckles and heard the frothy slosh as the boys plunged their buckets. As big around as a wagon wheel, and nearly man-height, it would hold a fair amount. Two such together, as Ector had, might supply a celebration such as ours for a day and a night—perhaps two even—but never three days and three nights.

"How much is in the vat?" I asked the nearest boy.

"Why, it is nearly full, Emrys," the boy replied.

"And the other? Empty or full?"

"It is full, lord," the boy replied.

"When last did you fill from it?"

The lad—I imagined him ten or twelve summers, judging from his voice—hesitated. "Lord?"

"The question is simple enough, boy," I said. "When did you last fill from the second vat?"

"But we have not touched it, lord," he answered. "This is the only one we are allowed to breach."

"That is true," confirmed an adult voice from the doorway behind me. "Wise Emrys," the man said, "I am Dervag, brew master to Lord Ector. Is there something wrong with the ale?"

"I remember you, Dervag. Your ale is excellent, never fear," I assured him. "Even so, it is suspiciously plentiful. This has pricked my interest."

"My lord Ector keeps three casks," Dervag explained, coming to stand with me. "These three: two ale, and one mead. The boys fill from the standing vat, and only when the last drop is drained from the first will I allow anyone to open the next."

"Then perhaps you could look for me and see that all is as it should be."

The amiable man stepped up on the stone beside the vat. "It is above two-thirds full yet," he announced, growing puzzled. He hurried to the second barrel. I heard a wooden cover lifted and quickly dropped back into place.

"This vat has not been touched." The brew master's tone had become wary and slightly accusatory. "What is happening here?"

"An apt question, Dervag," I replied lightly. "How is it that men feast three days and nights and the ale vat shows less sign of ebbing than yonder lake? Answer me if you can."

"But, Lord Emrys, I cannot answer. Since the warband's return, I have been day and night in the brewing house, preparing to refresh these vats when they are empty. I bethought myself that when the lad came to fetch me, it was to open the second vat. But this"—he struggled to make sense of it—"this is most unchancy."

"Nonsense!" declared the cleric, arriving with Ector just then.

Dyfrig, Bishop of Mailros, though a bighearted, cheerful man, maintained a precise and particular mind worthy of any scholar. He went to the cask, peered in, and declared that to his eye the vat appeared full.

"Yet this single observation is no true test," he stated.

"But we have drunk from this selfsame ale vat for three days," Ector insisted. "And it is no less full than when we first began."

"Be that as it may," Dyfrig allowed, "I was not here to see it." Turning to the boys standing by with their buckets and cannikins, he commanded, "Fill the lot, lads."

Dervag himself filled two buckets and, when the last one was full, the bishop again mounted the stone step. "You will all mark," his voice echoed from inside the great cask, "that I am reaching inside the vat and pressing my thumbnail into the wax. I have scratched a line at the level of the remaining ale."

He turned to us and stepped down. "Now then, my friends, we will watch. And I will look inside again when the cannikins have been refreshed for the third time."

"Go, lads," Ector ordered, "do your work."

We waited in the brewhouse—Dervag, Ector, Dyfrig and I—passing the time cordially. After a time, the serving boys returned, the buckets were replenished, and we waited again. After filling the buckets the second time, Ector ordered torches to be lit because it was growing too dim for them to see properly. We talked of the feast and of the splendid victory at Baedun.

In a little while, the lads returned for the third time and, as before, Dervag refreshed their cannikins from the vat. "Will you look now, Dyfrig?" Ector said.

Dyfrig mounted to the stone. "Give me a torch."

A moment's silence . . . and then a sharp intake of breath: "Upon my vow!"

"Do you see your mark?" Dervag asked.

"I do *not* see it," the bishop replied quickly, "by reason of the fact that the level of the liquid is now higher than when I made the mark."

"Let me see." I heard a scuffling sound as the brew master joined the bishop on the step, almost toppling him from the stone in his excitement. "It is as he has said," confirmed Dervag. "Bring the jars!"

The boys rushed forward and the jars were filled yet once more. Then the two of them looked again. "I see the mark!" the brewer shouted. "There it is!"

Bishop Dyfrig descended the step and stood once more before us. "It is a wonder," he said. "I am satisfied."

"What does it mean?" said Ector, demanding an explanation.

"Rejoice, Ectorius!" the bishop told him, "for even as Our Lord Jesu at the marriage feast turned water into wine and transformed five loaves and two fishes into a feast for five thousand, so has the Blessed Christ honored your feast with a rare and precious gift. Rejoice! Come, we must share the glad news."

Share it, he did. Word of this wonder carried everywhere. In time, the story of Ector's Excellent Ale Vat took its place beside the tale of Bran's Platter of Plenty and Gwyddno's Enchanted Hamper.

But on that night, when the good bishop finished telling the assembled warriors what he himself had witnessed, the gathering sat silent, pondering. Then up jumped Bors. He stepped from bench to table and stood in the midst of the gathering with his arms outspread.

"Brothers!" he shouted, his voice loud in the hall. "Is there now any doubt what is required of us?"

"Tell us!" someone cried; it might have been Gwalchavad.

"Here is Arthur!" He thrust his hand to the bemused Arthur. "Victorious Battle Chief, Conquering War Leader, acclaimed of men, and favored of the Great God. It is time we made our Duke of Britain a king!"

The warriors lauded the suggestion. "Well spoken," some shouted. "So be it!"

Bors, fists on hips, challenged them. "Then why do you yet sit here when there is kingmaking to be done? Up! Stand on your feet, brothers, I tell you not another night shall pass before I see the kingly torc on Arthur's throat!"

At these words those closest to Arthur leapt to their feet and pulled him from his chair. They hoisted him to their shoulders and carried him from the hall. "I think they mean to do it," observed Dyfrig. "Is there anything to prevent them?"

Ector laughed. "If all the battle host of Saecsland could not prevail against them," he said, "I do not think anything in this worlds-realm can prevent them now."

"It comes to this, Dyfrig," I told him. "Will you make Arthur king, or will I?"

"By your leave, Merlinus," the bishop said, "I will do the deed, and gladly."

"Come then!" Ector said. "We stand here flapping the tongue and we will be left behind."

Out from the hall and through the yard, down from Edyn's rock and through the glen, the war host of Britain bore Arthur. The warriors carried him to Mons Agned, also called *Cathir Righ*, for the number of sovereign lords who had taken their kingship on its throne-shaped summit.

And there, in the cool blue dusk of a long summer day, a scattering of stars alight in a high bright northern sky, Arthur was made king. Placing Arthur in the great rock chair, the warriors gathered at the base of the seat. Bors approached and, drawing the sword from the hilt at his side, placed the blade at Arthur's feet. "As I lay my sword, I lay my life, and hold myself under your authority." So saying, he stretched himself face down on the ground, whereupon Arthur placed his foot upon Bors' neck. Then Arthur bade Bors rise, and Cador also came and stretched himself upon the ground at Arthur's feet. Owain came next, and then Maelgwn and Idris and Ector— all of them hugged the earth and stretched the neck before Arthur in full sight of the war host and their own kinsmen. If you have never seen this, I tell you it is a powerful thing to witness proud lords humbling themselves before a heaven-blessed king.

The Cymbrogi, Companions of the Heart, passed before Arthur then and, laying aside their spears, they knelt and stretched forth their hands to touch his feet. Cai, Bedwyr, Rhys, Bors, Gwalchavad, Llenlleawg, and all the rest. Each swore faith to Arthur, and pledged him life for life and owned him king.

When all had been observed as it should be, I came before the Bear of Britain. "Arise, Arthur!" I declared, raising my rowan rod over him. "By the witness of those who have pledged fealty to you, lords and kinsmen, I do proclaim you king of all Britain."

The warriors extolled this with jubilant shouts and wild cries of acclamation. Oh, it was good to hear their strong voices ringing out as if to fill the Island of the Mighty with a glad and happy sound. When the cheering had abated somewhat, I said, "All praise and worship to the High King of Heaven, who has raised up a king to be Pendragon over us! All saints and angels bear witness: this day is Arthur ap Aurelius made king of all Britons."

Turning to the gathered warriors, I raised the rowan and, in the bards' voice of command, I called, "Kneel before him, Cymbrogi! Fellow countrymen, stretch forth your hands and swear binding oaths of fealty to your lord and king on earth—even as you swear life and honor to the Lord of All Creation!"

They knelt as one, and as one plighted troth with Arthur. When this was done, I turned again to Arthur. "You have heard your sword brothers pledge life to life with you, Arthur. Is it your will to receive these oaths?"

"I do receive the oaths plighted me," he answered.

Upon receiving this assurance, I summoned the waiting Dyfrig. "Come here, friend, consecrate this lord to his sacred duty, and make him king indeed."

The Bishop of Mailros stepped to the rock seat. In his hands he held a torc of gold, which he raised, and in a loud voice charged Arthur, "Declare this day before your people the God you will serve."

Up spoke Arthur. "I will serve the Christ, who is called Jesu. I will serve the God, who is called the Father. I will serve the Nameless One, who is called the Holy Spirit. I will serve the Holy Trinity."

To this, Dyfrig demanded, "And will you observe justice, perform righteousness, and love mercy?"

"With Blessed Jesu as my witness, I will observe justice; I will perform righteousness; I will love mercy."

"And will you lead this realm in the true faith of Christ so long as you shall live?"

"To the end of my strength, and the last breath of my mouth, I will lead this worlds-realm in the true faith of Christ."

"Then," Bishop Dyfrig declared, "by the power of the Three in One, I raise you, Arthur ap Aurelius. Hail, Arthur, Protector of Britain!"

"Hail, Arthur!" shouted the warrior host in reply, their voices resounding in the twilight. "Hail, Protector and Pendragon of Britain!"

I thought that the bishop would place the torc of kingship on Arthur's throat then, but he gave it to me instead. I felt the cool, solid heaviness of the golden ornament between my hands as I stepped once more to the stony seat. Arthur's touch, light but steady, directed me to the mark. I spread the ends of the torc and slipped it around his neck, feeling the warm pulse of blood flutter beneath my touch.

Then, pressing the soft yellow metal carefully, I closed the circle once more and stepped away, leaving Arthur to glory in

the loud acclaim of lords and men. The long dusk had given
way to a clear bright twilight, and the glad cries shook the very
hills, as Arthur took up his long-denied sovereignty in the Region of the Summer Stars.

2

  IF THEY HAD BEEN JUBILANT BE-fore, the warrior host became ec-static. They embraced their new king with such zeal and enthusiasm, I be-gan to think he would not survive their adulation. They seized him and up! up! they raised him, high upon their shoulders. Down from the rock they carried him, and through the glen, singing all the way. Upon returning to Caer Edyn, Arthur bestowed gifts on his lords and men—gold and silver rings and brooches; he gave knives and swords, cups, bowls, armbands, and precious stones.

"I would honor my crowntaking with gifts," he explained to Dyfrig, "but I think you would not esteem gold rings or silver cups. I am thinking a strong roof over those ruins of yours would please you more."

"God bless you, Arthur," replied the bishop. "Gold rings are little use to a monk—especially when wind blows and rain falls."

"Therefore, I return to you all that the Picti and Saecsen have taken. And I entreat you to take from the battle spoils as much as you require to rebuild your abbey—and not only Mailros, but Abercurnig church as well. For I am persuaded that winds blow and rains fall at Abercurnig ever as much as anywhere else."

"In Christ's name, I do accept your gift, Arthur," replied Dyfrig, well pleased.

"Then I would ask a gift of you in return," the new-made king continued.

"Ask, lord," Dyfrig said expansively, "and if it is in my power to grant, be assured I will give it."

"I would ask you to take as much more from the spoils to cause a chapel to be built at Baedun."

"A chapel?" wondered the bishop. "But we have an entire abbey nearby. What do you want with a chapel?"

"I would have the monks of Mailros employed there to sing the Psalms and offer prayers for our brothers who now sleep on Baedun's slopes. I would have good prayers made for Britain perpetually."

This request delighted the bishop. "It shall be done, lord," replied Dyfrig. "Let there be Psalms and prayers day and night, perpetually, until the Lord Christ returns to claim his own."

Nor was Arthur content to allow his honor to rest there. Early the next morning, he rode out to the settlements surrounding Caer Edyn to offer gifts to the widows—wives of men killed defending their homes, or fallen to the Sea Wolves in battle. He gave gold and silver from his battle chest, and also sheep and cattle so they should not suffer want in addition to their grief.

Only then did Arthur return to Caer Edyn to celebrate his kingmaking. I let him enjoy himself for a time, and when I judged the moment most propitious, I gathered my cloak around me and took up my rowan staff and tapped my way to the center of the hall. In the manner of a druid bard, I approached the place where he sat at table with Cai and Bedwyr, Bors and Cador, and the Cymbrogi.

"Pendragon of Britain!" I called aloud.

Some of those looking on thought I meant to offer a song. "The Emrys is going to sing!" they said to one another and hushed their talk to hear me. Quickly, the hall fell silent.

It was not a song I intended, however, but a challenge.

"May your glory outlast your name, which will last forever! It is right to enjoy the fruit of your labor, God knows. But you would find me a lax and stupid counsellor if I did not warn you that away in the south part of this island there are men who have not yet heard of Baedun and know nothing of your kingmaking."

Arthur received this with puzzled amusement. "Peace, Myrddin." He laughed. "I have only just received my torc. Word will reach them soon enough."

I was prepared for this reply. "Blind I may be, but I was not always so, and I am persuaded that men believe their eyes more readily than their ears." This observation met with general approval.

"True! True! Hear him, Bear," Bedwyr said; Cai and Cador and others slapped the board with their hands.

"So it is said," agreed Arthur, growing slightly suspicious. "What is your meaning?"

I held out my hand to those gathered in the hall. "Fortunate are the men of the north," I told him, "for they have ridden beside you in battle and they know your glory full well. But it is in my mind that the men of the south will not be won with such news as comes to them in time."

"There is little I can do about that," Arthur observed. "A man may be made king but once."

"That is where you are wrong, O King," I told him flatly. "You are Pendragon of Britain now—it is for you to order what will be."

"But I have already taken the crown here," he said. "What need have I of another kingmaking?"

I answered: "What need have you of two eyes if one sees clearly enough? What need have you of two hands if one grips the sword tightly enough? What need have you of two ears—"

"Enough!" cried Arthur. "I understand."

"But it is *not* enough," I replied. "That is what I am telling you."

"Then also tell me what must be done to quiet you, and you may be certain that I will do it at once."

"Well said, Bear!" cheered Cai, and many laughed with him.

"Hear your Wise Bard," Bedwyr called. "Myrddin speaks the simple truth."

"Very well," Arthur said. "What would you have me do?"

"Send the Dragon Flight to summon the lords of the south to attend you in Londinium, where they shall witness your crowntaking. Only then will they believe and follow you gladly."

Arthur liked this. "As ever, your words are wise, Myrddin," he exclaimed. "For I will be king of all, or king of none. Let us go to Caer Londinium and take the crown. North and south have been divided far too long. In me, they shall be united."

Truly, the south had ever given Arthur trouble. Those proud princelings could not imagine anything of import happening beyond the cramped borders of their narrow horizons. The nobles of the western realms, men like Meurig and Tewdrig, knew differently, of course; they understood the value of the north, as well as its vital strategic significance. But, from the times of the Romans, most southern lords held the north in lowest esteem and deemed the people there beneath their regard. That is why, if Arthur was to be High King in more than title only, he must make good his claim in the south.

As laudable and necessary as his kingmaking at Caer Edyn, more so was his crowntaking at Londinium. This was where his father took the crown. *This* was the kingmaking I wanted for him: the same ceremony Aurelius enjoyed.

For men had become confused. Many did not even remember Aurelius anymore—alas, his reign was too short! Most remembered Uther, and imagined Arthur was Uther's bastard boy. Therefore, I was keen to proclaim Arthur's true lineage, and demonstrate his true nobility.

I mean Uther no disrespect. God love him, he was all the king we needed at the time, and better than we deserved. Still, he was but half the man his brother was. For this reason, I was eager to establish Arthur firmly in his father's light—especially where the lords of the south were concerned. Arthur had amply demonstrated his uncle's courage and cunning; if he could achieve his father's skill at kingcraft, Britain might yet elude the darkness even now engulfing the world.

That is what I thought, and that is what I believed. If you, O Great of Wisdom, secure in your toplofty perch, think otherwise, then look around: how much of what you see now would exist if not for Arthur? Meditate on that!

So the next day we rode to the shipyards at Muir Giudan to board ships and sail south along the coast and up the turgid Thamesis to Londinium. Like his father before him, Arthur found little to love in the tangled sprawl of dwellings and footpaths of this much-vaunted *civitas*. On his first visit—when coming for the Sword of Britain—he told me it appeared nothing more than a midden heap floating on an uneasy morass of bogland. The stink filling my nostrils gave me to know that the place had not improved. Oh, there were a few fine buildings of stone still standing: a basilica, the governor's palace, a wall or two, and such. Truth be told, however, the church alone was worthy of its place.

It was to Urbanus' church that we proceeded. The messengers, who had raced ahead to inform the settlements along the way, were waiting for us. Also waiting was Aelle, War Leader of the South Saecsens, those of the Saecsen Shore who had kept faith with Arthur. With the *Bretwalda* were his entire retinue of house carles, and all their wives and children. I believe they would have brought their cattle, too, they were that eager to honor the new British king and renew their vows of fealty.

In this, these rude barbarians showed themselves more noble than many who esteemed themselves the highest of our wayward island brood. For his part, Arthur greeted the Saecsen War Leader like one of his own Cymbrogi, and gave Aelle and the battlechiefs with him such gifts as they prized: horses, dogs, and objects of yellow gold.

We then formed ranks and passed through the gates and into the tight-crowded streets of the decrepit fortress. Our arrival occasioned considerable interest. Once the people of Caer Londinium glimpsed the young king with his subject lords before him they understood that someone of consequence had appeared in their midst. But who?

Who was this brash young man? Look at him; look at the way he is dressed. Look at his retinue. Certainly, these are not civilized men. Is he a Pict? A Saecsen, perhaps? More likely, he is some fool of a northern nobleman parading his rustic vanity in the capital.

Thronging the way, the jaded folk of Londinium shouted from the rooftops. "Who do you think you are, stranger?" they called. "Are you Emperor Maximus? Do you think this is Rome?"

Some laughed at him; others jeered aloud, calling him arrogant and a fool, flinging abuse in half a dozen languages.

"*They* are the fools," Cador grumbled. "Do not listen to them."

"I see Londinium has learned no love for me," Arthur replied unhappily.

"Nor I for them," Bedwyr answered. "Take the crown, Bear, and let us be gone from this miserable dung heap."

"How long do they think their precious walls would stand if not for you, Artos?" grumbled Cai.

"Let the barbarians have it and be done."

Thus we made our sullen way through the noise and stench of the city. The messengers had done their work and had informed the southern lords and Archbishop Urbanus of Arthur's imminent arrival and kingmaking. Both Paulus, who styled himself governor of Londinium, and his legate were waiting on the steps together as we turned into the long street leading to the governor's palace.

I had met this governor before: a bandy-legged sybarite with a wide, self-satisfied smile and small pig eyes, behind which twitched a rancorous and devious mind. Paulus, by name, was a cunning and oily adversary, and he did not take Arthur's arrival kindly. There was no welcome cup, nor did the fat governor invite us into his house to refresh ourselves from our journey.

"Greetings, Artorius." He chortled—the unpleasant sound brought his round, fleshy face before my mind's eye. "On behalf of the citizens of this great *civitas*, I welcome you. It is an especial honor for me to meet the famed *Dux Britanniarum* at last."

"Arthur is the High King and Pendragon," the legate corrected gently. "And I, too, welcome you, Artorius. And welcome, Merlinus. I trust your voyage was agreeable?"

"Artorius *Rex*, is it?" mused Paulus in feigned surprise. "Oh, then I am honored indeed. I hope you will allow me to introduce you to some of Londinium's fair daughters. We have many women who would like to meet the illustrious northerner."

Turning to me, Paulus said, "Merlinus? Certainly not *the* Merlinus Ambrosius, of whom so much is storied and so little known?" Clearly, he did not remember me.

"The same," I answered. Bedwyr, Cai, and Cador stood nearby, looking on—each of them worth any hundred of Londinium's self-flattering citizens. But Governor Paulus did not deign to notice them.

"I am delighted," Paulus said. "Now then, when is this ceremony of yours to take place?"

"On the coming Sabbath," the legate said quickly. "Merlinus, since receiving word I have been extraordinarily busy on your behalf. I have spoken to the churchmen, who assure me that everything will be ready according to your instruction."

"Splendid," enthused Paulus. "It does not appear you will require the aid of the governor." He was so anxious to distance himself from the proceedings that I thought he might do himself an injury.

"No," Arthur replied, his voice hard. "It seems I do not require the assistance of the governor. Though I thank you for the thought."

"Yes, well . . ." Paulus hesitated, trying to make up his mind about the unusual young man before him. "If you find you should welcome my aid, I will of course be only too pleased to assist you in every way."

"Again," Arthur said, "I thank you, but I cannot think of

any possible help you might be to me. Still, I will bear it in mind."

Oh, Arthur had the measure of Governor Paulus and was not deceived. The legate, embarrassed by Paulus' obvious slight, begged the governor's leave to withdraw, claiming the pressure of duties. "If you wish, I will conduct our visitors to the church," he offered, "and place them in the archbishop's care."

"I think we can find our own way to the church," I volunteered. Blind as I was, I would still rather flounder through the streets alone than be seen in the company of Paulus' toad.

"Of course, of course, by all means, go if you must," said Governor Paulus. "But return this evening, Artorius—you and one or two of your men. We will sup together. I have some excellent wine from the provinces of southern Gaul. You must come and drink with me."

At Arthur's hazy promise to give the invitation careful consideration, we departed, continuing on our way to the church.

"That man is a poisonous lizard, Artos," Bedwyr muttered sourly. "And I would not drink a single drop of his Gaulish wine if I were you—not even if I were dying of thirst."

"Patience," Arthur advised. "We satisfy the law in coming here. Nothing more."

"Law?" Cai demanded. "What law is that?"

"Great Caesar's law," Arthur informed them. "Established when he first set foot in Ynys Prydein."

"Yes?" inquired Bedwyr. "What is it?"

"Every ruler must conquer Londinium if he is to hold Britain," the king explained. I smiled to hear my thoughts echoed in Arthur's words.

"I know of no such law," Cador muttered. "What is so exalted about this crumbling cow byre?"

Gwalchavad, who had been following this exchange closely, added, "Londinium stinks of slops and urine. And from what I have seen, the people here are more kin to barbarians than to Britons."

"Peace, brothers! We will not stay here one moment longer

than necessary," Arthur assured them. "When I have achieved what I came here to do, we are away to Caer Melyn." He stopped, and smiled to himself. "Did you see how relieved Paulus was when we declined his invitation? Perhaps we should sup with him anyway. *That* would make the old toad squirm."

"I say we should do it," Cador urged. "And let us bring all the Cymbrogi with us and let them drain his precious wine to the dregs."

They talked like this until we reached the church, where we were met by Archbishop Urbanus, and Uflwys, who was now Bishop of Londinium. "Hail, Arthur! Hail, Merlinus! Greetings, good friends. In the name of our Lord the Christ, we do welcome you," said Urbanus. "May God's holy blessing be upon you."

"How have you fared?" asked Uflwys. "If you are hungry we have bread and ale."

"We can do better than that for the High King of Britain, Uflwys," the archbishop said. "You will find that we have not been idle since receiving word of your arrival."

Arthur thanked the archbishop, and suggested to Uflwys that the Cymbrogi stood ready to serve. "We are well used to making our own preparations," he said.

"While in Londinium," Archbishop Urbanus replied, "you must allow us to serve you. After all you have done for Dyfrig at Mailros, it is the least kindness we can perform."

By this the archbishop revealed his affliction; he suffered the same peculiar blindness as the southern noblemen. The Cymbrogi war host under Arthur's command had, at hideous cost, saved Britain from its deadliest danger, and all Urbanus could see was that an obscure northern abbey would receive a new roof and altar. Oh, but they are an ignorant fetch, these haughty southern patricians.

Nevertheless, we stayed in the precinct of the church, and in the next days it hummed like a bee tree in high summer. Riders came and went with messages both to and from various lords and noblemen. Even before entering the city, I had sent word to Dyfed in the west, as it was in my mind to have Bishop Teilo and Dubricius the Wise perform the crowntaking ceremony.

For, despite the archbishop's apparent blessing, I knew that he was not the man to bestow the Sovereignty of Britain. It was not a question of his esteem for Arthur; he did honor Arthur—in his own way. But Urbanus had lived too long in the city; too long had he feasted at the tables of rich and powerful men. Their thoughts had become his thoughts—rather than the other way. In short, the archbishop cared more for the friendship and good opinion of men like Paulus than for that of God. That is the sad truth of it.

The Kingdom of Summer required pure hearts and hands to guide it. In Arthur, the Summer Realm had found its lord; and in Arthur's kingship, a new age was being born. I did not care to allow a power-worshiping sycophant like Urbanus to midwife such an important birth. Therefore, I sent to those whom I knew to be holy men, as pure and undefiled in their faith as they were fierce in its protection.

When Urbanus heard what I had done, he reckoned it a slight. But I told him, "As Arthur is a man of the west and north, and will return there to establish his reign, I think you will agree it is only fitting that those who must serve with him also commission him to his rule."

"Ah, yes, of course," replied Urbanus, even as he struggled to calculate the degree of affront offered him. "When you put it in that light, I do agree with you, Merlinus. I will leave it in your hands, and in God's."

Within a few days, the first visitors began arriving in Londinium. A trickle to begin, the arrivals rapidly swelled to flood stage. From the Three Fair Realms of Lloegres, Prydein, and Celyddon they came, from Gwynedd, Rheged, and Dyfed, Mon and Ierne and Dal Riata, from Derei and Bernicia.

Aelle and his kinsmen were already there, but the presence of the *Bretwalda* caused other lords of the Saecsen kind to appear: Cynric, Cymen, and Cissa, with their carles and kith. Ban of Benowyc in Armorica, who had supported Arthur as he had Aurelius, arrived with two ships full of noblemen and servants. Meurig ap Tewdrig, King of Dyfed; Idris of the Brigantes, Cunomor of Celyddon, Brastias of the Belgae, and Ulfias of the Dubuni. King Fergus of Ierne, who owed Arthur tribute, received the summons and obeyed.

Each and every lord among them brought gifts for the new High King. The Dragon Flight, the Cymbrogi elite, were charged with assembling and guarding the tribute which flowed like a river of wealth into the church: gold and silver objects of all kinds—beakers, bowls, bracelets and brooches— many of them set with jewels and gemstones; there were swords and spears and shields and knives, and handsome carved-wood chests and chairs; there were bows of horn with silver-tipped arrows, and gifts of mead and ale, as well as grain and smoked meat—whole halves and haunches of pork and beef and venison. There were horses and hunting hounds by the score . . . the tribute of kings brought to seal the bond of fealty.

And when at last the day came to assemble in the church for the kingmaking, there was not enough room for everyone beneath that holy roof. The yard outside the church was scarcely less crowded than the sanctuary inside, and still there were those who were forced to stand in the street with the citizens of Londinium, who had lately become very impressed with this northern upstart and wanted to attend his crowntaking, out of curiosity if not homage. Even so, many who came simply to gawk stayed to venerate the new High King.

And this is the way of it:

We awakened before dawn on the appointed day to pray and break fast. Then, taking up my rowan rod, my hand on Bedwyr's shoulder to guide me, I led Arthur, who was flanked by Cai and Cador, across the crowded churchyard and into the church. Directly behind Arthur came young Illtyd, Dubricius' aide, who held a golden circlet in his hands. Bishop Teilo and Dubricius followed in their long cleric robes, each clasping a holy book.

The church was already full to overflowing, and at our appearance, the throng gasped: Arthur, arrayed like a Celtic prince, seemed a creature conjured from the strange, shifty light of the west or the enchanted mists of the north. He wore a pure white tunic and green trousers with a belt made of overlapping disks of finest red gold. His golden torc gleamed at his throat, and on his shoulders hung a fine red cloak.

Looking neither right nor left, he approached the altar to the chants of the assembled monks. *"Gloria! Gloria! Gloria in Excelsis Deo!"* they sang, filling the church with praise for the High King of Heaven, as at the altar Arthur knelt. Dubricius and Teilo took their places before him, placing their right hands upon his shoulders.

Raising my hands, I called out, making my voice resound within those walls. "Great of Might, High King of Heaven, Lord of the High Realms, Maker, Redeemer, Friend of Man, we worship and honor you!"

Like a bard of old, I turned to the four quarters and offered up the prayer Blessed Dafyd had offered for Aurelius on his crowntaking:

> *Light of sun,*
> *Radiance of moon,*
> *Splendor of fire,*
> *Speed of lightning,*
> *Swiftness of wind,*
> *Depth of sea,*
> *Stability of earth,*
> *Firmness of rock,*
> *Bear witness:*
>
> *We pray this day for Arthur, our king;*
> *For God's strength to steady him,*
> *God's might to uphold him,*
> *God's eye to look before him,*
> *God's ear to hear him,*
> *God's word to speak for him,*
> *God's hand to guard him,*
> *God's shield to protect him,*

God's host to save him
From the snares of devils,
From temptation of vices,
From everyone who shall wish him ill.

We do summon all these powers between him
    and these evils:
Against every cruel power that may oppose him,
Against incantations of false druids,
Against black arts of barbarians,
Against wiles of idol-keepers,
Against enchantments great and small,
Against every foul thing that corrupts body and soul.

Jesu with him, before him, behind him;
Jesu in him, beneath him, above him;
Jesu on his right, Jesu on his left;
Jesu when he sleeps, Jesu when he wakes;
Jesu in the heart of everyone who thinks of him;
Jesu in the mouth of everyone who speaks of him;
Jesu in the eye of everyone who sees him.

We uphold him today, through a mighty strength,
    the invocation of the Three in One,
Through belief in God,
Through confession of the Holy Spirit,
Through trust in the Christ, Creator of all creation.
So be it.

Then, coming once more before Arthur, I said, "Bow before the Lord of All, and swear your fealty to the High King you will serve."

Arthur prostrated himself face down before the altar, stretching out his hands to either side in the manner of a vanquished battlechief before his conqueror. Teilo and Dubricius stood at either hand, with Illtyd at Arthur's head.

Dubricius, at Arthur's right hand, said, "With this hand you will wield the Sword of Britain. What is your vow?"

Arthur answered, "With this hand I will wield the Sword of Britain in righteousness and fair judgment. By the power of God's might, I will use it to conquer injustice and punish those who practice harm. I will hold this hand obedient to my Lord God, used of him to do his work in this worlds-realm."

Teilo, standing at Arthur's left hand, said, "With this hand you will hold the Shield of Britain. What is your vow?"

"With this hand I will hold tight to the Shield of Britain in hope and compassion. Through God's will, I will protect the people who keep faith with me. I will hold this hand obedient to my Lord Jesu, used of him to do his work in this worlds-realm."

And then Illtyd, standing at Arthur's head, said, "Upon your brow you will wear the Crown of Britain. What is your vow?"

"Upon my brow I will wear the Crown of Britain in all honor and meekness. By the power of God's might and through his will, I will lead the kingdom through all things whatever shall befall me, with courage, with dignity, and with faith in the Christ who shall guide me while my body holds breath."

At this, the good priests replied, "Rise in faith, Arthur ap Aurelius, taking the Christ to be your lord and savior, honoring him above all earthly lords."

Arthur rose and Illtyd placed the slender golden circlet upon his head. Dubricius turned to the altar and took up Caliburnus—that is Caledvwlch, or Cut Steel, Arthur's great battle sword—and placed it in the king's right hand. Teilo took up Arthur's great battle shield, Prydwen, washed white and painted anew with the Cross of Jesu, and placed it in his left hand.

I stepped close and, finding the brooch by touch, unfastened the cloak from Arthur's shoulders. Teilo and Dubricius brought forth a fine new cloak of imperial purple with gold edging—an emperor's cloak, and its significance would not be lost on men like Paulus and Urbanus. This cloak the blessed priests fastened at Arthur's shoulder with the silver stag-head brooch of Aurelius.

Raising my staff once more, I cried, "Go forth, Arthur Pendragon, to all righteousness and good works; rule justly and live honorably; be to your people a ready light and sure guide through all things, whatever may befall this worlds-realm."

Gripping the sword and shield, the new purple cloak around his shoulders, Arthur turned to gaze upon his subject lords.

"People of Britain," I called, "here is your High King! I charge you to love him, honor him, serve him, follow him, and pledge your lives to him even as he has pledged his life to the High King of Heaven."

As if awaiting these words, the great doors of the church burst open with a tremendous crash. Cai and Cador, somewhere below the altar, shouted to the Cymbrogi. The crowd roiled with alarm and confusion. I heard steel sing out as weapons were drawn.

"Do not move, Myrddin!" Arthur shouted, dashing away.

"What is it, Arthur?" I demanded. "What is happening?"

Just then Dubricius cried, "Hold, men! There will be no bloodshed on this holy day. Put up your weapons."

I heard the sound of their footfall on stone as the intruders advanced. I gripped my rowan staff tightly. "Bedwyr!" called Arthur. "Stay with Myrddin!"

In the next heartbeat, I felt Bedwyr's hand tight on my arm, pulling me aside. "Stay back, Myrddin," Bedwyr said. "I will protect you."

"Who are they, Bedwyr? Do you know them?"

"I have never seen them before," answered Bedwyr, his voice tight. "There are twelve. They carry spears and—" he paused, wonderingly—"these strangers—they all look like Llenlleawg! And there are—" He halted again.

"What? Tell me, Bedwyr. What do you see?"

"I do not believe what I am seeing."

"Nor will I, unless you tell me. I cannot *see*, Bedwyr," I reminded him hopelessly.

"Maidens, Emrys," he replied. "Twelve—no, sixteen of

them, I think—all wear mantles of white and . . . what is this? Each maiden holds a white dove between her hands. They enter the church behind the warriors and advance to the altar. They are coming towards us, Myrddin.''

He halted again and I heard the sharp crack of the butts of spears upon the stones. There was silence for a moment, and then the crowd gasped. I could tell someone had entered the church.

"Bedwyr!" I demanded harshly. "What is happening? Tell me, man!"

"Why, it is Gwenhwyvar," he answered, mystified. "I think she has come to honor Arthur."

Stupid man! I thought, divining at last the significance of the maidens and doves. "Honor him!" I snapped. "Bedwyr, she has come to claim him!"

3

 AH, GWENHWYVAR! WHITE GOD-
dess of DeDannan's enigmatic tribe,
deeply did I resent you on that day,
and deeply, deeply did I fear you.
Perhaps I may be forgiven my rancor and alarm. Dearest of
hearts, I did not know you.

Let it be said that you never repaid my resentment with
spite, nor held my fear against me, less yet gave either of them
justification. In those next years you proved your nobility a
thousand times over. Gwenhwyvar, you were never less than
a queen.

I saw Arthur as the Lord of the Summer Realm, and that
vision cast all else in unreckoning shadow. But you saw Arthur
as a man; he needed that, and you knew it. Gwenhwyvar, in
the wisdom of your sex, you were a very druid. And more! It
made my heart soar to see how you and Arthur grew to one
in honor and courage. I do not wonder that God himself
formed you for Arthur.

Let it also be known that never did you deserve the slanders
that gathered thick about your name. It is ever the way of
small-souled creatures to pull down the giants in their midst.
Strangers to virtue, they cannot abide such nobility; lacking it
in themselves, they will not tolerate it in others. So they gnaw
away at it, as the insect gnaws at the root of the oak, until the
mighty forest lord falls. Christ knows, they have their reward.

Still, on your marriage day, I was no friend to you. For, as
Arthur was king of all Britons, it was in my mind to get for

him a British wife. Most canny of your kind, you knew better. Arthur, like the Summer Kingdom, was larger than Britain only. You taught me that, Gwenhwyvar—though I was long in the learning.

Bending low before Arthur, as Bedwyr described it, the Irish queen placed her white spear crosswise on the floor. Gwenhwyvar then stood and pressed the white dove she held into Arthur's hands. Seizing Caledvwlch from Arthur's side, she raised the naked blade to her lips, kissed the crosspiece of the hilt and cradled the Sword of Britain to her breast.

"Swords and doves, Bedwyr!" I said. "Think what it means!"

"Am I a bard?" growled Bedwyr. "Tell me, Myrddin."

"It means she has claimed him for her husband," I told him. "Does Arthur accept the dove?"

"He does," Bedwyr replied. "He holds it in his hand."

"Then he has accepted the match," I told him, realizing the ruin of the day. It was over before I could make a move to prevent it.

In truth, I should have known it was finished the day Fergus brought the treasures of his tribe to Arthur as tribute, placing his daughter and his champion in Arthur's care. In accepting Fergus' tribute he tacitly accepted the proposed match.

From the moment Gwenhwyvar set eyes on Arthur, she had chosen him for her mate. That is the way it is done among Ierne's royalty. For the sovereignty of the Eireann Island race runs through its women. That is to say, a man derives his kingship through his wife. Among the Children of Danna, kings enjoy their season, but the queen is queen forever.

And Arthur, innocent of the significance, made no complaint. Why would he? She was beautiful: hair black as a raven's breast, plaited in hundreds of tiny braids, each one bound with a golden thread and gathered to fall around her shoulders and neck—blackest jet against pale white skin. Her eyes were gray as mountain mist; her brow was high and smooth, and her lips cherry red.

Never forget she was a warrior queen. She carried a spear,

a sword, and a small round shield of bronze; her fair form she clothed in silver mail, of rings so small and bright they rippled like water when she moved. And Llwch Llenlleawg, her champion and battlechief, served Arthur well and took his rightful place among the Cymbrogi; but the tall Irishman was the queen's guardian first, last, and always.

It was true that the kings and lords of Britain would never have tolerated a High King whose wife was not a Briton born. But Gwenhwyvar, shrewd and subtle, had already triumphed. Before anyone knew it had begun, the contest was over. She simply waited until Arthur had claimed the kingship; then she claimed him. True, she waited not one moment longer than necessary lest any rival enjoy even the slightest chance. On the day that Arthur took the crown for the second time, that day was Arthur also wed.

We stayed in Londinium six days in all—feasting the kings and lords who had come to pay homage and tribute to the new High King. The feast became Arthur and Gwenhwyvar's marriage repast as well, and no one enjoyed the celebration more than Fergus of Ierne, Gwenhwyvar's father. I do not think I ever knew a happier man.

Arthur was pleased, as well he might be. He admired Gwenhwyvar for her boldness, and stood in awe—almost everyone did—of her beauty. Still, he did not love her. At least, not yet. That would come; in time they would learn a love which bards would celebrate a thousand years hence. But, as is so often the way with two such strong-willed mates, their first days of marriage chafed them both.

When the last lord had departed to his hearth, we also departed: the Cymbrogi with Cador and Bors to Caer Melyn, and the rest of us, Cai, Bedwyr, Llenlleawg, myself and Arthur, to Ierne with Gwenhwyvar. It is a short voyage and the weather stayed fair.

I remembered Ierne as a green gem set in a silver sea. It is a shallow bowl of an island, lacking Prydein's rough crags; what hills Ierne boasts are gentle and wooded, and its few mountains are not high. Expansive and numerous are its plains, which grow good grain in plenty. If the island's contentious kings ever stopped slaughtering one another, they might find themselves possessing grain-wealth enough to attract trade from the east for the upbuilding of their people.

It is a damp land, alas, suffering almost continual inundation by both sea and sky. Even so, the rain is soft, filling the rivers and streams with sweet water. The ale of the Irish is surprisingly good, for all they make it with scorched grain—yet another mystery concerning this baffling race.

We sailed into a bay on the northeastern coast. I heard a loud whoop, and Cai, standing beside me at the rail, said, "It is Fergus, bless him. He is wading out to welcome us." Even as he spoke I heard the splash of someone striding through the tidewash.

Fergus shouted something which I did not catch, and a moment later, a strange, shrill wail sounded from the beach. "What is happening, Cai?"

"Fergus' bards, I think. He has his retinue with him, and the bards are making a sort of music for us with pig bladders." He paused. "Most peculiar."

I had encountered the instrument before: an odd conflux of pipes which in their hands produce a laudable variety of sounds: now crooning, now crying, now piercing as a scream, now sighing and low. When played with the harp, which they often did, this piping made a most enjoyable music. And the voices of Eire's bards are almost as good as those of the Cymry.

Many among the Learned Brotherhood hold that the men of Green Ierne and the black hills of Prydein were brothers before Manawyddan's waters divided them. Perhaps that is the way of it. The people are dark, for the most part, like the mountain Cymry, and they are keen-witted and as ready for laughter as a fight. Like the Celts of elder times, they are generous in all things, especially song and celebration. They love dancing, and think themselves ill-treated if they are not allowed to move their feet when their *filidh* play the harp and pipe.

Fergus was lord of a small realm on the northern coast in

Dal Riata; his principal stronghold was called Muirbolc after one of his noble kinsmen. His hall and holding, as Cai described it to me, was fashioned on the old style: a number of small round houses—dwellings, grain stores, craftsmen's huts, cookhouses—surrounded a great timber hall with a high-pitched roof of thatch. An earthen wall topped by a palisade of sharpened timber had been flung around the whole. Beyond the wall were fields and cattle pens, and forest.

Inside the hall, which served as the king's house as well as the gathering place for all his folk, the great stone hearth blazed both day and night. Along the walls on either side of the hearth were booths with wicker-work walls where people could rest or withdraw more privately, and at the head of the hearth stood an enormous table, the king's table, fixed to the rooftrees on either side.

Fergus led us to his stronghold and stood before the gate. "You are welcome in Fergus' dwelling, my friends. Enter and take your ease. Let your cares be as the mist that melts at morning's touch. Come, let us eat and drink, and celebrate the union of our noble tribes together."

He greatly prized the marriage of his daughter and regarded Arthur as both kinsman and dearest friend. Never have I seen a lord so desirous of pleasing his guests as Fergus mac Guillomar. His good humor never flagged, and bounty, such as he could command, flowed from him like the waters of the silver Siannon. Fergus' fortunes, while still scant, had nevertheless improved since allying himself with Arthur. He possessed a fine herd of horses, and bred hounds second to none. He gave gifts to us all, and to Arthur he also gave a hound pup, which would be trained to battle and the hunt.

Fergus' daughter, too, was desirous of securing our good favor. Gwenhwyvar had brought Arthur to Muirbolc to deliver her dower to him, and a most unusual gift it was. But before I tell of it, I must first tell of the miracle that took place while we sojourned in Eire.

There were priests in the region who constantly sought to persuade Fergus to grant them lands on which to build a church and community for themselves. They also wished the king to join the *Christianogi*, of course, though they would settle for land.

Fergus did not trust them. He had got it into his head that once a king bent the knee to the Lord Christ, he became impotent. As Fergus was a man who greatly enjoyed the company of beautiful women, of which his realm abounded, it was a difficult thing for him to look favorably on any belief which threatened his pleasure.

"That is absurd," I told him, upon discovering the source of his reluctance. "Do not the priests take wives like other men? I tell you they do—and children are born to them. Their faith does not make them less potent than other men, God knows. You have swallowed a lie, Fergus."

"Oh, I am certain these priests are excellent in every way. I hold no enmity for them," he agreed lightly. "But why tempt calamity? I am happy—never more so than now that my daughter is wed to the High King of Britain."

"But Arthur himself is beholden to Christ," Bedwyr informed him, joining the discussion. "Faith has not made him impotent. Look at the two of them together—reclining together in their nook, drinking from the same cup. Ask Arthur if his faith has stolen his manhood. Better yet, ask Gwenhwyvar; she will tell you."

"It is the way of the Britons," the Irish King allowed, "to hold strange gods and stranger practices. We all know this. But it is not our way."

"It is the way of many of your kinsmen, Fergus," I countered. "Many now embrace the Lord Christ who formerly held to Crom Cruach. I ask you again, where is the harm?"

"Well," Fergus said, "they have grown accustomed to it, I expect, and it does them no harm. But I am not so accustomed. I fear it would go ill with me."

Nothing anyone could say would convince him. But, several days later, a group of monks arrived and sought audience with the king. As always, Fergus welcomed them and gave them gifts of food and drink—for they would not accept his gold.

Curious, I went to the hall to hear their appeal.

The leader of this group of wandering brothers was a priest named Ciaran. Though yet a young man he was already strong in the faith and very wise. Learned in Greek and Latin, articulate and well-spoken, his renown was such that many fellow monks, both British and Irish, had pledged themselves to his service to aid him in his work among the heathen clans of Eire.

"We heard that the great War Leader of the Britons is here," Ciaran declared. "We have come to pay homage to him."

This impressed and pleased Arthur. He did not imagine that his name was known outside Britain.

"You are welcome at my hearth," Fergus told the priest. "For Arthur's sake, I give you good greeting."

"May Heaven's King richly bless you, Fergus," Ciaran replied. "And may the High King of Heaven honor his High King on Earth. I give you good greeting, Arthur ap Aurelius."

Arthur thanked the priest for his blessing, whereupon Ciaran addressed himself to me. "And you are surely the Wise Emrys of whom so many wonderful tales are told."

"I am Myrddin," I answered simply. "And I stand ready to serve you, brother priest."

"I do thank you, Wise Emrys," he replied. "This day, however, it is for me to serve you." I sensed movement before me as he stepped closer. "We heard that you were blind, and now I see for myself that this is so."

"It is but a minor annoyance," I answered. "I am content."

"A man of your eminence would bear any hardship lightly, and I expected no less," observed Ciaran, and those with him murmured approvingly. "Perhaps it is as our Lord Jesu has said: 'This affliction has been given so that the glory of the Father may be revealed.' If that is the way of it, then perhaps I may be the instrument of that unveiling. Will you allow me?"

The hall hushed to hear what I would say. The audacious priest was offering to heal me. Well, what *could* I say? I had been telling Fergus of the power of the Risen One. If I refused Ciaran's gentle challenge, then I would be shown a liar. If, on the other hand, I accepted his offer and he failed, I would be shown a fool.

Better a fool than a liar, I thought, and answered, "As for myself, I am content. But if the Ancient of Days desires my healing for his benefit, I stand ready to oblige."

"Then so be it."

Stepping close, Ciaran unwound the bandage and raised his hands before me; I could feel the heat from his palms on my skin, as if I had raised my face to the sun.

"God of Creation," the priest said, "I call upon your Divine Spirit to honor your name and demonstrate your power before unbelieving men."

So saying, Ciaran touched my eyes, and the heat of his hands flowed out from his fingertips. It felt as if my eyes were bathed in burning white light. There was some discomfort—a little pain, but mostly surprise—and I flinched away. But Ciaran held me, his fingers pressing into my eyes. The unnatural heat increased, burning into my flesh.

It felt as if my eyes were on fire; I squeezed them shut and clenched my teeth to keep from crying out. Ciaran took his hands away then and said, "Open your eyes!"

Blinking away the tears, I saw a throng of people looking at me in blank astonishment, their faces glowing like small, hazy suns. Arthur gazed at me in wonder. "Myrddin? Are you well?" he asked. "Can you see me?"

I raised my hands before my face. They shimmered and shone like firebrands, each finger a tongue of flame. "I see you, Arthur," I answered, looking at him. "I am healed."

This happy event caused a tremendous sensation in Fergus' house; they talked of nothing else for days. Even Bedwyr and Cai, who had seen wonders enough in their time with me, confessed amazement. Blindness is a wearisome nuisance, and I was greatly relieved to be quit of it. I felt suddenly lighter, as if I had shed a weighty and unwieldy burden. The hazy glow gradually faded and my sight became keen once more. My heart soared.

"But what if you had not been healed?" Bedwyr asked me later. "What if this priest had failed?"

"My only worry," I told him, "was what doubters like Fergus would think if I refused. Since I could do nothing about the healing in any event, I agreed."

"But did *you* doubt?" he persisted. He meant no disrespect; he genuinely wanted to know.

Did I doubt? No, I did not. "Hear me, Bedwyr," I told him. "I believed the One who made men's eyes could restore my sight. After all, is that any more difficult than filling Ector's ale vats? A miracle is a miracle. Even so, I have lived long enough in the Great King's care to know that whether I am blind as a bump or own the eyes of an eagle is a matter of such small regard it does not bear thinking about, much less worrying over."

In truth, I was powerfully grateful to have my sight returned to me. Yet, lest men think that I cared only for the Gifting God in what I could get from him, I kept my joy to myself. Fergus, however, was much excited by this show of power. He took it as a sign of great import and significance that this wonder should have taken place beneath his roof.

He leaped from his chair and seized Ciaran by the arms. "Earth and sky bear witness, you are a holy man, and the god you serve is a remarkable god. From this day you shall have all that you ask of me—even to the half of my kingdom."

"Fergus mac Guillomar mac Eirc," replied Ciaran, "I will not take one thing from you unless you give your heart into the bargain."

"Tell me what I must do," Fergus answered, "and be assured the sun will not set before it is accomplished."

"Only this," the priest answered. "Swear fealty to the High King of Heaven, and take him for your lord."

That very day Fergus pledged life and faith to the True God, and all the members of his clan with him. They embraced their new faith with much devotion and even more zeal. Fergus granted the good brothers leave to sojourn in his realm. He charged them also with the teaching of his household.

The king's bards were far from pleased with this develop-
ment. They grumbled against the king's new allegiance. But
when I related what Taliesin had told Hafgan about the faith
of Christ, they allowed themselves to be persuaded. "It need
not mean the end for you," I assured them. "If you, who seek
the truth of all things, would embrace a higher truth, you will
find your rank is not diminished, but increased. A new day is
dawning in the west; the old ways are passing, as you must
know. The man who will not bend the knee to Christ will
find his place given to another."

Gwenhwyvar, who had learned the faith from Charis during
her sojourn in Ynys Avallach, praised her father's courage. Fergus embraced his daughter. "It is not courage, my soul," he
said. "It is simple prudence. For if I did not acknowledge what
I have seen this day, then I would be more blind than Myrddin
ever was."

"I would that more British kings displayed such prudence,"
observed Arthur.

In all, we spent a fine time with Fergus and his people. No
doubt we might have stayed with them a goodly while, but as
the days passed, Arthur began looking more and more across
the sea towards Britain. I knew he was thinking of his Cymbrogi and the day of leaving was close at hand. One night as
we sat at the hearth with our long flesh-forks in our hands,
spearing tender morsels of savory pork from the caldron while
the bards sang, Gwenhwyvar approached with a bundle in her
arms. The bundle was wrapped in soft leather bound with
cords. She held it as if it were a child, and I thought at first
that it was.

"Husband," she said, cradling the bundle, "in respect of our
marriage, I would bestow a gift." She advanced to where he
sat. Arthur lay aside his fork and stood, watching her intently,
holding her with his eyes as he would clasp her in his arms.

Extending the leather bundle to him, Gwenhwyvar placed
it in his hands and then proceeded to loose the bindings. Layer
upon layer of leather fell away to reveal a vellum scroll. I had
heard of such before; they had been common in the days when

the Eagles ruled in Britain. But I had never before seen one.

Arthur regarded the object with bemused pleasure. So far was it from anything he might have expected, he did not know what to make of it. He looked to his wife for explanation and wisely held his tongue. Bedwyr and Cai exchanged bewildered glances, and Fergus beamed with magnanimous pride.

Taking the scroll, Gwenhwyvar carefully unrolled it. I could tell by the way she touched it—gently and with utmost reverence—that it was of immense age and priceless in her eyes. This intrigued me. What written there could be so valuable?

She spread the scroll before Arthur's eyes, and he bent his head over it. I watched his face intently, but his bewilderment did not abate—if anything, it increased. Indeed, the more he studied the scroll, the more perplexed he became.

Gwenhwyvar watched him with a wary, yet knowing air. Gray eyes alert, dark brows slightly arched, she was waiting for his reaction, and testing him by it. Was he worthy of this gift? She was thinking, was Arthur the man she took him to be? Was the gift of her life entrusted to one who could respect its value?

And Arthur, bless him, knew himself entangled in a decisive trial. He studied the scroll for a time, and then raising his head, smiled confidently and cried, "Come here, Myrddin, and behold! See what my queen has given me!"

It was a canny remark. Gwenhwyvar was well pleased, for she heard in it what she wanted to hear. And Arthur, seeing her reaction to his words, beamed his pleasure, for he had extricated himself most shrewdly. Fergus smiled happily, knowing the treasure of his tribe had found a worthy protector. Only I was unhappy now, for Arthur had cleverly shifted the burden to my shoulders; it depended on me to appraise the gift and offer an opinion of its value.

I hesitated, curiosity and reluctance warring within me. I could decline Arthur's offer and force him to declare his ignorance. Or I could go to his aid. Arthur was waiting. Curiosity won over reluctance, and I rose and went to where

Arthur and Gwenhwyvar held the scroll stretched between them.

They turned the scroll towards me. I looked at the pale vellum, expecting to see a picture rendered there, or words of one kind or another. There was a picture, yes, and words, too—but in all it was like nothing I had ever seen.

4

  I NOW APPRECIATED ARTHUR'S discomfort, and why he had called upon me as he did. I stared at the proffered scroll and the strange markings on it. I opened my mouth to speak, thought better of it, and studied the scroll once more.

There were several long columns of words scratched out in a language I did not know: neither Latin nor Greek, which I can, if pressed to it, make out. And there was a picture—not one only, but several: one large drawing flanked by three smaller ones. The drawings were almost as inscrutable as the words, for they showed a strange hive-shaped object resting on a short stack of thin disks and floating in a blue firmament—water perhaps. But it was not a boat, for there was an entrance, or at least a hole in the side which would let the water in. The smaller pictures showed the same object, or similar objects, from different views. The thing was without markings of any kind, so I could get no hint of its function.

I knew Gwenhwyvar was awaiting my appraisal. "This is indeed remarkable! I perceive you have treasured it long in your clan."

"The vellum scroll before you has been given hand to hand from the first days to this," Gwenhwyvar explained. "It is said that Brigid, queen of the Tuatha DeDannan, brought it to Eire."

"That I can well believe," I told her. "And can you yet read the words written here?" I indicated the delicate tracery of symbols.

Gwenhwyvar's face fell slightly. "Alas, I cannot. That art is long vanished from our kin—if indeed any ever possessed it," she replied. "It was my hope that you, Wise Emrys, might read them out for me."

"I wish I could," I told her. "But I am unused to studying script, and would no doubt make a poor assessment." Then with sudden inspiration I said: "Still, it may be that the priest Ciaran knows this script and can tell us what it means. If you agree, we might take it to him tomorrow."

"Your counsel is good," replied Gwenhwyvar, "but let Ciaran be summoned here. It is not right that our treasure should be carried through the realm as if it were a thing of little value." Fergus agreed with his daughter, and dispatched a messenger at dawn to bring the priest to Muirbolc to view the scroll.

"What do you think it pictures, Myrddin?" wondered Arthur the next morning while we waited for the monk to arrive. We were sitting on the rocks above the shore. The day was bright and the sea calm as it washed back and forth over the rocky shore below.

"It would appear to be a dwelling of some kind," I replied. "More than that I cannot say."

He fell silent, listening to the seabirds and feeling the sun's warm rays on his face. "A man could grow to love it here," he murmured after a while.

Cai and Bedwyr, who were beginning to look longingly towards home, approached then. They settled themselves on either side of us. "We thought you were readying the ship," Bedwyr said. "We did not want you to forget us here."

"Arthur was just saying he did not wish to leave at all," I told them.

"Not return to Britain!" Cai exclaimed. "Artos, have a care. If we must endure any more of their piping we will certainly go mad!"

"Peace, brother," Arthur soothed. "Myrddin is jesting. We leave tomorrow as planned. Even now the ship is being readied." He opened his eyes and pointed down the beach a short distance to where our boat was drawn up. Several of Fergus' men, and our own pilot, were shaking out the sails.

"We came to tell you that Ciaran has arrived," Bedwyr informed us. "Fergus is waiting for you and Myrddin to join them."

Arthur jumped to his feet. "Then let us attend him. I am determined to solve at least one riddle before I leave this place."

Ciaran greeted us happily. "You will have good weather for tomorrow's sailing," he told us. "I will come to see you away."

"Oh, do not talk of leaving," Fergus cried. "It is my heart you are taking from me when you go."

"Your place is assured with me," Arthur told him. "Come visit us when you will."

Gwenhwyvar approached with the scroll and proceeded to unwrap it. The priest was eager to see it, and pronounced it a prize beyond price. "I have seen such before," he said, bending his head over the close-worked script. "When I was pupil to the sainted Thomas of Narbonne, I attended him on a journey to Constantinople. The priests of that great city preserve the world's wisdom on scrolls of this kind. It is said that the oldest come from Great Alexandria and Carthage."

Fergus smiled, well pleased with this assessment. "Can you tell out the marks?" he asked.

Ciaran bent his head still lower, pulled on his lip, and then said, "No, I cannot. It is not Greek or Latin, or any other tongue I know. But," he continued, brightening, "that is of little consequence, for I know well the object represented here."

"Then tell us!" urged Arthur.

"It is called a *martyrion*," explained Ciaran. "There are many kinds, and this is—" Seeing our confusion, he halted.

"If you please," I said, "our learning in these matters is not as great as yours, good monk. Is this *martyrion* a building to the memory of the illustrious dead?"

"A House of Honor," Gwenhwyvar affirmed. "That is what the old ones called it."

"Yes! Of course!" Ciaran agreed eagerly. "Forgive my presumption. What you are seeing here—" he lightly traced the painted picture with a fingertip—"is indeed a House of Honor—of the kind called *rotonda*, for its round shape. And, you see, it is tabled, for it is raised on many *mensi*." He traced the round stone tables which formed both the foundation and steps leading to the entrance.

"These are known in Rome?" wondered Arthur. Cai and Bedwyr still appeared perplexed.

"Not even Rome boasts such constructions," Ciaran informed him. "The art of their making is lost to Rome now. And there is but one in the City of Constantine, and it is a very marvel. I know because I saw it."

"Can this House of Honor be made from the drawing here?" Arthur asked, turning his eyes from the priest to me as he spoke.

"It is possible," I allowed cautiously. "Taking the drawing as a guide."

"But that is the purpose of this scroll!" cried Ciaran. "It is meant to guide the builder. You see?" He indicated a row of numbers in one line of the script. "These are the very measurements and ratios the builder must use as he assays his work. The *martyrion* is meant to be built."

"Then I will build it," Arthur declared. "I will raise this Tabled Rotonda to the memory of the Cymbrogi who died on Baedun. And they will have a House of Honor such as cannot be boasted even in Rome."

That night we drank the king's good ale and vowed to visit one another often. Arthur had found in Fergus a boon companion, a king whose loyalty was secured through mutual respect and strengthened through marriage. God knows, the lords of Britain had caused Arthur enough heartache and trouble. Ierne allowed Arthur to escape the petty kings and the clamor of their incessant demands.

Thus, when we put to sea the next morning it was with renewed vigor for the rest we had enjoyed, but with some small reluctance as well. Fergus promised to attend Arthur at Caer Lial, where we would observe the Christ Mass together. Even so, Arthur and Gwenhwyvar stood long at the rail, watching the green banks of the island disappear into the sea mist. They looked like exiles cast adrift on the fickle tide.

We sailed along the northern coast, intending to follow the channel and cross over to Rheged where the sea is narrowest. As the boat passed the last headland and came into the narrows, we saw the black sails of strange ships. They were yet some way off to the south, but were drawing swiftly nearer.

"I make it seven of them," said Bedwyr, scanning the glittering sea. The day was clear and the sun shone bright on the water, making it difficult to see. "No—ten."

"Who are they?" wondered Arthur aloud. "Do you know them, Cai?"

"The Picti, and some, like the Jutes and Danes, will fly blue," Cai replied, eyes narrowed. "But I know of no tribe that flies black sails."

Arthur thought for a moment, and then said, "I want to see them. We must get closer." He turned and called the order to the pilot, Barinthus, who dutifully swung the boat onto a new course.

We watched, standing at the prow, shading our eyes with our hands as we stared into the white sun-glare. "I count thirteen now," Bedwyr said after a moment.

"The ships are large," observed Cai. "Larger than any we have. Who can they be?"

More sails appeared. "Twenty," Bedwyr informed us, straining forward to count the sails. "Yes, twenty, Myrddin, and they are coming toward—"

"I see them," I reminded him, gazing at the black ships hastening across the water. "And I like not what I see."

"I cannot see anyone aboard," remarked Gwenhwyvar. "They hide themselves from us—why?"

Closer, more sails were becoming visible as still more ships sailed into view. "Twenty-eight!" called Bedwyr. "No . . . thirty!"

"Arthur, who besides the Emperor has a fleet so large?" asked Cai.

"Rome perhaps. Though the Romans would be reluctant to launch such a fleet in northern waters, I think."

We allowed the nearest vessel to come within spear-throw, and then steered onto a parallel course. Huge round leather-covered shields hung from the rails below a rank of raised oars, ten on either side, and spears jutted out from between the shields. Long wooden bankers formed a narrow roof over the rowing benches, and provided a platform for the warriors. The square sail bore the image of an animal crudely outlined in white against the black. "What is that?" wondered Cai, squinting at it. "A bear?"

"No," I answered, "not a bear—a pig. It is a boar."

The two ships held their courses for a time, and then the black ship veered suddenly towards us. In the same instant strange warriors leapt onto the platform—big men, wide shouldered, with black hair and pale skin—screaming, jeering, brandishing spears.

"They are attacking!" shouted Bedwyr, leaping for his spear and shield.

A heartbeat later, the first enemy spears flashed up into the air. All fell short, save two—one spear glanced off the side, and the second struck the rail. Llenlleawg leaped to the rail and snatched up the spear before it fell into the sea. It was a thick, ungainly thing of scraped wood fixed to a heavy iron head, more suited to thrusting than throwing.

Gwenhwyvar took up her shield, and Cai likewise. Only Arthur remained unmoved. He stood staring at the oncoming craft while those around him armed themselves. The enemy keel slashed the waves, driving nearer. Spears flew, arcing up and falling. Fewer fell short this time; several struck the sides, and one snagged the sail.

"Arthur," I said, "do you mean to fight them?"

He did not reply, but stood looking at the oncoming ship, eyes narrowed against the sea-glare. Bedwyr, holding out Prydwen, urged Arthur to take it. But Arthur made no move.

"What would you have us do, Bear?" Receiving no answer, Bedwyr glanced quickly at me.

"Arthur?" I asked.

Turning from the rail at last, Arthur called to the pilot. "Turn aside!" he ordered. "Back to Ierne! Fly! We must warn Fergus!"

The ship veered away from the oncoming enemy ship. The enemy gave chase, but our smaller, lighter vessel steadily pulled away, increasing the distance between us. We were soon beyond spear-throw, and seeing they could not catch us, the enemy fell back and returned to their previous course.

Flying before the wind, we made for the Irish coast. "Faster!" Arthur yelled. Though we would make landfall well ahead of the enemy, there was not an instant to spare.

Soon the coastal hills loomed before us, and we came in sight of the bay from which we had put forth. "Saddle the horses," Arthur commanded.

"Let us get them on land first," Bedwyr suggested.

"Do it now." Arthur turned to the pilot. "Barinthus! You know the bay. Run the ship aground."

Cai, Bedwyr and Llenlleawg saddled the horses, and they were ready to ride as we came into the bay. Barinthus did not strike the sails, but steered the craft straight towards land. I watched the shore sweeping nearer and braced myself for the collision. Not Arthur; as the keel drove into the hard shingle, Arthur swung himself into the saddle.

We struck the shingle with a tremendous crack. The rudder splintered and the mast burst its bindings. Even as the ship lurched and shuddered to a halt beneath him, Arthur lashed his mount forward. "Hie! Hie!" he cried.

The horse lifted its forehooves and leapt over the side,

plunging to the hocks in seawater. Another leap, and Arthur was clattering away up the beach. Gwenhwyvar followed Arthur's example, with Llenlleawg close behind, still clutching the enemy spear.

"Look at them," muttered Cai, shaking his head. "They will break their necks riding like that. They should have a care for the horses if they have none for themselves."

Bedwyr replied from the saddle. "Tell that to the barbarian battlechief when his spear pricks your backside." He lashed his mount and leaped overboard with a shout. "Hie! Yah!"

Cai followed, and I gathered my reins. As I swung into the saddle, I called to the pilot. "I will wait for you, Barinthus."

"Nay, lord. Do not wait for me," the seaman replied, working to secure the loosened mast. "I am soon finished here and will follow."

"Make fast the boat, then, but do not linger." I urged my mount over the side. The horse reared and plunged, splashing seawater over me. And then I was pounding over the beach. Cai had reached the cliff-track leading to Fergus' stronghold, and Bedwyr was laboring up the steep track; Arthur and the others had already disappeared.

Upon reaching the track, I paused to look back. The bay was yet empty. The enemy had not followed us to shore—likely, as we had outraced them, they would wait to make landfall when they had the support of numbers.

By the time I reached Muirbolc, the alarm had already sounded. Everyone was rushing around: men to secure the fortress, women and children to hiding, warriors to their weapons, herdsmen to gather their cattle and bring them within the protection of the caer.

Fergus and his battlechief stood in the center of the yard with Arthur and Gwenhwyvar before him. Gwenhwyvar, at Arthur's side, was saying, "Listen to him, Father. There are too many. We cannot fight them here."

"Ten shields on each side—that is at least twenty warriors in each ship, maybe more," Arthur told him bluntly.

"And there are thirty ships—maybe more. If they make landfall here, they will be sitting in your hall before the sun sets."

"Our only hope is to flee the caer and rally the clans," Gwenhwyvar insisted. "At least that way we might have a chance. We know the land and they do not. We will rally Conaire and the men of Uladh. When they learn the danger, they will not turn us away."

Fergus pulled on his chin and frowned as he turned the matter over. "Fergus," Arthur said gently, "we cannot save Muirbolc, but we can save our lives. If we stay here we will lose both."

"Very well," Fergus agreed reluctantly. "I will do as you say." He turned to his battlechief and, with a word, sent the man away. "We must gather provisions," the king said, turning back. "It will take time."

"There is no time," said Arthur. "We must leave at once."

"Bad enough to abandon my stronghold," Fergus replied. "Skin me alive if I also abandon the treasure of our clan."

Arthur relented, "Then make haste. I will ride with Cai and Bedwyr to the headland to see where the enemy makes landfall."

"I will ride with you," Gwenhwyvar said.

"Stay here, lady," Arthur told her. "We will return soon."

Gwenhwyvar made to protest, but thought better of contending the matter and held her tongue. To me, Arthur said, "You will come with me, Myrddin."

Bedwyr, Cai, and I rode out with Arthur, and met Barinthus at the gate as he arrived. "They did not follow us, lord," he said. "I waited to see, but they have not entered the bay."

"Remain here and keep watch," Arthur commanded him. "Alert Fergus if you see anything. We ride to the headland."

We galloped along the coastal path, searching the sea below for any sign of the black ships. But we saw nothing until reaching the high bluffs of the headland. And then, as we crested the hill and the broad expanse of the sea to the north and west came into view, our hearts sank.

For, spread out upon the water all along the northern coast, were forty or more black sails, clustered thick like carrion birds on a glassy plain.

5

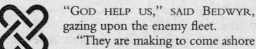"GOD HELP US," SAID BEDWYR, gazing upon the enemy fleet.

"They are making to come ashore there," replied Arthur, pointing to the bay farther along the coast. "Likely they will be on foot—I saw no horses—so it will take them some little time to march inland." He glanced at the sky. "The sun will set before they can form a raiding party."

"Then we have one night at least to prepare," Cai said.

"This night only," Arthur confirmed. Wheeling his horse, he started back down the track. Cai followed, but Bedwyr and I sat looking at the enemy ships for a moment longer.

"There must be a thousand warriors or more," Bedwyr mused. "I wonder how many these Kings of Uladh can command?"

"That, I very much fear, we will soon discover," I replied gloomily.

We returned with haste to Muirbolc, where the people had begun leaving the caer; the first groups were already melting into the forest. Fergus stood at the gate as his people passed before him, urging them to courage and speed. Arthur, Gwenhwyvar, and Llenlleawg stood together in deliberation. Cai was nowhere to be seen.

Arthur raised his head and waved us to join him. At our arrival, he said, "Bedwyr, you and Cai will stay to aid Fergus and his battlechiefs. Gwenhwyvar, Llenlleawg and I will raise the Uladh lords."

"Someone should warn Ciaran and his brother monks," I pointed out. "I will go to them."

"If we have difficulty with the lords, I want you with me," Arthur insisted.

"The good brothers are not far," Gwenhwyvar said. "We can take word to them on the way."

"So be it." To Bedwyr, Arthur said, "When Cai returns from the bay, tell him what we have done."

"If all goes well," Gwenhwyvar added, "we should return here before sunrise with help."

We remounted and, bidding Fergus farewell, rode out at once. Llenlleawg led the way. We passed through a wood and crossed a stream, then reached a broad, gently sloping lea where we turned south and came after a short ride to a rough holding—little more than a field camp, where the monks had settled.

Ciaran greeted us and offered food and drink. "God be good to you," he said. "We would be honored if you will stay to sup with us."

"Nothing would please us more," Gwenhwyvar told him. "But we cannot stay. We have come to warn you. There is trouble coming. Invaders have been seen. Even now they are making landfall along the northern shore not far from here."

"Invaders." The priest mouthed the word, but showed no fear. "Who are they? Do you know?"

"They are a tribe I have never seen before," Arthur told him. "But I can tell you this: they have a fleet as large as the Emperor's, and their ships and sails are black."

"Vandali," said Ciaran.

"Do you know them?" I asked.

"I know of no other barbarian host to own a fleet," the priest replied. "They are known in Constantinople. That is where I heard about them and their black-sailed ships."

"And did you also hear how they may be defeated?" inquired Arthur.

Ciaran shook his head slowly. "Sadly, no. In truth, I heard that they cannot be defeated. Of all barbarians, the Vandali are the most fierce and cruel. They kill for pleasure, and possess no respect for life—neither their own nor anyone else's. They hold no thing as sacred, save their own valor, and they live only for the sport of killing and the plunder to be won with the points of their spears." The priest paused, measuring the effect of his words. "I would be lying if I told you that anyone could stand against them. The Vandali are feared by all who know them. Even the Goths flee them on sight." Ciaran paused, then added, "That is all I know. I wish I could tell you more."

"And I would hear more, but I am grateful for this little," Arthur replied. "Fergus and his people are leaving the caer. If you go at once, you can join them in hiding."

"We are going to rally the kings," Gwenhwyvar said. "We ride first to Conaire at Rath Mor."

"May God go with you, my friends," Ciaran said. Raising his hands, he blessed us with a prayer as we continued quickly on our way.

The stronghold of Conaire Crobh Rua, or Red Hand, was much the same as that of Fergus, only larger, and a great ogam-carved pillar stone stood at the entrance to the caer. His war-band was accordingly larger, too, boasting five warriors to every one of Fergus' men, and no fewer than four tributary kings supported him as well. Each of these small kings maintained warriors at his own expense which Conaire could command at need.

He would be a powerful ally. Consequently, winning him was crucial to Ierne's survival.

Gwenhwyvar understood this necessity and the terrible urgency of raising a host swiftly. Upon reaching Rath Mor and finding the gate open, she rode into the caer, ignoring the shouts of the lax gatemen to stop and be recognized.

She rode straight to the hall and shouted, "Conaire! Come out, Conaire! We must talk, you and I."

The people heard and began hastening to us. The door to the hall was a simple white ox hide with a hand painted on it in red. The head of a man appeared from behind the skin and declared, "The king is deaf to all demands but his own."

"Just you tell your deaf king that he is a fool to sleep within his hall while his realm suffers invasion," she snapped, her dark brows lowered. The head promptly disappeared. "Did you hear that, Conaire?" she shouted.

A moment later the ox hide was thrown aside and a tall man with fair hair and a red-brown beard stalked out. A fine, handsome man, he folded his bare arms across his chest. "Ah, Gwenhwyvar," he said upon seeing her, "I should have known it was you making all this tumult." He glanced quickly at those of us accompanying the queen. "I thought you were in Ynys Prydein. Is it to marry me that you have come here?"

Gwenhwyvar favored him with a disdainful smile. "Conaire Crobh Rua, I will never marry you. The man you see beside me is my husband—"

"Then you can say nothing I care to hear." The Uladh king started back to his hall.

"My husband," Gwenhwyvar continued, "Arthur, High King of the Britons."

Conaire stopped and turned. "Indeed?" He looked Arthur up and down, and then, as if deciding he had seen nothing worth troubling himself over, dismissed Arthur with a sneer. "I did not know the Britons had got themselves another new king," he said. "Now that I see him, I wonder why they bothered."

Arthur regarded the Irish lord coolly, but without rancor. He said nothing. Gwenhwyvar, however, stiffened in the saddle; her face flushed red with anger. Yet it was the silent Llenlleawg who answered Conaire's insult.

"Your ignorance is exceeded only by your arrogance, Conaire," he said. "This night you must decide whether you will live or die."

The Irish lord glared lethally at Llenlleawg. "It seems," he said, his voice tight with loathing, "that I will not be alone in making that decision."

"It will not be Llenlleawg's spear that steals the breath from your body," Gwenhwyvar said. "While we stand here barter-

ing insults, the enemy invader claims our land. We have one
night to make good our defense, or our realm is surely lost."

Conaire's eyes swung slowly from Llenlleawg to Gwenhwyvar. "What invader?" he demanded dully.

"They are of a tribe called Vandali," Gwenhwyvar told him.
"And they have come in force to plunder Ierne."

The Irish king drew himself full height. "This danger can
be but small, or I would have heard of it. Still, I am not surprised that Fergus has sent you to plead for him—the least sign
of trouble and he comes begging my protection. Tell him I
will consider the matter, and reply when it suits me."

He made to dismiss us and turn away.

"Stay!" I roared. Holding him with the bardic voice of command, I said: "Hear me, Lord Conaire. I have known many
kings: some have been fools, and others haughty. But few have
been both and outlived their imprudence."

The proud king bristled at this. His eyes flashed quick anger.
But I did not give him opportunity to speak.

"Know this: We have come here to warn you and seek your
aid. You know nothing of the force arrayed against us. I tell
you the truth, unless we stand together when the battle begins,
not one of us will survive the onslaught."

Conaire frowned. He fairly squirmed under my authority,
but I held him with my voice. "This *is* the way of it. If you
doubt me, why not ride with us to the coast and see for yourself
that what you have heard is no mere fancy of the fainthearted?"

The Irish lord glared murderously at me, but kept his mouth
firmly shut.

"Well?" asked Gwenhwyvar. "What say you, Conaire?"

He turned to one of those who stood looking on. "Bring
my horse," he barked angrily. To Gwenhwyvar he said, "I will
ride with you, and see for myself. If it is as you say, I will
protect you." He allowed himself a sly, sneering smile. "But
if it is otherwise, you must deliver to me the thing that I shall
demand of you."

Conaire stared at Gwenhwyvar as he said this, and it was
not difficult to guess what was in his mind as he spoke. Arthur's

face darkened at the mindless provocation. Nor did I fault him. Had I been Arthur, I would have split him crown to crotch at a single stroke. But Gwenhwyvar intervened. "Make no demands you would not wish yourself to fulfill, Conaire."

Without a word, Conaire turned on his heel and disappeared into the hall. Gwenhwyvar allowed herself a self-satisfied smile. "Well," she said, "that was better than I hoped."

"Is this Red Hand always so agreeable?" Arthur asked.

Gwenhwyvar answered, "It was ever in his mind to have me for his wife. He has a wife, of course, and two cumal-wives also. But he contrives to make himself a king after the manner of Rory and Conor mac Nessa. That is why he has ever sought me to agree to marry him."

"If his courage is half as great as his vanity," Arthur remarked, "then the black-sailed Vandal will soon be fleeing back over the waves as fast as the wind can carry them."

"When the time comes for spear-play, you will not be disappointed," Llenlleawg suggested. "A bard with a harp does not make sweeter music."

"This I want to see," replied Arthur.

Conaire reappeared and, his horse having been brought, he mounted at once and led us out from the caer and along a well-worn trail through a wood. We came eventually to a low, treeless rise giving way to a series of downward-sloping ridges which ended in sharp cliffs overlooking the northwestern coast. Even before reaching the cliffside we could see the thick-sown black sails close-clustered on the sea. Many ships had already made landfall, and more were coming in with every wave; but we saw no one on shore, and no sign of horses aboard any of the boats.

"Forty ships," observed Bedwyr. "No more have joined them. That means they have all arrived."

"Unless this is merely the advance force sent to spy out the land," Cai pointed out. Both men lapsed into silence at that unsettling thought.

The Irish king stared at the spectacle before him for a long time. "Never have I seen such an audacious invader," he said at last. "Such insolence incurs a heavy debt, and I mean to collect my share."

"Well said, Conaire," Arthur told him. "Together, we will drive these barbarians into the sea."

Conaire, the westering light in his eyes, turned to Arthur and looked him full in the face. "Lord, I am a man of impulse and quick temper, as you have seen," he said. "I spoke without due consideration and my words were not worthy. And now I am sorry. For I think you are a very king among your kind, and it is not meet for two such noble allies to enter battle with malice between them."

"I agree," replied Arthur nicely. "I think it will be toil enough to fight the Vandal horde without also bearing a heavy dislike for one another."

So saying, the High King of Britain held out his arm to the Irish king. Conaire clasped his arm and the two embraced like kinsmen, animosity forgotten.

But Conaire was not finished. He turned next to Gwenhwyvar and said, "Lady, you know I have always held you in highest esteem. That is why I deeply regretted your leaving Eirinn to take a husband of British blood. And though I bear the loss, I understand your choice and even find it in my heart to approve. You have made a laudable match and found a man above all worthy of you. Lady, I commend you. And I offer you my hand, as I would gladly have offered you my life."

"I will take your hand, Conaire," Gwenhwyvar answered, leaning close, "but I will have your cheek as well." Taking his hand, she pulled him to her, put her lips to his cheek and kissed him.

The Irish king grinned broadly and, lifting the reins, urged his horse forward. We raced to Rath Mor, and had almost reached the shelter of the wood when, with a sudden cry, an enemy warband burst out from among the trees.

Within two heartbeats we were confronted by fifty warriors—large men, fierce, pitiless eyes glittering like chips of jet in their sallow faces. They advanced on foot, warily, and carried no swords, only the thick black spear and heavy wooden shield we had seen on the ships. They hesitated only a moment, then the enemy battlechief gave a shout and they rushed upon us, black spears leveled, screaming as they ran.

6

 ARTHUR LASHED HIS MOUNT TO speed and raced to meet the charge head-on. "Follow me!" he called, setting his shield as he flew towards the enemy.

Llenlleawg was first to react to Arthur's lead. He blew past me and took up position to the left and just behind Arthur so that the barbarians could not come at the king from his blind side.

Conaire was suddenly beside me, holding out his spear. "You have no spear," he said. "Take mine."

"Keep it," I told him. "I prefer the sword."

Gwenhwyvar lashed her mount to speed, unslinging her shield and drawing her sword at full gallop. "Oh, heart of my heart," said Conaire, watching her go, "is that not a sweet sight?"

"Come, Irishman," I called. "They are leaving us behind!"

Arthur reached the enemy line and hurtled through, scattering foemen in all directions. Llenlleawg, right behind, did not give them a chance to regroup. He ran down three or four as they fled and slashed two more. The line gaped wide, allowing Gwenhwyvar to ride through unopposed. She gained the edge of the wood and then turned back, charging again into the re-forming rank.

I saw where she intended to strike and swerved to join her attack. Conaire, on my right, loosed a wild, joyous whoop and rode straight to the center of the line—spear high, shield outflung, and reins flying loose. One glimpse of the three of us sweeping down upon them and—mouths gaping in unintelligible shouts, shields thrown high—the strangers scrambled for the cover of the wood.

Arthur and Llenlleawg met them, however, swinging up from behind. The Vandal warband was neatly sliced in two—those closest to the trees made good their escape, but the rest found themselves the center of an attack by five swiftly converging horsemen. The disordered rank folded inward upon itself to become a confused knot. Gwenhwyvar and I reached this knot first and stabbed into it. Conaire slashed in from the side, and Arthur and Llenlleawg charged in from the rear.

They fell before us. Confused, crying out in panic and rage, lunging desperately with their short, clumsy spears, they threw themselves at us, and we trampled them down. The soft green turf blushed bright crimson in the lowering sun and the shadows stretched long.

The enemy warriors fled the fight, leaving their dead and wounded on the ground as they disappeared into the shelter of the wood. Llenlleawg would have pursued them, but Arthur called him back.

"Warriors!" Conaire hooted in derision. "I have never seen such hopeless warriors. If that is the best they can do, give me a gang of boys with sharp sticks and I will conquer the world!"

"They were a scouting party only," replied Arthur. "Our horses scared them."

"But they attacked us!" argued Conaire. "They wanted to fight. Fifty against five! And we routed them without breaking a sweat."

"Arthur is right," I remarked. "They were only searching out the land and we surprised them. And now that we have shown them what manner of men inhabit this place, we should not expect them to make the same mistake again."

"Bah!" Conaire growled. "What do I care what you call it? We beat the thieving barbarians. Let them try again and we will give them the same."

Arthur shook his head gravely. "Speed and courage saved

us today, Conaire. We should account ourselves fortunate to have escaped with our lives." He swung himself from the saddle and walked to where the enemy warriors lay on the ground. He stooped briefly over two or three of them, and then called, "This one is still alive."

"I will soon put that right," Conaire answered, quickly jumping down from his horse.

"No," Arthur said, halting the Irish lord. "Let us take him back to the caer and see what we can learn from him."

Conaire frowned. "We will get nothing from him. Let us kill him now and save ourselves the trouble of carrying him back."

However much I agreed with Arthur, I strongly suspected Conaire was right. One look at the strange features—high cheekbones and narrow, almost slanted eyes above a long thin nose, and skin the color of old ivory, he seemed to have come from another world—and I concluded that we would learn nothing of value from the injured man. Nevertheless, we picked him up and slung his unconscious body across Llenlleawg's saddle. The Irish champion shared Gwenhwyvar's horse and we made our way quickly back to Rath Mor, where Conaire summoned his druids, informed them of the danger, and then dispatched messengers to rally his lords and chieftains. The barbarian was taken to one of the nearby round houses to be guarded until he awakened.

"I have sent word to Fergus to join us here," Conaire explained. "He and his folk will be safer in this stronghold than wandering around in the forest where the barbarians can get at them."

"I do thank you, Conaire," Gwenhwyvar said. "Your consideration will not be forgotten."

"I do it for you, lady," he answered. "And for this husband of yours. I tell you I like him well, and mean to account myself worthy in his eyes."

"That you have done already," Arthur told him, which pleased Conaire immensely.

"Then come into my hall," the Irishman said. "We will lift

cups together and drink our fill. My alemakers are champions of their craft, and tonight may be the last chance we have to savor their subtle art. Come, Arthur! Come, Gwenhwyvar! Come, Myrddin Emrys and Llenlleawg! Let us drink to the health of our enemy's enemies!"

Arthur took two steps towards the hall and stopped. "I would enjoy nothing more than to drink with you, Conaire," he said. "But I think the enemy will not be celebrating tonight. Therefore, I suggest we look rather to the defense of the people."

The Irish king's face clouded. "We have done all we can," Conaire said stiffly. "What more would you have us do?"

"The enemy have yet to assemble their war host. We will never have a better opportunity to attack."

"But it will be dark before we can assemble our own battle host," Conaire pointed out.

"Better still," replied Arthur with a grin. "Let darkness hide our numbers, and let us strike them before they strike us! Come, Conaire, we will carry the battle to them on the shore even while their ships are making landfall."

Conaire hesitated; he was not inclined to such tactics and distrusted them. Arthur understood his reluctance. Conaire's experience of warfare was that of an elder time, when kings met to wage combat in the morning and then rested and refreshed themselves to fight again in the evening, breaking off at dusk to return to their strongholds.

Arthur, nurtured on ruthless necessity and desperate cunning, had learned a keen and lethal shrewdness. He never considered the battle without also assessing the shape of the war. I never knew him to take the field without a thought to the next day's battle. And that was what lay behind his thinking now: anything they could do to harry the enemy on this night would be to their advantage next time. And, as Arthur knew, we would need every benefit we could command.

I believe Conaire sensed the wisdom of acting on Arthur's counsel, even if he did not fully perceive its source. Even so, Arthur did not coerce the Irish king—he coaxed; he cajoled.

"Ah, the sky is clear, and the moon will shine bright. It is a good night for a ride along the sea. Gwenhwyvar has told me of the beauty of the Eireann coast. I think I would like to see it by moonlight. What say you, Conaire?" asked Arthur. "Will you ride with us?"

"By my father's head, Lord Arthur," Conaire replied, "you are a very man. Well then, since we are going, let us at least lift a cup while we wait for our companions to join us."

Gwenhwyvar stepped between the two men and, taking each by the arm, turned them towards the hall. "Well said, Conaire, we will drink to the friendship of kings. And then we will show this Briton the delights of these favored shores by moonlight."

By the time the sun set, the first of Conaire's warbands had arrived. The chieftains strode noisily into the hall to Conaire's acclaim. He pressed cups into their hands, drank with them, and made much over our first skirmish with Vandal foe. Fergus and his people arrived last, and Cai and Bedwyr with him. Arthur quickly explained what he had seen, and described the encounter with the enemy.

"Where is this captured foeman?" asked Bedwyr when he had heard the tale. "Perhaps we should see if he is of a temper to speak to us."

As Conaire was occupied with his lords, Arthur and I, Cai and Bedwyr, left the hall and went to the round house where the barbarian had been taken. He lay on his side on the dirt floor of the house; his hands and feet had been bound with a rope of braided leather. He sat up and scowled defiantly at us as we entered. The warrior guarding him acknowledged us, and said, "He has made no sound since waking. He just sits and glares like a sun-sick lizard."

"We will watch him now," said Arthur. "You may join your kinsmen in the hall."

The warrior departed eagerly, and we stood for a moment looking at the captive. Tall—nearly as tall as Arthur—he was thick-limbed and brawny. His arms and legs were covered with small, even-spaced scars. His hair and eyes were black, and he wore no beard or mustache—indeed, save for his head, all the hair had been scraped from his body. His thin, faintly slanted eyes watched us sourly, without interest. Arthur nodded to Bedwyr, who stepped before him, questioning, "Who are you, Vandal? What is your name?"

The captive merely curled his lip.

"Answer me, and it will go well with you," Bedwyr said, speaking slowly. "Do you hear me?"

The barbarian offered no reply; neither did he give the slightest indication that he understood Bedwyr's speech.

"That is not the way to do it," grumbled Cai. He stepped before the captive and, thumping himself on the chest, said, "Cai. I am . . . Cai." He pointed a finger at the barbarian's chest. "You?" He made the word a question, and to my surprise the barbarian answered.

"*Hussa!*" he growled in a low voice. "*Hussa the groz.*"

"You see?" said Cai, turning his head. "That is how—" But at that moment the barbarian pitched forward and rolled into Cai's legs, knocking him to the ground. Bedwyr, who was nearest, leaped to Cai's aid, pulling the captive off as Cai kicked himself free.

Bedwyr helped Cai to his feet and the barbarian lunged away. "That was foolish," Cai said. "I will not make that mistake again."

"What is he doing?" Arthur said, pushing past them. He rushed to the captive and rolled him onto his back. The barbarian clutched Cai's dagger in his bound hands. He grinned viciously and spat in Arthur's face.

"You filthy—" cried Cai, diving towards him.

Before Cai could lay hand to him, the barbarian turned the knife and plunged the blade into his own gut. His eyes bulged with the sudden shock. And then, hands and arms shaking with the effort, he forced the blade up under his own ribs and into his heart.

The savage smile became a rictus. A tremor shook the body and the barbarian slumped back, blood bubbling suddenly from his mouth. His legs twitched and he lay still.

"So," observed Bedwyr, "we will get no more from him now."

"We learned his name at least," Cai said, feeling the place at his belt. "Why did he have to use *my* knife?"

"Was it his name?" I mused, looking at the stranger's corpse. "I wonder."

We returned to the hall and told Conaire what had happened. "It is for the best," the Irishman reflected. "He would no doubt have been unhappy to remain here any longer."

The first stars were shining in a skybowl of deep blue as we rode out from Rath Mor to meet the enemy host encamped on the shore.

We lay on our stomachs and gazed down upon the night-dark shore by the light of a bright half moon. The easy roll of the sea upon the strand sounded like the breathing of an enormous beast, and the campfires strung along the coast glinted and glimmered in a shimmering line into the sea-misted distance. Other lights shone across the water where enemy ships rode at anchor.

"Still but forty ships, and only half have come ashore," observed Bedwyr. "That is good."

"Oh, that is very good," muttered Conaire.

"I make it between four and six hundred warriors," Bedwyr continued. "Less than a thousand, anyway."

"With as many more to follow," said Arthur.

"Why have they come here?" wondered Cai.

"Be grateful that they *are* here," I said.

"Grateful!" Bedwyr scoffed.

"Would you rather they were in Britain?" I asked.

Bedwyr looked at me for a moment. "I did not think of that."

Conaire rose to his feet. "I have seen enough. Let us begin."

"We will strike the first camp," said Arthur, pointing to the nearest of the campfires. "And you, Conaire, will strike to the south—there." He pointed to the next cluster of fires up the coast. "Create as much havoc as possible and retreat," Arthur said. "Then we will assemble once more and strike again—moving south down the coast."

Fergus sat his horse at the head of his warband and waited, holding the reins of our horses. "It is a good night for a battle," he said, drawing the air deep into his lungs. "I wish I were riding with you."

"There will be opportunity enough for that in the days to come," Arthur told him.

The men of Uladh numbered three hundred and thirty, along with their five lords, and all were mounted; one hundred and fifty horsemen were placed under Arthur's command, and the same number under Conaire's. It had been decided that a smaller warband of thirty would remain behind to maintain a rear guard and prevent an enemy force from circling round behind us; that task had fallen to Fergus, Gwenhwyvar and me.

The two warbands departed, leading their horses silently down the cliff track to the strand below; there, they would remount and take up their attack positions. Once they had reached the strand and moved off, we were to follow and guard our retreat. Arthur was determined that there should be no chance for the enemy to sound the alarm, so he and Conaire would attack at will, and without warning.

When the last of the warriors had descended the cliff track, we started down. Although the trail was steep and rough, the moonlit path was easy to see and we had no difficulty making our way down. The others had already vanished by the time we reached the strand. I wondered that so many warriors could melt so quickly and quietly into the darkness. We remounted and established a guard on the cliff trail, and another a short distance along the shore.

Then we settled ourselves to watch and wait, our weapons in our hands. I could see the enemy campfires stretching into the distance. The nearest lay only a few thousand paces from where we waited, and although I could not see any of the Vandali in the darkness, I could hear their voices—the sound carried inland on the sea breeze—a coarse, broken speech, harshly uttered. And with this, the clink and clatter of men making rough camp.

All at once, there came a shout from up the beach, brutally truncated in mid-cry. A heartbeat later, the invader camp was in turmoil. Shouts echoed along the cliffside. I glimpsed the forms of horses moving against the firelight, and the swift, flashing glint of weapons as they rose and fell. The darkness itself seemed to swirl and swarm.

As abruptly as it had begun, the attack was over. Almost before the enemy could arm themselves, the defenders had struck and vanished. And before the alarm could spread to the next camp, that camp, too, was under attack. In this way, the assault traveled up the coast away from us, and we gradually lost sight of our warriors—although the sound of the havoc they created continued long after they had gone.

Still we watched and waited. The night passed in a tense but idle vigil. Gwenhwyvar dismounted and walked a little way along the strand. I joined her. We walked a short while in silence, eyes and ears straining into the darkness. "Do not fret for him," I told her. "He will be well."

"Fret for Arthur? I wish I were *with* him."

The sky was growing gray in the east when a call came from the clifftop above. We turned to see a dark figure making its way down the cliff track. "Lord Fergus," said the man, running to meet us. "Conaire has returned. He is waiting for you."

"And Arthur?" asked Gwenhwyvar, betraying a shred of concern after all.

"He has not yet returned," the messenger replied.

"You go, Myrddin," Fergus said. "I will wait here a little longer for Arthur."

Gwenhwyvar and I left Fergus and ascended to the clifftop where Conaire and his warriors were waiting, exhausted and bruised from their night's work, but jubilant.

"I regret you were not there to see us," the king said. "When you hear the tale, you will rue your misfortune that you missed it. Oh, it was a beautiful fight, I tell you."

His battlechiefs agreed loudly. "The enemy runs away at

first sight of a horse!" some said. "And their leaders cannot command them." Others offered, "They hardly know how to use their own weapons!"

The Irish were ecstatic at their easy mastery of a much more numerous foe. In this, I saw Arthur's genius at work: he had designed this exercise not only to harass the enemy, but to inspire the Irish at the same time. They had gained confidence in their ability to attack and rout the invader with small risk to themselves. Thus, when next the two forces met, the Irish would hold themselves superior no matter how many foemen faced them across the line.

A pale white sun was showing above the eastern rim when Arthur finally returned. Like Conaire, he had suffered no loss greater than his night's sleep. Unlike Conaire, he was far from jubilant. He kept his distress to himself, however, until we were alone at Rath Mor.

"What is troubling you, Arthur?" I asked. As he had seemed ill-disposed to talk on the way back, I waited until Gwenhwyvar had gone to bed before challenging him outright.

"I do not like these Vandali," he said darkly.

"Conaire is very well pleased with them," I remarked. We sat at the far end of the hut the Irish king had provided for their quarters; Gwenhwyvar slept in the bedplace behind the wattle wall.

"Yes," granted Arthur, "but the Irish have little experience dealing with barbarians. They think that because the enemy fears our horses, he can be easily beaten."

"What do you think?"

"I think they are waiting for their lord. He has yet to come ashore; when he does, it will begin."

"Indeed. But why would he wait?"

Arthur shrugged heavily. "Who knows why the barbarians do anything? Their ways are past reckoning."

"That is true." I paused, then asked the question foremost in my mind. "Can the Irish defeat them?"

The High King of Britain considered this for a long time before answering. "No," he said at last, shaking his head.

"They are skilled horsemen and warriors," he allowed, "but their courage is brittle and they are easily given to despair. Also they are wayward and contrary, Myrddin, I swear it. Tell them one thing and they do another." He paused. "But that is not what disturbs me most."

"What then?"

"We cannot drive these invaders away without the aid of the British kings," he said gloomily.

I finished his thought: "And British kings will never risk their lives and kingdoms to aid the Irish."

"They will sooner cut off their own arms than lift sword to defend Ierne," he muttered. "Even so, how long do you think the barbarian will content himself with this scrag of turf and rock when Britain stands ripe for the plucking? Even the Irish do not content themselves with raiding one another, but ever and always leap across the sea to our fair shores when seeking easy plunder."

He had read the situation aright, and I told him so.

"Aye," he agreed grimly, "when the barbarian has plundered here, he will turn greedy eyes towards Ynys Prydein. Pray that does not happen, Myrddin. We have just put down the Saecsens—Britain cannot survive another war."

7

 "WAYWARD AND CONTRARY!" Gwenhwyvar cried. "Easily given to despair!" She charged into the room and planted herself before us, fists on hips.

"Gwenhwyvar," Arthur said, somewhat startled. "I thought you were asleep."

"Listen to the both of you," she scolded. "I will tell you what troubles me, shall I? You haughty Britons think you are the only men alive who know how to throw a spear."

"Calm yourself. I did not mean—" began Arthur.

"You think you are the only men under God's blue heaven who know how to defend your land and people from enemy invaders! You think—"

"Enough, woman!" Arthur said, rising to his feet. "I am sorry! I did not mean for you to hear."

"Sorry!" Gwenhwyvar stepped nearer, her nose almost touching his chin. "Sorry that I heard your scurrilous talk, or sorry for what you said?"

"I feel the way I feel," Arthur told her, growing angry. "I cannot change that."

"What do you know, you big stump?" Gwenhwyvar pushed her face into his, though she had to stand on toe tip to do it.

Arthur's jaw bulged dangerously. "I know what I see with my own eyes."

"Are you blind then?" Gwenhwyvar scoffed. "For a truth

you know nothing of Ierne's people. You know nothing of our courage. You know nothing—"

Taken by fury, she leaned too far and fell forward. Arthur, red-faced and furious, without a thought reached out, took her elbow and steadied her.

Quick as a lash, Gwenhwyvar snapped, "Take your hand from me, Briton!" placed both hands against his chest, and shoved him backwards. Caught off-balance Arthur went down, and Gwenhwyvar, supremely triumphant, stormed out of the house.

Arthur sat astonished for a moment. Then: "It is as I told you, Myrddin. They are a contrary race, and hasty. And that is the end of it."

I put out a hand to help him up. "What will you do now?" I said, ignoring the squabble.

"We must return at once to Britain," he said. "We must raise the support of Britain's kings and persuade them to pledge warriors to the fight."

"Easier to persuade the invaders to turn their ships and sail away," I replied.

"You know them too well," Arthur agreed. "Yet, I see no better hope for Ierne. Indeed, it is Britain's best hope as well. For if we can defeat the Vandali here, Britain will remain unscathed."

I left Arthur to his rest then, and went in search of a place where I might sit alone with my thoughts. I found a sheltered nook in the shadow of the wall, wrapped myself in my cloak, and settled down to contemplate the magnitude of the disaster that had befallen us.

Oh, it was a calamity and I knew it. Britain was newly united, the alliance still soft; it would harden in time—given the chance. But the British kings had suffered at Baedun, and they needed time to heal their wounds and rebuild their warbands. Even Arthur's most loyal lords would view a war across Muir Eireann with cold eyes. The Irish had long been a thorn in the British flesh with their incessant raiding. Few Britons would see the prudence of Arthur's summons—much less understand it—and none would welcome it.

At the very least they would resist. Worse, I feared, they would turn against him. And should worse come to worst, the fragile alliance would shatter; our hard-won peace would be but a memory, and the Kingdom of Summer would die in its infancy. It had long been all my care to aid that birth, and the last thing I desired was to see that long and arduous—and life-costly—work undone. Great Light, I would do anything, *anything* to prevent that.

I thought long and hard, and was drawn from my contemplation at last by the jangling clang of the alarm. Conaire, like the chieftains of old, had a strip of iron hung from a post outside his hall. When need arose, the iron was struck with a hammer and the people ran to answer the alarm.

Stirring myself, I rose and made my way to the hall among the scurrying Uladh folk. I saw Cai, with his distinctive hobbling gait, hurrying across the yard, and called to him. He joined me and we walked together to the assembly place.

Conaire stood with the hammer in his hands and a fierce look on his face. "The enemy approaches!" he shouted, and began ordering the defense of Rath Mor.

"Where is Arthur?" Cai wondered, looking around the crowd.

"Asleep, I suppose. You'd best go wake him." Cai hastened away. Warriors were already rushing to arm themselves and take up defensive positions on the wall.

Bedwyr and Llenlleawg appeared. "What is happening?" Bedwyr yawned. "Trouble?"

"We are being attacked," I answered. "Reprisal for last night's raid, no doubt."

"Where is Arthur?"

"Cai has gone to rouse him."

"Did he need rousing?" wondered Bedwyr.

My eyes flicked to his face, and then to where he was looking. I saw Arthur emerging from the round house, doing up his belt. And then I saw what Bedwyr had seen: Gwenhwyvar, face flushed, emerging behind him, her hair awry and her laces undone.

"Perhaps not," I replied. "It appears he was already well roused."

Llenlleawg smiled, and Bedwyr observed, "The barbarians will rue the day they called the Bear of Britain from his den."

Arthur joined us and received word of the enemy advance calmly. "How many?" he asked.

"Conaire did not say," Bedwyr informed him.

Arthur gave a nod to Llenlleawg, who dashed away at once, and it came to me that Arthur had begun trusting more and more to the Irish champion. Not that he neglected Cai and Bedwyr, mind, but he now included Llenlleawg in his confidence. Where there had been but two, there were now three. I wondered where Gwenhwyvar would fit in this triumvirate.

Still, judging from what I had seen in the hut, Gwenhwyvar could speak for herself. I had no doubt she would make a place for herself precisely where she wanted it. She joined us now and took her place beside Arthur. "How many?" she asked.

"I have sent Llenlleawg to determine," Arthur replied. There was no trace of vexation or ire in either of them. Like a summer storm over Loch Erne, it had all blown over without a trace, leaving the sky brighter and the sun warmer than before the wind and rain.

Conaire summoned his bards and chieftains to attend him, and pushed his way into the hall. The Irish king was outraged that the Vandal horde should appear at his gates. "They tracked us from the beach," he shouted as we entered the hall. He threw an angry fist in Arthur's face, the previous night's euphoria forgotten in the new day's crisis. "This would never have happened if you had not attacked them. Now they have come here for their revenge."

Arthur bristled at the king's accusation. "It was to be expected," he replied coolly. "Or did you think they would not march against you if you let them take your land?"

This reply made Conaire even angrier. "This is your doing! I should have known better than to listen to a British tyrant.

On my father's head, I will not allow myself to be beguiled again."

"Conaire Red Hand!" It was Gwenhwyvar in full cry. "It is a wicked thing you are doing. Stop it! You disgrace yourself and I will not hear it."

Fergus joined his daughter. "If not for Arthur, the enemy would have overwhelmed us before now. The Britons have faced barbarians before. I say we listen to them." He turned to Arthur. "Tell us what you would have us do."

I believe Conaire felt some relief at having the decision taken from him. In his heart, he was secretly grateful to Arthur for his superior battle cunning. But, lest his bards and lords account this a weakness, he felt he must rant against Arthur. Thus, it was all bluff and bluster, and there was no real wrath in it.

Arthur did not wait to be asked again. "I say we move against them at once. We must not allow them to establish themselves outside our walls, or we will be trapped inside."

Conaire drew himself up. "That is just what I was going to suggest myself. It is good to see that the British battlechief agrees with me." He turned to his lords. "We will assemble as before. Those of you who followed Arthur last night will do so again. The rest will follow me."

He turned back, and regarded us with an imperious gaze. "When you are ready, Britons," he said, as if we were recalcitrant children. "The enemy awaits."

Gwenhwyvar regarded him with an angry stare. "That swaggering butt of a man," she said. "Does he think he is Emperor of Rome to treat us this way?" She turned to her husband. "We should leave him to the Vandali."

"Truly," replied Arthur, watching as the Irish lords noisily left the hall. When they had gone, we followed.

Out in the yard, the stablers and boys were saddling the horses, and warriors strapped on armor and swords while their kinsmen scurried about on desperate errands. Gwenhwyvar went to fetch her arms and ready herself for battle. Arthur stood at the door of the hall and looked on the tumult for a moment, then said, "If we live to see the end of this day, Myrddin, I swear upon my sword that I will yet teach these Irish some order."

The turmoil quickly abated, however, and we were soon ready. All that remained was for Llenlleawg to return with word of the strength and position of the enemy forces. We waited, growing anxious and apprehensive. "Something has happened to him," Cai grumbled, jabbing the end of his spear into the dirt.

"Not Llenlleawg," Bedwyr replied. "He is too slippery an eel to fall foul of any barbarian net."

Still we waited. Cai was for going after Llenlleawg to discover for himself what had happened. Arthur advised against it. "He knows the hiding places in the land. He will return when he can."

"Oh, aye," Cai agreed. "Aye. I know. But I would feel better for knowing the enemy's strength and position."

"So would I, Cai," Bedwyr said, "and trust Llencelyn to bring us word in time."

Cai laughed aloud at Bedwyr's epithet, and Arthur chuckled.

"Llencelyn?" I asked. "Why do you call him that?" It was a play on the Irish champion's name with the word for storm. I saw the humor, but was curious to hear Bedwyr's reason, for it meant they had begun to admit the Irishman into the intimate fellowship enjoyed by Arthur's Cymbrogi.

"You have seen him, Emrys. We all know he fights like a whirlwind."

"Indeed," Cai concurred, "he is a very tempest."

Gwenhwyvar joined us then, all gleaming points and keen edges. Her mail shirt shimmered like a wet skin, and the spike of her spear blade shone. She wore a kilt of leather and high leather boots. Her hair was gathered and bound tight at her neck; and, like the warrior queens of her people, she had daubed her face and arms with bright blue woad: spirals, stripes, sunbursts and serpents. She appeared fierce and beautiful, almost lethally dangerous to behold.

I had never seen her so, and remarked at my surprise in her transformation. She took my astonishment for flattery. "You have never seen me lead a warband against an invader," she replied. "But you are fortunate indeed, Myrddin Emrys, for this woeful lack is soon redressed."

"Lady," Bedwyr said, "I reckon myself fortunate that I do not have to lift blade against you, and I can but pity the luckless wretches who do."

Arthur, deriving great pleasure from his wife's appearance, grinned and put his hand to her chin. He took a dab of woad onto his finger and applied it to his own face: two slashes high on his cheeks beneath each eye.

"Allow me," said Gwenhwyvar, taking some of the paint from her arm. She put her fingertips to his forehead and drew two vertical lines down the center of his brow. In a stroke, the Bear of Britain became a Celt like the warrior kings of old who first faced the Roman Eagles across the ditch.

"How do I look?" he asked.

Cai and Bedwyr were as taken with the transformation as I was, and acclaimed it by demanding marks of their own. "I will have woad-paint made for all of us," Gwenhwyvar told them as she dabbed their faces. "From now on we will greet the enemy with the blue."

A shout came from the platform above the gate. "A rider approaches!"

"Llenlleawg returns," Arthur said, starting towards the gate as the gatemen hastened to admit the rider. The sound of hooves reached us, and a moment later, Llenlleawg pounded through the gap and into the yard. He slid from the back of his mount and, ignoring Conaire and the Irish chieftains who called out to him, strode instead directly to Arthur.

"They want to talk to you," Llenlleawg told him.

"Do they indeed?" wondered Arthur. "When and where?"

"On the plain," Llenlleawg answered. "Now."

"How many have come?" asked Bedwyr.

"A thousand and two hundreds at least, maybe more."

While the others strove to take this in, he added, "I think they have all come ashore now."

"God save us," Bedwyr muttered under his breath. "Twelve hundred to our three."

"Treachery for certain," Cai declared.

Conaire arrived, angry at being made to run to Arthur for word of what Llenlleawg had discovered. "Am I to beg for every scrap from your table?" he demanded. "Will someone yet tell me what is happening here?"

"They want to talk to us," replied Arthur simply.

"By all means," spat Conaire, "let us talk to them. Our spears will be tongues, and our swords teeth. We will give them such a splendid conversation."

"They say that if we do not talk to them," Llenlleawg continued, "they will rub us out and burn everything. Then they will strew the ashes in the sea, so that nothing will remain."

"If this is how they parlay, then we are speaking to the wind," Cai replied.

"Who told you this?" I asked Llenlleawg. "How did you come by this message?"

The lean Irishman's face fell and he blushed with shame. He drew a deep breath and confessed: "I was taken prisoner, Emrys."

"How could this happen?" wondered Fergus.

"I alone am to blame. I saw the foemen assembled on the plain, and thought to ride close." He paused. "I rode into a band of enemy chieftains scouting ahead of the host. They were in the wood and I did not see them until it was too late."

"Why did you not fight them, man?" demanded Fergus.

"I would have welcomed such a fight!" declared Conaire.

"Let him speak!" shouted Arthur, growing annoyed.

"They surrounded me," Llenlleawg said, "and before I could draw sword one of them began shouting to me in our own tongue. He begged me to save my own life and that of my kinsmen by taking word back to our lords."

"You did well," Arthur told him. "Let us hope it is the saving of many lives."

"It is a coward's ruse," Conaire announced. "They can have nothing to say that we care to hear."

"No doubt," allowed Arthur judiciously. "Still, we will listen all the same."

"Listen? Let *them* listen! I mean to give them words of my own to chew on," boasted Conaire. He was becoming exasperated at finding himself pushed aside by this turn of events.

"They want to speak to Arthur alone," Llenlleawg told him. "They said they would only speak to the king who ordered the night raid."

Fergus shook his head. "It is surely a trick," he warned. "Revenge for last night's attack."

Cai agreed. "Hear him, Artos. Fergus may be right. We cannot allow you to meet them alone."

Arthur made up his mind at once. "Very well. We will go out to them together," he said, "then Myrddin and I will advance to speak to them."

We mounted the war host and rode to the wide grassy plain south of the stronghold where, as Llenlleawg had said, the Vandal horde waited. The ground sloped slightly away towards the west, rough and uneven with hillocks of turf and rocks. A ragged little stream meandered through the center of the plain, dividing it from north to south. We rode to the head of the plain and halted to overlook the battleground.

"Earth and sky bear witness!" Bedwyr gasped when he saw the battle throng. "Twelve hundred only? It seems twice that many at least, or I never drew sword."

The barbarian swarmed thick across the western half of the plain in untidy clusters around standards of various kinds: some of skin, others of cloth, or metal, but all of them bearing the image of a black boar in their design. These were, I decided, their clan groupings. Like the Saecsen, the Vandali entered battle surrounded by their kinsmen, under leadership of their tribal chieftain.

Continuing on, we advanced slowly onto the plain. At our

approach, a knot of barbarians drew apart from the center mass, crossed the stream, and marched towards us. One of the chieftains carried a standard—the head and pelt of a great black boar fixed upon a pole. The boar's mouth was open, his curving yellow tusks exposed.

We proceeded to within a hundred paces of one another, whereupon the barbarian delegation stopped. "This is far enough," Arthur said. "Stay here." The war host halted, and Arthur and I rode on to meet the Vandal chiefs.

Like the others we had seen, they were big, well-muscled men; they carried the heavy wooden shield and stout black spear. Naked to the waist, they wore either leather leggings or coarse-woven cloth breeches. Their flesh was the color of pale honey or aged parchment; and, to a man, their hair was black— they wore it long and braided thick. Several had thin mustaches over their wide mouths, but most did not; none wore a beard. Their eyes were strange—sly and narrow, slanting upwards in their broad, brutal faces—keen and wary, and set deep under heavy brows; made more mysterious by a thick band of black paint slashed across their wide cheeks.

A tall, lanky man stood with them; his skin was milk-white and his hair the color of flax. On his neck he wore a thick iron ring, with slightly smaller bands on each wrist. Ragged scars of vicious slash marks, livid still, marked the flesh of his chest and stomach.

It was this man who addressed us, speaking in our own tongue. "In the name of Amilcar, War King of the Vandal nations, we greet you," he said. "It is Amilcar's war host you see before you; it is by his hand that you are alive this day."

By way of reply, Arthur said, "It is not my custom to exchange greetings with any who threaten war against me or those I have sworn to protect."

The tall man replied with benign indifference. "I understand, lord." Touching his neck ring he said, "I am often made to bear tidings others find offensive."

"Since you are a slave, I will assume that the words you speak are not your own. Therefore, I hold no enmity toward you." The slave said nothing, but inclined his head slightly, giving us to know that Arthur understood his predicament aright. "What is your name, friend?"

"I am Hergest," he said. "And though I am a slave, I am a learned man."

"As you are a Latin speaker," Arthur said, "are you also a holy man?"

"I own no king but the Lord Christ, High King of Heaven," Hergest answered proudly. "Formerly, I was a priest. The barbarian burned our church and killed our bishop along with many of our brothers. The rest were made slaves. I alone survive."

At this, the slave lifted his hand as if presenting the barbarian company to us. Instead, he said, "You may speak freely. They understand no tongue but their own."

"Have you been long with them?" I asked.

"It is three years since I was taken," Hergest replied.

"You must have proven your value to them many times over," I observed.

"Indeed," replied the slave, "I must prove it anew with every day that passes, for I know I will not outlive my usefulness by so much as a single breath."

One of the big-shouldered barbarians grew impatient with the talk and grunted something to Hergest, who answered him in his own tongue. "Ida says you must come down from your mount if you are to speak to him." Hergest paused, allowing himself the shadow of a smile. "They fear horses greatly."

"Tell him," Arthur replied calmly, patting the horse's neck, "that I will come down from my mount, but only to speak to one of my own rank and authority."

"Arthur!" I whispered. "Have a care!"

The slave started. "Arthur?" he asked in surprise. "You are Artorius—also called the Bear of Britain?"

"I am known by that name," Arthur answered; indicating the staring barbarian, he replied, "Now tell them what I said."

Hergest repeated Arthur's refusal to dismount and, to my surprise, the barbarian simply nodded, conceding the situation with placid acceptance. He and several others began discussing the matter between them. One of them—who seemed to be the youngest of the chieftains—spoke earnestly to Hergest, who pointed at Arthur and gravely intoned the words "Artorius Rex! Imperator!" The chieftain called Ida cast a dubious sidelong glance at Arthur, then turned abruptly and began striding across the plain to where the horde waited.

"That was well done, lord," Hergest told us. "They wished only to make certain that you were a king worthy of treating with their own leader. Mercia here"—he nodded to the young chieftain—"thinks that because you are young like him you must be a warrior of little worth or consequence. I assured them that you were greater even than the Emperor of Rome."

Arthur smiled, "You might have restrained your enthusiasm for my sake. Still, I will try not to make you out a liar."

The barbarian chieftain had reached the battle host. He addressed someone there, and then turned and pointed at us. A moment later, a figure emerged from the mass and walked toward us. The first chieftain fell into step behind this person, with two standard-bearers on either side.

The man was even taller than those around him—a champion of imposing stature, with wide, heavy shoulders, a powerful back, and thick-muscled limbs. Like those around him, he watched us with quick, intelligent dark eyes, above high cheekbones—all but obscured beneath a wide band of black paint. A thick mustache flowed over fleshy lips, and a long, black, double braid hung over one shoulder. In his right hand he carried a slender iron rod with the image of a boar in hammered gold at its top.

At his approach, the other barbarians moved aside, each man striking his chest with the flat of his hand as his lord passed. He came to stand before us, whereupon Arthur dismounted.

Hergest, standing between them, said something in the guttural speech of the Vandali, then turned to Arthur and said, "Lord Arthur, the man you see before you is Amilcar, War King of Hussa, Rögat, and Vandalia."

The barbarian king raised his iron rod and placed his left

hand upon the golden boar. He grunted something to Hergest, but his eyes never left Arthur's.

"As you are called the Bear of Britain," the slave explained, "the mighty Amilcar desires that you shall call him by the name his enemies have learned to fear."

"What is that?" asked Arthur.

"Twrch Trwyth," answered Hergest. "Black Boar of the Vandali."

8

"WHY ARE YOU HERE?" ARTHUR asked, his voice calm and steady as his gaze.

The slave Hergest spoke Arthur's words to the Vandal king, who replied impassively. "Twrch would have you know," related the slave, "that he has heard of the deeds of the British Bear and has given command that your realm should not be destroyed at this time. For the Black Boar is also a mighty war leader and it is a sorrowful waste of wealth when two such champions fight."

Amilcar spoke some more, and Hergest continued. "Twrch asks you to consider his elation when he learned the Bear of Britain was here."

"It is difficult to imagine," Arthur replied amiably. "Tell Twrch Trwyth that I am waiting to hear why he has seized land belonging to another."

"He has taken land for his camps—nothing more."

"Does he intend to stay?"

Hergest consulted the barbarian warlord and answered, "Twrch says he intends to plunder the land until he has enough wealth to continue his journey."

"Does his journey have a destination?" I asked the learned slave.

"We have come from Carthage," Hergest explained. "The Emperor of Great Constantine's city sent soldiers to banish the Boar and his people from the land they have held for many generations. So now they search for another home. However, their departure was made in haste and they came away with nothing; thus they require wealth to continue the search."

"I see," replied Arthur. "And does he expect this wealth to be given to him?"

The Boar King and his slave conversed a moment, whereupon Hergest answered, "Twrch says that in honor of your renown and the great esteem in which he holds you, he will not kill you and ravage this weakly defended island—a deed he could easily perform since the vast number of warriors you see before you are but the smallest part of his war host, and more are coming here even now. Twrch says it is a very great gift he offers you. In return for this kindness, he expects you to make a gift of equal value. For he has vowed to destroy both Eiru and the Isle of Britons unless you grant his desire."

Arthur stared implacably at the massive battlechief. "What is his desire?"

Hergest turned to Amilcar and conveyed Arthur's question. The barbarian replied with a grunt.

"Everything," Hergest reported. "He says you must give him all."

To his everlasting credit, Arthur allowed the Vandal chief no support for his greed, nor any hope that it would be rewarded. Neither did he provoke the barbarian with an outright refusal. He turned his eyes to the sky as if pondering the inconstant clouds.

"As you know, these lands are not under my authority," replied Arthur at last. "I could not give you a grain of sand or blade of grass, much less anything else. I know a man of your rank will understand this."

He paused to allow his words to be translated for the Boar King. When Hergest turned back to him, Arthur said, "Therefore, I will take your demand to those who hold authority over this realm—though I do not believe they will grant it."

Arthur's reply was delivered with such confidence and dignity, the Boar King could not but agree. "Take my demand to the rulers of this realm," Amilcar conceded through Hergest. "If, when the sun stands over the battleground, I have not heard their reply, then I will attack and you will all be killed like dogs."

"Well," I observed, as we rode slowly back to the waiting battle host together, "we have gained a span of time at least. Let us use it wisely."

"Was he telling the truth, do you suppose?" wondered Arthur. "Does he really have more warriors on the way?"

"Difficult to say," I replied. "No doubt we shall see."

I expected Conaire and the Irish lords to greet the Vandal's demand with the contempt it deserved, and I was not disappointed.

"Everything?" Conaire hooted. "I say they will have not so much as the breath in their nostrils when we have finished. Let the battle begin at once. They will get nothing from my hand but the sharp end of a spear."

"It is not what you will give them," Arthur said. "It is what the enemy has given us."

"He has given us nothing but the outrage of his assault! Must we also endure the insult of his absurd demands?" Conaire glared at Arthur and at me.

"Why, the Vandal battlechief has given us the victory this day," Arthur replied. "For he has allowed us to determine how the battle will proceed. And I tell you, that is worth the small insult."

We began discussing how best to make use of the boon we had been granted. Conaire grew impatient with the talk. "This makes no sense," he complained. "We have horses and they do not. I say we attack them and ride them down when they flee. We all know they will not stand before our horses."

Bedwyr put him straight. "With all respect, Lord Conaire, there are too many of them. While we attacked one warband, the others would quickly surround us. It is four of them to every one of us, mind. We would soon find ourselves unable to move at all—horses or no."

"Then let us form the line," Conaire suggested. "We will charge them and drive them back to the sea with the points of our spears."

"Nay, lord," Cai replied. "Our force would be spread too thin; we could not sustain the line. They would have only to sever it in one or two places to separate us. Once divided, they would easily overwhelm us."

"What, then?" demanded the Irish king, his brittle patience shattering at last.

"As you rightly say, they fear nothing more than our horses," Arthur told him. "If we hold to the course I will devise, that fear will become a weapon we can wield against them."

At once, Arthur began ordering the fight. In full view of the enemy, we laid our battle plan while the Black Boar stood looking on, waiting, the sun rising higher and hotter all the while. When he had finished, Arthur said, "I will speak with Twrch Trwyth now. While we are together you will lead your warbands into position."

"But they will see us," Fergus suggested. "Would it not be best to surprise them?"

"Another day, perhaps," replied Arthur. "This day I would have them ponder their predicament and let foreboding grow within them."

Arthur and I returned to where the Vandal battlechiefs waited. Amilcar, not at all happy to be made to stand idle while we talked at length, scowled at us. Arthur did not dismount, but spoke to him from the saddle, making the Boar King squint into the sun.

He growled something at us, and Hergest said, "Amilcar demands to know your answer."

"The lords of Ierne say that you shall have nothing from them but the sharp end of the spear," Arthur replied.

Hergest smiled at this, and relayed Arthur's words to his master, who glowered even more fiercely. "Then you will all be killed," the Vandal said through his slave. "Your settlements and strongholds will be burned and your women and children slaughtered; your treasure will be carried off, and your grain and cattle also. When we have finished, not even your name will remain."

When Hergest finished, the Vandal lord added, "I know these are not your people. And though you have refused my gift, I will yet extend my hand to you, Bear of Britain. Join with me, you and your men. Two such mighty war leaders in alliance could win much plunder."

"I care little for war, and less for plunder. Thus, I cannot accept your offer," Arthur answered. "Yet, for the sake of those who own you lord, I will make you an offer in return: take your men and go back to your ships. Leave this island as you found it, taking nothing with you but the sand that clings to the soles of your feet."

"If I do this, what will I receive?"

"If you do as I say, you will receive the Bear of Britain's blessing. Further, I will bid the priests of my realm to make heartfelt prayer to the High King of Heaven, who is my lord, to forgive any crimes you have committed in coming here."

Amilcar recoiled at the suggestion. "Can I fill my treasure house with these prayers?" he sneered. "Who is this lord of yours that I should heed him? Your offer is a mockery, and worthy only of contempt."

"So you say," Arthur replied equably. "Even so, I do not withdraw it."

Just then, one of the Vandal chiefs attending Twrch grunted at him, calling his attention to the movement of our warriors. The Boar King turned to see our force divide itself in three— a main body with two smaller wings to the right and left; these advanced, and the central body withdrew so that it was well behind the protecting wings.

Amilcar barked a stream of commands and questions to his chieftains. They answered with shrugs and worried looks, whereupon he turned to Arthur. "What is this?" he demanded, speaking through Hergest. "Why do you array yourselves for battle in this way?"

"This is to help you understand," Arthur replied, "that we mean to defend our land and people. If you would steal from us, you must be ready to die." These last words were spoken with the cold certainty of the tomb.

The Vandal king's face darkened. His eyes narrowed. He looked again at the odd battle formation. He spoke a few words to Hergest, then turned and walked back to his waiting horde. "Lord Twrch says that he has talked enough. From this day, he is deaf to all entreaties. Expect no mercy—none will be granted."

We sat our horses and watched the Vandal chiefs withdraw. Arthur waited until they had almost reached the stream and rejoined their warbands, and then: "Yah!" He slapped his mount and raced towards them. They turned to the sound of hooves, saw the horse thundering down upon them, and scattered. Arthur swerved at the last moment and snatched away the boar's head standard from the grasp of the astonished Vandal holding it.

None of the enemy knew what had happened until Arthur was already galloping away again. He rode out of spear-throw, stopped and lofted the standard. "Here is your god!" he shouted at them. Then, slowly, so that every eye would see and there could be no question of his intent, he lowered the standard and drove it head first into the ground.

The Vandali did not take this desecration calmly. As the boar's head touched the earth, an enraged cry went up. But Arthur ignored them and, turning serenely away, rode back to where our warriors waited, leaving the boar's head standard in the dirt behind him. The enemy roared the louder.

"That was well done!" cried Fergus as we rejoined them.

"Hoo!" cheered Conaire. "By Lugh's right hand, you are a rascal, Lord Arthur!" He gestured with his spear towards the Vandal host. "Listen to them! Oh, they are angry with you!"

"But do you think it wise to provoke them so?" wondered Gwenhwyvar.

"It is worth the risk, I think," answered Arthur. "How else could I be certain they would be drawn to the center?"

"It is a good ploy," I told him. "Let us hope it works."

The infuriated enemy did not wait to be further disgraced. They loosed a resounding shout and rushed forward, splashing across the stream. They came in a reckless, heedless swarm, running into battle.

It had been a long time since I sat a horse in battle. I had vowed never to fight again, but I felt the sword hilt in my hand, and the old familiar thrill quivered through my spine. Well, it would do no harm to fight today, I reckoned; besides, every blade was desperately needed. Thus, without considering the consequences, I found myself in the forerank of the battle host.

I watched them draw nearer, my heart quickening. I heard the enemy's feet pounding a dull drumbeat on the earth, and saw the sun hard on spear shaft and shield rim. I looked along the line of our own warriors, our swift *ala*. The horses hoofed the ground and tossed their heads, the sundering shout of the enemy making them skittish.

To the right, Cai sat at the head of his wing of fifty. Opposite him to the left, Bedwyr waited with his fifty. Both wings angled inward to force the enemy in towards the center. They ran over the rough ground, screaming as they came.

Gwenhwyvar at my right hand looked across to me. "I have never fought beside Arthur," she mused. "Is he as canny as they say?"

"They do not tell the half of it, lady," I replied. "I have fought beside Uther and Aurelius, and they were warriors to make others pale with envy. But Arthur far outshines his fathers on the unfriendly field."

She smiled with admiration. "Yes, this is what I have heard."

"The Lord of Hosts formed Arthur for himself alone," I told her. "When he rides into battle, it is a prayer."

"And when he fights?" asked Gwenhwyvar, delighted with my acclaim of her husband.

"Lady, when Arthur fights it is a song of praise to the God that made him. Watch him now. You will see a rare and holy sight."

Conaire, sitting opposite me on the other side of Gwenhwyvar, heard our talk, and turned his face to me. "If he is such a fierce warrior," he scoffed, "why do we sit here waiting for the foemen to overwhelm us? A true warrior would meet their attack."

"If you doubt him," I said, "then by all means join the host of vanquished Saecsen who thought they knew something of war. Join the Angli and Jutes, and Frisians and Picti who belittled the Bear of Britain. Speak to them of your superior wisdom—*if* you can find any who will hear you."

Closer and closer the enemy came. Only a few hundred paces separated us from them now. I could see their faces, black hair streaming, mouths agape in savage howls.

"How long must we wait?" demanded Conaire loudly. Some of the Irishmen muttered agreement with their lord. "Let us strike!"

"Hold!" countered Arthur. "Hold, men! Let them come. Let them come."

Llenlleawg, sitting at Arthur's right hand in the front rank, turned in the saddle to face Conaire. "Shut your mouth!" he hissed. "You are scaring the horses."

Fergus, at Arthur's left hand, laughed, and the Irish king subsided with an angry splutter.

The enemy fully expected us to charge them. They were prepared for that. But they were not prepared for us to stand waiting. The nearer they came, the more time they had to think what was to happen to them, and the more their fear mounted within them.

"Hold!" Arthur called. "Stand your ground."

The Vandali reached our outflung wings. As Arthur anticipated, they did not know what to make of the wings and so ignored them in their drive to take the center.

I could almost see what they were thinking—it showed in their faces. Surely now, they were thinking, the Bear of Britain will make his attack—and then we will swarm him and pull him down. But no. He waits. Why does he delay? Does he fear us?

They rushed past the wings and surged on in a wave. Closer, and yet closer. I could see the sweat on their shoulders and arms; I could see the sun-glint in their black eyes.

I felt a thin chill of fear snake through my inward parts. Had Arthur misjudged the moment? Great Light, there were so many!

And then . . .

Arthur raises his sword. Caledvwlch shimmers in his up-raised hand. He leans forward in the saddle.

Still, he hesitates.

The Vandal enemy is wary. Even in their greedy rush they are watching. They know he must charge. They brace themselves for the command, but it does not come. They are drawing swiftly closer, but the command does not come.

Why does he delay? Why does he hesitate?

I can see the doubt in their eyes. They are almost upon us, but Arthur has made no move. The sword hovers in the air, but it does not fall. Why does he delay?

The enemy falters. All eyes are on Arthur now.

It is a slight alteration of gait, a small misgiving. Their step is now uncertain. Doubt has seized them in its coils. They waver.

This is what Arthur has been waiting for.

Caledvwlch falls. Like fire from heaven it falls.

Hesitation ripples through the enemy forerank, passing backward through the floodtide.

The signal is given and the enemy braces for the impact. Still, we do not charge. We make no move towards them. Confusion. Bewilderment. The signal has been given, but no attack comes. What is happening? What does it mean?

Oh, but the trap is sprung. They do not see it. Their doom has come upon them and they do not know it.

Cai slashes in from the right. Bedwyr on the left thrusts forward. The two wings are now jaws with teeth of steel snapping shut. The outwitted barbarians turn to meet the unexpected attack and are instantly divided. Half turn one way and half another.

The center is exposed.

This time there is no hesitation. Caledvwlch flashes up and

down in the same swift instant. And then we are racing forward, flying into the soft belly the enemy host has revealed.

The hooves of the horses bite deep, flinging turf into the air. We shout. The Vandal host hears the cry of our warriors. It is the ancient war cry of the Celt: a shout of defiance and scorn. It is a strong weapon.

And we are flying towards them. I feel the wind on my face. I can smell the fear coming off the enemy warriors. I can see the blood throbbing in their necks as they stumble backwards.

The center collapses. The onrushing Vandal tide is turning. Those in the rear force their way forward even as the forerank folds inward upon itself.

The horse glides beneath me. It undulates slowly and I am part of its rolling rhythm. I see a barbarian turn to meet me. A black spear rises. The sword in my hand sweeps down and I feel the fleeting resistance as the body before me falls away.

Another enemy appears. He leaps forward, jabbing upward with the spear. My blade slashes and the man spins away, clutching his head. I hear his scream and suddenly the clash of frenzied chaos around me slows, dwindling down and down to the barest movement, languid and listless and slow. My vision grows hard-edged and keen as the battle *awen* seizes me.

I look and see the battlefield spread before me, the enemy upon it moving as if in a torpor. Their hands swing in lazy, languid strokes; the spearblades edge cautiously through the air. The Vandal faces are rigid, their eyes fixed, unblinking; their mouths hang open, teeth bared, tongues lolling.

The battle sound throbs in my head. It is the roar of blood pulsing in my ears. I move into the crush and feel the heat of striving bodies; my arm strokes out its easy cadence; my dazzling blade sings out an unearthly melody. I smell the sick-sweet smell of blood. After long absence, I am Myrddin the Warrior King once more.

9

  I MOVE LIKE A STORM-DRIVEN SHIP through the tide. Enemy rise before me—a massive sea-swell of warrior-flesh breaking upon the sharp prow of my blade. I hew with fatal and unforgiving accuracy, death falling swiftly as my unswerving sword. Blood mist gathers before my eyes, crimson and hot. I sail on, heedless of the tempest-waves of foe.

Up and up they rise, and down and down they fall. Death rakes them into heaps of twitching corpses before my high-stepping steed. The spears of the enemy seek me; I have merely to judge the angle of thrust to turn aside their feeble jabs. Every stroke follows a leisurely contemplation in which my mind traces the arc of each movement, and the next and the next. No wasted motion, no effort unrewarded. I kill and kill again.

If death ever wears a human face, this day its face is mine.

The barbarian foreranks cannot stand before us, nor can they retreat—they are too tight-pressed from behind to give feet to their flight. With Cai and Bedwyr forcing the sides into the center, and the center caught between the onrushing horses and their own rear guard still pushing in from behind, the enemy can but stand to our cruel, killing blades.

Eventually, the advance slows, the surge falters, and the tide begins to turn. The foe is flowing away, rear ranks first. The front ranks, feeling the sustaining wall behind give way, fall back. The battleline breaks; the invaders turn and flee the field, leaving their dead and dying heaped upon the earth.

They run screaming, crying their fear and frustration to the unheeding sky. They run in shameful disarray, without thought for their wounded kinsmen. They simply abandon the battleground and all upon it in their flight.

I leap after them, exulting in triumph. My victory song resounds across the plain. The foemen give way before me, stumbling in their haste to save themselves. I drive on and on, lashing my horse to speed.

And then Arthur is beside me, his hand on my sword arm. "Peace! Myrddin! Stop—it is over. The battle is finished."

At his touch, I came to myself. The battle frenzy left me. I felt suddenly weak, drained, my chest hollow; my head throbbed, and I heard a sound like the echo of a mighty shout receding into the heavens, or perhaps into realms beyond this world.

"Myrddin?" Arthur gazed at me, concern and curiosity sharp in his ice-blue eyes.

"Pay me no heed. I am well."

"Stay here," he ordered, urging his horse away. "The pursuit is outpacing us. I must call the warriors back."

"Go," I told him. "I will remain behind."

Our warriors gave chase as far as the stream. But there Arthur called off the pursuit lest the enemy regroup and surround us. Then he returned to the blood-soaked battleground to deal with the wounded and dying barbarians.

"What should we do with them, Bear?" asked Bedwyr. He was scratched and bleeding in several places, but whole.

Arthur gazed across the corpse-strewn field. Crows and other carrion birds were already gathering, their raw calls foretelling a grisly feast.

"Artos?" Bedwyr asked again. "The wounded—what will you have us do?"

"Put them to the sword."

"Kill them?" Cai raised his head in surprise.

"For the love of Christ, Arthur," Bedwyr began. "We cannot—"

"Do it!" Arthur snapped, turning away.

Cai and Bedwyr regarded one another with grim reluctance. Conaire saved them from having to carry out Arthur's order. "I will do the deed, and gladly," the Irish lord volunteered. He called his chieftains together and they began moving among the fallen. A sharp blade-thrust here, a short chop there, and silence soon claimed the battleground.

"Sure, it is a hateful thing," Cai observed sourly, rubbing the sweat and blood from his face with his sleeve.

"Their own kinsmen would do the same," I reminded him. "And they expect no less. Better a quick, painless end than lingering agony."

Bedwyr gave me a darkly disapproving look and stalked off.

Quickly gathering up our own wounded—our losses were uncommonly light—we left the field and returned to Conaire's stronghold. My head still ached with the beating throb of the battle frenzy, and every jolt of the horse sent a spasm through me. Gwenhwyvar's voice stirred me from my self-absorbed regard.

"Did you see him?" she asked, her voice low.

"Who?" I wondered without looking up.

"It was very like you said," she replied. "But I could not have imagined it would be so . . . so splendid."

I turned my head, wincing at the pain. Gwenhwyvar was not looking at me, but at Arthur a little distance ahead. Her skin was glowing with the sheen of exertion, and her eyes were alight.

"No, I did not see him," I told her simply.

Her lips curled with the hint of a smile, and she said, "I do not wonder that men follow him so readily. He is a wonder, Myrddin. He must have killed three score in as many strokes. I have never seen the like. The way he moves through battle— it is as if he were tracing the steps of a dance."

"Oh, yes. It is a dance he knows well."

"And Caledvwlch!" she continued. "I believe it is as sharp

now as when the battle began. My blade is notched and bent as a stick, but his is fresh still. How is it possible?"

"The weapon is not called Caledvwlch for nothing," I told her. She looked at me at last, but only to see if I were mocking her; she turned her gaze to Arthur once more, repeating the word softly. "It means Cut Steel," I added. "It was given him by the Lady of the Lake."

"Charis?" she asked.

"None other," I replied. "My mother may have given him the sword, but the way he uses it, his uncanny skill—that is his own."

"I have seen Llenlleawg fight," Gwenhwyvar reflected. "When the battle frenzy comes upon him, no one can stand against him."

"Well I know it," I replied, recalling the Irish champion's extraordinary ability to turn himself into a fighting whirl-wind.

"The battle frenzy grips him and Llenlleawg loses himself," she continued. "But with Arthur I think it must be the other way: he finds himself."

I commended her perception. "A most astute observation, lady. In truth, Arthur is revealed in battle."

She fell silent then, but the love and admiration in her gaze increased. It is the way of women sometimes, when the man they know so well surprises them, to exult in their discovery and cherish it. Gwenhwyvar hoarded her discovery like a treasure.

We rested through the day, delivering ourselves to the care of those who had remained at Rath Mor. We ate and slept, and roused ourselves at dusk to celebrate the victory we had been granted. By then men were thirsty and hungry, and wanting to hear their feats lauded in song. We ate and drank, and listened while Conaire's bards vaunted the achievements of the warriors, praising one and all with high-sounding words. Cai, Bedwyr, and Arthur were mentioned, of course; but among the kings involved, Conaire shone like a sun among so many lesser lights, though his part in the battle was actually quite small.

This chafed the Britons. "Are we to sit here and listen to this uncouth noise?" Cai demanded. The third bard had just launched into a lengthy retelling of the battle in which the Irishmen featured most prominently, and the British received no mention. "They are telling it all wrong, Myrddin."

"They only praise their king," I replied. "He is the one who feeds them."

"Well, they praise him too highly," Bedwyr put in. "And that is not right."

"They steal the High King's glory and dish it out to Conaire and his brood," Llenlleawg complained. "Do something, Lord Emrys."

"What would you have me do? It is Conaire's right. They are his bards and this is his caer, after all."

The three desisted then, but maintained an aggrieved and peevish silence. Thus it did not surprise me greatly when, as soon as the bard finished his laudatory song, a shout went up from Cai.

"Friends!" he said, leaping to his feet. "We have enjoyed the singing of Irish bards as much as we are able," he said tactfully. "But you would think us Britons a tight-fisted and greedy race if we did not tell you that beneath this roof sits one whose gift in song is owned as one of the chief treasures of Ynys Prydein." He turned and flung out a hand to me. "And that man is Myrddin ap Taliesin, Chief Bard of Britain."

"Is this so?" wondered Conaire loudly. He was feeling the heady effects of flattery and drink, and it made him wonderfully expansive. "Then let us share this treasure you have been hoarding. Sing for us, Bard of Britain! Sing!"

Everyone began pounding on the table and calling for a song. Bedwyr rose and borrowed a harp from the nearest bard; he brought it to me. "Show them," he whispered, placing the harp in my hands. "Show them what a True Bard can do."

I looked at the instrument, considering what I might

sing. I looked at the boisterous throng, red-faced and loud in the clamor of their cups. Such a rare gift should not be wasted on the unworthy, I thought, and passed the harp back to Bedwyr.

"Thank you," I told him, "but it is not for me to sing tonight. This celebration belongs to Conaire and it would be wrong for me to diminish the glory he has rightly won."

Bedwyr scowled. "Rightly won? Are you mad, Myrddin? If there is any glory this night *we* have won it, not Conaire." He offered the harp to me again, and I refused again. "Earth and sky, Myrddin, you are a stubborn man."

"Another time, Bedwyr," I soothed. "We will have our night. Let it be this way for now."

Seeing he could not persuade me, Bedwyr desisted, returning the instrument to its owner with a shrug. Cai gave me a look of supreme disapproval, but I ignored him. Since it was clear I would not sing, and since no more songs were forthcoming, the celebration ended and men began drifting off to their sleeping places.

Just before dawn the next morning, Arthur sent Cai and Bedwyr with a small warband to the coast to observe the movements of the Vandal host. We had slept well, and rose to break fast. I observed the haughty confidence of Conaire's warriors—they swaggered and laughed loudly as they sharpened blades and mended straps—and I remarked on it to Arthur. "Give them one simple victory and they think they have conquered the world."

He smiled grimly. "They think it will always be so easy. Still, I will not discourage them. They will learn the truth soon enough."

Yet, when Bedwyr and Cai returned, they said, "The Boar and his piglets are leaving."

"Truly?" wondered Conaire.

"It is so, lord," replied Cai. "Most of the ships have gone."

"Indeed," added Bedwyr, "only a few remain, and those are even now sailing from the bay."

"Then it is as I thought!" Conaire crowed. "They were only looking for easy plunder. When they saw we meant to fight, they took their search to other shores."

Gwenhwyvar, who had come to stand beside Arthur, turned to him. "What do you think it means?"

He shook his head slightly. "I cannot say until I have seen it for myself."

As quickly as horses could be readied, we rode to the clifftops overlooking the bay, and gazed out on a calm, bright sea speckled with the black sails of departing Vandali ships. The last had left the bay only a short while before we arrived, and were following the others, sailing back the way they had come.

"You see!" cried the Irish king triumphantly—as if the sight vindicated him in some way. "They will not soon forget the welcome they received at Conaire Red Hand's hearth."

"I see them leaving," Fergus replied thoughtfully. "But I am asking myself where they are going."

"That is what I am wondering, too," said Arthur. "And I mean to find out." He turned quickly and summoned Llenlleawg to him; they spoke quietly. The Irish champion nodded once, mounted his horse and rode away.

We returned to Rath Mor, and spent the day resting and waiting for Llenlleawg's return. I slept a little in the heat of the day, and woke to a scattering of low clouds and a freshening wind off the sea. The caer was quiet as I made my way towards the hall.

Bedwyr called to me as I entered the yard. "Myrddin!" he rose from the bench outside the hall and crossed to me quickly. "I have been waiting for you. Arthur asked me to bring you as soon as you stirred."

"Has Llenlleawg returned?"

"No," he replied, "and I think that is why Arthur wishes to see you."

I turned towards the hall, but Bedwyr caught my arm.

"Conaire is there, and he has had too much to drink. Cai is keeping watch inside. Bear is in his hut."

We walked quickly to the hut Arthur and Gwenhwyvar shared. Bedwyr ducked his head and pushed through the ox hide covering. "Bear, I have brought—" he began, then halted abruptly and backed out the door again quickly.

I heard Gwenhwyvar laugh, and Arthur called out, "It is all right, brother, there are no secrets between us."

Bedwyr glanced at me and muttered, "Not anymore."

"Come in," urged Gwenhwyvar. "Come in, both of you. It is all right." The laughter in her voice reminded me of my own Ganieda, and the memory pierced like an arrow through my heart. Ganieda, best beloved, we will yet be together one day.

Bedwyr and I entered the hut. Gwenhwyvar was tying her laces and rearranging her clothing; her hair was tousled and her smile was full. Arthur was reclining. He raised himself on his elbow and offered us places on the hide-covered floor. "You might have told me to delay a little," Bedwyr said, blushing lightly.

"And you might have announced your arrival," Arthur replied with a laugh.

"Dear Bedwyr," Gwenhwyvar said softly, "there is no hurt, and hence no blame. Be easy."

"Llenlleawg has not returned?" Arthur said.

"Not yet." Bedwyr gave his head a slight shake.

"It is as I feared."

"Then you do not know him," Gwenhwyvar began. "He will—"

Arthur did not let her finish. "It is not Llenlleawg's welfare that concerns me. I know full well that he is more than match to any trouble that finds him. But if the invaders had simply sailed away, he would have returned by now. I think it likely the Vandal host has come ashore again farther south. And *if* Amilcar's boast about having more warships waiting—" He left the unsettling thought hanging.

In the wisdom of warcraft, Arthur had no equal. Likely, he

was right. I might have asked him how he had arrived at this conclusion, but I accepted it instead, saying, "What do you propose?"

"Conaire must ride south at once to renew the defense. I will return to Britain and raise the war host."

"Will they agree to fight, do you think?" wondered Bedwyr.

"They have no choice," Arthur said bluntly. "How long will the Island of the Mighty remain secure with the Rampaging Boar just across Muir Eiru?"

"I agree, Bear. All saints bear witness, your words are prudence itself," Bedwyr affirmed. "But prudence is a virtue in short supply among the bull-necked British lords, as you well know. It may be that they will require something more to convince them."

I agreed with Bedwyr, but Arthur remained confident in his ability to reason with the Lords of Britain and win them to the campaign. "We leave at once."

"The ship must be readied," I pointed out.

"I have already sent Barinthus ahead with some of Fergus' men," Arthur said. "Bedwyr, fetch Cai."

Bedwyr rose and paused at the door. "What of Conaire?"

"I will tell Conaire what is to be done," Arthur answered.

"Allow me," Gwenhwyvar offered. "You must not delay or the tide will be against you. Go now. I will explain to Conaire." She saw the question in Arthur's eyes, and said, "Spare no thought for me, my love; I will be well. Besides, Llenlleawg will soon return."

Arthur rose. The matter was concluded and he was eager to be gone. "Very well."

We waited in the yard as our horses were made ready. Fergus and Cai emerged from the hall. "It is better we were gone," Cai told us. "That Conaire is itching for a fight and I fear he will have one before this day is through."

"You go," Fergus said. "Leave Conaire to me. I know him, and I will see no harm is done."

"I leave it to you then," Arthur said, swinging himself up

into the saddle. "Do what you must, but be ready to ride south as soon as Llenlleawg returns. I will send men and supplies as soon as I reach Caer Melyn."

"Fare well, my love," Gwenhwyvar said.

Arthur leaned down and gathered her in a quick embrace, and we then rode from Rath Mor and hastened towards the coast. The ship was waiting when we arrived, and the tide was already flowing. Wasting not a moment, we boarded the horses, slipped the line, and pushed off. Once into the bay, Barinthus raised the sail and the ship took wings back to Britain.

10

  WE ENTERED MOR HAFREN AS soon as it was light and came within sight of the hills surrounding Caer Melyn. For two nights and a day, Barinthus and his crew had wrested speed from contrary and fitful winds to reach the trail to Arthur's southern stronghold as the sun broke the horizon in a blaze of red and flaming gold. Once more in the saddle, we flew through shadowed valleys blue with hanging mist. By the time we reached Caer Melyn, I could feel the heat of the day to come.

And I felt something else: a stab of foreboding, sharp and quick. My senses pricked.

At our approach, the gates of the fortress were thrown open wide and, as the others entered the yard to the acclaim of their sword brothers, I paused before passing the threshold. There was a cloying closeness in the air, a stillness that stifled, and seemed to me more than just the early warmth of a hot summer day. It was as if an enormous, suffocating presence, unseen as yet, though near, was shifting its immense weight towards us, thickening the air around it as it came. I could feel the ominous advance as that of a silent squall line of storm cloud drawing over the land. But there were no clouds; nothing could be seen.

Yet, despite the glad greeting we received from the Cymbrogi, my heart remained troubled by this strange feeling of oppression.

Arthur wasted not a moment. Even while he washed and

189

pulled on clean clothes, he called commands to his battlechiefs. He sent riders to make for the realms round about to summon all the nearest lords to council and ordered ships to take word to the north. Gwalchavad, ever eager to plow the sea fields, led the ship-borne messengers; they departed the caer at once and were gone before the sound of their greeting had faded in the air. Arthur then commanded the Cymbrogi to ready the remaining fleet. There were provisions to load, weapons to assemble, horses to gather in from the grazing lands as, once more, the *Dux Bellorum* prepared for war.

I had little part in the preparations. My place was with Arthur in council, and I readied myself in the best way I knew to receive the southern noblemen: I prayed. Arthur thought the warbands would rise to his call; but I knew it would take more than a polite request to move British kings to pursue a war on Irish soil.

This, of course, I tried telling Arthur, but he would not hear it. "And *I* tell *you*, Myrddin, it is either fight the Boar on Irish soil, or fight him here. Blood will be spilled either way, I do not deny it; we can at least save the destruction of our lands."

"I do believe you. However, the Lords of Britain will want a better reason," I insisted, "to fight shoulder to shoulder with those who have dealt them so much heartache through the years."

"That is past and forgotten."

"We are an unforgiving race, Arthur," I continued. "We have long memories. Or have *you* forgotten?"

He did not smile at my meager jest. "They will listen to me," he maintained. His confidence brooked no opposition.

"They will listen, yes. They will sit down and discuss the matter until the cock crows, but will they act? Will they raise so much as an eyebrow to aid you in what every last one of them will regard as a quarrel between barbarians? Indeed, most of them will think it divine punishment on the Irish for their thieving and warring ways."

It was clear that Arthur would not hear it, so I stopped telling him. I took my leave and left him to his plans. Stepping from the hall, I nearly collided with Rhys, Arthur's steward, hurrying away on some errand or other. "Ah, Rhys! There you are. I have been looking for you."

"I give you good greeting, Emrys," he replied quickly, and asked: "Is it true we are joining the Irish in a boar hunt?"

"Yes," I answered, and told him the boar we were hunting was human. Then I asked, "Where is Bors?"

"A message came two days ago from Ban," Rhys explained. "Bors was summoned home."

"Trouble?"

"I think so. But Bors did not say what it was. He only said he would return as soon as he had seen to his brother's affairs."

"Have you told Arthur this?"

"No," he answered. "I have been running since you arrived, and—"

"Well, tell him now." Rhys looked past me into the hall. "Yes, at once. We will talk again later."

When he had gone, I slung my harp upon my back and walked out from the caer and down to the little Taff river to find a shady place to sit and think.

In the shaded valley, down among the green rushes, I sat myself upon a moss-covered rock and listened to the water ripple as it slid along the deep-cut banks. Bees and flies droned on the lifeless air and water bugs spun in small circles on the slow-moving water. There with the ancient elements of darkness, earth, and water, I cast my net of thought wide. "Come to me!" I whispered to the air. "Come to Myrddin. Illumine me . . . illumine me."

I sat bent over the polished curve of my harp as if I might pluck the knowledge I sought from the song-laden strings with my fingertips. But though the harp gave forth its quicksilver melody, I was not enlightened. After a while, I put the harp aside and took up my staff instead.

It was, I reflected, a venerable length of rowan, the stout wood smoothed with use. Bedwyr had made it for me following my ordeal with Morgian. The thought brought a fleeting twinge of fear—like the shadow of a circling crow touching my face.

I pushed the hateful memory from me, however, and gradually felt the peace of the valley, like its deep, still warmth, enfold me. I fell into a waking sleep, a reverie, and I began to dream. I saw the mountains of Celyddon, dark-clothed in their sharp-scented pines, and beyond them the barren, windy heathlands of the Little Dark Ones, the Hill Folk. I saw the members of my adopted family, the Hawk Fhain. I saw Gern-y-fhain, the Wise Woman of the hills, my second mother, who taught me the use of powers even druids have forgotten—if they ever knew.

Thinking on these things, I let my mind wander where it would. I heard the riversound, the gentle ripple of water lapping, and the dry twitch of grass where a mouse or bird passed. I heard the click of a moorhen, and the sawing buzz of a fly. These sounds faded away slowly, replaced by the rasping hiss of a whisper, broken by time and distance, but gradually growing stronger. Words began to form. . . .

Dead? . . . Dead. . . . But what do you mean? How can it be? . . . No! No! The anguished voice faded away in a stifled scream and was replaced by another: *I am burning. . . . I cannot see . . . Lie down, Garr. I will help you. Do not try to stand. . . .* I heard a child's voice crying: *Wake up, Nanna. Wake up!* The small voice dissolved into sobs, and was mingled with other cries which grew into such a wailing and shrieking that I felt their distress as a keening lament. My soul writhed in sympathy; tears came to my eyes. And yet, no hint of what was happening, or where.

Great Light, comforter of all who mourn and are heavy-laden, sustain those who need your strength in the day of their travail. This, for the sake of your Blessed Son. So be it!

I prayed and remained silent for a time. But the voices did not return, and I knew they would not now come again. I had sometimes heard voices in the past; and now, as then, it did not occur to me to doubt their veracity. That I should hear them did not surprise me; it merely confirmed once again the capricious blessing of the *awen*.

Thrice blessed is the Emrys of Britain! It is the blessing of my mother's race to make me long-lived, just as it was the blessing of my father, singing the very life into my soul, which awakened the *awen*. The blessing of Jesu called me forth to serve in this worlds-realm.

Oh, but I am a wickedly slothful servant, dim-sighted and slow of understanding, preferring my warm dark ignorance to wisdom's cold light. When men speak of Myrddin Emrys in years to come—if they should remember me at all—it will be as a blind beggar, the fool in the courts of kings, the simpleton whose ignorance was exceeded only by his pride. I am not worthy of the gifts I have been given, and I am not equal to the tasks those gifts beget.

High King of Heaven, forgive me. There is no truth but it is illumined by you, Great Light. Though I see, I am a blind man still. Lord Christ, have mercy on me.

So the river ran, and so ran my thoughts. The mind of man is a curious thing. Seeking knowledge, I was confronted with my own ignorance; I could but admit my poverty and embrace mercy instead.

The first of the summoned lords had arrived with his war-band by the time I returned to the caer. Ulfias, whose lands were nearest, was with Arthur in the hall. They sat at table together, with Cai, Bedwyr and Cador attending. Ulfias, looking grim and uncertain, lifted his head as I entered, but did not rise. Arthur glanced up, grateful for my arrival. "Ah, Myrddin, good. I thought to send the hounds after you." He turned to Rhys, hovering nearby. "Fill the cup." As Rhys produced a jar, Arthur continued, "I have been telling Ulfias about the Vandali invading Ierne."

Having taken the measure of Ulfias, I looked the wavering lord in the eye and demanded, "Well then, will you support your king?"

The young lord swallowed hard. "It is a very difficult thing, to be sure," he muttered. "I would like to hear what the other lords say."

"Cannot you determine your own mind?"

My question shamed him. He actually winced. "Lord Emrys," he said in a disconcerted tone, "is it not to be decided in council? What the council agrees to do, that will I do. You have my pledge."

"A pledge is but a paltry thing," I scoffed. "And if the council decides to bare its bottom and sit on the dung heap? Will you do that as well?"

Cai and Cador laughed.

"Beware," warned Bedwyr under his breath. "You go too far."

But Arthur said, "Never fear, Ulfias. It may not come to that. But if it does, no doubt you will enjoy the close companionship of your friends."

Oh, Arthur was astute. Though he made light of my remark, he would allow Ulfias no dignified means of retreat. The Dubuni lord was caught in his own indecision; he must remain unmoved and endure the scorn, or redeem himself.

"Come, Ulfias," Cador urged amiably, "let us support our king as we have sworn to do. And who knows? We may grow to love Ierne."

Ulfias swallowed his pride and said, "Very well. If the women there are all as fair as Gwenhwyvar, I may even take an Irish wife."

"I do not wonder that you say so," Cai told him solemnly. "I have seen the Dubuni tribe, and you could do worse than choose an Irish maid—if you can find any who would have you."

Ulfias smiled doubtfully. This gentle taunting was better than my mockery. So, one more lord was added to our number. Cador's loyalty was beyond question. Indeed, he would not allow Arthur to humble himself by asking what he was more than willing to give outright. Cador, holding Caer Melyn in his lord's absence, had sent word to his battlechiefs within moments of Arthur's return.

The others we might have counted on—Idris, Cadwallo, Cunomor, and the Lords of the North—would not receive word for many days. Meurig, however, arrived at dusk, and Brastias the following morning. Accompanying Brastias was a kinsman, a young nobleman named Gerontius, whom the elder lord was grooming for command.

Ogryvan of Dolgellau and his neighbor lord, Owain, arrived at midday, bringing with them their sons: Vrandub and Owain Odiaeth, who—in this season of peace following the Saecsens' defeat—had been given charge of their fathers' warbands.

Arthur welcomed the noblemen and gave them food and drink. No sooner were they settled than Urien Rheged arrived with his warband, and suddenly the caer was overflowing with warriors. "We will begin now," Arthur decided.

"What about the other lords?" wondered Bedwyr. "A day or two more and they will arrive. You will need them."

"I cannot wait any longer. Every day we delay means another day of plunder for Twrch Trwyth." So saying, Arthur invited the nobles into the hall with their warriors and began the council even as the welcome cups were filled and passed.

"Your swift answer to my summons gladdens me," Arthur declared, standing before them at the board. "Be sure that I would not have asked you to attend if the need were not already sharp. I will keep nothing from you; the reason for the summons is this: the barbarian horde of one Twrch Trwyth has invaded Ierne and I fear that island is lost if we do not rally to her aid."

"A small enough loss, it seems to me," observed Brastias sourly.

Cador was quick to respond to this impertinence. "You speak, Brastias, like one who has never had to defend a coast against marauding Sea Wolves."

"What have the Irish ever given us but the point of a spear if we were foolish enough to turn our backs to them?" Brastias demanded. "Sooner aid the barbarian, I say, and have done with the Irish for once and all."

"For myself," put in Ogryvan, laying aside his cup, "I have lost much to Eriu's thieves." He looked at Arthur. "Even so, I give my support to the king if it will secure the safety of my coast."

"Well said, Lord Ogryvan," Arthur commended him. "That is the price I will demand for Britain's aid. From what I have seen of the Black Boar, the kings of Ierne will pay that price and gladly." He told them then of our encounters with the Vandali, and warned, "Know this: Amilcar has vowed to destroy Britain as well as Ierne. Unless we stop him there, we will see our own homes burned and our kinsmen slaughtered."

The lords sat in contemplation. Arthur had put the matter before them plainly. What would they do?

Meurig was the first to speak. "This is a most distressing report. And I could wish it came at a better time." He stretched a hand towards Arthur. "We have only just defeated the Saecsen. Our provisions are depleted and, God knows, our warriors could use a season of rest."

"Trouble knows no season, brother," old Ogryvan growled. He raised his head and looked around the gathering. "I am with you, Arthur," he said. "My warriors are your own."

Owain, sitting next to Ogryvan, added his support. "Our sons must soon rule in our places," he said. "Let them fight beside our War Leader as we have done, and learn the true cost of peace."

"You will not regret your decision," Arthur told them, and turned again to Meurig. "You have heard your brother lords. What say you?"

"The Lords of Dyfed have ever stood beside their War Leader in battle." Meurig glanced sideways at Brastias. "We will support our High King to the last man."

Brastias did not like this insinuation; he glared the length of the table. Clearly, the deliberations had taken an unexpected turn. He did not want to appear less willing than his peers, neither did he want to aid Arthur.

"Well, Brastias," the High King asked. "What is it to be?"

"If they see fit to lend aid in exchange for peace," Brastias allowed stiffly, "then I will not withhold it. But should this venture fail, I will hold you to blame."

That was Brastias, true to nature: already shedding responsibility, and he had not even mounted horse nor drawn blade. Arthur let the remark pass, and turned to Ulfias. "You have heard the others," he said. "Do you take back your word, or keep it?"

Well done, Arthur, I thought, make the wavering prince declare himself before the others; give him a place to stand, yes, but make certain he stands when the time comes. Ulfias seemed to shrink in upon himself. "I will keep my word," he said, glancing up quickly, his voice barely audible.

Of the assembled lords, only Urien Rheged had yet to declare himself. All eyes turned towards him. "Come, Urien," Ogryvan urged, "let us hear your pledge."

Of all the lords, I knew least about Urien. He was a raw young man, big-boned and brawny, with long hair, wild like a lion's mane, and dark. Watchful eyes and a brooding mouth gave him a shrewd, almost devious appearance. I had heard he was a Lord of Rheged, one of Ennion's kinsmen. The estimable Ennion had been wounded at Baedun Hill and died a day or two later. No doubt Urien fought in that battle, too; I do not remember.

But Urien Rheged held his kinsman's place now, and I found myself wondering what kind of man he was. Young, certainly—even, I think, younger than he appeared—he masked his youth with the kind of gravity older men sometimes possess. He was given to few words, which made him appear wise, and took his time answering, which made him seem thoughtful.

When at last he spoke, he said, "For myself, I am sick of warring. Let the Irish feel the fire now, I say; we have felt it long enough." This was said with great weariness, as if he himself had borne the brunt of more battles than could be told. "But since my brothers deem it best to aid this campaign, I am willing." He paused again and looked around to see if all eyes were on him, then, drawing himself up, he announced, "Urien of Rheged will do his part."

His heart was not in it, but honor bound him to pursue a repugnant course—at least that was the impression he meant to impart. And others, I noted, were persuaded by it.

Arthur struck the board with the flat of his hand. "Good!" he said, his voice filling the hall. "Then it is settled. We sail for Ierne as soon as men and supplies can be assembled."

Within moments the peace of the stronghold dissolved in the high-purposed commotion of a battlehost on the move. Rhys, and the small troop under his direction, busied themselves through the day and into the night with the daunting task of loading wagons and moving weapons and supplies down from the caer to the ships. After the third or fourth course of wagons had departed, Bedwyr came to me. "There is not enough food," he announced bluntly, "or anything else, come to that. It is as Meurig said: we need a season of peace to fill our storehouses and granaries. I do not see how we can fight on nothing."

"Does Arthur know?"

"God love him," Bedwyr replied, shaking his head, "as long as there is a drop left in his cup, he thinks there is enough for everyone, evermore."

That was true. Arthur, who had never owned anything outright for himself, had as little regard for the ebb and flow of wealth as for that of the tide. "Leave the matter with me," I told him. "I will see that Arthur is apprised."

But it was not until the next day, when the last of the warriors were boarding and the first ships were already poling their way out into deeper water, that I found opportunity to speak to Arthur alone.

"The council went well," he said, pleased to be moving again.

"Did it? I noticed you did not tell them how many Vandali stood against us. The lords may have second thoughts when they see the size of the barbarian host." Arthur dismissed my qualms with a toss of his head, so I turned to the concern uppermost in my mind: "Bedwyr tells me we do not have enough provisions to feed the war host."

"No?" He glanced at me to assess the gravity of the problem. "Well, we will raise all we can here and obtain whatever is lacking in Ierne," he concluded simply. "The Irish kings will support us."

That was, on the face of it, a logical solution; and we had no better choice in any event. "Very well," I replied, "but we must inform Conaire as soon as we arrive. He may need time to raise enough tribute."

The return voyage was maddeningly slow. The winds of summer can be fickle in any event, but these were mere breezes, sighs that billowed the sails one moment and died away to nothing the next. All day long Arthur urged his doughty pilot to make haste, only to be told in the same dry, uncompromising tone that unless the king could wring wind from a calm sea and cloudless sky he must be satisfied with what little speed he got.

In the event, we all took a turn at the oars. Fully three days later we passed through the narrows and rounded the northern tip of Ierne and, half a day after, reached the bay from which the enemy fleet had fled. There were, of course, no ships to be seen there, so we continued south along the coast, searching the innumerable nameless coves for the black ships.

At last, at last, we sighted the Vandali fleet massed in the center of a sheltered bay high up the west coast. Arthur, almost beside himself with impatience, ordered the ships to make landfall a little to the north, out of sight of the Vandali fleet. No sooner were the men, horses and supplies ashore than the ships put out to sea again—there were too many Britons to cross all at once, so the ships must make a second voyage to bring the rest of the men and whatever additional provisions Rhys had obtained.

As soon as his horse was on dry land, Arthur was in the saddle, leading the war host inland. "Do you know where you are going, Bear?" asked Bedwyr as we created the sea bluffs and began descending to the wooded lowlands.

Arthur thought the question foolish. "I am following the Black Boar, of course."

"Should we not rather be looking for Gwenhwyvar and Fergus?"

Arthur did not bother to turn his head to answer. "The Black Boar is ashore now, and where he is to be found, there we will find the defenders."

Find them we did: the Irish war host—his own queen among them—at the end of a long shallow valley with their backs to a rocky escarpment, surrounded on three sides by the screaming barbarian swarm.

11

"MUST I BE EVERYWHERE AT once?" Arthur's cool blue eyes sparked quick fire as they played over the battleground where the surrounded Irish were fighting for their lives. "By the Hand that made me, someone will answer for this!"

Caledvwlch came ringing from its sheath at his side; he lofted the great sword, raised himself in the saddle, turned to look behind him, and gave a mighty shout: "For Christ and glory!"

A heartbeat later, the Flight of Dragons thundered to the attack. Our war host was divided into three. Arthur led the Cymbrogi, Bedwyr led the western bands, and Cai those of the south. At Cador's horn blast we swept down into the valley as one—separating into our contingent groups only at the last so that the enemy could not anticipate where we would strike.

The Vandali, emboldened by early success and hopeful of an easy victory over the ill-prepared Irish, had not posted a rear guard. Arthur, anxious to divert the foe—and they were so easily diverted!—drove down upon them with all the tumult at his command. The enemy heard the sound, turned, and lost all expectation of victory. One look at flight upon flight of mounted British warriors sweeping down upon them and they fell into confusion. The battle suddenly shifted front to back: the Vandal foreranks with their guiding battlelords were trapped behind the press of their own men; and those in the rearward ranks, more lightly armed, found themselves facing a ferocious attack with no one to lead them.

Slashing with spear and sword, we thrust into the midst of the foe, reckless in our attack. The Cymbrogi raised their battle cry, making as much noise as possible to announce their arrival and divert the Black Boar.

I saw the fearful expressions on their broad faces as they turned on stumbling feet, weapons slack in their hands, and pitied them. They were so ill-prepared. Even so, I knew they would have killed us all without remorse. Heavy-hearted, I struck; we all struck the killing blows, driving them down and running them over. The screaming of those frightened, dying barbarians was bitter to hear.

A Vandal battlechief appeared before me. He drew back his great shield and swung it, slashing edgewise at the horse's head and neck. I pulled back hard on the reins, lifting my mount's forelegs off the ground. The animal was well trained to battle; a hoof lashed out, catching the foeman on the chin. His head snapped back with a crack and he sank like a stone beneath the onrushing wave of battle.

I felt a hand on my sword arm. Glancing down, I saw a warrior clutching my arm and clawing desperately for a better grip. I threw the reins to the side. The horse wheeled away and the clinging warrior was lifted off his feet and thrown through the air to land hard on his back. He made to rise, but could not, and fell back, fainting.

The force of our charge carried us deep into the Vandal battle cluster. Surrounded by frightened, confused enemy warriors, we drove deeper still, hacking our way through them. Blood mist rose in our eyes; the pungent sweetness of warm entrails assaulted us.

I let my horse have its head, and smashed through the enemy with the flat of my shield, striking here and there with my sword as opportunity allowed. The killing was easy. There was no glory in it—not that there ever is. Though when two skilled warriors meet and prowess alone decides their fate, there is a kind of honor in the contest.

The Vandali lacked skill, but tried to redeem this lack by the force of numbers. This might have worked for them in the walled cities of the East, and on less able defenders. But it would take more than numbers alone to overcome the battle-wise Cymry.

Since Twrch could no way mount a counterattack, he had no choice but flight. The fight was short and sharp, and sent the enemy howling in rage back down the valley. We pursued as far as we dared, but Arthur was wary of carrying the pursuit too far lest we become ensnared.

While Cador and Meurig guarded against the enemy's return, the Cymbrogi liberated the Irish. Clearly, we had arrived at the most providential moment: the Irish defenders were exhausted; they stood swaying on their legs, barely able to raise their arms. Most of their horses were dead, and far too many warriors.

Gwenhwyvar stood at the forefront of the Irish, her shield riven and her clothing filthy and blood-spattered. At her side, Llenlleawg—wild-eyed, his mouth flecked with foam—gripped the remains of a splintered spear, bloody at both ends.

"Greetings, husband," Gwenhwyvar said as we rode into their midst. She lifted an arm and drew her sleeve across her forehead, smearing gore and grime. Her sword was ragged and notched. "I would we had devised a better welcome for you."

"Lady," Arthur said gently, "the sight of you whole is welcome enough. Are you hurt?"

"No," Gwenhwyvar said, shaking her head, frustration and humiliation making her voice hollow. "I am only sorry you were obliged to rescue us."

"Not half as sorry as you would be if I had not," Arthur replied. "How did this happen?" He looked around, his relief quickly giving way to anger. "Where are the other Irish lords?" he demanded.

The question was apt. I saw only those defenders we had left behind—and far fewer of those than before. Where were the others Conaire had vowed to rally?

"There are none," Fergus shouted angrily. He lurched to where we stood, and leaned on his spear, breathing heavily. "There are none because Conaire would not ask."

Cai was mystified. "For the love of God, man, why not?"

"Conaire thought to vanquish the Vandal unaided," Gwenhwyvar explained, giving an involuntary shudder of disgust.

"He would share the glory with no one," Fergus continued bitterly. "Least of all a Briton."

Arthur turned to confront Conaire, who stood glowering at us a short distance away. "Is this true?" the Bear of Britain demanded.

The Irish king drew himself up. "I will not deny it," he growled. "And I would have defeated them, too, but for the treachery of my own battlechiefs."

"Treachery! Treachery?" cried Fergus. "I call it prudence. We were being cut down like timber where we stood."

"I counted on you to attack," Conaire argued. "Your thoughtless retreat cost us the battle."

"It was retreat or be slaughtered!" Fergus insisted.

"Enough," Gwenhwyvar snarled. "Both of you!"

"Perhaps you did not see how many Vandal stood against us!" Fergus charged. "Perhaps you thought the Black Boar would turn tail and run away when the Mighty Conaire Crobh Rua appeared!"

Conaire, growing red in the face, shouted, "It was you who turned tail and ran away!"

"Mallacht Dé air!" Fergus spat on the ground.

"Silence!" roared Arthur. The two sputtered and subsided. "Never," said Arthur, speaking deliberately and low so that only the chieftains would hear, "disgrace yourself before men who must follow you in battle. We will speak of this in private. I advise you to gather your wounded and return to your stronghold before the Vandali recover their courage."

Conaire turned on his heel and stalked away. Fergus glowered at him, and then moved off. Gwenhwyvar said, "I am sorry, Arthur. It was against my will that we allowed ourselves to be party to this—"

"Calamity." Arthur supplied the word for her.

Gwenhwyvar's eyes sparked quick fire, but she swallowed, bent her head, and accepted his judgment. "I hold myself to blame," she offered, shame making her meek. "I should have prevented it."

"*Someone* should have prevented it," Arthur agreed curtly. "We will rue the loss of these warriors," he said, gazing around at the carnage, his mouth a hard, thin line. "A cruel waste—the more since it was pointless." He turned again to his wife and demanded, "What were you thinking?"

Gwenhwyvar's head rose. "I am sorry, my lord," she whispered. There were tears in her eyes.

Only then did Arthur relent. He turned away from her and began ordering the Cymbrogi to bury the dead and remove the wounded. I stepped close to Gwenhwyvar. "He is angry with Conaire, and he—" I began.

"No," she stopped me, pushing the tears away with the heels of her hands, "he is right." She drew a deep breath, steadied herself, and turned to the task at hand. She picked up her sword and asked, "Is he always right?"

I offered her a smile. "No," I replied gently. "But he is rarely wrong."

The stronghold was an abandoned hillfort which Conaire had found in lands long neglected. Rock-bound and hilly, the soil thin and unproductive, it had been many years since any Irish lord had laid claim to the realm. There were few settlements, and those were not large. All the better for the Black Boar—it provided him a safe haven from which to raid more prosperous lands to the north. And this, Conaire's negligible presence notwithstanding, he had proceeded to do.

During our absence, the Vandal warlord had successfully carried off cattle and plunder from the nearby small holdings, and had destroyed the strongholds of three noblemen as well. Most of the Irish had fled north and east, out of harm's way. This in itself was unfortunate, for if they had gone south, they might at least have alerted the southern lords to the invader. As it happened, the better part of twelve hundred Vandali warriors now lay between us and direct passage to the south, effectively cutting off communication with any support we might receive.

The rickety fort was not large enough to house the gathered British warbands, so they were forced to make camp outside the stronghold below earthen banks. While the kings of Ynys Prydein saw to the crude comfort of their men, Arthur held council with Fergus and Conaire in the ruined barn that passed for a hall in that place. Most of the roof thatch had blown off, and part of one wall was collapsed, but the hearth was intact and the board and benches were serviceable enough.

So, we sat over our cups in the hall listening to Fergus recount all that had transpired since we were last together. Arthur's face grew darker and his eyes harder by degrees as Fergus explained how the matter stood. After the debacle of Conaire's defeat, Arthur was in no humor to view our plight in any but the harshest light. The Bear of Britain scowled, taking the news in grim and prickly silence.

For his part, Conaire had grown suitably contrite. He wore his chagrin like a battered crown; his back bent under the weight of disgrace and his head drooped in sympathy with his shoulders. He had not breathed a word since returning from the battlefield.

"Tomorrow," Arthur said, with controlled and quiet fury, "we will undertake to hold the invader in the valley and prevent him from making any more raids or moving farther into the land. And *you*, Conaire Crobh Rua, will take three of your best men and ride to rally the southern lords."

The Irish king nodded glumly, but said nothing.

"Go now," Arthur commanded. "This matter is ended."

Conaire rose and, looking neither right nor left, walked slowly from the ruined hall.

"You crushed him, Bear," Bedwyr said when Conaire had departed.

"He will recover," Arthur grumbled. "Which is more than can be said for many of the men who trusted him with their lives."

"Better the slap of a friend," observed Fergus, "than the stab of an enemy."

Arthur turned cold eyes on Fergus. "And you," he said in a tone of tight restraint, "will ride to the settlements round about—if any are left intact—to raise tribute for us. We have had to come away with only what we could carry, and there is not enough food or drink to sustain us."

"It will be done." Fergus rose and walked out, pausing at the threshold for a moment to say, "I never was so glad to see a man with a sword in his hand as when I saw you today, Arthur ap Aurelius. I thank you." He ducked his head through the door and disappeared.

"My father is right," Gwenhwyvar murmured. "If not for you, we would all be dead now."

"It is God you must thank," Arthur told her. "If the winds had been contrary, or a storm had raised the waves—or if I had chosen to spend the night in my bed rather than in the bottom of a boat . . . " He looked at his wife, considering the implications. "I thank God you are alive," he said. "We are fortunate indeed."

Gwenhwyvar leaned close, took up his sword hand and pressed it to her lips. "Well I know it, husband," she whispered. "Well I know it."

The British lords, having settled their men, began arriving in the hall just then. Gwenhwyvar kissed Arthur quickly, rose, and departed. Her fingers lingered along the line of his shoulders as she passed behind him.

Cador sat down beside Arthur. "You did not tell us that there were so many barbarians," he chided.

"If I had told you," Arthur replied easily, "you might have found it more agreeable to stay home."

"At least I would have had a bed." Cador drew a hand through his hair and rubbed his face. "These Vandali are certainly strange-looking creatures."

One of Fergus' men appeared with more cups and jars of ale. He proceeded to fill and distribute the cups among the lords as they sat down. "Where is their homeland?" wondered Meurig.

Arthur invited me to answer. "They have come from Carthage, where they have lived for many years," I replied. "The Emperor of the East has driven them from that place, and so now they search for new lands, and plunder as they go."

"You know this truly?" mused Owain.

"They have with them a slave—a priest named Hergest, who speaks our tongue," Arthur answered. "He has told us the little we know."

"But who are they?" demanded Ogryvan. "And who is their king?"

"They are a northern race," I answered, "led by one, Amilcar, who styles himself Twrch Trwyth, the Black Boar of Hussa, Rögat, and Vandalia. He is a rapacious lord whose greed is exceeded only by his vanity."

We talked of this for a time, and then the conversation turned to the lack of any worthwhile Irish presence. The British kings were sharply critical of the circumstance, and allowed their opinions free rein. They decried the catastrophe on the battlefield.

"I would have welcomed a little more support from the Irish," Ogryvan suggested delicately.

"Support?" sneered Brastias. "Even my cowherds are better able to defend themselves. Can they not be bothered to protect their own lands?"

"Hold, Brastias," Bedwyr warned. "They know their mistake. Arthur has dealt with them. The matter is ended."

The lords stared uneasily into their cups, and it was only when the haunches of venison appeared and men began to eat that tempers eased. Still, it was not a good beginning; the lords trusted Arthur, yes, and for now were content to extend that trust to include the Irish. But for how long?

That was the question concerning me. Taking the matter into my own hands, I left the lords to their repast and went in search of Conaire. I found him sitting with three of his chieftains beside a small fire; I did not wait to be greeted. "May I join you?" I asked.

Conaire raised his eyes and I glimpsed genuine surprise in his expression. "Sit," he said. "You are welcome here, bard."

He returned his gaze to the fire. I decided a clean cut was best. "Arthur holds no ill will for you, Conaire," I told him. "But we cannot drive the invader from the land without the aid of the southern Irish. You must see that now."

Conaire nodded glumly.

"I know what happened," I continued, drawing him out. "You saw how easily Arthur repelled the first attack, and you thought it would be the same with you."

"That I did," replied Conaire, staring into the fire.

"Well, there is no shame in it," I said. "Some of the best warriors the world has ever seen have tried their hand."

"Truly?" wondered Conaire, glancing up hopefully.

"Truly," I answered solemnly. "The grave mounds are full of Saecsen war leaders who thought they knew how to best Arthur."

Caught, the Irish king squirmed. "Is he a god then, that he never puts a foot wrong in battle?"

"No, Arthur is a man," I assured him. "But he is not like other men when it comes to a fight. The ways of war are meat and drink to him, Conaire. His skill is like to the genius of a bard, and—"

"A bard of battle." Conaire sniffed in mild derision.

I paused, checking my anger. "Mock me, Conaire, I do not mind. But the men who died under your command today deserved better."

"Do I not know that?" His voice was anguished. "I sit here with my head in my hands and it is all I am thinking."

"Then while you sit there, add this thought to your thinking. You may not like the Britons—"

"A true word there," muttered one of the Irish chieftains.

"Even so," I allowed, "Arthur has risked much to bring those Britons here. I do not say you should like it, but you should be grateful at least."

Conaire shrugged, but said nothing. His insolent silence angered me. "Think!" I demanded. "Which is easier: raising a warband and sailing to a foreign land to engage a fearsome enemy, or remaining secure in your own realm and enjoying the fruit of your reign?" The four of them stared dully at me. "Tell me, if you know." Contempt dripped from my words.

"You make it more than it is," Conaire insisted weakly.

"So?" I challenged. "If it is a matter of such small consequence, then tell me this: which of you would do the same for him?"

Conaire's eyes shifted to one and another of his chieftains and then back to the fire. None of them made bold to reply.

Suddenly sickened by the Irish king's misplaced pride and selfishness, I wanted nothing more to do with him. Rising at once, I bade him consider well my words. Then I removed myself from that miserable company.

Great Light, they are but children! Breathe on them the breath of wisdom, strengthen their hearts and souls, for in the heat-rage of battle we need not children, but men!

12

 WE MET AMILCAR AND HIS HORDE
the next day in a narrow valley beside
a lake. The foe displayed a guile not
seen before. Instead of simply over-
whelming us with their numbers, they split the main body of
their force into three divisions and attempted to draw and separate the British defense. It was clumsily done, however, and
Arthur easily avoided the trap. The attack, confined and con-
stricted by the steep sides of the glen, quickly collapsed and
the invaders withdrew in all haste. In this they showed freshly
acquired wisdom.

"The Black Boar is growing canny," Cai observed, watching the Vandal host streaming from the valley.

"They are learning respect," Bedwyr suggested.

Llenlleawg, overhearing the remark, said, "They are learning cunning. It will not be long before they overcome their
fear of our horses."

"Pray that does not happen," Arthur replied. "Our ships
will arrive soon, and if Conaire succeeds in rallying the south
Irish we may have a large enough force to defeat the Boar and
his piglets, or drive them back to the sea."

Our ships did arrive later that day, bringing the remaining
men and horses, but only a fraction of the provisions we required. "I am sorry, Lord," Rhys apologized as we stood looking at the scant heap of provisions stacked on the shingle. Men
slogged ashore through the shallows, leading horses, or carrying

weapons. "I swear it is all I could raise. If I had had more time to range farther . . . " he paused. "I am sorry."

"Where is the blame?" Arthur asked. "I find no fault with you. Fret not, Rhys."

"But it is a shameful portion for men who must fight."

"True," the king agreed, but added optimistically, "Still, it may be enough—if the campaign is short."

"Oh, aye," Rhys said, eyeing the meager heap doubtfully, "if we conclude the conflict tomorrow or the day after. The supplies will last that long at least."

We did not fight Twrch the next day, nor the day after—although we did keep close watch on the enemy. Arthur set scouts in a wide ring around the Vandal encampment, and charged them with reporting even the smallest movement, day or night—requiring them also to bring back any game for the pot. When, for the third day, the Black Boar again refused to take the field, Arthur grew suspicious.

"Why does he wait?" Arthur wondered. "What can he be thinking? He must know that the longer he delays the stronger our forces grow."

And indeed, Conaire arrived the following day with five Irish kings and their warbands—over nine hundred men in all, though less than half were mounted. This brought the number of defenders to nearly two thousand in all. Arthur was well pleased with the southern lords' support. Unfortunately, they seemed to have come empty-handed, expecting food and supplies to be provided by the Britons.

"I commend you, Conaire," Arthur said, hailing him loudly and with praise in the hearing of his brother kings. "You have richly increased our numbers. I do not doubt that with such support as you have won, we will soon drive the foe from your lands."

"And it had best be soon indeed," Gwenhwyvar added. "We have but one day's feeding for our own warriors, and not even that if we must share it with all."

Conaire's smooth brow creased in concern, and the gratified smile faded from his lips. "Is this so?" He swung accusingly towards Arthur. "I thought you would bring food supplies with you."

"I brought all I could raise," Arthur answered. "The peace of Ynys Prydein is but new-won; the war was long and our storehouses and granaries are empty still."

"Besides," continued Gwenhwyvar severely, "this is not Britain's fight. Do you expect the British-folk to feed us as well as fight for us?" She cast him a withering glance. "See here, Conaire Tight Fist, you must open that worm-eaten trove of yours and part with some of your treasure."

Conaire rolled his eyes and puffed out his cheeks. "The wealth of the Uladh is no concern of yours, woman!" he sputtered. "Why, are there no deer on the hills, nor fish in the lakes?"

"If we are fishing," Gwenhwyvar replied, arching a pretty eyebrow dangerously, "we cannot be fighting. Or is it in your mind to frighten the Vandali away by waving fishnets at them?" She whirled away imperiously, denying Conaire any rebuttal.

"Ach! But she is a sharp-tongued terror," the Irishman muttered. "If she were not also a queen—" He glanced at Arthur and left the thought unfinished. The southern lords drew near just then, and Conaire squared himself and straightened.

"It is simple truth," I suggested, "and plain as our need: we lack food. As this is your realm, Conaire, we must look to you to supply it."

Conaire, still smarting under the lash of Gwenhwyvar's rebuke, did not wish to appear niggardly under the watchful gaze of noblemen from Connacht and Meath. He drew himself up full height. "Never fear," he said expansively, "stand back and watch what I will do. There is no lack when Conaire Red Hand is near."

"I leave the matter with you," Arthur said. He turned to the southern lords and greeted them, then presented himself saying, "I am Arthur, King of the Britons, and the man with me is Myrddin Emrys, Chief Bard of Lloegres, Prydein and Celyddon."

"To be sure, the names of Arthur and the Emrys are not unknown among us," one of the kings replied. "I am Aedd of clan Ui Neill. Kinsman to Fergus I am, and it is my good pleasure to greet you, Arthur, King of the Britons. My men and I are at your service and yours to command." Then he inclined his head in a slight bow of respect.

Turning to me, he said, "But there is surely some error here: you cannot be that Emrys renowned in story. I had thought you full of years, yet here I see but a shaveling youth."

Aedd spoke with such simple grace and goodwill that both Arthur and I found ourselves warming to him at once. "Do not let appearances deceive, Lord Aedd. The old man of the stories and myself are one."

Aedd expressed his astonishment. "Then it is true! You *are* a very Prince of the Otherworld."

"My people wear our years more lightly than most, I cannot deny it; but while we live we walk this world and not another," I told him. "So, in the name of the One who made us all, I am pleased to greet you."

The remaining four now pressed in, eager to be recognized by us. Aedd, to Conaire's vexation, took it upon himself to introduce his fellow kings: Diarmait, Eogan of the Ui Maine, Illan, and Laigin—all four young men and strong, at ease with themselves and with their men, confident in their abilities. Each displayed an easy wealth: they wore bright-colored cloaks—red-and-blue striped, broom yellow, and emerald green; their torcs were huge gold bands of twisted coils which, together with their rings and bracelets, could have kept a governor's household; their boots and belts were good leather, and the swords on their hips fine steel, long and sharp-edged.

The five displayed an easy assurance to match their wealth. I did not begrudge it them. Yet I was mindful that Conaire, for all his confidence, was woefully ineffectual. Still, I thought, if swagger alone could prevail against the Vandal horde, we would not have to put hand to sword.

Each of the Irish chieftains deferred to Arthur, acknowledging his renown and placing themselves under his command.

Aedd and Laigin, dark-haired handsome men, seemed particularly earnest in securing Arthur's good favor. This pleased and gratified Arthur, nor did it pass Conaire unnoticed. As this natural warmth began to flow between Arthur and his Irish brothers, Conaire grew increasingly tight-lipped and aloof.

We dined together that night, British and Irish together, noblemen all. And though the meal was far from sumptuous, it became a feast in the glow of new-kindled friendship. The Irish kings ceaselessly plied the British with questions about hunting and riding, battles won and lost, matters of kingcraft and kinship. They professed themselves delighted with all they learned. For their part, the British were pleasantly surprised by their Irish companions.

Most of the Britons had come harboring long-standing resentment, if not hostility, towards the Irish. As I have said, they or their fathers had fought Irish raiders too many times to think well of them; and Conaire's poor showing and worse manners had not altered opinion for the better. For Arthur's sake alone they had come, not from any goodwill towards the inhabitants of Ierne. Now, however, seated side-by-side along the weathered board with a hole in the roof and the summer stars looking down, the British lords, like Arthur before them, found genuine affection springing up between them and the Irish chieftains.

Nor was it drink making them feel that way: we had only enough to wet our tongues with a welcome cup and the supply of ale was exhausted. Rather was it the inborn charm of DeDannan's children: their graceful flattery beguiled and enchanted. Like their music—which, along with nearly all else, they stole from Ynys Prydein years ago—their words spin and dance in beautifully intricate patterns, delighting both ear and soul.

"How they talk. It is like the angels, surely," Cai chuckled, entranced by the lightness of their speech.

"They spin fine wool," Bedwyr agreed, "only you must not let it droop over your eyes, Cai." He was reluctant to give himself to them wholeheartedly; having grown to manhood on Britain's western coast, Bedwyr had bloodshed to balance his opinion.

Laigin, sitting across from Bedwyr, overheard the remark. "For shame," he said, his smile wide and comfortable, "is it to bruise my heart that you speak so?"

"I fear for you, friend," Bedwyr answered readily, "if your heart is so easily bruised. Life must be a perpetual injury to you."

Laigin laughed. "I like you, Bedwyr. And had I a drop left in this cup of mine, I would drink the health of Britain's Bright Avenger." He raised his empty cup, cradling it in both hands: "To the most noble warrior who ever drew sword or lofted spear."

Bedwyr, resting his elbows on the board, allowed himself to be cozened by Laigin's flattery. "It seems to me you need nothing in your cup," Bedwyr replied, "for words alone suffice to cheer you."

"He is drunk indeed," Cai observed dryly, "if he thinks *you* the most noble warrior under this roof."

"Again, I am wounded," Laigin declared, placing his hand over his heart.

"Well," Bedwyr allowed, "I suppose we must offer some remedy for this injury."

Laigin leaned forward eagerly at that. I saw that we had come to the kernel of the young lord's concern—and also how adroitly he had directed the conversation to his own ends.

"Allow me the honor of riding beside you in battle tomorrow," Laigin said, eager as a boy for his father's approval.

"If that would console you," Bedwyr began.

"It would encourage me wonderfully well," Laigin put in quickly.

"Then so be it." Bedwyr raised his hand in assent. "If you ply the blade half as well as you employ your wit, we shall be the most feared warriors on the field of battle."

Cai gave a little snort to show what he thought of the notion. Up spoke Aedd from two places away, and I realized he had been following the conversation closely, overhearing every word. "Let them console themselves with their pitiful belief if they can, brother Cai," he said. "Take no heed. Only allow me to ride beside you and we will show one and all what can be accomplished by men who know the sharp end of a spear."

"Well said, my Irish friend!" replied Cai, slapping the board with his palm. "Let the foe beware."

"And friend as well," said Bedwyr.

They then fell into an amiable dispute about who should fare best in the next day's combat, and boast gave way to boast. I looked beyond them down the length of the board and saw the remaining British and Irish nobles head-to-head in equally agreeable discourse, with Arthur and Gwenhwyvar ruling over this affable assembly, gently encouraging the new-born concord to deepen and thrive.

Great Light, may brotherhood succeed! Send your sweet spirit to soothe the hurts and grudges of former days.

When at last we rose from the board and made our way to our beds, it was as if we had all discovered kinsmen closer to us than the blood kin left behind. Of all present, Conaire alone was in no a better humor and disposition when he stood up than when he first sat down. The serpent of jealousy had gotten its sharp tooth in him and begun to gnaw.

With the warriors assembled and ready, and food supplies short, we did not wait for the Black Boar to attack again, but carried the battle to him. Though still woefully outnumbered, Arthur, determined to make the most of the fear and confusion caused by our horses, proposed another night raid.

Throughout the day, guided by the reports of our spies, we established positions in the low hills encircling the Vandal encampment. By stealth, like a great stalking cat, we slowly, silently gathered our strength for the assault. As the sun dipped below the rim of the horizon, we were ready to pounce.

Darkness came eventually, but even when night's cloak overspread the valley, the sky remained light. Arthur crouched in the dusky shadow of an elm on the flank of the hill, idly plucking grass from the turf and watching the enemy campfires. I crouched beside him. Strung out along the hilltops all around the camp, unseen in the twilight, our warriors awaited Arthur's signal.

The night was still. We could hear the sounds of the camp below as they prepared the evening meal: the clink and clatter of cooking utensils, the murmur of voices around the fire . . . the common sounds of ordinary life, innocent in themselves. The Vandali were human creatures, after all, more alike in their ways than different.

"I did not choose this," Arthur murmured after a time. His thoughts were running with mine.

"Amilcar did," I reminded him. "You gave him the choice."

"Did I?" He spat out a blade of grass he had been chewing.

After a while, the moon rose, shedding a soft silver light over the valley. A chill crept into the air as the warmth of the land gradually cooled in the absence of the sun. Behind us, ready, growing anxious for the fight, our warriors fidgeted, the need for still, watchful silence chafing them.

Still Arthur waited.

The moon made its slow, stately way across the skybowl and, little by little, the sounds of the enemy camp diminished. Keen-eyed in the night, Arthur crouched, mute and immobile as a mountain. Yet I sensed in him an inner agitation—or did I only imagine it? Regardless, it seemed to me that he warred within himself, doubting the wisdom of the course he pursued. And so he hesitated.

Sensing his thought, I said, softly, "The battle plan is sound. It is but the waiting makes you doubt it."

He turned his face to me. I could see his eyes hard and bright in the moonlight. "But I do not doubt it," he replied.

"Then why do you hesitate?"

"If I hesitate," he replied, "it is from certainty, not doubt. Our raid will succeed." He returned his gaze to the valley and peered into the darkness—like a seaman trying to fathom an unknowable depth.

"Strange cause for concern," I observed, trying to comfort him somewhat.

"I tell you the truth, Myrddin," he said, and though he spoke softly I heard the iron edge to his words. "I fear this victory, for I cannot see beyond it." He paused, and I thought he would not speak again. But after a moment he went on, "Streams of consequence flow from every action, and from every conflict there are two paths by which events may go. Always, before I draw sword in battle, I look ahead to see which path may offer the better resolution, and I move the battle towards that path if I can." He paused again, and I waited, letting him come to it in his own time. "Tonight," he continued at last, "tonight I look, but I cannot see where either path may lead."

"And that frightens you?"

"Yes, it frightens me."

"Then I am greatly encouraged," I confessed.

"Are you indeed?" He regarded me closely once more.

"I am," I told him, "for it tells me you are but flesh and blood after all, Arthur ap Aurelius, though some have begun to think otherwise."

I saw his teeth glint white in the darkness as he smiled. He rose abruptly, reaching down to help me to my feet. "Come then, disagreeable bard," he said. "It is time to discover which path we shall take—and trust God to meet us on the way."

BOOK THREE

THE
FORGOTTEN
WAR

1

ALL YOU WHO LOOK UPON THE land now and raise your unholy complaint, tell me: where were you when the Black Boar gouged our sacred earth with his tusks and shook the very hills of Ynys Prydein with his ungodly bellowing?

Tell me! You, who from the lofty battlements of your superior intellect scan all that passes in the world and pronounce upon it, tell me now that you divined the disaster that came to pass. I defy you! Instruct me, Wise Ones, in how it could have been prevented.

O Great of Knowledge, secure in your wide intelligence as you regard the calamity of Twrch Trwyth, tell me: did you also foresee the Yellow Ravager?

When the dread Comet passed over the Island of the Mighty and scourged Lloegres with its tail, where were you? I will tell you, shall I? You sailed for Armorica!

Who left the land of your birth to barbarians? Who left your shores undefended? Who turned away from Britain in its day of peril and dread? Not Arthur. Never Arthur.

Why do you complain? Why do you demean him now? I demand an answer! Tell me: why do you grieve heaven with your tedious contention?

The caviling of the false-hearted is the mewling of sick cats. It signifies nothing—save a pinched, ungenerous spirit, perverse in spite and rotten with envy. The weak-willed always decry those who, when the day of strife breaks, fill their hearts with courage and cast safety to the wind. Fear is man's first enemy, and his last. Hear me now; I tell you the truth: conquer fear and your reward is assured.

On the night that Arthur sought light along conflict's shadowed paths, he found only fear. Even so, being Arthur, he put fear behind him and strove instead in faith. Thus, all that came after will yet be accounted him as righteousness. This is something small-souled men will never understand.

We triumphed that night, but our victory sowed the seeds of a bitter harvest. We purchased liberty for the Ereann Isle, but at great cost to Ynys Prydein. For Ierne's freedom meant hateful travail for Britain.

At Arthur's word, Rhys sounded a short, piercing blast on the horn, and it was answered no fewer than seven times across the valley. At the horn's second sounding, we lashed our horses to speed. Down we struck, falling like lightning from a cloudless sky.

We drove into the sleeping camp. The Vandali, living by constant warfare and accustomed to it, overcame the shock and reacted swiftly. Leaping from their round tents, they ran screaming to their weapons, and within moments the battle was joined. It was then that Arthur's genius revealed itself anew.

For, by employing so many points of attack, he spread the enemy and forced them to remain on the defensive. Though each of our attacking forces was small, the more numerous barbarian host could not afford to ignore any of them, for every lapse was punished severely. The Black Boar and his warlords could neither unify nor concentrate their defense, and thus were robbed of the advantage their vast numbers gave them. The swift-moving raiders struck and retreated to strike and strike again.

The tactic would not have worked in the daylight. But it was perfectly suited to a night raid, where darkness multiplies the ordinary confusion and chaos of battle into a potent force all its own. Arthur manipulated this force, wielded it like a

weapon. A harp singing under the touch of a true bard is but
a dull, stifled thing compared to the song of a weapon in Arthur's hands. And I thrilled to it.

I rode in the front rank with him—Llenlleawg and Gwenhwyvar on his left, with me on his right, backed by Cador and
Meurig and their warbands. From time to time, I caught fleeting glimpses of other warbands as they darted in and out along
the battleline. It was in Arthur's battle order to resist engaging
the enemy head-to-head, so we delivered only glancing
blows—striking and breaking off before they could muster
their forces to trap us, which was ever their chief intent.

Arthur continually searched the heaving sea-swell of battle
for the Black Boar's standard; if he chanced upon Twrch
Trwyth in the fight, the opportunity of crossing swords with
the Vandal war leader would not pass him by. As the fortune
of combat decreed, Arthur received his chance. For on one of
our swift-breaking forays, I saw the boar standard rise up before
us, and in the same instant heard a full-throated battle cry as
Arthur sped past me, making for the place. I lashed my mount
forward, striving to keep pace with him. I saw Llenlleawg's
sword flash in the firelight as he matched Arthur stroke for
stroke.

The two of them pushed into the churning mass before us.
Turning to my right, I saw Gwenhwyvar struggling to follow.
"Lady!" I shouted. "Here! This way!"

She was beside me at once and together we struck into the
bristling wall of defenders. I slashed with my sword, my arm
rising and falling, the quick blade hacking a grudging path
through the stubborn press. All at once the way parted, and I
saw before me the huge Vandal chieftain, surrounded by his
bodyguard, and Arthur, high on his rearing mount, Caledvwlch a reddish blur in his hand.

Twrch Trwyth, angry, his eyes mere slits of hatred, met
Arthur's assault. He leapt forward, throwing his spear before
him, slashing at Arthur's throat.

But Arthur was swift. Up came his blade. The Black Boar's
weapon splintered and the spearhead spun away. Disarmed,

Amilcar fell back, taking cover behind his upraised shield. Crack! Arthur struck the shield a bone-breaking blow. Then another and another.

The Vandal chieftain staggered and fell back. I saw him stumble as his bodyguard surged forward, encircling him once more. Then the tide of battle bore him away. The foemen swarmed us and it was either break off the attack or be dragged down. There was nothing for it but to disengage.

We regrouped just out of spear-throw. "I had him!" shouted Arthur in frustration. "Did you see? I had him!"

"I saw," Gwenhwyvar said. "You hurt him, Arthur. He went down."

"Aye, he went down," Llenlleawg confirmed. "But I think he was not wounded."

"I was this close!" cried Arthur, slapping his thigh. The shield rattled on his arm. "I had him in my grasp!"

"He will not long elude you," Gwenhwyvar said. "Few men feel the Bear of Britain's bite and remain alive to tell it."

Cador reined in beside us. "Too bad. You will have another chance, Artos."

"If that is to be," answered Arthur, scanning the melee, "it will be another battle. This one is finished."

"Finished?" Cador protested. "Artos, we are just beginning to make our mark here."

"And the enemy has begun throwing off his confusion." He pointed with his sword. "Soon Twrch will realize he can repel us. I would rather we were gone before that time."

We looked along the line. The Vandali were everywhere moving to the offensive. At last emboldened, they were fighting back; the tide of battle was turning. It was time to withdraw.

"Rhys!" shouted Arthur. "The horn! Sound the retreat!"

Thus with the sound of the hunting horn ringing in our ears, we fled, flew back up the long slopes and into the dark. We paused at the crest of the hill to look back upon our night's handiwork. The enemy camp swirled in turmoil: tents burned, men screamed and cried, running here and there. Around the perimeter, however, the silent dead lay thick-strewn on the ground.

"Victory," Arthur muttered. "It swells your heart with pride, does it not?"

"Amilcar will understand his aims cannot succeed," I replied. "It may be that you have saved the lives of many this night."

"Pray God you are right, Myrddin," the king replied. Then, turning his mount, he rode down the hill away from the valley.

We did not return to the abandoned stronghold, but rested beside a stream a short distance away from the battleground. At dawn one of the scouts Arthur had posted to watch the enemy camp appeared to rouse us.

"The enemy is striking camp, lord," the rider said. "They appear to be moving."

"Show me," Arthur said. He summoned Cador and myself to attend him, and, in a gesture of reconciliation, Conaire as well. We arrived at the crest of the hill overlooking the Vandal camp just as the sun broke fair in the east.

We stared into the valley, the red-rising sun in our eyes, and watched as a line of warriors extended from the mass and began threading along the stream, heading west. Soon the entire invading host was moving, flowing like a dark river towards the sea.

"They are leaving," observed Cador. "The triumph is yours, Artos! You have defeated them."

Cocking his head to one side, Arthur gazed long at the retreating floodtide. When he turned away at last, "Follow them" was all he said.

Then Arthur and I returned to our men, leaving Cador, Conaire, and the scout to oversee the retreating foe. The kings and lords were awaiting word, and Arthur lost no time: "It appears the enemy host is leaving the valley. I have set Cador and Conaire to follow and bring word of their purpose."

So we settled down to wait, and the day progressed. Men looked to their weapons and nursed their wounds, grateful for the rest. As the sun passed midmorning, Fergus arrived to great acclaim with much-needed provisions—including a small herd of cattle on the hoof. He set those with him to distributing the food and came to us. Ciaran, the priest, was with him.

"What am I hearing?" Fergus demanded, almost stumbling in his excitement. "The enemy routed? That is what they are saying. Is it true?"

"So it does appear," Gwenhwyvar informed him. She rose and greeted her father with a kiss. "The Black Boar has left the valley—Conaire and Cador follow to learn where he has gone."

"And here I am with meat and grain enough to last the summer," Fergus complained good-naturedly. "What am I to do with it now?"

"The food is no less welcome for that," Cai told him. "Waiting is hungry work. I am starving."

"Say no more, my friend." Fergus turned and called a string of commands which brought men running with ready-baked loaves, haunches of roast meat, and skins of ale. The Irish lord had, it seemed, snatched bread from the ovens and meat from the spit, gleaning the very crumbs from beneath the tables of those from whom he obtained his support.

"Oh, they were happy to give it," Fergus explained when Bedwyr commented on the astonishing largesse. "Once I had sufficiently aroused their sympathy, they could not give me enough. Bless them."

"Fergus mac Guillomar!" Gwenhwyvar cried. "You robbed Conaire's settlements?"

"Tch!" sniffed Fergus. "You wound me, daughter! Did I steal a mouthful? I never did." He gazed around him and, finding few believers, appealed to Ciaran. "Tell them, priest. You were there."

"It is true," Ciaran affirmed. "All gave freely. But upon my life, I still do not understand how it is that those most reluctant in the beginning gave the greater share in the end."

Fergus grinned. "Ah, it is my winsome way. I find that once

a man properly understands what is required of him, he is more than happy to oblige."

"And the presence of armed warriors crowding the threshold had nothing to do with it, I suppose," Gwenhwyvar remarked.

"Daughter, daughter," Fergus chided, "do you expect me to go scurrying through the land unprotected? Listen to you now. I rode with stout warriors—I freely confess it. How else was I to fend off the Vandali and bear away the supplies entrusted to my care?"

Everyone laughed, much amused by Fergus' explanation. "Friend Fergus," Arthur said, "however you came by the meat and ale, it is more than agreeable. I thank you, and can but praise your diligence."

"You are good to commend me so," the Irish king replied. "Still, I would rather I had been here last night with you. I missed a good fight, I think. If only I could have seen it."

"Well, I was there," Cai told him, wiping his mouth on his sleeve and raising the cup in his hand. "And I tell you the truth, the foam in this cup is a far better sight to my eyes than any I saw last night."

The day grew warm—another hot, cloudless day—and, after their meal, the men lay down to sleep, taking what shelter they could find under trees and bushes round about. In this way we passed the time, waiting for Conaire and Cador to return with word of the Vandal retreat.

It was not until dusk the next day that the awaited word arrived. The two lords and their scout appeared out of a crimson sunset, hungry and thirsty, having ridden far and fast to report that the barbarian horde had boarded their ships and sailed away.

2

 "THEY KNOW THEY CANNOT stand against us," Conaire boasted. "We have driven them away." The nobles were inclined to agree with Conaire; most lords viewed the barbarian departure in an auspicious light. Arthur knew better.

"The Black Boar has not given up the fight," the High King told the onlookers. "He has merely gone to easier plunder elsewhere."

"What do we care about that?" Brastias countered. "He has left Ierne, and that is all that matters."

"Is it?" Arthur turned on the unruly lord. "Amilcar has left before—only to appear again farther down the coast." He summoned the Irish lords. "You know your island best," he began, "therefore you must ride the coasts to determine where the Black Boar has gone."

"It will take time," Conaire warned. "There are more wrinkles in the shore than stars in the sky."

"Then you must go with all haste," Arthur bade him. After a short discussion it was determined that each king, leading a scouting party of six men, would search out a different portion of coastline, thus making a complete circuit of the island. They would then hasten back with the report. Meanwhile, Arthur's own ships would begin a sweeping search—some working north, around the headlands and then south, through the narrows, others sailing south down the west coast, then around to the east and up.

"It is a most inelegant plan," Arthur observed as the first scouting party rode from the camp. He paused, his brow heavy-furrowed as he watched the riders depart. "God knows, I can think of no other way."

"There is no other way," Bedwyr replied. "You have observed the most prudent course, and there is nothing more to be done until the scouts return. Put it from your mind, Bear."

But Arthur could not put it from his mind. The days passed—and how they creep with numbing slowness for those who wait. After six days had gone, Arthur posted sentries on the high ground to watch the approaches from the east, west, north, and south, charging them to bring word the instant they saw anyone returning.

While the rest of the camp settled back to wait, the High King prowled the perimeter—a most restless bear; he ate little and slept less, growing more irritable by the day. Gwenhwyvar and Bedwyr tried to pacify him, and when their own attempts failed, they brought the problem to me.

"Such anxiety is not good for him, surely," the queen said. "Myrddin, you must do something."

"What do you suppose I can do that you cannot?"

"Talk to him," suggested Bedwyr. "He always listens to you."

"And what would you have me tell him?" I countered. "Shall I say: Do not worry, Arthur, all will be well? He is right to worry. Amilcar has placed us in perilous difficulty and Arthur knows it. Think, Bedwyr: we cannot move from here until we know where the Boar has gone. Meanwhile, the barbarians are free to strike where they will."

"I know that," Bedwyr said icily. "I only meant that it does Arthur no good to fret about it."

"He is the king! Should he not fret for his own?" I replied.

Bedwyr rolled his eyes. "Bards!"

"It is no help to quarrel among ourselves," Gwenhwyvar interposed. "If we cannot calm Arthur, at least we need not add to his worries."

In the evening of the ninth day, two riders under Fergus' command returned to say that the northwestern coast from Malain Bhig to Beann Ceann had been scoured. "No enemy ships sighted anywhere," the scout said. "Lord Fergus presses the search north to Dun Sgeir."

Four days later, scouts returned from the east coast. "We ranged as far south as Loch Laern," they said, "and saw naught but your own ships working down the narrows, lord. The pilot said they had seen no sign of the Vandali either."

Seven days more brought further news: no enemy ships anywhere on the west coast from Dun Iolar to Gaillimh Bay. After that the reports came more rapidly—one or two a day—and all with the same account: no enemy ships; the Vandali were nowhere to be found. If any thought this information would cheer Arthur, they were mistaken. Despite the encouragement of his lords, he greeted these reports with deepest dread—as if each negative sighting confirmed a dire suspicion.

The only variation in the pattern came from the last of the parties led by Laigin, whose scouts had searched out the remote and sparsely populated finger-thin peninsulas of the south coast. "There were ships, I believe; but we did not see them," the Laigin said. "The people of the Ban Traigh say that many ships were there, although no invaders attacked."

"When?" asked Arthur.

"That is the strange thing," the Irish lord answered. "It seems they were there when the Black Boar was fighting here."

"That cannot be," suggested one of the Britons; I think it was Brastias. "They are in error. It must have been before the battle—"

"Or after, more like," suggested Owain.

"What difference can it make now?" wondered Urien. "They are gone, and that is what matters."

Arthur glared at the man, but could not bring himself to answer such foolishness. He wrapped himself in his stifling silence and stalked off. Nor could he be persuaded to speak again until two days later when his own ships returned. Barinthus, having directed the undertaking, came before his king with the final report. "We have encircled the island entire, and have seen neither hull nor sail in any hiding north, south, east, or west. The black ships have gone from these waters."

"Say it loud!" cried Conaire, pushing himself forward. "The enemy is defeated! What further proof is needed? We have won!"

Fergus, eager to offer his thanks, took up the cry. "Hail, Arthur! Ierne is free! The barbarian is defeated!"

At this, the entire camp loosed a wild, heart-stirring cheer. The celebration, long denied, began then and there; the Irish kings called for their bards to compose victory songs, and the ale was poured anew. The campfires were built up and several head of fat cattle quickly butchered and set to roast on spits over the flames. The long, anxious wait was over: Ierne was free, the victory complete.

After days of inactivity, the lords and warriors leapt at the chance to release their anxiety in revelry. It was as if the entire camp had been holding its breath until now, and found, to its great relief, that it could breathe once more. While the meat roasted and ale splashed from skin to jar to cup, the bards began reciting their songs, extolling the virtues of the assembled warbands and their champions. At the conclusion of each recitation, the warriors applauded with noisy acclaim. The best efforts also had their material reward—the patron lords bestowing on their Chiefs of Song lavish ornaments of silver and of gold—inspiring ever more exalted feats of praise and wordplay.

But Arthur stood apart and watched the rejoicing with a cold eye. Gwenhwyvar, having borne her concern with great fortitude for so many days, could not but reproach him for his gloom. "Your scowl could sour honey," she told him. "Ierne has shaken off the invader. That is the best news we could receive."

He turned his scowl upon his wife. "That," he told her curtly, "is the worst news of all. The very thing I feared most has befallen us." He flung a hand to the roistering warriors. "The saving of Eiru is the ruin of Ynys Prydein!"

With that he stormed into the center of the gathering and, snatching the hunting horn from Rhys, raised it to his lips and gave a loud blast. Expecting a speech of commendation and the bestowal of gifts, the crowd called for silence and pressed close about to hear what the High King would say. When he knew that they could hear him, Arthur spoke. "The victory is won for Ierne, but you must continue your celebration alone. For I must return to Britain at once." Arthur then commanded the Britons to begin preparing to leave.

"Nay, Arthur. Nay!" Fergus cried. "You have suffered much for our sake; therefore you must stay, take your rest, and let us feast you three days. It is but a small thing in light of your toil on our behalf."

"I thank you, and my lords thank you," Arthur replied. "It may be that we will all meet again, if God wills, to renew our feast in better times. I fear we have waited here too long already."

"One day more, at least," Fergus insisted. "You must allow us to pay proper homage to the victory you have won for us. For I swear by head and hand, without you there would be no free man drawing breath this day."

Conaire, lurking nearby, heard this and grimaced with distaste. "Lord Arthur has spoken, Fergus. It is not meet to keep such exalted men from their lofty affairs."

Some of the nearby British lords heard the remark, and bristled at it. Urien leapt to his feet, fists clenched. "Irish filth!" he growled, his voice low.

Gerontius started forward. Brastias threw out a restraining arm. "Be easy, brother."

Owain, nearest Arthur, rose to his feet. "Lord Arthur," he called loudly, "we have waited this long; one day more will make no difference. Whether in feast or fight, I would have these Irish kings know that Britain stands foremost," he concluded, eyeing Conaire with cool defiance.

The other Britons quickly assented to Owain's suggestion—repudiating Conaire's discourtesy. But Arthur would not be moved.

"Not a moment more may be spared," he insisted. "Gather your men, Owain—you and your brother lords—and make for the ships. We sail for Ynys Prydein at once."

The High King's decision was thoroughly resented by all the warriors and most of the lords. Only those who knew Arthur best accepted his command, even if they did not understand it. Only Cai, Bedwyr, Cador, and myself thought he had acted wisely; the rest regarded his behavior as rash, uncouth and inconsiderate.

Nevertheless, the ships were soon full-laden and the arduous process of moving Britain's war host began once more. As on the previous crossing, the wind refused to aid us in any but the most ineffectual manner; we made up for its lack by plying the oars—which most warriors regarded as tedious punishment. When resting from their labors, the Cymbrogi drowsed or talked, filling the long summer day. As the sun plowed its slow furrow across the empty skyfield, I stood at the prow, listening to the talk around me and the slow, rhythmic splash of the oars, gazing at the heat-haze dancing on the flat level horizon. I felt the sun hot on my head, smiting me with peculiar intensity. And I began to wonder how long it had been since the last rain. How long since I had last seen a sky gray with clouds and felt a cool north breeze on my face?

Deep in thought I heard a voice call out to me: *We have no choice. Burn it down. Burn it to the ground.*

This strange intrusion startled me. I turned to see who had spoken—but all was as before: men in their various positions of repose, no one paying particular attention to me. It took me a moment to realize I had not heard the voice at all—not with my ear, at least. The voice had come to me as voices sometimes do.

I strained to hear more, but it was gone already. "No choice," I whispered to myself, repeating what I had heard. "Burn it down."

What did it mean?

Another long hot day followed, and another; we glimpsed

the cragged west coast of Britain in the twilight, but it was dark when we entered Mor Hafren, and the tide was flowing against us. Rather than disembark in the dead of night on the rocky coast, our small fleet anchored, waiting for the tide to turn before making our way up the estuary channel to the landing-place below Caer Legionis.

It was not until daybreak that we were able to proceed. As ours was the lead ship, we were first to taste smoke on the morning air, and first to sight the dark, ugly haze smudged across the eastern sky. Alas! We were first also to behold that sight most dreaded in our race's long experience: the black bank formed by the massed hulls of enemy ships.

The hateful keels had been driven hard aground, and the ships—scores of them, in all shapes and sizes, enough to serve an emperor!—hundreds of ships, lashed together rail-to-rail and put to the torch. The sails and hulls must have burned for days—even now the smoke rolled heavenward from the smoldering masts and keels.

Oh, but there were so many! Score upon score of enemy ships—many times more than we had encountered in Ierne—and all of them fired to the waterline. We gazed with shock and dismay at the loathsome sight, and rued the meaning in our bones.

For the Black Boar was loose in the Island of the Mighty. And, Blessed Jesu have mercy, he meant to stay.

3

Coldly furious, Arthur ordered Barinthus to make landfall farther up the estuary, and sent Bedwyr, Llenlleawg, and the Cymbrogi to scout the way ahead. He stood in water to his knees, commanding his battlechiefs as they disembarked. The last ships had not even touched shore before the first divisions were armed, mounted, and moving away.

The Vandali had left a wide trail along the valley floor—grass trampled into the dry dirt by thousands upon thousands of trampling feet.

The trail led directly to Caer Legionis. The city itself, such as it was, had been abandoned in the days of Macsen Wledig when the legions left; the people had moved back into the surrounding hills and built a hillfort there, returning once more to an older way and more secure.

We skirted the deserted town and continued on to Arthur's fortress at Caer Melyn. As we drew nearer, we met Bedwyr and two scouts returning. "They sacked our stronghold," he reported, "and tried to burn it. But the fire did not take hold. The gate is broken."

"And those inside?" asked Arthur.

"Dead," answered Bedwyr. "All of them—dead."

When Arthur made no reply, Bedwyr continued. "They took what they could carry off, and moved on. Shall I send Llenlleawg and the others ahead to discover where they have gone?"

Still Arthur made no reply. He seemed to look through Bedwyr to the hills beyond.

"Artos?" said Gwenhwyvar. She was coming more and more to recognize and understand her husband's moods. "What are you thinking?"

Without a word, he lifted the reins and continued to the caer. If the Black Boar had wanted to devastate the fortress, not a single timber would have remained upright. As it was, however, aside from the broken gate, the stronghold appeared intact—quiet, but undamaged. It was not until we entered the yard that we saw the fire-blackened walls and smelled the death stink. A party of Cymbrogi were already at the sorrowful chore of dragging out the dead, preparing to bury them on the slope of the hill below the timber palisade.

We joined in this heartbreaking labor, then gathered on the hillside in the twilight to offer up prayers for our fallen brothers as we consigned them to their graves. Only when the green turf covered the last corpse did Arthur enter the hall.

"They were careless," Cai observed. "They were in haste."

"How do you know this?" wondered Urien. Since the last days in Ierne, he had dogged Arthur's steps, insinuating himself into the group closest to the High King. If anyone else noticed his presence, they gave no sign.

"If Twrch Trwyth had desired its destruction," Cai answered curtly, "the caer would be ashes, and those scattered to the winds."

Embarrassed by his failure to discern the obvious, Urien withdrew and said no more.

"It is fortunate we have the war host with us still," Bedwyr said. "That great horde on foot—"

"Our horses can easily overtake them," Cai put in, finishing the thought. "They cannot have traveled far."

"But the war host is fewer now than it was in Ierne," Cador pointed out. "Without the support of the Irish lords, I fear we will fare less well than before."

"Gwalchavad will have reached the northern lords with our

summons," Bedwyr reminded him. "Idris, Cunomor, and Cadwallo will arrive soon."

Cador nodded, but the frown did not leave his face. "We need more," he said, after a moment. "Even with the northern warbands it is still ten or twenty Vandali for every fighting Briton."

"Bors and Ector should arrive any day," Cai added. "Together they will bring above six hundred."

There followed a reckoning of numbers; warbands were estimated and tallied. At best we could count on four thousand, perhaps more—though likely far fewer. However, lack of fighting power was not the uppermost concern. Men must eat if they are to fight. And the talk soon turned to the persistent problem of provisions. Warriors require a constant, uninterrupted supply of food and weapons. We had not enough of arms or food to sustain a lengthy campaign.

"We must send to the settlements for our support," Cador observed gloomily. "And that will take men away from battle."

"If we do not send them," Gwenhwyvar replied, "it will cost the lives of more. There is no other way."

"There is another way," Arthur said quietly, finding his voice at last. "We will use the treasure of Britain to buy grain and cattle in Londinium." Turning to Cador, he said, "I give this task to you. Take everything we have saved from the Saecsen wars and use it in the markets."

Bedwyr shook his head in amazement. "Bear, God love you, we were plundered! Amilcar has it all!"

"All?" wondered Arthur aloud; this problem had not occurred to him.

"Not all, I suppose," Bedwyr allowed. "We have that left which was hidden under the hearth, and the little we had with us in Ierne."

"It is enough? That little is enough?"

"Perhaps," Bedwyr said doubtfully.

"Artos," Gwenhwyvar said, "whatever we lack can be made up from the churches. They have gold and silver aplenty. Go to them. Let them help us now as we have helped them."

"Tread lightly," I warned. "Separating holy men from their worldly wealth is not without consequence."

"Listen to your queen," Bedwyr urged. "What good will their gold and silver do them when the barbarians come and carry it off? They will lose both their treasure and their lives. But if they give their gold to us, they may at least keep their lives."

"So be it," said Arthur, having heard enough. To Cador he said, "Stop at the churches on the way and raise whatever you can. Tell them Arthur has need of it. When you reach Londinium, see you bargain well—our lives depend on you."

Cador accepted reluctantly. "As you will, lord," he said. "I will leave at first light tomorrow."

Arthur stood. "I am going to my chamber—what is left of it. When the lords have settled their men, let them attend me in council here."

Thus, as a woeful sliver of moon rose to shine upon the ruined caer, the lords of Britain sat down to plan the defense of the island. Having had a taste of the Vandal way of fighting, the Britons were all for blunt confrontation. "Give them the edge of the sword, I say," Ogryvan argued. "They shake with fear whenever they see our horses. We can catch them and ride them down."

"He is right. A bold attack will send them back to their ships, smart enough," added Brastias. "They are cowards and we are swiftly done with them."

Meurig spoke up. "The sooner we engage them, the sooner we are rid of them. We must ride at once."

"And then we will not need all the supplies you deem necessary to purchase," Ulfias put in hopefully. "We can finish this business before harvest."

The High King abruptly banished all such thoughts from their minds. Up he rose, fists clenched. "Did the sight of burning ships mean nothing to you?" he shouted. The noblemen glanced at one another warily. When no one made bold to answer, Arthur said, "Hear me now: it will not be as it was in Ierne. The Boar has changed. He knows well what awaits him here, and yet he comes. I tell you the truth, Amilcar has become a new and more dangerous enemy."

"How so, lord?" demanded Brastias. "He tramples, he burns, he runs away. It is the same reckless enemy. You may mistake carelessness for cunning, but I reckon it well when I see it."

Gerontius made to press the argument, but Arthur cut him off with a chop of his hand. "Am I surrounded by fools?" he asked, his voice tight with fury.

"Tribes and families!" he shouted. "Their ships burned behind them. Think!" He glared the length of the board, towering in his anger. When he spoke again, his voice was a tight whisper. "The Black Boar will no longer content himself with plunder only. He means to settle."

Before the noblemen could frame a reply, Arthur continued. "The entire realm is unprotected—and Twrch Trwyth knows this. He runs before us, laying waste the land as he goes." The High King's words were finding their mark at last; the lords kept their mouths firmly shut and listened. "Only now does the enemy begin to show his true likeness, and it is an aspect I greatly fear."

Having made his point, Pendragon concluded simply, saying, "Return to your men. Tell them we ride in pursuit. We leave at dawn."

While the battlechiefs made ready to ride, I sat alone in the empty hall and considered the meaning of the change in the Black Boar's designs. Arthur had discerned the matter aright: enraged, or at least frustrated, by Arthur's opposition to his intended plundering of Ireland, the Black Boar had moved on to easier pickings. What better place than an undefended Britain? With the war host of Ynys Prydein in Ierne, the Vandal chieftain could plunder here to his heart's content, amassing great wealth before he was caught.

Arthur had read the signs aright, certainly. Even so, misgiving gnawed at me. Amilcar knew—and knew beyond any doubt whatsoever—that the lords of Britain would soon arrive to put an end to his plunder. Having faced Arthur and suffered defeat at every turn, why risk confronting the Bear of Britain again?

More importantly, if he meant to settle, why choose Britain? Did he not fear Arthur? Did the Black Boar believe he would not be hunted down and killed?

Something drove Amilcar to this extremity. Was it desperation? Revenge? Something of both perhaps, but there seemed to me also a portion of shrewd defiance. How was that to be weighed?

I went to sleep with an uneasy mind and was roused a short while later by Rhys. Declining to break fast, I went out to walk the ramparts of Caer Melyn until it was time to leave. I watched the sky lighten in the east. Away in the south, white clouds crept along the coast, but these faded even as I watched and with them vanished any chance of rain. The day before us would be the same as those just past: scorching hot.

I turned my eyes to the hills. The grass was beginning to wither and dry. Already the trails were turning to dust. If it did not rain soon, the streams would begin to dry. Drought is not unknown in Britain, God knows, but it is rare and always betokens hardship.

As I stood looking out upon the slowly parching land, these words came again to mind: *Burn it. . . . We have no choice.* "We have no choice," the voice had said. "Burn it down. Burn it to the ground."

Words of despair, not anger. They spoke of resignation and defeat, of a last hopeless extremity. Burn it down. What calamity, I wondered, did burning resolve? What emergency was served by fire?

We have no choice. . . . Burn it to the ground. I looked down upon the caer, busy with the surge of men preparing for battle. Yet, even as I looked, the commotion changed before my eyes: the men were not warriors anymore, and the disturbance was of a very different order. I heard weeping and shouting. Men bearing torches flitted among the dwellings, pausing to set the roof-thatch alight and hurrying on. Smoke drifted across the yard. And there, in the center of the yard—corpses stacked like firewood for a pyre. A man with a torch approached this gruesome heap and touched the flame to the kindling at the base of the heap. As flames licked up through the bodies, a woman dashed forward as if to throw herself onto the pyre. The man with the torch caught her by the arm and pulled her back, then threw the torch onto the stack. Leading the woman, he turned, shouted over his shoulder to others looking on, and walked from the caer, consigning the dead and the empty stronghold to the flames.

Smoke passed before my eyes, and I heard someone call my name. When I looked again, I saw Rhys hastening to his horse at the gate. Cai and Bedwyr were already mounted, and the Flight of Dragons stood by their horses. Shaking with the force of the vision, I thrust the unsettling image from me and went to my horse. Below the caer, word of the impending departure was shouted from camp to camp. In a moment we would all ride from Caer Melyn, some to search out and gather provisions, most to engage the invader. Many who stood now blinking in the sunlight of a new day would not return.

Great Light, we ride today on paths unknown. Be a bright flame before us. Be a guiding star above us. Be a beacon pyre behind us. We are lost each one unless you light our way. Raising my hands in a bard's blessing, I said:

> *Power of Raven be upon us,*
> *Power of Eagle be ours,*
> *Power of the Warrior Host of Angels!*
> *Power of storm be upon us,*
> *Power of tempest be ours,*
> *Power of God's holy wrath!*
> *Power of sun be upon us,*
> *Power of moon be ours,*
> *Power of eternal Light!*
> *Power of earth be upon us,*
> *Power of sea be ours,*

> *Power of the Heavenly realms!*
> *All Power of Heavenly realms to bless us,*
>   *and keep us, and uphold us.*
> *And a Kindly Light to shine before us,*
>   *and lead us along the paths by which we must go.*

Satisfied with this benediction, I hurried to my place, took up the reins, and swung myself into the saddle.

Like countless invaders before them, the Vandali followed the Vale of Hafren, striking deep into the heart of the land. There were few settlements directly in the Black Boar's path—spring flooding kept the valley folk on higher ground for the most part—until he reached the broad midlands where the valley gave way to meadows and fields around Caer Gloiu, the old Roman town of Glevum.

If Amilcar had already reached that far, the whole of Lloegres' soft middle would lie open before him. The barbarian hordes would then spill out over the low, fertile meads, and there would be no containing them.

Thus we rode with dire urgency, stopping only to water the horses, pressing on through the heat of the day. The long time waiting in Ierne had given Amilcar a fair start on us, and Arthur was determined to find and engage the enemy without delay. Day's end found us far down the valley, but, aside from the much-trampled earth, we had seen no sign of barbarians.

"They move more swiftly than I imagined," Arthur observed. "Fear drives them at a relentless pace, but we will catch them tomorrow."

We did not catch them the next day, however. It was not until the sun had fallen behind the hill-rim two days later that the enemy finally came into sight. Though we had been watching their dust clouds before we came upon them, that first sight still took breath away: a great restless swarm surging like an angry flood up the wide Hafren valley. These were not a new breed of Sea Wolf looking for spoils and easy plunder, these were whole tribes on the move, a people looking for a place to settle, an entire nation searching for a home.

One glimpse of the Vandali host, asprawl like a vast dark stain spreading over the land, and Arthur ordered the columns to halt. He and his chieftains rode to the nearest hilltop to assay the predicament. "God help us," Bedwyr murmured, still struggling to take in the immensity of the throng before us. "I had no idea there could be so many."

"We saw the ships," Cai said, "but this . . . this—" Words failed him.

Arthur surveyed the multitude with narrowed eyes. "An attack now would only push them farther inland," he decided at last. "We must strike from the far side."

Upon returning to the waiting columns, Arthur summoned the lords and told them his decision. Having chased the enemy for the better part of three days, the noblemen, anxious to engage, were not pleased to have the anticipated battle denied them.

"Go around?" demanded Gerontius. "But they stand waiting before us! They are in no position to fight. We have only to attack and they are defeated." This view found favor with others, who added their endorsement.

"If it were so certain," Arthur replied wearily, "I would have given the order before you thought to complain. But victory is far from assured, and I would sooner force Twrch Trwyth back along a path he has previously trampled than offer him opportunity to venture farther afield."

"Is that prudence?" inquired Brastias, not quite concealing the sneer in his tone. "Or plain folly? If we look to our swords, sparing nothing in the attack, I have no doubt at all that this will be concluded before nightfall."

Arthur turned his face slowly to the disagreeable lord. "I wish *I* could be so easily convinced," he replied. "But for the sake of all who will raise sword beside me, I must own my doubts. And, since I am High King, the matter is not at issue." He turned in the saddle. "We go around."

"And waste another day at least!" protested Brastias. He and Gerontius had apparently taken it upon themselves to question

Arthur's every move. In this they were to be pitied, for there is no cure or comfort for this sort of blindness, and men who fall victim often find it fatal.

Circling the enemy meant a long day toiling through the rough-wooded hills to the north of the Hafren valley—an arduous task to move so many men quickly and quietly. The first stars were already showing in the sky when we finally descended to the valley once more, no great distance ahead of our slower-moving foe. After setting sentries along the hilltops to either side, we made camp by the river and remounted before dawn to take up our attack position.

We were assembled in a crook in the valley, ready and waiting when the Vandal horde finally appeared. They came on in a great dark flood, like a tidal wave pouring through the valley, pausing, swelling, flowing—inundating the land. We waited and listened—the sound of their advance rumbled like dull thunder upon the earth. The dust from their feet clouded the air like smoke.

Closer, we heard more particular sounds: the cries of children and sometimes laughter, the barking of dogs, the lowing of cattle and sheep, the sharp squeal of swine.

Arthur turned his face to me, his blue eyes dark with worry and lack of sleep. "They advance with women and children at the fore."

He quickly summoned his battlechiefs.

"Bairns on the battlefield!" Cai protested. "What kind of war leader would force his people so?"

"Amilcar must know we would not willingly slaughter women and children," Bedwyr pointed out. "He uses them as his shield."

"I do not care," said Brastias gruffly. "If they are fool enough to wander onto the battleground, they deserve whatever happens to them." Others agreed.

"But women and children," Gwenhwyvar protested. "They have no part in this." She looked to her husband. "What will you do, Artos?"

He thought for a long moment. "We cannot give in to

Amilcar. The attack will commence as planned, but let each warn our warbands that innocents advance before the battle host, and they are not to be killed if it can be helped."

"Even so, many will die," Gwenhwyvar insisted.

"That is as it may be," Arthur conceded. "I know no other way." Yet, unwilling to give the order, he asked, "Does anyone suggest a better plan?" The king looked to each of his chieftains in turn, but all remained silent. "So be it," he concluded. "Return to your places and prepare your warbands. I will give the signal."

The High King's commands were relayed quickly through the ranks: the British war host advanced to their positions and made ready to charge. The forerunners became aware of us then, for a shrill, blatting horn sounded and all at once the leading edge of the dark flood froze. The sudden halt sent rippled waves coursing back through the oncoming throng.

"May God forgive us our sins this day," said Arthur grimly. And, without another word, raised his hand to Rhys, who put the battle horn to his lips and sounded the attack.

4

  ARTHUR INTENDED TO HALT THE
enemy's advance—which our attack
accomplished admirably well. One
look at the flying hooves and leveled
spears hurtling towards them and the Vandali fled.

Pressed between the valley's steep sides, the invading host
shrank from the impact. The mass shuddered, surged, and began to move away, effectively trapping the main body of warriors in the rear and keeping them from ever reaching the fight.
We did not even unsheathe our swords.

Having so easily succeeded in his aim, Arthur commanded
Rhys to signal the lords to break off the charge. This brought
cries of outrage from the British kings.

"Why have you called us back?" demanded Gerontius,
flinging himself from the saddle. Brastias and Ogryvan galloped
to where Arthur, Gwenhwyvar, Bedwyr and I stood together.
"We could have defeated them once and for all!"

"Look!" shouted Brastias, gesturing wildly in the direction
of the fast-retreating horde. "We can catch them still. It is not
too late. Resume the attack."

Meurig joined the group then; Ulfias and Owain were not
far behind. Llenlleawg and Cai sat their horses, looking on.

"What has happened?" demanded Owain. "Why have we
broken off the attack?"

"Well you might ask!" cried Brastias. "Let Arthur explain
if he can. It makes no sense to me."

Owain and Meurig looked to Arthur, who replied, "This day's fighting is done."

"Madness," spat Gerontius.

"Madness?" challenged Bedwyr, his temper flaring instantly.

"We had victory in our grasp and threw it away," answered Gerontius hotly. "I call that madness, by God!"

"They were women and children!" Bedwyr replied, his face growing red. "Oh, a very great victory to slaughter sheep and babes in arms. By all means, trample down the defenseless and count it a triumph!"

"Aghh!" growled Gerontius in frustrated rage. He opened his mouth to renew his protest, but Cai restrained him.

"Enough, Gerontius. Say no more," advised Cai, "that way you will have less to regret."

Brastias put a hand to his friend's arm and made to turn him away, but Gerontius shook off the hand and stabbed his finger in Arthur's face. "We might have settled it today but for your damnable caution. I am beginning to wonder if it is not cowardice instead."

"If you value your tongue, stop it flapping," warned Bedwyr, stepping towards him.

Gerontius glared at Bedwyr, then at Arthur, and stormed off. Brastias went after him, calling him back to make his objections known before all. Though the others said nothing, I could tell they also faulted Arthur's decision. They had supposed an easy victory and saw it snatched away. After an awkward silence, they slowly dispersed, frustrated that the first battle fought on British soil should be cut off without at least punishing the invader for his audacity.

"It was the right thing to do, Bear," offered Bedwyr, hoping to soothe. Instead, he produced the opposite effect.

"Little you know me, brother, if you imagine I care what a fool like Gerontius thinks," Arthur replied hotly. "Or that his words will sway me." He turned on his heel and ordered Llenlleawg to lead the Dragon Flight in making certain the retreat continued.

When they had gone, Gwenhwyvar and I sat down with

Arthur. "Do they truly believe this war will be won in a day? Or that a single battle will decide it?" he asked, shaking his head. "Have they fought at my side so long, yet even now can speak of cowardice?"

"It is nothing," Gwenhwyvar told him. "Less than nothing. Pay it no mind, my love."

"They are not with me in this yet," Arthur said. "Is it not enough that I must fight Amilcar? Must I carry those faithless lords on my back as well?"

"Was it ever different?" I asked.

Arthur glanced at me, and then allowed himself a slow smile. "No," he admitted. "In truth, nothing has changed. But I thought that taking the High Kingship might have granted me a whit of authority."

"It only gives them reason to fear you all the more," Gwenhwyvar said.

"Why should they fear me? Is it Arthur invading their lands? Is it Arthur plundering their treasure and making widows of their women?"

"Let me go to Fergus and Conaire," Gwenhwyvar urged. "They will show their loyalty and shame the Britons."

Arthur gently declined; he rose and said, "Come, we must make certain the Vandali do not overcome their fright and turn back."

Remounting our horses, we continued on down the valley, leading the warbands of Britain. The Dragon Flight were already far ahead, the dust from the hooves of their horses rising up to mingle with that of the fleeing enemy. I saw the white pall hanging over the valley and grew suddenly light-headed.

I entered a waking dream.

It seemed as if I were lifted out of myself—as if my spirit took wings to glide above me. For I felt a rush of movement and looked down to see myself riding beside Arthur; Gwenhwyvar and Cador rode at his right hand, and behind us the warbands in three long columns: a Roman *alá*, though no one now alive, save me, had ever seen one.

And I recalled the day I gazed out from my Grandfather

Elphin's hillfort into the dale to see Magnus Maximus, *Dux Britanniarum*, leading the Augusta Legion south. I did not know it then, but soon that great general would lead his army across the Narrow Sea to Gaul, never to return. He is remembered now as Macsen Wledig, and has become a fabulous figure: an illustrious British Emperor. But he was Roman through and through; and though he fought well to preserve us from the barbarians, he was no Briton.

How long ago was that? How many years have passed? Great Light, how long must I endure?

I lifted my head and soared higher. When I looked again, I saw the dark stain on the land, the cancer that was the Black Boar's invading host, flowing through the valley. There were so many of them. So very many! It was a migration, an entire civilization on the move.

Above me I saw, beyond the pale blue sky, bright beams of starlight, fixed and frozen in their empty firmament. The stars shone down, shedding their light upon us by day and night, untouched and uninfluenced by the deeds of men. What are men, after all? Frail creatures, frail as the grass that grows green one day and withers the next, blown away on every wind.

God help us, we are mingled starlight and dust, and we know not who we are. We are lost unless we find ourselves in you, Great Light.

Out across the wind-tossed waves I saw Gaul and Armorica, and beyond them the Great Mother of Nations, Rome, once a beacon to all the world. The light had already flickered out in the east; hungry darkness now stretched its claws toward tiny Britain. But I saw Ynys Prydein, the Isle of the Mighty, like a sea-girt rock, solid amidst storm-tossed waves—a many-favored land, shining like a Beltain blaze in a wilderness of night, alone among her sister nations yet holding the all-devouring darkness at bay. And this by the virtue of a lineage which united the fiery courage of the Celt with the cool dispassion of Roman discipline, distilled into the heart of a single man: Arthur.

Before Arthur there was Aurelius; and before Aurelius, Merlin; and before Merlin, Taliesin. Each day raised up its own champion, and in each and every age the Swift Sure Hand labored to redeem his creation. Look you! We are not abandoned, nor do we strive with our own strength alone. Call on your Creator, O Man, cling to him, and he will carry you. Honor him, and he will establish guardian spirits round about you. Though you walk through flood and fire, you will not be harmed; your Redeemer will uphold you. Bright armies of angels go before us, surrounding us on every side if we could but see!

Oh, but there were haughty lords among us, proud men who bent the knee willingly to no one. Arthur, embodying all that mortal power could boast, was hard put to unite them—and him they knew. What they would not grant to an earthly king, they would scarce yield to an unseen spirit. No power on earth, or up above, can force the human heart to love where it will not love, or honor where it will not honor.

How long I drifted in this strange flight, I do not know. But when I at last came to myself again, it was twilight and a still, quiet camp lay around me. I awoke to find myself sitting on a calfskin by a fire, a bowl of stew untouched in my hands.

"Hail, Myrddin. We welcome your return," Arthur said as I stirred. I looked across the fire to see him watching me, concerned by the dazed expression on my face. "You were surely lost in your thoughts, bard."

Gwenhwyvar lifted my dish slightly. "You have not tasted a bite of your food."

I looked into the bowl cupped in my hands. The dark liquid within became a squirming, seething mass of yellow maggots. I saw human bones, smoldering with inexplicable fire. And I heard again the echo of those mysterious words: *We have no choice . . . burn it down.*

I saw again the mound of corpses, bloated and stained a hideous blue-black, piled high and burning, greasy smoke assaulting a dry white sky. The gorge rose in my throat; I gagged and threw the bowl from me.

Gwenhwyvar put her hand on my arm. "Myrddin!"

Sudden knowledge burst within me; the hateful word formed on my tongue. "Pestilence," I answered, choking on the word. "Even now death is moving like a mist through the land."

Arthur's jaw was set. "I will defend Britain. I will do all that may be done to defeat the Vandali."

He misunderstood my meaning, so I said: "There is an enemy more powerful than the Boar and his piglets, more dangerous to us all than any invader who has breached these shores."

Arthur regarded me sharply. "You speak in riddles, bard. What is this death?"

"It is called the Yellow Death," I replied.

"Plague!" Gwenhwyvar gasped.

"There has been no word of plague from any of the lords," said Arthur. "I will not allow such rumors to be spread amongst men preparing for battle."

"I have no interest in rumors, O Great King. Even so, there is no doubt in my mind—nor should there be in yours—that the Yellow Death is even now loosed in Britain."

Arthur accepted the rebuke in my words; staring into my eyes he asked, "What is the cure?"

"I *know* no cure," I told him. "But it comes to me," I added on a sudden inspiration, "that if any remedy exists it may be that the priests at Ynys Avallach know of it. Their experience is wide and their knowledge deep," I said, and remembered my mother telling me that the monastery was becoming a place of healing. But that had been years ago—would it still be so now?

"Then you must go at once without delay," said Gwenhwyvar.

I rose from my place.

"Sit down, Myrddin," Arthur said. "You cannot go now. It is dark and there are fifty thousand barbarians between you and Ynys Avallach." He paused, looking up at me in the firelight. "Besides, I sit in council tonight and I need you here."

"I cannot stay, Arthur," I said. "If anything can be done, I dare not wait. I must go. You know this."

Still Arthur hesitated. "One enemy at a time," he said. "We only squander our strength if we chase off in all directions. There is no cure for the plague, you said so yourself."

"I have no wish to defy you," I said stiffly. "But you have the Cymbrogi to attend you, and I may be of use elsewhere. This danger has been shown to me, and I cannot ignore it. I will return as soon as possible, but I must go. Now. Tonight."

"Bear," Gwenhwyvar implored, "he is right. Let him go. It may be the saving of many lives." Arthur's gaze swung from me to her, and she seized on this momentary hesitation. "Yes, go to them, Wise Emrys," Gwenhwyvar urged, as if this had been Arthur's plan all along. "Learn all you can and bring us some good word."

"I make no promise," I warned, "but I will do what may be done. As for rumors, say nothing to anyone about this until I return."

"So, it is settled," declared Arthur, though I could tell the decision did not sit well with him. He stood abruptly and cried out for Llenlleawg. "Myrddin must leave us for a time," he said. "Since the valley is swarming with Vandali, I would ask you to accompany him on his journey."

Llenlleawg inclined his head in assent, his expression impassive in the firelight.

"I thank you," I told them both. "But I will travel more swiftly alone."

"At least let him see you to the boat," Arthur insisted. "Then I will know the barbarians did not stop you."

Seeing he was determined to get his way in something, I relented. Bidding Arthur and Gwenhwyvar fare well, Llenlleawg and I went at once to the horse picket to retrieve our mounts. We rode from the camp as Arthur was sitting down to council.

I do not know which I pitied more: Arthur contending with his kings, or myself spending a sleepless night in the saddle. Likely, I had the better bargain.

5

LLENLLEAWG AND I KEPT TO THE
hilltops till we were well out of sight
of the barbarian encampment, turning our horses into the vale as the sun
broke red and raw in the east. Llenlleawg led the way, riding
a little ahead, keeping close watch on the trail and the bluffs
to either side, lest we encounter any straggling Vandali. But
the trail remained empty and safe—until, rounding a blind turn
just after midday, the Irish champion halted abruptly. "Someone is coming this way. Three riders, maybe more."

My eyes scanned the riverside trail before us, but I saw nothing. "There." The Irishman pointed to the rock-strewn riverbank ahead and to the right. The white sun high overhead
shrank the shadows, making everything appear flat and col-
orless. I looked where Llenlleawg indicated and saw that what
I had taken to be the gray shapes of boulders were in fact riders,
slowly picking their way along the riverside.

"Did they see us?"

He gave his head a slight shake. "I do not think so."

We sat motionless for a time, waiting for the strangers to
show themselves. Since the men were mounted, I did not think
they could be Vandali, but we waited just the same. The
strangers were also wary; they came on slowly, pausing often
to scan the trail ahead, and the instant they sighted us, one of
their number turned tail and raced back the way they had
come, leaving the remaining two to continue on.

"Let us meet them," Llenlleawg said, drawing a spear from

behind his saddle. We moved ahead slowly, and but a single spear-throw separated us when Llenlleawg gave a whoop and lashed his mount to speed. "It is Niul!" he called back to me. "Lot's man!"

He rushed ahead, hailing the riders loudly. I galloped after him as Llenlleawg and Niul, leaning from the saddle, embraced one another. "What do you here, cousin?" cried the one called Niul. "I thought it was a very *cruachag* rising out of the river to carry us off." He laughed, throwing back his head. One glance at the scars on his shield arm and the notched blade ready on his thigh gave me to know this battle-wise veteran feared little in this world.

Not waiting for Llenlleawg to present me, he turned and called: "Hail, Myrddin Emrys!" At my surprise, he laughed again. "You do not remember me, nor do I blame you."

As he spoke, a memory shaped itself in my mind. I remembered a room in a house—Gradlon the wine merchant's room in Londinium the first time I had met Lot. This man, one of Lot's chieftains, was there. "It is true that I do not remember your name, if I ever heard it," I confessed. "But you, I think, attended the first Council of Kings in Londinium. We shared a cup of beer together, as I recall, since Lot would drink no wine."

"By the God that made you, Lord Emrys—"Niul laughed, enjoying this meeting very much—"you are a wonder. True enough. My soul, I was but a boy then. Yes, we shared a cup of beer. Lot would drink nothing else. But where is Pelleas? How come you keep company with this wild beast of an Irishman?"

"Pelleas is dead," I told him. "Several years ago."

Sorrow stole the mirth from his smile. "Ah, a sad loss indeed." He shook his head. "Forgive me, I did not know."

Llenlleawg spoke up. "Niul's mother and mine were kin," he explained. "Niul was fostered in Fergus' house. We were raised together."

The urgency of my journey pressed upon me, so, at risk of rudeness, I said, "Is Lot here?"

"He follows directly," replied Niul. "He is with the warband but a small distance behind. Come, I will take you to him."

Curving around the foot of an enormous hill, the valley bent and widened as it passed. Once beyond the bend I saw, spread out across the valley floor, a warband of perhaps five hundred warriors—three hundred on foot, the rest on horseback: a most heartening sight.

From the forerank of warriors two horsemen rode to meet us. Lot I would have recognized anywhere: his bold checked cloak of black and crimson, his braided locks, his great golden torc, the blue-stained clan marks on his cheeks. He recognized me, too, and called out with evident pleasure. "Hail, Emrys! I give you good greeting. It is long since we last met—too long, I think."

I hailed him in return, and we embraced one another in true friendship. "Well, it is once again in the saddle with sword in hand—not so, Myrddin Emrys?"

"I would it were not so," I replied. "Still, I am glad to see you. In the name of the High King, I welcome you, Lot."

"We came upon Llenlleawg and the Emrys on the other side of the bend yonder," Niul put in. "They ride alone."

"And here were we expecting these fierce Vandali Gwalchavad warned us of," Lot offered by way of explanation.

"Continue on the way you are going and you will soon find as many as you care to see," Llenlleawg answered. "Fifty thousand or more."

"Truly?" wondered Lot. "Gwalchavad did not say there were so many."

"He did not know," I replied, "nor did we." Llenlleawg then told them where to find Arthur and how best to avoid the barbarians.

"Will you ride with us, Emrys?" Niul asked.

"Alas, we cannot," I replied. "Llenlleawg and I pursue other affairs, no less urgent."

"Then we will not delay you longer," Lot said. "Until we meet again, Myrddin, I bid you fare well and safe return."

We continued on our way, and they on theirs, and we soon

passed from one another's sight. The valley widened and, as the day dwindled, I could see the waters of Mor Hafren shining in the distance. We camped on the trail and were in the saddle again before dawn.

The sun had not risen above the surrounding hills when, high in the clear, cloudless sky I saw the dark shapes of carrion birds circling a place a little distance to the north. "That is Caer Uisc," I observed.

Without a word, Llenlleawg turned aside and made for the settlement. We arrived a short time later to find the place burnt to its post holes. I surveyed the blackened arena formed by the scorched timbers of the palisade. Here and there, under collapsed roof trees I saw a few objects recognizable still: the sphere of an overturned caldron, a tripod reduced to lengths of twisted iron, heat-shattered jars by the score, and—God have mercy!—half-buried amid heaps of dead ash, the charred corpses of plague victims, young and old alike. The birds worked at the dead, picking clean the bones.

"The Black Boar has done this thing," Llenlleawg declared bitterly.

"No," I told him, seeing the flames and hearing the weeping of my vision once more. Here was its confirmation—if any were needed. "Twrch Trwyth is not to blame. The people of Caer Uisc have burned their own settlement."

Llenlleawg started at this. "That cannot be!" he protested, and began to dismount in order to examine the scene more closely.

"Stay!" I commanded. "Touch not so much as an ash to your boot." Pulling himself back into the saddle, he opened his mouth to object. I silenced him with a word, and said, "You will know this killer soon enough. When you return to Caer Melyn, tell Arthur—only Arthur, mind!—what you have seen. Tell him also that Myrddin's vision was true. Do you understand? Say nothing of Caer Uisc to the others. We were never here, Llenlleawg."

Accustomed to taking orders, the man accepted my instructions. I turned away. "We best not linger. The day is speeding from us."

We rode on in all haste to the harbor at Caer Legionis, where Arthur's fleet, joined now by Lot's ships, lay at anchor. Barinthus hailed our approach; the doughty pilot had remained behind with a handful of men to guard and maintain the ships. "What word?" he called. "What word of the battle?"

"We fought but once," Llenlleawg answered. "A broken skirmish. There was no victory."

We dismounted and greeted the pilot; several others came running to hear what we had to say. I told them how the situation stood between Arthur and Amilcar, and asked, "Have you seen anything?"

"Lot arrived midday yesterday," Barinthus told us.

"Nothing else?"

"No one passes here without our notice," the bull-necked shipman answered. "We keep watch day and night, and neither friend nor foe has come this way—save Lot, as I say, and yourselves." He paused, anticipating my order. "I am at your service, Wise Emrys. Where would you go?"

"To Ynys Avallach," I answered, indicating the broad sweep of Mor Hafren glittering like hammered gold in the fading light of day. "I see the tide is flowing now. The need is such, I cannot wait."

"It shall be done," the pilot said. "I myself will take you."

"Also," I added, "it would be wise to move the ships away from the shore. We will not need them soon, I think."

"The thought had occurred to me," Barinthus replied, in a tone that made it clear I need concern myself no further with the safety of the ships.

He turned and began barking commands; those with him leapt to their tasks. I bade Llenlleawg return to Arthur then, and by the time my mount and I were aboard the boat, Arthur's fleet was already being moved to deeper water—well out of reach of marauding barbarians.

Riding the ebbing tideflow, Barinthus expertly guided the ship around mudbanks and swiftly brought us to the opposite shore at the place where the little river Briw met the larger Padrud, forming a great mudflat at low tide. "It looks to be a mucky landing," he warned. "This is as close as I dare go."

Thus was I forced to disembark in waist-deep water. Leading my horse, I splashed through the water and floundered across the mudflat to dry land—where I mounted and hastened inland. Night overtook me on the way, but I did not stop; I wanted to reach my grandfather's house as soon as possible. Pushing a relentless course, I came in sight of the tor as the sun rose once more.

There can be few more beautiful sights in this worlds-realm than the palace of the Fisher King by golden dawnlight. The slender towers and graceful walls of white stone—all rose-and-honey-colored in the morning light—made a richly glowing reflection in the lake that surrounded the tor with Ynys Avallach rising above the flat marshland like an island from a blue-green sea.

Years had passed since I last saw it—several lifetimes, it seemed. Even so, it remained as I recalled from earliest memory, and my heart swelled with a sudden yearning. Avallach's palace had ever been a haven to me, and I felt its old tranquillity beckoning, like a cool breeze over the shaded depths of the lake's many-shadowed pools, soothing the traveler's heat-fevered brow.

Oh, Blessed Jesu, keep this place close to your loving heart, and hold it in the palm of your Swift Sure Hand. If goodness anywhere endures in this worlds-realm, let it reign here, now, and for as long as your name is honored among men.

I made my way around the lake, passing beneath the hill where stood the abbey, and reached the causeway leading out across the water to the tor. Ynys Avallach, green as an emerald against the sun-fired sky, seemed some otherworldly place—an impression only deepened upon meeting those who dwelt there. Fair Folk indeed, graceful in every line, enchanting to look upon—even the lowest stablehand possesses a bearing of high nobility. Two young grooms dashed forward, running to take my horse. Avallach, last monarch of that dwindling race, appeared and called a greeting as I passed under the high-vaulted arch.

"Merlin!" His voice resounded like glad thunder. Before I had properly dismounted, he drew me from the saddle and gathered me in his strong embrace. "Merlin, my son, my son. Stand here. Let me look at you." He held me at arm's length, then seized me once more and crushed me to him.

Arthur—big as he is—is but a boy beside the Fisher King. I felt a stripling youth again.

"The peace of Christ be upon you, Merlin, my son," Avallach said, spreading wide his arms. "Welcome! Come into my hall—we will raise the cup together."

Leaving the stone-flagged yard, we crossed a roofed portico and passed through two great doors into the palace. "Charis is not here at present," the Fisher King informed me as the welcome cup arrived. "One of the priests summoned her this morning. They fetch her whenever she is needed at the shrine."

"Did they say why?" I asked with sinking heart, praying it was not what I feared. Could plague spread so quickly? I did not know.

"Sickness," Avallach replied, holding out the cup. When the cup was filled, the Fisher King pressed it into my hands. "Drink, Merlin. You have traveled far, and the journey was hot. The villagers say there is drought."

I smiled. Avallach called any and all who lived in the shadow of the tor "villagers"—as if he were a lord with thriving settlements full of loyal subjects. In truth, though a few folk still lived in holdings scattered around the marshes, most who passed through the Summerlands were pilgrims in search of a blessing at the shrine.

"Then I will find her at the abbey," I said, and sipped some of the good, rich beer before passing the cup to Avallach.

"So I imagine," he said, raising the cup, watching me over the rim. He paused, cocking his head to one side as he studied me. "Christ have mercy!" he cried all at once. "Myrddin, you can see!"

"Truly, Grandfather."

He gazed at me as if at a marvel. "But—but how did this happen? Your sight restored! Tell me! Tell me at once."

"There is little enough to say," I replied. "I was blind, as you well know. But a priest named Ciaran laid hands on me and it pleased God to heal me."

"A miracle," breathed Avallach, as if this were the most natural explanation—as if miracles were splendidly commonplace, as frequent as the sun rising in the east each day, as wonderful and as welcome. Indeed, in his world, perhaps they were.

Talk passed then to the small happenings of the marshland: fishing, the work at the shrine and abbey, the toil of the monks and the ever-widening circle of faith. I marveled, not for the first time, how little the trauma and turmoil of the day mattered in this place. Events of great moment in the wider world were either unknown here or passed as incidents of small consequence. The palace of the Fisher King, like its tor, stood aloof from the ravages and upheaval of the age, a true haven, a sanctuary of peace in a trouble-fretted world. Great Light, let it ever be so!

I would gladly have conversed with him all day, but the need pressed in me once more. Promising to return as soon as possible, I took leave of Avallach and walked to the abbey, glad to be out of the saddle. As I climbed the path from the lakeside, some of the brothers saw me and ran ahead to announce my arrival. I was met and conducted to Abbot Elfodd's chamber.

"Wait here, please," the monk said. "The abbot will join you as soon as he is free."

"Thank you, but—"

The monk was gone before I could stop him. I thought to call him back, but fatigue overwhelmed me and instead I sat down in the abbot's chair to wait. I had just closed my eyes when I heard the sound of footsteps outside the door.

"Merlin!"

I opened my eyes, stood, and was instantly enfolded in a strong, almost fierce embrace.

6

 "YOUR EYES . . . YOUR BEAUTIFUL eyes," Charis whispered, tears of happiness spilling freely down her cheeks. "It is true! Jesu be praised, you can see! But how did this happen? Sit down at once, and tell me. I must know. Oh, Merlin, I am glad you are here. What a delightful surprise. Can you stay? No, do not tell me; whether short or long, it makes no difference. You are here now and that is all that matters."

"I have missed you, Mother," I murmured. "I did not know how much I had missed you until this moment."

"How I have longed for you, my Hawk," Charis said, drawing me to her again. "And now here you are—a prayer answered."

Charis was, as ever, unchanged—save in small ways only: her hair she wore in the manner of highborn British women, thickly plaited with strands of golden thread woven into the braids; her mantle was dove-gray, simple, long, and utterly lacking any ornament. Slender, regal, she appeared both elegant and mysterious, the stark austerity of her garments enhancing rather than diminishing her royal mien. Her eyes, as they played over my face, were as keen as any inquisitive child's, and held a strength of authority I had not known before.

She saw that I had noticed the change in her attire, and said, "Your eye is more than keen, Hawk, to see what is no longer there." She smoothed her mantle with her hands and smiled.

"Yes, I dress more humbly now. Many of the people who come to the shrine have so little; they possess nothing—less than nothing, some of them—I do not wish to remind them of their poverty. I could not bear to offend them even by my clothing."

"He would be a miserable man indeed who found the sight of you offensive," I replied lightly.

She smiled again. "And why your own drab cloak, my son? I cannot find it fitting to your rank that you array yourself so."

I spread my hands. "Like you, I find it easier to pass through the world without proclaiming my lineage at every turn. Come, you are tired—"

"I was," she replied quickly, "but the sight of you has revived me completely. Sit with me. I would hear you tell me all that has passed in Arthur's court since I last saw you."

"And I would enjoy nothing more than to spend the day with you," I replied, "for there is much to tell. But my errand is urgent and I cannot stay one moment longer than necessary. I am sorry. I must return as soon as—"

"Leaving before you have properly arrived!" Both Charis and I turned as the abbot bustled into the room. Elfodd, in his white mantle and green tunic, greeted me warmly. "Welcome, Merlinus! Welcome, good friend. They just told me you had come. Sit, man, you look exhausted."

"I am pleased to see you again, good abbot. You are flourishing, I see." He appeared unchanged for the most part—a little plumper perhaps, with more gray in his hair, but the same Elfodd that I remembered. "Charis has told me you are busy as ever."

"Run off our feet, matins to evensong," he replied happily. "But we thrive. God is good. We thrive!"

"I am glad to hear it."

"Still—"he grew serious—"it is not so with some who come here. One died last night who was in our care, and two others with the same illness have been found—far gone they were, not even the strength to drag themselves up the hill."

He regarded me closely, weighing his next words carefully.

I felt I knew already what he would say. "Merlinus, it may not be safe for you here. I pray I am mistaken, but it seems very like plague. If so, the one who died last night is but the first of many."

"Trust me, there will be more," I told him, and explained the reason for my visit. "I hoped you would know some remedy. That is why I have come."

"Then Jesu help us all, for there is no remedy," he answered, shaking his gray head sadly. "The pestilence cannot be contained: it wanders on the wind; like tainted water, it poisons everything. No one is safe." He grew silent, contemplating the enormity of the predicament looming before him.

"I have been speaking to Paulinus," Charis began, excitement quickening her speech. "He is well learned in this—"

"Paulinus?" wondered Elfodd—memory broke across his blank features like sunrise. "Oh, praise God, yes! Paulinus! Blessed Jesu, of course. With all the tumult, I had quite forgotten."

"Paulinus has recently arrived," Charis began.

"Arrived from Armorica," the abbot broke in. "He spent some time in south Gaul and, I believe, in Alexandria, where he learned much of healing herbs unknown to us here."

"They have experience of plague in those places," Charis said. "We were speaking of this just before you came, Merlin. You must talk to him at once."

"Foolish servant," cried Elfodd, "what am I thinking?" He turned on his heel and called out in a loud voice: "Paulinus! Someone bring Paulinus to me at once!"

A monk appeared in the doorway behind him, acknowledged the abbot's call, and disappeared at a run. Though early morning yet, it was already hot in Elfodd's cell. "Let us await him in the cloister; it is cooler there."

We stepped from the closeness of the abbot's cell out into the colonnaded walkway. A single tree grew in the center of the courtyard, shading the square. The leaves on the tree were dry and drooping for lack of water. "I see we must bring some water from the lake for Joseph's tree," Elfodd said absently.

The land is athirst, I thought, and had my thoughts answered by a calm, deep voice which said, "The hammer of the Sun beats upon Earth's anvil. All that is green shall be brown; all that burns is consumed."

We turned to see an old, spare, bald-headed man step into the light. His face was lean and brown from many days, perhaps years, in the southern sun. Into my mind came the rejoinder to his quoted scrap of prophecy. "And all who pass through the fire will be purified," I added, holding his gaze with my own.

"So be it!" the monk said; he inclined his head in deference to Abbot Elfodd, who had summoned him. "Wise Ambrosius, my name is Paulinus. I am at your service."

He joined us, greeting Elfodd and Charis with simple grace. I saw, to my surprise, that he was much younger than I had first thought. His bald head, and the leathery appearance of his skin, made him look older than his years. But there was no mistaking the youthful intensity of his deep brown eyes. He was dressed in the humble undyed homespun tunic of the monks, but held himself with the bearing of a lord.

"I remember you, brother," I said, "and need no new introduction."

"By the Blessed Lamb!" he cried in amazement. "It cannot be! For I was but a lad the only time I saw you, and never a word passed between us."

I looked on his countenance, and recalled an elderly man helped along by a boy who carried his staff. The man was the aged Dafyd walking out from the Llandaff monastery; the apple-cheeked boy had shaggy dark hair and bright bold eyes—the same eyes that looked at me with such amusement now.

"You were at Llandaff with Dafyd," I told him. "Were you born there?" I do not know why I asked the question. There are always plenty of children at any monastery; that fact alone possessed no great significance.

"Well you know it!" He laughed. "Saints and angels, I thought I would never leave that place. Ah, but truly, there are times now I wish I never had."

He laughed again and I realized I had heard that laugh before, and that turn of phrase. Oh, yes, he was a Cymry through and through. "Are you Gwythelyn's son?"

"One of six, and good men all," he answered. "To my kinsmen in Dyfed I am Pol ap Gwythelyn. How may I serve you, Myrddin Emrys?"

As Charis had already discussed the possibility with him, I saw no need to soften the blow. "As you know, plague has visited Britain," I said. "I have come from the High King to learn what may be done."

Paulinus made the sign of the cross and, raising his hands and face to the sun, he said, "All praise the World Creator, and his Glorious Son, who works in mysterious ways his wonders to perform! Happy am I among men, for many are called but few are chosen, and this day have I been chosen. I am but a tool in the Master's Hand—yet my destiny shall be fulfilled."

Elfodd looked on, somewhat astonished by this outburst. Charis regarded him curiously.

"Do I take it you can help us?" I asked.

"All things are possible with God," Paulinus answered.

"Brother, your piety is laudable. Yet, I would thank you for a straight answer in simple words."

Paulinus accepted the rebuke with good grace, explaining how he had long questioned the guiding hand which had led him far into foreign lands in search of exotic cures and remedies, yet removed him from contact with the very people who could most benefit from his knowledge. In short, he had begun to feel his effort wasted: that he had mistaken his call.

"I wanted to be a healer," Paulinus continued. "I feared I had become a scholar instead. That is why I came to Ynys Avallach—the work here is known and respected, even in Gaul. And now God, in his infinite wisdom, has raised up his servant. My years of study will be justified; my gift will be honored. I am ready." He turned his face to the sun once more, and exclaimed, "Goodly Wise is the Gifting Giver and greatly to be praised! May his wisdom endure forever!"

"So be it!" I cried, to which Charis and Elfodd added a

hearty "Amen." Turning to the abbot, I said, "Elfodd, we must hold council at once. There is much to discuss."

"Of course," the abbot agreed. "Let us go to the chapel, where we can speak more privately."

He turned and I made to follow, but my vision blurred and I swayed on my feet. Charis reached out to steady me. "Merlin!" she cried, her voice sharp with concern. "Are you ill?"

"No," I replied quickly, lest they think the worst. "I am well, but overtired."

"You have not eaten since leaving Arthur," Charis declared, and I was forced to confess it. "Why?" she asked, and answered her own question: "There is trouble in Britain," she said, "and more than plague only."

Again, I admitted that she had read the situation aright. "Then come, Hawk," Charis said. "I am taking you back to the tor at once."

"It is nothing," I insisted.

"Elfodd and Paulinus will attend us there," she said, leading me away.

As I had neither the strength nor will to resist, I gratefully succumbed to her care and allowed myself to be taken to the Glass Isle.

7

 AFTER I HAD EATEN SOMETHING and rested a little, the clerics arrived to join Charis and Avallach in deliberation over the predicament before us. We met in the sunwell outside Avallach's chamber, where a canopy of red cloth had been raised to form a shady place. Chairs were brought and we held council under the awning, as beneath the cloth of a Roman camp tent. This was fitting, for our talk was as momentous as any military campaign, and no less urgent.

"From what you have said," Paulinus ventured, "I think it safe to say that the disease follows the Vandal fleet. Where their keels touch, the pestilence alights."

"If that is the way of it," I said, "I am wondering why the Cymbrogi remain untouched? They have been fighting the barbarian from the first, yet no one has fallen ill. Also," I pointed out, "the Vandali stormed Ierne before coming to Britain, yet we have heard no word of plague from anyone there."

The monk considered this carefully. "Then," he concluded at last, "it must arise from some other source." Turning to Elfodd, he asked abruptly: "The man who died last night—where was his home?"

"Why, he lived nearby," the abbot answered, "at Ban Curnig; it lies a little to the west. But he was a farmer. I do not think he had ever been on a ship—or even near one."

"I see." Paulinus frowned. "Then I do not know what to

say. I have never heard of plague arising anywhere but in a port, and we are a fair distance from the sea."

We all fell silent, thinking how this mystery might be solved. "What about the others?" I asked after a time. "Two more died; were they farmers as well?"

"I do not know," Elfodd replied, "and they can tell us nothing now."

"One of them was a trader," Charis said. "At least, I assumed so. I have seen a merchant's purse often enough to know one."

Avallach stood and summoned one of his servants. After a quick consultation the servant hastened away. "We will soon discover what can be learned from a merchant's purse."

"While we wait," Elfodd suggested to Paulinus, "tell us what you know of this pestilence." With that, the monk began to relate all he knew of the disease and the various means and methods he had learned for treating the victims. There were herb and plant potions thought to offer some relief; fresh water—that is, water drawn only from swift-running streams—must be maintained for drinking; grain must be roasted before eating, or be thrown away—especially grain tainted by rats; travel must be curtailed, for the disease seemed to spread most freely when men moved unrestrained. The dead must be burned, along with their clothing and belongings and, to be certain, their houses and grainstores too. Fire offered some protection, since once burned out the pestilence rarely returned.

"I will allow you no false hope," Paulinus warned. "There are several kinds of plague—all are deadly. With the Yellow Ravager, as in war, it is a fight to the death. Many will die, the weak and the old first. That cannot be helped. But the measures I have suggested will be the saving of many."

The servant returned shortly, bearing a leather bag which he gave to Avallach. "Now then," said the Fisher King, untying the thongs. He emptied the contents of the bag onto the table before us. Coins spilled out . . . nothing else.

"I had hoped to find something to tell us whence this trader came," Avallach said ruefully.

Gazing at the small pile of coins, I saw the glint of silver in the sunlight. Shoving aside the lesser coins, I picked up a silver denarius. Londinium! But of course, that open cesspit could spawn a thousand plagues!

"Grandfather," I said, holding up the coin, "the bag has spoken most eloquently. See here! The man has lately been in Londinium."

"How do you know this?" asked Elfodd, greatly amazed.

"Aside from Eboracum, that is the only place he can offer his goods in trade for silver like this."

"Truly," added Paulinus, "if he had fallen ill in Eboracum, I think he would have died before ever crossing the Ouse."

"And," put in Charis, "Londinium is a port."

Elfodd nodded, accepting the evidence laid before him. "So, our friend has lately been trading in Londinium and was returning home when he fell ill. How does this help us?"

Paulinus replied, "The city can be warned and sealed off, thereby greatly containing the disease. For it is known that even those who merely pass through a plague city may become ill."

"Very well," Elfodd concluded. "Now, to the matter of the curatives—"

"Speak not of curatives," Paulinus cautioned, "where none exists."

"Even so," I replied, "you mentioned elixirs that might offer some relief. How are these to be prepared?"

Paulinus, somber in light of the daunting prospect before us, replied, "With the ingredients in hand, preparing the potions is simplicity itself." He laid a finger to his lower lip. "I think . . . yes, the best I know makes use of a water-loving herb as its chief element. I believe the land here abounds with the very plant required—and the other herbs are easily gathered."

"We will need a very great quantity," Charis pointed out.

"The brothers will provide all that is needed," Abbot Elfodd promised. "We have among us men well skilled in such matters already, and they can teach others. Reaching every settlement and holding will be much more difficult."

"Leave that to me," I said. A plan had begun forming in my

mind. "Now, Paulinus, you must tell us everything you know about the making of this remedy and its use. Everything," I stressed, "to the smallest particular, mind, since your directions will be carried to every holding and city in the land."

Paulinus the reluctant scholar proved an able teacher, as he began describing the process by which the elixir was made and how it should be used for best effect. As he spoke, I found myself admiring the clarity of his disciplined mind. His years of learning were not in the least wasted on him, as he feared. What is more, I could well appreciate his elation at finally hearing the call he had waited so long to answer.

"Of course, it is infinitely better to prevent the illness," the learned monk concluded. "The small benefit offered by the remedy is useless if the potion is not given at the onset of the fever. With the potion there is small enough possibility of improvement. Without it," he warned, "nothing can avail, save prayer alone."

"I understand," I replied. Turning to Avallach, who had maintained a grim, watchful silence during our discussion, I said, "You will be in danger here. I would have you come to Caer Melyn with me, for the abbey will soon become a haven as well as a hospice."

"Son," replied Avallach kindly, "it is that already. This disease but increases the work. And, as the toil is multiplied, so too the glory. What God sends we will endure, depending not on our own strength but upon the One who upholds us all. And," he said, lifting his hand, palm upward, in the manner of a supplicant, "if prayer can avail, I will devote myself to it with a whole and willing heart."

I was clearly not persuading him otherwise, so I did not press the matter further. "May your prayers prove more potent than any elixir," I told him.

When our talk concluded a short while later, we left Avallach to his rest. Paulinus, Elfodd, Charis and I walked down to the lake, where the monk showed us the plant which gave the potion its healing power. Putting off his tunic and sandals, and rolling up his trouser legs, he waded into the water—bent-backed, hands on knees, dark eyes searching the cool, green shallows.

In a moment, he stopped and reached into the water and brought up a plant with long green leaves, clusters of small pale pink flowers on a fleshy stem. I knew the plant as that which the lake-dwellers called *ffar gros*. "This," he said, pointing to the thick brown root, "when crushed with the leaves and stalks of the *garlec* and the *brillan mawr* in equal measure—and the whole prepared as I have told you—provides such benefit as we can supply." Then, as if proving the taste of the imagined remedy, he added, "I think a little liquor of the *rhafnwydden* will make it more palatable."

Returning to the bank, he quickly secured the other plants he had mentioned. For indeed they grow readily in woods and along most watercourses throughout Ynys Prydein. Satisfied with his ingredients, Paulinus led us on to the abbey, where, after obtaining the necessary utensils, he set about preparing the potion, showing us how to strip the stems and roots of the plants before crushing and boiling them together with a small amount of salt water in a pot. The water turned yellow and smelled of rotten eggs.

When he judged it prepared, Paulinus dipped out some of the cloudy liquor with a ladle and blew on it gently. "There are several ways to determine if it is well made," he said, "but this is the best." With that he put the ladle to his lips and drank it down. "Yes. It is ready."

Offering the ladle to each of us in turn, he gave us to drink of the draught. "Taste," he urged. "There is no harm in it."

"Pungent," Charis concluded, wrinkling her nose slightly, "and bitter—though not disagreeable." She passed the ladle to me, and I sipped some down; the liquid tingled slightly on the tongue.

"If given when the fever first commences," Paulinus instructed, "the best result is secured, as I say."

I commended the monk's sagacity, and said, "This plague will be a match for any man's best. Your king could use you in the fight. Will you come with me?"

Paulinus was not slow to reply. "I will come with you, Lord Emrys." He turned in deference to his superior. "If, that is, Abbot Elfodd will permit my absence."

"Paulinus," Elfodd said in a fatherly tone, "you have received a summons from the High King. You must go. And, as we somehow endured here before you came, I daresay we shall make out when you have gone. Yes, go. I give you my blessing. Return when your service is completed."

Paulinus inclined his head. "I am your man, Lord Emrys."

"Good."

"We will prepare as much of the potion as we can before you go," Charis offered. "We will send you away with a goodly supply."

Elfodd approved her offer. "The brothers stand ready to serve. Many hands will speed the work."

"I thank you both. I knew it could not be wrong to come here." To Paulinus I said, "Hurry, now. We will leave as soon as you are ready."

Charis and I left Elfodd and Paulinus to their work and returned to the palace. She made no sound as we walked along, so I asked, "Are you frightened?"

"Of the plague?" she asked with slight surprise. "Not in the least. In my years on the Glass Isle, I have seen all that illness and disease can do, Hawk. Death no longer holds any terror for me. Why do you ask?"

"You have said nothing since leaving the abbey."

She smiled wistfully. "It is not from fear of plague, I assure you. If I am reticent it is because you will be leaving soon, and I do not know when I shall see you again."

"Come with me."

"Oh, Merlin, I dare not. Would that I could, but—"

"Why not?"

"I will be needed here."

"Indeed, your skill will be welcomed wherever you go," I told her. "Arthur would find a place worthy of your skill and renown." I paused. "I know he would like nothing more than to see you again—Gwenhwyvar, too."

"And I would like nothing more, I assure you," she replied. "But my place is here. I have lived so long upon my tor, I could not abandon it now—especially in these troubled days."

"I wish more had your courage."

"Bless you, my Hawk. Perhaps when this present difficulty is over, I will come to Caer Melyn and stay a while with you. Yes," she said, making up her mind. "I will do that."

While waiting for Paulinus to join me, I rode to Shrine Hill. It was in my mind to spend a moment at the small wattle-and-mud chapel in prayer before returning to the fray. The shrine, on its hump of a hill beside the tor, is kept clean and in good repair by the monks from the abbey. They venerate the place, since it was here the Good News first came to Britain with Joseph, the wealthy tin merchant from Arimathea. The shrine is a simple structure, lime-washed with a reed-thatched roof over a single room containing a small stone altar.

I dismounted outside and entered the cool, dark room to kneel on the bare earth floor before the altar. The feeling of the Savior God's presence in that crude sanctuary remained as potent as ever—it is an ancient and holy place. Here Arthur was given his vision and call, the night before he received the Sword of Sovereignty from the Lady of the Lake. Here, too, I saw the Grail, that most mysterious and elusive token of God's blessing and power.

Kneeling in that humble place, I said my prayers, and when I rose once more to continue on my way, it was with strength of heart and soul renewed.

Paulinus and I left Ynys Avallach a short while later; Arthur was waiting and I was anxious to set my plan in motion. It was this: all travel to and from Londinium must cease—every road and riverway sealed off; every settlement and holding must be warned and provided with the elixir. As to that, I would have Paulinus teach ten of the Cymbrogi how to make the potion; these ten, armed with this knowledge, would then range far and wide throughout Ynys Prydein taking word of the plague and instructing others how to combat it. Each monastery and abbey would, like the Glass Isle, become a refuge; the monks and clerics would make the healing potion and dispense it to surrounding settlements and holdings, instructing the people in the ways of combating the disease.

It was, I reflected, a poor strategy with which to fight so powerful an enemy as the Yellow Ravager. Still, it was the only weapon we had and we must use it however we could, seizing any advantage and every opportunity to strike—and strike swiftly.

Accordingly, Paulinus and I raced back along the Briw, retracing the trail to the landing-place where Barinthus and the boat waited. It was late the next day, and the sun was almost down, when I hailed the pilot. While he and Paulinus boarded the horses, I stood watching the gloom deepen across the vale of Mor Hafren, spreading like an oily stain over the water.

It was death I saw, the dissolution of the Summer Kingdom, that fairest flower extinguished in the first flush of its bloom before my eyes. My heart grew heavy within me, and cold.

Great Light, what more can one man do?

The sun had set by the time we reached the far shore, yet the night sky was light, so we hastened on our way, stopping once only to rest and water the horses. We rode through the next day and most of the next night—keeping close watch for the Vandali, but encountering none—and reached the British encampment before dawn. At our arrival, one of the night guards roused Arthur, who abandoned his bed to greet us.

I protested the intrusion, but he waved it aside. "I would have wakened soon in any event," he said. "Now we have a moment's quiet to speak to one another."

He bade me join him at his tent, where a small fire burned outside. "Gwenhwyvar is still asleep," he explained as we sat down at the fire.

"I thought I saw more ships on Mor Hafren," I remarked as we sat down by the fire.

"Lot is here, as you know," Arthur answered. "Idris and Cunomor have come at last, and Cadwallo arrived the day after you left. They are with Gwalchavad and Cador, who are leading a raid to the south. If all goes well they should return at dawn."

Rhys appeared bearing a bowl and some cold meat and stale bread. He offered the bowl first to Arthur, who pushed it towards me. "I will have something later," he said, "but you have ridden hard. Eat, and tell me how you have fared in the Glass Isle."

"It was God's own hand that led me there, Arthur," I told him, breaking the bread. "I was right about the plague."

"I know," replied Arthur, "Llenlleawg told me about Caer Uisc. I was wrong to oppose you."

I waved aside his apology. "I have brought word of a healing potion—among other things."

"I thought they said there was a monk with you."

To Rhys I said, "Fetch Paulinus; Arthur will receive him now."

Yawning—all but swaying on his feet with exhaustion—the monk was led forth. Arthur cast a dubious eye over him. "I give you good greeting, brother," he said amiably.

Paulinus inclined his head uncertainly. "And I you," he responded, but, oblivious to the honor paid him, made no further salutation.

"Paulinus!" I said sharply. "Shake off your lethargy, man. Should the High King of Britain not command your attention?"

Paulinus' eyes grew wide as he snapped himself erect. "Lord Arthur! Forgive me, my king; I did not know it was you. I thought—" He gestured vaguely towards the tent as if expecting a different king to appear still. "I thought that you would be a much older man."

Arthur enjoyed this. "Who then did you think me?"

"I took you for a steward," Paulinus blurted, much chagrined. "The Pendragon of Britain," he began. "Forgive me, lord. Jesu have mercy, I meant no disrespect."

"I forgive you readily," Arthur said. "I see you stand in need of sleep. I will not keep you from it. Come to me when you are better rested and we will talk." To Rhys he said, "Find this monk some place to lay his head where he will not be wakened by everyone who passes. And give him something to eat if he is hungry."

"Thank you, lord," said Paulinus. Then, grateful to be relieved of further embarrassment, he gave an awkward bow and scurried after Rhys.

The High King watched him go, shaking his head slightly. "I trust you know what you are doing."

"He will serve," I assured him. "He lacks experience of kings: he has spent more time in the company of plants and healing herbs than that of noblemen and princes."

"Then he is what we need now," Arthur said, and added in a sour tone, "not another grasping lord who thinks he knows better than his king how to wage war on the invader."

"It is going badly, then?"

Arthur picked up a stick, snapped it, and threw the pieces into the fire, deliberately, one after the other. "Some would say so."

"How does the matter stand?"

He frowned into the fire. Behind him the sky lightened to a clear dawn. "The Black Boar and his piglets have fled into the hills," he said, and I heard frustration in his tone, "and it is the devil's own work to get at them. With every raid we merely push them deeper into the glens." He threw another stick at the flames. "I tell you the truth, Myrddin, they are more stubborn than badgers to root out."

He paused and brightened somewhat. "Now that Lot, Idris, and the others have come we may begin to make better account of ourselves. Jesu knows we are doing all we can."

Gwenhwyvar, wakened by our talk, emerged quietly from the tent. She was dressed in a thin white mantle, her hair wound in a strip of soft white cloth. She settled easily beside Arthur, who put his arm around her shoulders and drew her to him. "Greetings, Myrddin," she said. "Have you a good word for us?"

"No, the word is not good. Plague is indeed upon us, and there is no remedy."

"Then we must prepare as best we can."

"Yet my journey was not without some small consolation," I added quickly. "For I have brought a monk who understands much about the disease; he is going to help us. I also learned this: the pestilence likely issues from Londinium—the harbors there serve many foreign vessels. Paulinus tells me that plague often follows the trading fleet."

Gwenhwyvar caught the full implication of my words at once. "Londinium," she gasped. "But Cador is on his way there now."

"He will be stopped," Arthur said. "It may be that he has not reached the city yet."

"Londinium must be sealed off," I said. "All roads must be guarded, and the rivers. No one must enter or leave until the disease has run its course."

"That means we cannot count on fresh supplies from Londinium's markets," Gwenhwyvar said. "Blessed Jesu. . . . " She leaned instinctively against her husband for comfort. "What are we to do, Artos?"

"We will fight this enemy like any other."

"But it is *not* like any other enemy," she snapped. "It spreads on the wind. It slays all without regard, and neither sword nor shield is proof against it."

"All that can be done, we will do."

"I must go to my father," she said, already thinking ahead. "They must be told."

"No," he told her bluntly. "You will not go."

"But I must warn my people. It may be that—"

"They will be warned," he replied firmly. "But I need you here." His tone removed all dissent.

"First, we must tell the noblemen," I suggested. "They will want to send word to their people. The disease cannot have spread far yet."

Arthur stood. "Rhys!" A heartbeat later, the High King's steward stood beside him. "Summon the lords to attend me at once." As Rhys dashed away, the king said, "What will come of this, God alone knows."

The lords answered Rhys' call and assembled around Arthur's fire, a ring of faces—some concerned, others merely curious. Arthur did not bid them sit down, but stood before them grave and solemn; he wasted no words. "Plague has come to Britain," he said simply. "You must send riders to warn your people."

The noblemen gazed at Arthur in astonishment, and looked to one another for explanation. "Is this so?" they wondered in shocked voices. "How can it be?"

"Trust that it is so," the king told them. "The plague follows the trading fleet; foreign merchants have brought this pestilence to our land."

"Tell us," called one of the kings, "what is the nature of this pestilence? How is it to be fought?"

Arthur indicated that I should tell them what I knew of it. "This plague is known from elder times as the Scourge of the East," I began. "It is the Yellow Death, a sickness which spreads with the swiftness and voracity of fire. By these signs it may be known: the flesh fluctuates between intense fever and numbing chill; the limbs tremble and shake; noxious fluids bloat the body, but there is no purging of the bladder. In the final extremity, the skin turns yellow and the victim vomits blood. Death brings release in the space of two days—three at most."

"Yet, we are not without some hope," Arthur continued. "We have with us a monk who knows how best to battle this Yellow Ravager. Now you will all summon such messengers as you deem best to ride to your clans and tribes and warn them of the danger."

"Messengers!" cried Ogryvan. "I will go myself. My people will hear of this plague from no mere messenger. I will not abandon my realm in its crisis."

Others made similar objection, but Arthur stood firm. "I need you here," he replied. "The battle is joined. You cannot leave."

"Cannot leave!" roared Brastias. "Cannot! I give my aid

freely, or not at all. I alone determine when I shall come and go."

"I am your king," Arthur reminded him, his voice hard-edged as Caledvwlch. "As you have pledged me fealty, I hold authority over you. It is my right to command, and I order you to stay."

"I, too, am a king," Brastias replied loftily. "The fealty I pledged is but token of the kingship I hold. If I may not rule even so much as my own movements, whether I stay or go, then I hold no more authority than the lowest servant in my house."

Arthur fixed him with a look of withering disdain. He checked his anger before answering. "You know best what manner of king you are," he replied, his voice low. "And I will not make bold to dispute your claim. But you do those you deem beneath you an injustice when you compare their rank to yours."

Brastias swelled with rage. Arthur allowed him no time to reply. "Time is precious to those we must warn, and we waste it chattering about rights and rule. Summon your riders and send them to Myrddin. He will instruct them."

Turmoil erupted at this command. The night's lingering calm was shattered by shouts of alarm as the fearful tidings spread from camp to camp. Arthur gathered the Dragon Flight and chose three from among the volunteers to ride north, bearing the warning to the lords who were on the way to join us—Ector especially—and any other settlements they passed. He also selected a force—two hundred men, who would be sorely missed from the ranks—to lay siege to Londinium. These he dispatched with all haste in the hope that they might stop Cador on his way to the markets.

As this guardian force departed, those closest to Arthur sat in council with him: Gwenhwyvar, Bedwyr, Cai, Llenlleawg, and myself. "Can anything be done?" asked Cai, speaking aloud the question foremost in everyone's mind.

"Pray," Arthur replied solemnly. "Pray God to remove this

pestilence from our land. Or, if that is not to be, to show us the way through it. Truly, I fear in my bones that unless the Lord God upholds us, this travail will prove the doom of Britain."

BOOK FOUR

THE HEALING
DREAM

1

DRY . . . DRY . . . DRY. AND HOT. The earth cracks. The rivers wane. No cloud touches the burning sky, and the land parches beneath an unrelenting sun. Sacred springs dry up, and holy wells echo to the sound of empty vessels. There is no breath of wind or breeze to cool the land. Animals thirst; their strength fails and they fall and, falling, die.

All the while, the pestilence snakes along the lowland tracks like an unseen fog. One after another, the caers, settlements, and holdings are visited by the Yellow Ravager. Strengthened by the drought, which drives men from their homes in search of water, the pestilence steals over the land. Children cry and women mutter in fear-fretted sleep; men complain bitterly that this is Arthur's fault.

The small kings blame him and plot treason in their hearts. "It would not be so if I held this land," they boast. "I would put an end to this invader and drive all sickness from our shores."

This they say as if the Vandal were no more than a drunken shepherd and the plague his mange-bitten dog. It steals the breath from my mouth to see how swiftly men abandon the one they pledged to serve through all things to the death. But when faith fails, men abandon all that sustains them. They flee the source of their uncertainty, rushing blind into betrayal and unbelief.

Behold! The Narrow Sea is plowed with a thousand furrows

as British boats sail for Armorica. With coward hearts once-brave men put oar to water, lest the land of their birth become also the land of their death.

Well and well, their fear can be forgiven. They merely do what their faltering courage allows. Far worse—and forever unforgiven—are those who strive to use the suffering and torment of others to advance their own bloated ambitions.

There are four openly against Arthur now: Gerontius, Brastias, Ulfias, and Urien. The first two I understand. Indeed, I know them only too well! Ulfias is weak and anxious to please his bellicose neighbor; he has decided that peace with Brastias is worth more than fealty to Arthur. In that, he is much mistaken.

If only they had left the camp—but no, they stamped around poisoning the very air with their complaints, stirring up resentment at every chance, swaying the less steady with their insidious slanders. Weaker brothers listened to them and were led astray—men like Urien.

I can only wonder at Urien. His fiery enthusiasm has burned itself out; his ardor, so bright and warm in the beginning, has grown cold. This is the way of it sometimes, God knows: the hotter the fire the more quickly it dies. Still, I had hoped for better from Urien Rheged. Young and raw, and painfully eager to please, it is true, he yet seemed a solid enough nobleman. Given maturity and experience, he might have grown into an able and honorable lord. He would have found in Arthur a steady and generous friend.

What, I wonder, turned him against Arthur? What failing did he perceive, or, more likely, imagine? What glittering inducement did Brastias offer, what irresistible promise, to turn Urien's fire-bright loyalty to sodden ash?

Sadly, even the most sacred vows are oft forgotten before the words die in the air. Ah, let it go, meddler! There is no binding a heart that will not be bound, less yet one that honors nothing higher than itself. So be it!

This, then, is how Lugnasadh found us: plague ravaging the people and the Black Boar ruining all the land.

Like the hounds of the Wild Hunt we pursued the invader north and east, driving deeper into the many-shadowed glens. Somehow the Vandali always remained just beyond reach. They refused to fight, preferring to flee, most often traveling by night. Moving along the ridges and river valleys, they were following Albion's ancient trackways into the rich heartland.

Arthur sent swift messengers ahead along these routes to warn the settlements of the invader's approach. Even this simple task was made difficult by the fact that the wily Amilcar had divided his forces, and then divided them again. There were now no fewer than seven enemy warbands loose in the land, each under the command of a Vandali chieftain intent on driving as far inland as possible, plundering every step of the way.

Twrch Trwyth seemed well pleased to allow his piglets to scatter while he escaped north and east with the main body of the Vandal host. There must have been a purpose to this mad design, but I could not discern it.

Still, we pursued relentlessly, catching them when we could, fighting when battle was offered—but mostly arriving a day behind their latest flight. Futility dogged us and the constant sun burned us black. Provisions ran low—a persistent problem, nagging as the ache in our empty bellies—for with Londinium quarantined, we were forced to buy grain and cattle from smaller markets as far away as Eboracum, and just getting enough was as tedious as it was time-consuming. Meanwhile, the small kings took to squabbling among themselves and disputing Arthur's command.

This alone would have been the undoing of many a lesser man. But Arthur had the plague to fight as well. And that proved no less stubborn than the Black Boar.

I see Paulinus, grown haggard and gaunt in his battle against the scourge. How not? He rests little and rarely sleeps. He toils like a slave demented, teaching, organizing, making and dispensing his medicine. The shy monk has become a valiant warrior, as relentless in his own way as any of Arthur's chieftains, engaged in a fight no less fierce than any fought with Amilcar.

At first word of a settlement or holding where the plague had taken hold, that was where Paulinus wanted to be. Taking no thought for himself, he gave all to the battle, winning renown in the war against the Yellow Destroyer. Others saw his example and were inspired to follow him. So, together with a handful of brothers from Llandaff who willingly joined him in the work, he shouldered the task of fighting the plague.

But the disease, like the invader, ran far, far ahead without slackening pace. There seemed to be no way to contain or subdue either of them. Thus, when his lords began deserting him, Arthur took it hard.

"Be at ease, Bear," Bedwyr said, trying to calm the king. "We do not need the likes of Brastias raising hackles at every turn."

We were gathered in the large council tent, but Arthur, angry with the wayward kings, had not summoned them. He sat with his elbows on the board, frowning, while those nearest the High King tried to lighten his gloom.

"Better to see the back of them, I say," Cai added.

"He is right, Bear," Cador put in. "They took but three hundred riders with them all told."

"Blessed Jesu, it is not the loss of a few horses I mind!" roared Arthur. "Three have defied me to my face. How long do you think it will be before the rot sets in with the rest?"

Gwenhwyvar, bright seraph in a cool white mantle, leaned close. "Allow me to go to my people," she soothed. "The Erean kings are willing. Indeed, they are eager to repay the debt they owe Britain. You need only ask."

"It would do no harm to replace the riders and warriors we have lost," Bedwyr argued. "It may be that the arrival of the Irish lords will shame the weak-willed and encourage the loyal."

"That would be no bad thing," Gwalchavad offered, adding: "I welcome any man who stands beside me in this fight."

Gwenhwyvar took Arthur's right hand in both of hers. "Why do you yet hesitate, my husband? There is neither shame nor harm in this." She clasped his hand and pressed it earnestly as she would press her argument. "The sooner away, the sooner returned. You will hardly know that I have gone."

Arthur considered this. He hovered on the threshold of yielding. "What say you, Myrddin?"

"Your wise counselors have given you good advice," I replied. "Why ask me?"

"But I *am* asking you," Arthur growled.

"Very well," I said. But before I could deliver my answer, the hunting horn sounded outside—a short blast, followed by two more.

"Someone has come," Cai said, jumping to his feet. He paused. "Do you want me to bring them to you, Bear?"

"See who it is first," Arthur said sourly.

Rhys' signal indicated a newcomer to the camp. Cai left and we prepared to receive our guests.

In a moment, Cai's voice called: "Arthur, you should come out. You will want to see these visitors."

Arthur sighed, pushed back his chair—Uther's great camp chair—and rose slowly. "What now?" Throwing aside the tent flap, he stepped out and I followed. Cai was standing a short distance from the tent, gazing down the hill towards the stream.

Mounting the slight rise towards us was a crowd of clerics: three bishops—no less—with thirty or more monks. The bishops wore rich priestly garb: long dark robes and glittering gold ornaments; they wore soft leather boots on their feet, and carried gold-headed oak staves in their hands. Those with them, however, were arrayed more humbly in undyed wool.

"Heaven preserve us," Gwalchavad muttered aloud. "What are *they* doing here?"

"Peace, brother," Bedwyr advised. "It may be they have come to lend their aid against the plague. Any help in that struggle would be most welcome."

"They do not look like men who have come to offer aid,"

Gwenhwyvar observed. "Far from it, I am thinking."

Her womanly perception was keen as her eyesight, for the knit brows and firm mouths of those who approached suggested solemn purpose and inflexible resolution. The leading bishop thumped the ground with his crozier as if he were pummeling snakes, and those around him walked stiff-legged, with shoulders tight and chins outthrust. Another time, it might have been cause for laughter. But not this day; the Bear of Britain was in no merry mood.

Rhys moved to take his place with Arthur as the churchmen came to stand before us. I recognized none of them, nor any of their followers. Their arrival had, of course, drawn the attention of the men in camp, curious to see what these important visitors would say. Soon a hundred or more had gathered, which seemed to please the bishops. Rather than come face-to-face with the High King, they halted a dozen paces away—as if to force Arthur to come to them. I took this as a very bad sign.

"Hail, brothers in Christ! Hail and welcome," Arthur called to them. "In the name of our Great Lord Jesu, I give you good greeting."

"Hail to you," the foremost bishop replied. He did not deign to recognize the High King's rank—neither did he, nor any of the others, offer his king the customary kiss, much less the simple cordiality of a kindly blessing.

A better man than I, Arthur ignored the churchman's unwarranted insolence. "You honor our rude war camp with your presence, my friends. Again, I give you good greeting in the name of our Lord and king," he said amiably—heaping, as it were, flaming coals upon their heads.

Gwenhwyvar, not to be outdone, spoke up. "We might have prepared a better welcome had we known you were coming," she said sweetly. "Still, we are not without common courtesy." I smiled at this gentle rebuke of the bishops' bad manners. She turned to Rhys. "Bring the welcome cup," she commanded.

"Nay, lady," the bishop said, holding up an imperious hand.

He was a rotund man, solid as an ale vat in his long robes, his chief adornment a huge golden cross which hung around his neck on a heavy chain of gold. "We will not share the common cup with you until we have spoken out what we have come to say."

"Speak, then," Bedwyr said, fairly bristling with menace at the churchmen's effrontery. "God knows, you have succeeded in pricking our curiosity with your audacity."

"If you think us too bold," the bishop replied haughtily, "then truly you are more timid men than we presumed."

"It seems to me," replied Cador, perfectly matching the cleric's icy tone, "that you presume too much." Then, before the irate bishop could respond, he changed tack. "Ah, but forgive me," he continued smoothly, "perhaps you do not know who it is that addresses you with such good grace." The young king raised his hand to Arthur and said, "I give you Arthur ap Aurelius, King of Prydein, Celyddon, and Lloegres, Chief Dragon of the Island of the Mighty, and High King of all Britain."

The pompous cleric almost burst at that. He glared at Cador and muttered, "We *know* who it is we have come to see."

Again Cador was ready with a choice reply. "Then I must beg your pardon once more," he said lightly, "for it did seem to me you were in some doubt regarding the rank of the man you addressed. I only thought to ease the burden of your ignorance—if ignorance it was—for I did not imagine such a grave insult could be intentional."

Realizing he was bettered, the gruff bishop inclined his head slowly. "I thank you for your thoughtfulness," he replied. Turning to Arthur, he said, "If I have offended the mighty Pendragon, it is for me to beg his pardon."

Arthur was losing patience. "Who are you and why have you come?" he demanded bluntly.

"I am Seirol, Bishop of Lindum," he announced grandly, "and these are my brothers: Daroc, Bishop of Danum, and Abbot Petronius of Eboracum." He raised his monkish staff to his fellow bishops, each in turn lifting a pale hand in the sign of peace. "We come with representatives of our churches, as you see." By this he meant the company of monks with them. "We come by authority of Bishop Urbanus of Londinium, who sends this with his sign." He produced a parchment roll bearing the bishop's sign and signature.

"You have wandered far from home, brothers," Arthur remarked. "Lindum is many days to the north—likewise Eboracum; and Londinium is no small distance away. The matter must be of some import, that you travel so far in such troubled times."

"Well you know it, lord," Seirol affirmed imperiously. "We have braved many hardships—and this so that you would not have cause to doubt our resolve."

"You seem most resolute to me," Arthur answered.

Bedwyr, who sensed approaching danger, warned under his breath, "Tread lightly, Bear."

Bishop Seirol's nostrils flared with anger. "I had heard of the rough ways of our great king." He said disdainfully. "I fully expected my share of abuse."

"If you think us too rough," Cai remarked, "then truly you are more delicate men than I presumed." Many of the onlookers laughed outright, and the churchmen shifted uneasily.

The bishop stared sullenly around. Raising his crozier slowly, he gave a sharp rap on the earth. "Silence!" he cried. "You ask why we have come here. I will tell you. We have come to perform our most righteous and holy duty in demanding that you, Arthur ap Aurelius, foreswear your kingship and yield the Sovereignty of Britain to another."

"What!" The incredulous voice was Bedwyr's, but the thought was in every head. "Arthur forsake the throne?"

"That is indeed a matter of some consequence," Arthur remarked drily. "Unless you are more fool than you seem, you must have sound reason for this grave suggestion. I would hear it now, churchman."

Bishop Seirol frowned, but failing to discern whether Arthur's reply slighted him or not, he drew himself up and launched into the explanation he had prepared. Flourishing his crozier, he proclaimed, "Since we have braved many dangers, do not think we will be easily discouraged. The land is in turmoil, and the people are hard pressed. All day long we are sore beset. Plague and war have proved the doom of many, and the land calls out for justice."

"We are not unmindful of these travails," Cador assured him. "If you do but look around, you will observe that even now you stand in a war camp at the forefront of the battle. Or did you think this was Londinium or Caer Uintan, and we were all hiding safe behind high walls?"

Bishop Daroc's anger flared. "Your impertinence is unbecoming, Lord Cador. Oh, yes, we know you, too. You would do well to heed our indictments, who hold sway over the eternal security of your soul."

"I had thought," Cador responded cooly, "that God alone held dominion over my soul. And since I have placed my trust in him, say and do what you will—I fear no mortal man."

Bishop Seirol pressed on with his attack. "Hear me, proud king! Do you deny that the enemy overruns the land with impunity? Do you deny that the land is wasted by pestilence?"

"How," replied Arthur slowly, "could I deny what is perceived by even the dullest eye? You must know that I have sent messengers far and wide throughout the land with the warning."

An expression of triumph transformed the bishop's face. He raised outspread arms and turned this way and that, exulting in his imagined victory. "Hear me, warriors of Britain!" Seirol cried in a thunderous voice. "These twin travails of plague and war have come upon us by the immorality of one man!" He flung a hand at Arthur and shouted, "Arthur ap Aurelius, *you* stand condemned of God. Truly, the evil ravaging the land flows from your iniquity alone, and from the wickedness of your reign."

The accusation hung in the air for a long, awful moment. Then Cai's voice cracked the stunned silence. "Iniquity and wickedness?" he hooted in sharp derision. "Bear, we have heard enough from this puffed-up toad. Allow me to run them out of camp with the flat of my sword."

"By what right do you come here like this to defame the King of Britain?" demanded Gwenhwyvar tartly.

"I am the Bishop of Lindum!" Seirol cried. "I speak for the holy Church of Christ on Earth. Since there is but one Savior, we are united in one body. Thus, when I speak, I speak for God."

"I am Caius ap Ectorius of Caer Edyn," Cai spat, stepping towards the churchman, his hand on the hilt of his sword. "I say you are an addled windbag, and I speak for every man here."

The absurdity of Seirol's charge defied us to take it seriously. But the bishops were in dead and utter earnest. They had worked themselves up to this preposterous indictment and meant to have their full say.

Bishop Petronius, his features convulsed in a murderous scowl, pushed forward. "Kill us if you will," he hissed. "We expected no less from you. All the world shall know that we were martyred in pursuit of our duty by vicious and spiteful cutthroats."

"Persist in speaking to your king thus," Bedwyr warned, his voice low with menace, "and we will not disappoint you, priest."

"Bloodshed and murder is all you know!" charged Bishop Daroc. "Death will not stop our voices. The truth will not be silenced! Our blood will cry calumny from the very ground!"

"Shall we put it to the test?" Gwalchavad inquired.

Arthur raised his hand. "Peace, brothers," he said, his tone even. He looked to Seirol. "You have made grievous complaint against me, friend. Now I would hear your proof."

The bishops exchanged glances and an expression akin to worry flitted across Seirol's flushed face. They had thought the charge self-evident and had not anticipated a direct challenge. So do the arrogant and self-righteous ever remain swift to observe the mote in others' eyes, while oblivious to the log in their own. They trembled now, for the first time beginning to doubt themselves.

"Well, I am waiting," pressed Arthur. "Where is your proof?"

"Beware, vituperous priests," I warned, stepping forward. "You stand in the presence of one whose honor is above reproach, but instead of praising him as you ought, you impugn him with foul slander. Woe to you, and shame! Were you men of honor you would fall on your faces and plead forgiveness for your sins. Were you true servants of Christ you would drop to your knees and beg pardon!" I shouted, and the air shivered. "Pray mercy from the king of kings on earth who rightfully holds the rule of this land from the High King of Heaven. Kneel before him, for I tell you the truth: you stand to forfeit your worthless lives."

No one had spoken to them like this before, and the perfidious monks gaped in horror and disbelief. Yet they were so consumed with condemnation and their own self-importance that they could not accept the truth as I spoke it.

Bishop Seirol, infuriated by my outburst, lunged forward angrily, recklessly. "You ask for proof!" he cried. "You ask for proof! I tell you the proof of my accusation stands beside you, O King."

With that, the bishop lofted his cleric's staff and gazed around. With a flourish of exaggerated pomp, he leveled the crozier and pointed. I felt my blood surge within me as I prepared to meet his allegation; I would meet and answer the slandering monk, stroke for stroke. But it was not me he pointed to.

No, that unjust honor fell to Gwenhwyvar.

"Behold!" the bishop crowed. "She stands brazen and unashamed in the sight of all. What need have I of further proof?"

Both Arthur and Gwenhwyvar were taken aback by this extraordinary outcome. The nature of the accusation escaped them. It did not escape me, however; I knew precisely what the foul churchman insinuated.

"For the love of Christ, man," I whispered harshly, "withdraw and say no more."

"I will not withdraw!" Seirol exulted. He now imagined he had won his case, and made bold to pursue his victory further. "This woman is Irish!" he said, his voice ripe with insinuation. "She is foreign and a pagan. Your marriage to her, O King, is against God's law. As sure as you stand beside her, you stand condemned."

Petronius, emboldened by Seirol's example, entered the dispute. "Since the beginning of the world," he charged, "never was there plague in Britain—until you became king and took this pagan Irish woman for your queen."

It was difficult to determine which he thought the worse: that Gwenhwyvar was pagan, or that she was Irish; or, indeed, that she was a woman.

Bishop Daroc thrust himself forward. "It is the judgment of God upon us for this immoral king's crimes. God is not mocked. His laws endure forever, and his punishment is swift."

Arthur, grave and calm, replied in a voice so even and restrained, that hearing it froze the marrow of those who knew him well. "I am no scholar of holy writ, that I freely confess. My life is otherwise spent."

"In bloodshed and strife is your life spent," sneered Petronius—and was swiftly silenced by the arch of Arthur's eyebrow.

"But tell me now," Arthur continued, raising his voice slightly, "is it not sin to bear false witness against a brother?"

"Well you know it," replied Seirol smugly. "Under God's law, those stand condemned who exchange the truth for a lie."

"And does not this selfsame law you invoke invite him who would condemn another to first present himself blameless?"

The bishop all but laughed in Arthur's face. "Do not think to turn that great teaching to your defense," Seirol crowed. "I was shriven at dawn and bear no taint of sin which can be reckoned against me."

"No?" wondered Arthur, his voice the warning rumble of thunder. "Then hear me, impudent monk. You have sinned three times since you came into this camp. And for those sins I call you to account."

"You dare malign a Bishop of Christ?" charged the outraged cleric. "I have not sinned once, much less three times."

"Liar!" roared Arthur, finally roused to the attack. He lifted a balled fist and slowly raised one finger. "You accuse me of iniquity and wickedness, and call down the judgment of God upon me. Yet when I demand proof of these accusations, you offer none. Instead, you carry the assault to the woman God himself has given me."

"Regarding Gwenhwyvar—" he slowly raised a second finger—"you call her pagan who is, like yourself, a Christian born of water—a baptism to which fact I can call to witness Charis of Ynys Avallach and Abbot Elfodd himself. And since, as you happily remind us, there is but one Savior and all who call upon him are united in one body, you do falsely judge her and call her pagan who is in truth your sister in Christ. Thus, you twice condemn one who is innocent."

Only then did the churchman feel the sand wash out from beneath his feet. The color drained from his face. Those with him did not yet perceive the fatal blow, though even as they watched the stroke was falling upon their uncomprehending heads.

Arthur raised another finger. "Lastly, you lie when you say you have no sin, for you have sinned in the sight of these many witnesses since first you began to speak. I have no doubt that you would continue adding sin to sin were I to allow you to go on speaking."

Bishop Daroc drew himself up. "We are not under judgment here."

"Are you not?" demanded Arthur. "He is ever under judgment who bears false witness against his brother. The sun has not yet reached midday and already you have, in your own words, 'exchanged truth for a lie'—and not once only, but three times. For this you stand condemned out of your own mouth."

Alight with righteous wrath, Arthur challenged, "What have you to say, churchman? I am listening, but I do not hear your answer. Can it be that when you have no lie in your mouth you have nothing to say?"

The chagrined bishop, having no reply to offer, glowered at Arthur, but kept his mouth firmly shut.

"Too late you show wisdom," Arthur told him. "Would that you had thought to exercise it sooner. As it is, you have wasted much in a long and dangerous journey to flaunt your foolishness. I am certain you could have accomplished that without setting foot beyond Lindum. Or is there yet a further purpose to your visit? Some other grievance against your king?"

Bishop Daroc could not resist flashing a brief glance in Cador's direction, thereby betraying the true essence of the priests' complaint. His ears flushed red and color rose in his cheeks.

"So!" Understanding broke like sunrise over Arthur's countenance. "Myrddin warned me about holy men and worldly wealth. How well he knows your kind."

"Indeed, lord," remarked Cador. "You should have heard their shrieking when I suggested we had need of the golden trinkets gathering dust in their treasure chests."

Arthur addressed the bishops with thunder in his voice. "You have lied to your king and borne false witness against your queen—for no better reason than because I sought relief and sustenance for my men in the wealth of the church I am sworn to defend. Your selfishness and pride—that only!—brought you here, and all who have witnessed this shameful exchange now see your naked greed and poverty of spirit." He shook his head slowly. "You are no Christian men.

"Hear me, sons of Vipers. For your sins you will be stripped and flogged and driven from this camp. You will be conducted to Llandaff, where the holy Illtyd, true priest of Christ, will decide your punishment. Pray that he has more compassion than I, for I tell you straight I will advise him to turn you out of the church lest you bring the Blessed Jesu himself into disrepute with your pride and ungodly conceit."

So saying, the High King reached out and lifted the gold

cross and chain from around Seirol's neck. "You will no longer need this, I think; and we can use it here to buy food and drink for hungry warriors."

He turned away from the sputtering cleric. "Gwalchavad! Cador! Take them to Llandaff and tell Illtyd all: charge him devise fit punishment."

Cai watched as the odious priests were led away. "You should have let me deal with them, Bear," he said. "God knows, they have already been the downfall of many."

"Their punishment best comes at Illtyd's hand," Arthur replied. "For he is a holy man and they will not be able to console themselves with the secret thought that they were misunderstood or compelled unfairly by a pagan."

He made to turn away, but Gwenhwyvar now stood before him, hands on hips, her shapely brows knit together and dark eyes ablaze. "This matter is not ended yet, O King," she said. "I have been reviled for my birth in the sight of everyone here. Honor demands satisfaction."

Suspecting a subtle trap, Arthur cocked his head to one side. "What do you propose?" he asked warily.

"Just this: that I sail at once for Ireland and summon lords who, by the strength of their devotion, will make faithless Britons everywhere weak with envy and sick with shame to see such homage as my noble race shall offer."

The last clouds of anger lifted then from Arthur's brow. He looked at his wife; sharp appraisal mingled with deep appreciation, and . . . what? Gratitude? Recognition, yes. He saw in her a soul as staunch and zealous as his own, fiercely loyal and steadfast through all things and, like himself, more than a match for a handful of fallacious monks and faltering lords.

The Bear of Britain smiled and relented. "Men of valor are ever welcome at my side," he said, speaking loud for all to hear. "And if the nobles of Ierne prove more loyal servants of Britain than Britain's own sons, so be it. Let those who abandon faith and fealty bear the shame of their disgrace. Wickedness and deceit have no place in my realm, and any man who embraces the truth is friend to me."

Gwenhwyvar kissed him then, and the embrace was lauded by the throaty cheers of all who looked on. The queen sailed on the next tide with ships enough to bring the Irish back; twelve ships and men enough to crew them. At Arthur's behest, Llenlleawg and I went with her.

2

 WE MADE LANDFALL IN THE BAY
below Muirbolc. Commanding Barinthus and his men to hold the ships
ready to sail, we made our way at
once to Fergus' stronghold, which we found utterly abandoned. The houses were vacant and the hall was silent, though
cattle stood in the pen and there were horses in the stable. We
dismounted and stood in the yard, wondering where they had
gone, and when. Gwenhwyvar moved towards the hall.

"Allow me," Llenlleawg told her, darting ahead. He disappeared inside and emerged but a moment later to announce:
"It is not long abandoned! The ash bed in the hearth is warm
yet."

Gwenhwyvar remounted her horse. "We will go to Rath
Mor," she said. "It may be that Conaire knows what has happened here."

We turned our horses and hastened into the wood on the
trail leading to Conaire's stronghold. We had not ridden far,
however, when Llenlleawg halted in the track ahead and held
up his hand. "Listen!"

I paused and attuned myself to the sounds around me. Birds
warbled overhead, and the horses champed and chafed the
ground with their hooves. Beyond that, the light breeze fluttered leaves in the higher branches, and higher still, a hawk
keened its lonely cry. Was this what had halted Llenlleawg?

No. There was something else. I heard it now—as if coming

on a wave of the wind: the wailing shriek I recognized at once as the screech of the Irish pipes.

"It is the *piobairachd* of battle," the Irish champion said. "There must be a fight."

"This way!" cried Gwenhwyvar, pushing past us and away. We continued on the trail for a short distance, then Gwenhwyvar led us off the track beside a small brook, reduced to little more than a bare trickle through the undergrowth.

It was cooler down in the little dingle, and as we splashed along I noticed the sound of the pipes growing gradually louder, until . . . mounting the bank of the brook, we burst from the tree-lined shade and onto a broad wood-surrounded meadow adazzle in the sun.

And there on the meadow were two mounted forces arrayed and positioned for battle. Between these, alone and on foot, facing one another were Conaire and Fergus, brandishing the huge two-handed *cláimor*, the ancient clan sword. Both blades glinted as the combatants whirled them around their heads.

Gwenhwyvar took one look at the flashing swords and lashed her horse. "Yah!" she cried, and galloped across the meadow, yelling, "Stop that! Stop it, I say!"

"Father!" the queen shouted, flying directly to the center of the clash. She slid from the saddle before her mount had stopped. "Are you mad? What are you doing?"

"Stay back, daughter," Fergus answered. He was stripped to the waist and gleaming with sweat and oil. He had been anointed for battle and the sunlight made every muscle glisten and gleam. There were leather bands at his wrists and binding his legs from knee to ankle. In all, he appeared a Celt from another time as he leaned upon his great weapon, breathless from his exertion. "This is a fight to the death."

"This is absurd," Gwenhwyvar contended. "Put up your swords, both of you!" Aside from a neat cut on Conaire's arm there was little evidence thus far of any deadly intent.

"Stand aside, woman," King Conaire told her. "This is between Fergus and me alone."

The pipes screeched on, skirling loudly. "Silence!" Gwenhwyvar screamed at the pipers, who faltered to a squawky stop. She turned back to the two kings, fists on hips, and, in a tone that brooked no foolishness, demanded, "Now tell me, why are you standing out here hacking at one another like Finn mac Cumhaill and Usnach Blue Shield?"

"Do not think to intrude here," Conaire growled. "We mean to settle this before the sun passes midday."

"Do your worst, Conaire Crobh Rua," Fergus said, tightening his grip on the great sword once more.

"Answer me!" commanded Gwenhwyvar, addressing Conaire. "Why are you fighting?"

Fergus spoke first. "He has heaped dishonor on the tribe of Guillomar, and I cannot allow such abuse to go unpunished."

"Come then!" cried Conaire. "We will see who is to be punished here. Stand aside, woman!" He made to raise the sword over his head.

Gwenhwyvar put her hand to the naked blade and held it; she confronted him, her face a hair's breadth from his. "Conaire Red Hand, you tell me what has happened and tell it now."

"I will not!"

"Conaire!"

"I—it was, it—" he stammered, the weapon beginning to waver. "It is all Fergus' doing. Ask him, for my sword speaks for me."

"You hold the fealty of five lords, and are bound by strong oaths to protect them," Gwenhwyvar told him, still holding the blade and keeping his arms aloft. "Therefore, I demand to know why you are attacking one of your own kings."

"I will tell you nothing. Ask Fergus!"

"I am asking you!"

Conaire was red-faced with anger, his arms trembling with the effort of holding the heavy sword above his head. "Woman, you do vex me most sorely!" he growled. "I have told you it is all Fergus' doing."

"Liar!" cried Fergus, pressing close. "Stand aside, daughter. Let me finish him now."

"Father! Keep still." She faced Conaire and demanded, "Will you speak yet, or must we stand here all day?"

I glanced at Llenlleawg and saw that he was smiling, obviously enjoying the dispute. Even so, his spear was in his hand and ready.

The huge sword trembling above his head, Conaire rolled his eyes and gave in to her demand. "You are worse than your father," he snorted in disgust. "Let my hands down and I will tell you."

Gwenhwyvar, satisfied with his reply, released the sword and stepped back a pace. "Well?"

"It is that accursed priest!"

"Ciaran has done nothing to you!" Fergus charged, thrusting forward.

Gwenhwyvar pushed him back, and addressed Conaire. "What about the priest?"

"He stole six of my cattle," the king complained weakly.

"Your cattle wandered away when your cowherd fell asleep," Fergus said. "The priest found them."

"And took them to his own pens!"

"He offered to give them back!"

"Oh, he *offered*! He offered—*if* I would come and get them he would give them back."

"Well?" demanded Gwenhwyvar, growing more exasperated with each passing moment.

"It is only so that he can rail at me with that—that creed of his," Conaire insisted. "He defies me to listen to him and says that he will make a Christian of me yet. But I will have none of it!"

"What are you afraid of, man?" Fergus challenged. "Hear him out and make up your mind. No one can make you believe anything you do not want to believe!"

"And you, Fergus mac Guillomar, are a fool!" Conaire rejoined. "You are beguiled with the babble of that priest. Most malicious of men, he has stolen your wit as well as reason. Christians! Look at you, Fergus, you cannot even fight your own fights anymore. I see what listening to priests has done to you, and I will not go down that path."

Gwenhwyvar spoke up. "I am a Christian, too, Conaire," she said, coolly. "Do you think me weak-willed and witless?"

Conaire raised a warning finger. "Stay out of this, you. This is no concern of yours."

"Is it not?" she asked. "I rather think it concerns all who hold the Christ as lord over them."

"Then draw your weapon and stand behind your father," Conaire told her. "And I will give you stroke for stroke what I give Fergus."

"Go to it then!" cried Fergus. "Do your worst!"

"Oh, stop it—both of you," Gwenhwyvar snapped. "Conaire, we do not have time for this. If it is a fight you want, listen to me now. The Vandal host is laying waste to Ynys Prydein. I have come to raise the warbands of Eiru to aid Arthur."

Fergus was only too happy to be distracted from the tussle at hand. "Did you mean to keep it from us, daughter? Why, my men and I are ready; we will put to sea at once." He turned to his warriors, who stood looking on. "Bid your kin farewell, men. Arthur needs us." Turning back to Gwenhwyvar, he said, "Arthur in need? Say no more. That is good enough for me."

Conaire frowned. "Well, I care little for that. I will not go."

Gwenhwyvar could scarce believe the man's stubbornness. "After all Arthur has done for you?" she challenged. "Is this the thanks of a noble lord? Britain suffers now because Arthur helped you."

"What sort of king leaves his realm unprotected?" Conaire sniffed, putting on a brave display of indifference.

"He did it to save you!" Gwenhwyvar declared.

"More fool he," replied the Irish king smugly. "I did not ask his help, nor did I need it."

"If not for Arthur you would be dead now—you and all your people with you, Conaire Red Hand!"

"And if I were dead I would not have to keep hearing about Arthur!"

Gwenhwyvar, her face flushed with rage, spun from him. "Go, Father, ready your ships and men. Llenlleawg and I ride to rouse the southern lords."

"This lord will not be roused," Conaire insisted. "Nor any beholden to me."

"Go your way, Conaire," Gwenhwyvar told him. "You are of no consequence anymore."

"I will not go—"

"Well and good!"

"—and neither will I allow my lords to sail to Britain," he said. "This is no concern of the Uladh or its kin."

"Arthur needs help and I am pledged to give it," Fergus said. "All I have I owe to him. More, he is my kinsman through the marriage of my daughter. I am going to help him."

"And I say you will not go."

"And I say I will!"

"You will not—"

"Silence!" Gwenhwyvar screamed. She faced the Irish king squarely. "You can choose not to help us," she said, anger seething from every pore. "That is your right. But you cannot prevent Fergus from going if he is so resolved."

"No," allowed Conaire, growing sly, "I cannot prevent him from going. But—" he turned a defiant gaze upon Fergus— "if you leave, your lands are forfeit."

"Snake! Snake!" cried Fergus. "You cannot do that!"

"Stand back and watch what I do!"

"Do not listen to him, Father," Gwenhwyvar said. "Go and ready the men."

"Since you are going," Conaire continued, "I advise you to take your priests and people with you, for I tell you the truth: there will be no home for you if you return."

"Take the land!" Fergus bellowed, drawing himself up with immense dignity. "And I take back my oath of fealty to you. I once pledged myself to a true king, but you are not that man. Go your way, Conaire Crobh Rua. I am done with you."

"What need have I of a faithless lord like you?" Conaire sneered. "I will give your lands to men who honor their oaths and do not go chasing after priests of strange religions."

Fergus drew breath to reply. Gwenhwyvar put her hands on his chest and turned him. "Go now. Say nothing more."

"Indeed," her father replied, "there is nothing more to say."

He turned and hastened back to his waiting warband and the gathered throng of his tribe. In a moment they began moving away.

"I leave also, Conaire," Gwenhwyvar said. "My only regret is that I may not deal with you as you deserve. But hear me now: the day will come when you rue your shameful behavior, and on that day may your stone gods save you."

She turned, leaving him gaping after her. Gwenhwyvar swung into the saddle, wheeled her mount and galloped away.

Conaire turned to me and put out a hand, as if he would explain. "You have had your say, O king," I told him. "May your hasty words be a comfort to you as you sit in your friendless hall." I paused, allowing him to think about this. "But it does not have to end that way. Put conceit behind you; join Arthur and help him now as he helped you."

His handsome face tightened like a fist. "That I will not do."

"So be it." I turned my mount and rode after the others.

When Fergus reached Muirbolc a short time later, he was less happy with his decision. He sat downcast on a stool while around him the clan prepared to leave their home for ever. Gwenhwyvar did her best to console him, but she was anxious to be away once more.

"I am sorry," Fergus sighed. "I lost the land—land our fathers have held since the dew of creation was still fresh on the earth."

"You did well," Gwenhwyvar assured him. "Better an empty bowl with a true friend than a feast with an enemy."

"I lost the land." He sighed, shaking his head sadly. "I gave it to him."

"Arthur has a surfeit of land," she told him. "I am certain he will reward your loyalty most generously." That was all she said, but it remained with me for some time after.

Leaving Fergus to oversee the work, we three continued on. Llenlleawg led as he had recently come this way on an identical task. We rode first to Aedd—perhaps the most ardent supporter of Arthur among the southern Irish, and also the nearest—and, two days later, received a hearty reception.

"Hail and welcome!" Aedd called as we dismounted before his hall. The sun was well down, stretching our shadows long; we were travel-weary, and glad to quit the saddle. "I give you good greeting, my friends." The Irish king spread his arms wide in welcome. "I have been hoping to see you again, but I did not think it would be so soon."

We greeted and embraced him, and Gwenhwyvar said, "It is no happy chance that brings us."

"There is trouble," Aedd said, glancing from one to the other of us. "I see that it is so."

"We have come to—" Gwenhwyvar began.

But Aedd would not allow her to demean herself by asking his aid. "You have come to share the welcome cup with one who would be numbered among your many friends," he said quickly. "Come, take your ease."

Gwenhwyvar, agitated at her inability to make herself understood, tried again. "Would that I could," she said, "but, I fear we must—"

"You must not worry about anything while you are here," Aedd said. He took her hand and drew her away with him towards the hall.

"Perhaps you should explain, Lord Emrys," Llenlleawg suggested, watching his queen disappear into the hall.

"Let us trust Aedd in this," I said. "In any event it is late and we can go no farther this day."

"I could ride to Laigin on my own," the stalwart champion proposed.

"Stay," I advised. "Let us eat and rest and see what tomorrow brings."

Aedd could not do enough for us. He commanded servants to wait upon us while we were with him—a man each for Llenlleawg and myself, and a maiden for Gwenhwyvar. He summoned forth the best of food and drink, and directed his chief bard and harpers to sing soothing music. When we finished eating, he engaged us in amiable conversation, but would not allow any talk of the trouble that had brought us to him. Thus we rose and went to our beds well satisfied with all, save the most important part of our task.

"I *will* speak to that man in the morning," Gwenhwyvar vowed. "I will not be put off again. It is well for him to sit before the hearth spinning his nets of fine words, but I am not a salmon so easily caught. I will speak to him at first light, and he *will* listen."

"Then let it rest until the morning," I remarked. "It is a fine gift he has given us. We have enjoyed a night's peace, and the friendship of a generous lord—far from the battle clash and the carping of small-minded men."

The queen bit her lip uncertainly. "I hope you are right. I keep thinking of Arthur, and how he needs the aid we must bring."

"That is a worry for tomorrow, Bright One."

She smiled at the epithet and did indeed brighten. "Then I will leave it there." She leaned close, raised her lips to my cheek and kissed me. "God be good to you, Myrddin. Sleep well."

Gwenhwyvar's maid appeared with a rushlight to lead the queen to her sleeping-place. I watched them go, thinking how fortunate was Arthur to have a wife with such intelligence and courage. And so thinking, I asked forgiveness of the Great Light. "More fool the man who regards her lightly," I whispered. "There beats the heart of a lioness beneath that breast of beauty. Yes, and an iron-clawed will sheathed in a lithe and supple form."

3

I WAKENED THE NEXT MORNING to an ill-hushed commotion outside my sleeping-hut. I sat up. The sun had risen, but only just; the light was thin, the air still, yet ringing with the sound that had roused me: the jingle of a horse's tack.

In a moment the sound came again, but it was not that of a single horse. Meanwhile, the slap of bare feet gave way to the whisper of excited voices. I threw aside the lambskin covering and rose from the pallet, quickly pulling on my clothes. Seizing my staff, I went outside.

Upon emerging from the hut I saw the first horses arriving and knew at once what Aedd had done. Without word or hint to us, the canny king had dispatched messengers to each of the other southern lords and these had instantly assembled their warbands, riding through the night to arrive at dawn. This he had done to delight his guests.

"God love him," Llenlleawg said when he saw the warriors standing in the yard. "Here breathes a noble Celt indeed."

Like a sovereign of an elder time, Aedd had seen to the needs of his guests with a graceful, self-effacing generosity. It was a virtue still lauded in song, but now rarely encountered. One could be forgiven for believing that it had passed out of this worlds-realm altogether. But here was a man, king in more than name only, holding to the old way. This nobility lifted him up and exalted him in our eyes, and in the esteem of all who would hear of it in the days to come.

The three southern lords had come: Laigin, Diarmait, and Illan; with their massed warbands—numbering in excess of two hundred, and all on horseback. Aedd's stronghold could not contain them all, and most waited beyond the bank and ditch. Gwenhwyvar, likewise roused by the noise, appeared and hurried to where Llenlleawg and I stood watching Aedd as he gave orders to the warriors.

Seeing that we had discovered his surprise, Aedd joined us. "Have you told them of Arthur's need?" Gwenhwyvar asked.

"And demean that great king?" Aedd replied, chiding her gently. "I would never say such a thing."

Gwenhwyvar watched the teeming yard and wondered, "But you must have revealed something of the urgency of our distress to bring them at such speed."

"Lady"—Aedd smiled expansively—"I have simply told them that Arthur is desirous of increasing his joy with the pleasure of their company in his various adventures. I may have mentioned the merest possibility of a battle. They fought among themselves to be the first to respond to the summons."

"My lord and I thank you," the queen said. "I pray your kindness will be rewarded many times over."

Aedd inclined his head, then with a sudden sweep of motion, caught up her hand and kissed it. Gwenhwyvar blushed prettily. "This is my reward," he told her. "I desire nothing more. As for these—" he lifted a hand to the assembled lords and warriors—"the chance to fight alongside Arthur and encourage him with Irish valor is all they ask."

One of the lords, approaching us just then—Illan, I believe—overheard this remark. "Arthur has rightly shown his virtue," he said. "Now we must demonstrate ours, or for ever hold ourselves men of small regard."

Again, I heard the echo of an older sentiment in his words. Llenlleawg had recognized it and named it, and he was right. Here in this Emerald Island, the old ways still lingered on. The Irish, for all their failings, yet held to the ideals of their ancestors and clung to the beliefs of an earlier age—when kings were more than power-hungry hounds ever attacking one another and killing off the weaker members of the pack.

Oh, there were Irish kings as grasping as any, of course. But it warmed my heart to see that these few, at least, were not like their brothers.

"I must warn you," Gwenhwyvar was saying, "there is sickness in Britain. Plague is there, and more are dying of fever than ever see a Vandal."

"One enemy is much like another," Aedd answered. "Each will be fought in its own way. The plague will be to us only another enemy to be met and matched. We will not shrink from the fight."

Laigin called, "Are we to grow old standing here? There is honor to be won, and I mean to get my share."

"Hear him!" shouted Diarmait. "Why do we linger even a moment longer when we could be gaining everlasting renown?" At this the gathered Irish sent up a great clamor to be away.

Gwenhwyvar, overcome by the eager affection of her countrymen, turned once more to thank the king. But he would hear nothing of it. "You see how it is," Aedd said. "They will have their share of glory. Send them now, for I can no longer hold them back."

Gwenhwyvar stepped a few paces nearer the lords. "Kinsmen and friends," she said, "if Arthur were here before you he could in no wise offer you greater thanks than I do now. Go and join him—you will be welcomed. Even so, do not think to increase your renown. For I tell you truly—" she paused, tears shining in her eyes—"any glory you win in battle cannot match that which you have already earned this day."

The Irish lords, and those men close enough to hear, were greatly cheered by Gwenhwyvar's words. No sooner had she finished than Diarmait shouted, "A blessing! Send us with a blessing!"

Aedd turned to me. "Myrddin? Would you?"

I took my place beside Gwenhwyvar and raised my staff. Stretching my other hand high, palm outward, I said:

Strength of fortress be yours,
Strength of kingship be yours,
Strength of love and pride of homeland
  sustain you through all things.
The circling of Christ to protect you,
The shielding of angels to guard you,
The aiding of God to support you
  in the hot rage of battle and the
  twistings of the fight.
Be the Holy Christ between you
  and all things hurtful,
Be the Holy One of Heaven between you
  and all things wicked,
Be the Holy Jesu between your shoulders,
  turning every harm to good,
Upholding you with his Swift Sure Hand,
Forever upholding you with his Swift Sure Hand!

So saying, I sent them on their way to Muirbolc and the waiting ships. Aedd bade us dine with him before leaving. Gwenhwyvar declined. "We will break fast in the saddle, I think, or we shall be left behind."

We departed the fortress as soon as the horses were saddled. Aedd summoned his chief bard and one of his noblemen and directed them to hold the caer in his absence, saying, "I give you full freedom to serve me in every cause while I am away. Should evil befall, I bid you to seek the best for the people. If your lot is good, then I urge you to seek its increase and impart the benefit to all within your care."

Both bard and chieftain vowed to uphold the king's will and extend his renown, whereupon Aedd bade them farewell and we left the stronghold in a white haze of dust.

Upon reaching Muirbolc once more, we dismounted and stood on the cliffside overlooking the bay while the warriors and crewmen undertook to board the horses, a task made difficult by the swirling surge of the tideflow. Once the animals were blindfolded, however, the boarding process proceeded smoothly. Soon the first ships were putting out to sea.

Turning to Aedd, Gwenhwyvar put her hand on his arm. "Thank you, my friend," she said. "You do not know how much your courtesy and thoughtfulness have encouraged me."

"Never say it," Aedd replied. "What I have done is but a small kindness when held against all that you and Arthur have given me."

"Lord," Gwenhwyvar wondered, "what have we given you—save the chance to die on foreign soil fighting an enemy that is no more threat to you?"

"Lady," the Irish king answered, "you have granted me the opportunity of raising sword alongside the most exalted hero of this age. If I die, so be it. At least my blood will be mingled with that of champions, and I will enter heaven's fair hall in the company of men of vast and terrible renown. What warrior dares hope for more?"

We joined the ships then, picking our way down the cliffside to the shore. As Llenlleawg boarded the horses, Aedd, Gwenhwyvar and I hurried to our ship waiting a little way out in the bay. The Irish used small round hide boats—hardly larger than leather shields—to carry us so that we would not have to wade through the surf.

Barinthus helped us aboard, leaning low over the side to steady the small coracle. "The wind is fair for a change and the sea is running. I would we were away, Lord Emrys," he said as soon as we were all aboard. "We will make good sailing if we leave at once."

"Then do so, man," I urged. "Lead on, the rest will follow."

He scurried back to his tiller and began shouting commands to all within sound of his voice. The big square sail swung up on creaking ropes, ruffled in the wind, puffed out, and the ship swung away from the land. Within moments we were running before a fresh wind. The low-riding sun sent yellow rays glancing off the green waves, setting every crest alight and seeding the watery furrows with gold.

Gradually, the greens and gold of water and light deepened to the blues and grays of night as eventide stole over the wide sea-field. Beneath a clear, star-filled sky, the sea danced and glittered, divided at our passing by the ship's sharp prow, swirling in pools of molten moonlight in our wake. The air remained warm, occasionally wafting cool crosscurrents that splashed across my face. I remained awake, watching the lively sky and the slow progress of the glowing moon across heaven's vaulted dome.

To be alive to the wonder of the commonplace, I thought, *that* is the very gift of a wildly generous Creator, who ever invites his creatures to contemplate the exuberance of his excellent handiwork. There is a deep and abiding joy at work in this worlds-realm, and we who toil through our lives do often forget this, or overlook it. But look: it is all around! Ceaseless, unrelenting, certain as sunrise, and constant as the rhythm of a heartbeat.

I stood, as I say, at the prow through the night, the stars and silent, watchful Barinthus my only companions. Toward morning I saw the rich darkness of the eastern sky begin to fade. I watched the sunrise with eyes beguiled by night's veiled mysteries.

Dawnlight streaked the sky with the red of blood and banners, staining the deep-hued water. The play of liquid light and sinuous shadow cast me into a melancholy mood. I felt the coming of day as the approach of a predatory presence. My scalp tingled; my stomach tightened. My vision grew keen.

The boat rode the tideflow and the sunrise glinted like molten metal in flux, swirling, bubbling, moving. I lifted my eyes to the opposite shore, now in shadowed silhouette against a burning sky. It seemed to me as if the boat were no longer moving through water, but gliding over endlessly coiling clouds—passing like a phantom through the very essence of this worlds-realm.

Behind me the world of sense and substance, stark and solid, faded from view; before me opened the glimmering, insubstantial Otherworld. The boat, its bull-necked pilot, and my fellow passengers vanished—as if stolen by an all-obscuring mist. I felt the rising upsurge of my spirit as it shook off the dull, unfeeling flesh and soared free. Fresh wind rushed over my body; I tasted sweet air on my tongue. In the space of three heartbeats, my feet touched a far distant shore.

A woman wearing a long gown of gleaming sea blue stood waiting for me. Fair of face and form, she raised a slender hand and beckoned me to follow. I moved as one without thought or will, shielding my dazzled eyes with my hand. I looked for the sun, but could see it no more. The sky itself glowed with the intensity of brilliant white gold, a radiant firmament reflecting a great hidden source of light that was everywhere present, casting no shadows.

The woman led me to the foot of a high hill a short distance from the shore; the estuary had disappeared and a sparkling green sea stretched to the far horizon. We walked up the hill, the broad flank covered with grass so green it glowed in the golden light like sun-struck emerald.

Atop the hill a standing stone pointed like a long finger towards the shining sky. The woman, her long hair black as polished jet, her green eyes shining with wisdom's undimmed light, lifted her hand to the stone and, in a voice soft as the breeze rippling the grass on the hilltop, asked, "Can you read the stone, little man?"

I stepped to the stone and saw that its rough surface was deeply carved with the spirals, knotwork, and maze-like patterns of old. I gazed at the ancient designs, letting my eye follow the intricate tracery of the cunning lines. Though I had seen it countless times before, I could make no sense of it.

"I cannot read them," I confessed, and turned away from the stone to see the woman's face cloud and tears begin to fall from her lovely eyes. She buried her face in her hands and her slender shoulders shook with sobs. "Lady," I said, agitation making my voice tight, "why do you weep?"

"For sorrow that this confession should fall from your lips," she said. "For you, above all men, should heed the signs carved in the stone."

"I read words," I countered. "Give me words and I will discern their meaning."

She raised her tearful eyes and gazed upon me with an expression of deepest grief and mourning. "Alas and woe," she said, "now is our doom come upon us! Once there was a time when you would have beheld these selfsame signs and their meaning would have been clear to you. This is my lament: you then, O Son of Dust, might have read them as men now read their precious books."

This last was said as she turned and walked away. I started after her, but she held up her hand and bade me stay. "There will come after me another, one who will lead you back the way you came."

By this I thought that I would return to the world I had left behind. Either I was mistaken, or she meant something else, for I waited and no one appeared. Yet something held me on that high hill through a day and a night.

I slept through the dark period and awoke to see a maiden approach. She came to stand beside the tall stone. "I give you good greeting," she said, and smiled. Her teeth were even and white, her brow high and smooth; her eyes were bright. She was dressed in a mantle of green and gold, and her feet were bare.

In her hands she held a cloth-wrapped bundle, which she opened to reveal a harp. The harp was none other than my own, for I recognized it.

"What is this?" she asked in a voice to charm small birds from the sky. And before I could answer, she added in a warning tone, "Though you think you know it, surely you know it not at all."

"I would be ignorant indeed not to know what I myself have held and played a thousand times," I replied. "It is my harp."

She shook her head sadly. "Though you say it is a harp and speak the word forthrightly, it is clear you do not know it. For if you had spoken in truth, this instrument would have sung its name aloud. The sound of your voice alone would have called forth music."

The maiden turned away, and with a world-weary sadness,

rested the harp against the rune-carved standing stone. "There will come after me another who will lead you back the way you came," she said, and disappeared, leaving me alone once more.

Three days and three nights passed, and I awoke on the fourth day to see a tall youth standing beside the stone—so still he might have been a part of it. Like the woman, his hair was dark and his eyes green. His cloak was blue like the sky, and his shirt leaf green, his trousers yellow gold, and his belt white as a cloud. He carried a large cup, or bowl, in his hands.

Upon seeing him, I rose and stood before him. "I have been waiting for you," I told him, suddenly irritated at the delay.

"Though every heartbeat was a thousand years," he answered, "you have not tarried half so long as I have waited for you." Anger leapt in his eyes like lightning seaming black storm clouds with fire. "I have waited all my life for you."

"Who are you?" I asked.

"I am the King of Summer," he replied.

I knelt before him. "I am your servant, lord."

"Stand on your feet, little man. You were never servant to me," he sneered. "For how is it that the servant does not recognize his lord?"

"But I have never seen you," I insisted. "Even so, I stand ready to serve you through all things."

"Get you away from me, False-hearted One. For if you had been my servant you would have heard my call. And you would know what it is I hold here in my hands."

"When did you call me, lord?"

"Myrddin," he replied in a voice aching with sorrow, "I have ever called you. From before the beginning of the world I have sung your name."

"Please, lord," I cried, "forgive me. I did not hear . . . I did not know."

With a look of mingled sorrow and disgust, he placed the cup he carried beside the stone next to the harp. He then started away. "Lord, I beg you!" I called after him.

He paused and looked back. "After me will come another who will lead you back the way you came."

The Summer Lord vanished then, and I was alone once more. I contemplated the stone and its carved symbols; I gazed upon the harp, but did not play it; and mused over the meaning of the cup.

Three days passed on my lonely hilltop, and three dark nights. A sound came to me as I slept, and I awakened. I rose and stood, listening for the sound that had roused me. Almost at once, I heard someone singing in a clear, strong voice. My heart beat more quickly. I knew the voice . . . though I had heard it only once before—for there is none like it in all the world or any other. I heard it, and, oh! I knew it.

Taliesin!

... packed and ready that Charis will come with you, ... you will find you need more than you might ...

The Summer Lord, and say to him, 'Avallach cares ...

... I have endured the storm of the sea ... would ...

... the land, and that his wrath hangs over me like the ...

... sky ...'

I have given you my counsel. Hinge, and you ... go ... A friend may offer advice, but a wise man makes ...

4

 I GAZED ACROSS THE HILLTOP TO see a man striding towards me: a fine and handsome man. His hair gleamed like shimmering flax, his cloak was blue as the night sky and full of stars; his tunic was white, an... his trousers soft leather. He carried a stout rowan staff in h... right hand and a harp slung over his shoulder on a strap. In a... he looked a mighty bard—Penderwydd, champion amon... bards. My heart ached to see him, for I realized there were n... more of his kind in the world.

Great Light, where are the men of power and vision, whos... words bring life from death and kindle goodness in the colde... hearts? Where are the men who dare great things, whose dee... are legend?

"Hail, Taliesin!" I called, casting aside my grief and runnin... to meet him.

He seemed not to hear me, for he strode on as if to pass by... "Taliesin, wait!" I shouted. He halted and turned aside, b... did not greet me.

"Do I know you, little man?" he asked, and the questio... cut through me like the thrust of a sword.

"Know me? But I . . . Taliesin, I am your son."

He gazed at me, searching me head to toe. "Is it you... Myrddin?" he asked at last; his mouth bent in a frown of dis... approval. "What has become of you, my son?"

"Why?" I asked, my heart breaking. "Have I changed s... much?"

"I tell you the truth," he replied, "if you had not spoken my name just now I would not have known you."

He pointed to the instrument lying against the standing stone. "That is Hafgan's harp," he said. "Why is it sitting there?"

Embarrassed to have left it untended, I retrieved the harp and cradled it to my shoulder. And though I stroked and strummed, I could but conjure a meaningless tangle of noise from the instrument. I opened my mouth to sing, and could produce only a strangled, halfhearted sound.

"Stop!" he cried. "If you can play no better than that, cast the thing aside. It is useless as a rotten stick in your hands."

He then led me to the crown of the hill and pointed to the blue-green sea stretching below us like some vast swath of billowy silk. He bade me look and tell him what I saw.

"I see Mighty Manawyddan's realm," I replied, "deep as it is wide, dividing the island nations one from another."

"And what see you there?" He indicated the long sweep of the strand along the coast.

"I see the waves, ceaseless in motion, white-crested servants of the Lord of the Wave-Tossed Sea."

Taliesin's hand dropped to his side. "They are *not* waves," he said. "Look again, Ignorant One, and look closely this time. Tell me what you see."

Still, I saw the waves, and only the waves, washing back and forth upon the shore. Taliesin was not pleased with this answer. "How is it possible that you look and do not see? Has the light of discernment abandoned you?"

He raised his hand level to the horizon and spread his fingers wide. "They are not waves," he said again. "They are the boats of the people fleeing their homeland. The Britons are leaving, Myrddin, in such haste and in such numbers as to agitate the ocean."

As he spoke those words, the waves turned into boats—the white crests became sails and the rolling motion the wake flung back from each and every prow—and there were hundreds upon hundreds, and thousands upon thousands of them, all fleeing the shores of Ynys Prydein in great waves of home-leaving.

"Where are they going?" I asked, aware that I was witness-ing a disaster unknown in the Island of the Mighty from the days of its creation.

"They are fleeing to realms much inferior to the land of their birth," Taliesin answered sadly, "where they will live brutish lives under rulers unworthy of them."

"Why?" I asked. "Why do they abandon their lands and king?"

"They leave because they are afraid," Taliesin explained simply. "They are afraid because their hope has failed and the light which sustained it is extinguished."

"But Arthur is their hope and his life is their light," I objected. "They are surely wrong to leave, for the High King is yet alive in Britain."

"Yes," agreed Taliesin, "Arthur lives, but how are they to know? There is no one to sing his deeds, no one to uphold him in song, no one to extol him with high-sounding praise and so fire the souls of men." He turned accusing eyes on me. "Where are the bards to sing Arthur's valor and kindle courage in men's hearts?"

"I am here, Father," I said.

"You? You, Myrddin?"

"Since I am Chief Bard of Britain," I said proudly, "it is my duty and my right. I sing Arthur's praise."

"How so?" he demanded. "You cannot read what is written on the stone; you cannot coax music from the heart of the oak; you cannot drink from the exalted cup. Chief Bard of Ants and Insects you may be, but you are no True Bard of Britain."

His words stung me. I hung my head, cheeks burning with shame. He spoke the truth and I could make no reply.

"Hear me, Son of Mine," Taliesin said. And, oh, his voice was the wild wind-force trembling the hilltop with its right-eous contempt. "Once you might have sung the shape of the world and the elements would have obeyed you. But now you voice has grown weak through speech unworthy of a bard. You have squandered all that has been given you, and you were given much indeed."

I could not stand under this stern rebuke. "Please, Father," I cried, falling to my knees, "help me. Tell me, is there nothing I can do to turn back the waves?"

"Who can turn back the tide? Who can recall the arrow in flight?" Taliesin said. "No man can replace the apple on the bough once it has fallen. Even so, though the homeleaving cannot be halted, the Island of the Mighty may yet be saved."

I took heart at these words. "I pray you, lord, tell me what I am to do, and it shall be done," I vowed. "Though it take my last breath and all my strength, I will do it."

"Myrddin, beloved son," Taliesin said, "that is the least part of what it will cost. Still, if you would know what is to be done, know this: you must go back the way you came."

Before I could ask what he meant, Taliesin raised his hands in the bardic way—one above his head, the other shoulder high, both palms outward. Facing the standing stone, he opened his mouth and began to sing.

Oh, the sound of his voice filled me with such longing I feared I would swoon. To hear the sound of that bold, enchanted voice was to know the power of the True Word. I heard and inwardly trembled with the knowledge of what I had once held in my grasp, and somehow let slip away.

Taliesin sang. He raised his head and poured forth his song; the cords stood out on his neck, and his hands clenched with the effort. Wonder of wonders, the standing stone, cold lifeless thing, began to change: the slender pillar of stone rounded itself and swelled, stretching, thickening, growing taller. Stubs of limbs appeared at the top—these lengthened and split, becoming many-fingered branches which swept out and up into the handsome crown of a great forest oak. Leaves appeared in glossy profusion, deep green and silver-backed like birch.

This tree spread its leafy branches wide over the hilltop in response to Taliesin's glorious song. My heart swelled to bursting at the splendor of the tree and the song that shaped and sustained it—a song matchless in its melody: extravagant, spontaneous, rapturous, yet reckless enough to steal the breath away. Then, as I stood marveling, the tree kindled into bright flame and began to burn. Red tongues of flame sprouted like dancing flowers among the branches. I feared for the destruction of the beautiful tree, and made to cry out in alarm. But even as I stretched my hands toward the blaze, I saw that the shimmering flames halved the tree, dividing it top to bottom: one half stood shimmering, dancing, alive, red-gold against a blue night sky; the other half remained full-leaved and green in the bright light of day.

Behold! In the time-between-times, the tree burned but was not consumed.

Taliesin stopped singing and turned to me. Gazing with the sharp scrutiny of a master challenging his wayward pupil, he asked, "Now tell me. What do you see?"

"I see a living tree where once was a stone," I replied. "I see this tree half in flames and half green-leaved and alive. The half that burns is not consumed, and the half that resists the flame puts forth leaves of silver."

My father smiled; I felt his approval and my heart quickened. "Perhaps you are my son after all," he said proudly.

Lifting his hand to the tree, he spread his fingers and the flames leaped higher, sparks flew up into the night sky and became stars. Birds flocked to the green half of the living tree and took refuge in its branches. Small golden apples appeared among the leaves; the birds ate the apples and were nourished and sustained.

"This," he said, turning to me, "this is the way by which you must go, son of mine. See and remember." He gripped my shoulder tightly. "Now, you must leave."

"Let me stay but a little," I pleaded. "There is so much I would ask you."

"I am ever with you, my son," he said gently. "Fare well, Myrddin, until we meet again."

The next I knew I stood alone on the hilltop before the half-flaming, half-living tree. There I remained for a time—

whether short or long, I do not know—puzzling over the meaning of this conundrum, repeating the words: *this is the way by which you must go.* But I came no nearer to an answer. The weather changed; a sharp wind gusted around me, raw and cold. Hard rain began to fall, stinging where it touched my skin, driving me away.

Gathering my cloak around me, I peered over my shoulder one last time. The solitary oak had become a grove and I understood that it was for me to enter there. I stood for a moment, hesitant, fearful. The way back led through the grove; there was none other. I understood . . . still, I hesitated.

"Great Light," I said at last, "go before me into this dark place. Be my Savior and my Guide through all things, whatever shall befall me. And if it please you, Lord, oversee my safe return. I place myself under the protection of your Swift Sure Hand, and entreat you to surround me with Heaven's Champions. Though I go into the pit, there let me find you. Though I ascend the heights of moon and stars, there let me find you. Where I go, I go in faith, knowing that wherever I am, there will you be also; I in you, and you in me. In life, in death, in the life beyond, Great Light, uphold me. I am yours."

So saying, I entered the grove.

The path lay silent, the air heavy and redolent of the tomb. No kindly ray illumined my passage. It was as if I walked in the shadowlands, alive yet cut off from the realm of the living. The trees—their thick, gnarled trunks black with age and scarred by the gnawing ravages of time—seemed stout pillars holding aloft a canopy so green and dark that it formed a shroud over me. I walked steadily, but no eye marked my passing, no sound of footfall attended my steps.

I had entered a sanctum, a holy remove from the wider world, a *nemeton*. What is more, moving among the trees I felt a strange familiarity. With a shiver of recognition, I realized where I was: *Bryn Celli Ddu*, the sacred grove on the Holy Island. Hafgan, dear, blessed Hafgan, had told me about it when I was a boy.

Within this secluded remove, I sensed the spirits of the

Druidkind still lingering in the dense and dusky silence. Old beyond reckoning, the trees were ancient when Rome was still a muddy cattle pen. They had witnessed the ascent and decline of princes, kings, and empires; they had witnessed the slow ebb and flow of the years and seen Fortune's Wheel revolve in its ceaseless turning. These trees had watched over the Island of the Mighty since the first days, when the dew of Creation was still fresh on the ground. Brutus of Troy, Alexander, Cliopatra, and great Constantius had come and gone beneath their steady and unyielding gaze. The Learned Ones had held discourse under their twisting branches, and many yet slept in the bare earth beneath them.

Hafgan had told me, too, about that terrible day long ago when the Legions of Rome attacked the grove on the Holy Island. The Bards of Britain were felled like trees, hacked to death by Roman swords without protection of armor or weapons. For all its genius, the Roman military mind failed to recognize that the grove, not the Learned Brotherhood, was their true enemy. Had they burned it down or uprooted the trees, they would have triumphed that day, for they would have cut the Bardic Fellowship to its heart.

Relentless realists, men of practical habits and cool logic, the Romans never imagined that the trees, the symbol of the druid, must be conquered. The canny druids knew that flesh is weak, it lives out its span, dies and is no more. They sacrificed the perishable to the imperishable. The dying served the everliving, and thereby gained the eternal. The hardheaded Roman generals, watching the slaughter with cold eyes, never guessed it was their own downfall they beheld. For every drop of druid blood secured a future victory, and every druid death a triumph.

The Romans are gone now, but the Learned Brotherhood lives on. Many, very many, have realized the end of Truth's quest in the Cross of Jesu. The Wise Ones of the Oak have become the Brotherhood of Christ. The power of the holy grove is now the provenance of the Holy Church. The Great Light moves how he will. So be it!

In a little while, my steps led me to the mound I knew I would find in the center of the grove: a round hump of stone covered by earth and turf, its entrance barely visible in the gloom. It was a tomb—both actual and symbolic, for as everyone knows actual symbols are always the most potent. Actual, for the dead were truly buried within. But symbolic, too; for here among the bones of the illustrious dead of elder days, the Seeker could lie down in figurative death that his living bones might commune with the age-brittle remains of his fathers.

Now it was my turn; I was the Seeker.

Stepping to the mound entrance, I raised my face to the sky but could see nothing through the dense thatch of interwoven branches save a dull golden glow. The boles of the mighty yews showed iron-black against the uncanny gloaming. It was the time-between-times and I could already feel my feet on the path. Raising my hands to either side of my head, I cried out in supplication:

> *Traversing glens, traversing forests,*
> *   traversing valleys long and wild,*
> *Fairest Jesu be upholding me,*
> *Christ triumphant be my shield!*
> *Great King of Mercy be my peace:*
> *In every pass, on every hill,*
> *In every stream, headland, ridge, and moor;*
> *Each lying down, each rising up,*
> *Whether in this world or some other.*

Thus emboldened, I bent my head and stepped into the mound. Once inside, I was able to stand; I did so and walked farther into the mound, passing stone chambers on either side. I came to another threshold, crossed it, and continued. More chambers, some still bearing the bones of the ancient dead. I came to a third threshold and crossed it, entering yet another chamber—round as a womb and almost as dark. My shadow shattered and danced on the walls around me, quickened by a strange, flickering light behind me.

The walls of this chamber had been limed with white and painted with blue designs: the spiral and sundisk, the Mor Cylch and Cernunnos' horn. But the white had flaked away and the blue was little more than a stain on the rock. There were bones piled neatly against one wall: skulls round and white as river stones, thin curved ribs, arms and thighs.

I considered the impermanence of all things flesh, and the timeless moment that is eternity. I pondered the Eagle of Time sharpening his beak upon the granite mountain of this worlds-realm: when the stone mountain has been worn away to a single grain of sand, the eagle will fly away to the eyrie whence he came.

I meditated on these things as I stooped and stretched my hand towards a slender shinbone. All at once the ground beneath my feet gave way—as if a pit had suddenly opened under me. The chamber where I stood was hollow and the floor, weakened over time, could not hold my weight. I plummeted down into the blackness of *Annwn*; the Underworld realm had swallowed and claimed me.

I spun into the abyss.

Darkness, blacker than the cold embrace of death, swarmed over me. The world of light and life vanished somewhere far above, extinguished like a rushlight in a gale. I cast aside all hope and clung to my failing senses as a man hurled into the teeth of the storm.

I fell, tumbling, turning, dropping down and down and down past roots and rocks, past springs and pools and underground streams. Far, far below, I heard the clash and clatter of water breaking on rock in a vast hidden cataract. Falling swift and straight, I struck the dark water and struggled to swim, to rise, but my clothes were heavy and my limbs exhausted. I plunged beneath the surface and sank without hope into my cold deepwater grave.

In a rictus tight as rock, my body was seized and borne along by swift currents. Over naked spires and crevices yawning wide in unending night, over a landscape barren as it was bleak, I flew. Far beneath the roots of the world, I drifted, deeper than the deepest whale, deep in *Afanc*'s realm I soared in a slow, undulating flight.

Through eons of earth ages, I existed in my elemental wandering: without breath, without sight, without sense, a pure spirit pulled along by the slow circulation of *Annwn*'s unseen ocean. Bereft of all volition, I moved where the currents moved me. I became light and tenuous as a single thought, possessing only a thought's ineluctable freedom.

In this way was Myrddin Emrys reduced and undone: I became nothing—less than nothing. Trackless was my journey, unknown and unbeheld by any save God alone. Outward and inward, drifting over broken vistas of the Underworld and my own arid soul—the two were one and the same to me. The darkness of the pit was my inner darkness, its emptiness my own. I was a ripple on the crest of a secret wave. I was a fleeting disturbance in the hidden deep.

I was nothing.

The silence of the tomb engulfed me—a stifling, suffocating quietude, solid as granite and as heavy. I shouted my name aloud in defiance, but my voice could not penetrate that dense oppression and the word fell at my feet like a bird, dead, from the sky. I felt the mass of this deadweight silence on my skin, as if I were immersed in an ocean of fire-thickened pitch.

I wandered I know not where, creeping with utmost care over a rough stone floor that slanted away from me, descending with every step, down and down and down into a darkness immense and greedy.

Occasionally, I passed a fissure where I glimpsed the dim flicker of lurid flames crackling up from a deep-chambered cell below. At one such crevice I felt the hot blast of vented gas—like the belch of a fire-throated dragon. The heat gust washed over me in a great hissing gasp. My eyes stung and nostrils burned with the acrid, sulfurous stink.

Tears streamed from my eyes; my nose ran and my breath came in racking gulps. Choking, gagging, I stumbled on, bowed by the rack in my lungs and the pain in my eyes, each step a cry of defiance. Gradually I came to feel the presence of another with me in the gallery, walking but a short distance ahead as it seemed to me. I say that I became aware of this presence, for I think the stranger had been with me from the first step, but I had been too absorbed in my own misery to perceive her.

Yes, I knew, as one knows in a dream, that a female presence went before me, leading me along the death-dark corridor, matching my steps with hers—stopping when I stopped, moving when I moved.

Once I stumbled and fell down on hands and knees. I heard the footsteps continue a little way ahead of me. "Wait!" I shouted, lest I be left alone once more.

My voice struck the rock surface like the flat of a hand. But the steps ahead halted and then turned back. They came towards me. I heard the soft footfall return—closer, until the woman stood directly over me. Though I could not see her, I knew she was near.

"Please," I said, "wait but a little. Do not leave me here alone."

I expected no reply from my phantom companion. Nevertheless, my plea was answered. "Then get you up, Merlin," the woman commanded sternly. "Or I *will* leave you."

That voice . . . I knew it!

"Ganieda! Is it you?"

The footsteps started away again. "Wait! Please, wait!" I shouted, scrambling to my feet once more. "Do not leave me, Ganieda!"

"I have never left you, my soul," she answered, her voice echoing back to me from somewhere ahead. "And I never will leave you. But you must hurry."

I raised myself and lurched onward, desperate now. I must catch her! Dragging myself along, striking the solid jutting stone walls now and again with hands and arms and elbows . . . however fast I moved, she remained that many paces ahead of me; I could not gain so much as half a pace on my beloved guide.

I ran, growing breathless in the pursuit. My chest heaved with the effort, but I did not slacken my pace. Just when I thought I must faint, I felt cool, fresh air on my face and perceived a lightening of the darkness ahead—a slight but discernible graying of the all-pervading shadow in which I moved.

A dim, gray pall like false dawn hung over the room into which I stumbled. No more than a dozen paces ahead of me stood my beloved Ganieda. She appeared as she had on our wedding day: dressed in a fine white linen mantle with a golden bell on each and every tassel of her hem, her black hair brushed to shining and braided with silver threads, and on her fair brow a circlet of spring flowers. Folded over one shoulder, she wore a cloak of imperial purple and sky-blue check of the northern tribes, the folds fastened with a splendid golden brooch; gold bracelets and bands graced her slender wrists and arms, and white leather sandals held her feet.

All this I beheld with ease, for a light radiated from her, dim and diffuse, but distinct—as if her clothing glowed with a will-o'-the-wisp light. She gazed at me intently, her face at once severe and lovely, her hands clasped before her.

"Ganieda, you are—" I began, moving towards her.

She threw out a hand to halt me. "Come no nearer!" she said harshly, then added in a softer tone, "It is not permitted, best beloved."

"Then why have you come? If we are not to be together—"

"Torment me not, beloved," she said, and oh, I thought my heart would break. "We will be together—that I promise you—but not yet, my soul, not yet. You must endure yet a little longer. Are you willing?"

"I am—if by enduring I may secure the promise you have given."

"Then hear me, my husband. Believe me when I tell you that Britain will fall to the invader's sword. Through rapine and slaughter the land will be lost and the people destroyed.

Kings shall die unmourned, princes shall go to their graves unmarked, and warriors curse the day of their birth. The holy altars of Prydein will be baptized in the blood of her saints and flames destroy all they touch."

"This is more bitter to me than my own death," I replied mournfully. "These are not words to steady a faltering heart."

"My darling," she said in a voice of utter compassion, "you above all men must know that where great danger threatens, there hope abides. Faith ever erects her tent in the shadow of travail." Ganieda smiled, shaking her head slowly. "Is darkness stronger than light? Is not even the frailest good more powerful by far than the most eminent evil?"

She spread her hands and I saw, all around her, the forms of warriors—scores of warriors, hundreds of them, and each one arrayed for battle: shield over shoulder, strong hands gripping sword hilt and spear. They lay still, their eyes closed.

"Tell me, Ganieda, are they dead or do they sleep?"

"They live," she said. "As long as men love courage and honor, they remain alive."

"Then why do they sleep?"

"They await the battlehorn to call them forth," she explained.

"Only tell me where it is and I shall sound it," I replied. "Britain has need of such men."

"Yes," she agreed readily, "and so shall she ever need them. But these"—she made a circling motion with her hand—"their time is not yet. Be assured, you will know when it comes."

"Am I to see this tribulation?"

Ganieda turned sorrowful eyes upon me. "Yes, heart of my heart, you will live. For it is you alone who must summon the warriors to their mighty work. And it is you who must lead them." She paused, letting her gaze linger on the forms of the warriors around her. "I show you this so you will know without doubt that you go not alone into the evil day. Your sword brothers go with you, Merlin. They only await your call."

I looked upon the warriors once again, and I saw among them faces that I knew: Cai was there, yes, and Bedwyr, and Gwenhwyvar, Llenlleawg and Gwalcmai, Gwalchavad, Bors and Ban and Cador, Meurig and Aedd. There were others as well, the brave dead of previous battles: Pelleas, Custennin, Gwendolau, Baram, Elphin and Gwyddno Garanhir, Maelwys, Pendaran Gleddyvrudd—men of hard purpose, fearless, right-loving warriors who shrank before nothing, valiant heroes all.

"It is not for me to lead such warriors," I demurred. "Though I would gladly stand beside the best of them, the call is not mine to give. Certainly, a worthy king can be found to lead them."

"If that is what you wish," she said, and stepped aside. And I saw behind her another warrior, a lordly form, a figure I knew well.

"Arthur . . . " I gasped. "Say he is not dead."

"I have already told you," Ganieda replied.

"As long as men love courage—I know," my voice grew tight with desperation. "Please, say it all the same."

"He lives," she stated firmly. "But he, like all the others, awaits your call. And he will lead the war host of Britain in the battle to come. Use them well, my soul. They are the last, and when they are gone the world will never more see their like."

She turned and began walking swiftly away. "Now come with me," she called, "there is more I would show you. But we must hurry, for my time with you is almost finished."

Taking a last look at the sleeping warriors, I hastened after Ganieda and soon found myself in another gallery—this one of uncut stone, a natural tunnel. After several hundred paces, we entered a rough cavern. Water glimmered dully in the center of the floor; ragged teeth of stone dripped water into the black pool, drop by solitary drop.

Ganieda stood at the edge of the pool. "Come stand beside me, Merlin," she said, beckoning me nearer. "Look upon the water."

"A Seeing Bowl," I remarked, thinking the pool filled with the black oak water of druid lore.

"It is the Seeing Bowl of Annwn," she confirmed. Dread filled her voice; she stretched forth her hand. "Look you, and tell me what you see."

I looked and saw the dull glimmer of the water's surface, agitated by the steady slow drops from the stone teeth above. But beneath the ripples I perceived a young woman. "It is a maiden," I said.

The maiden turned as if looking up at me from the pool. But no, she could not see me, for she turned away again and began walking. All at once I could see all around and beyond her. "She is moving through a forest," I continued. "It is an ancient forest and the path is narrow, but she knows it well. The maiden hurries, but not from fear. She is not afraid, for she knows where she is going. Ah, there, she has come into a meadow in the wood. . . . "

I watched, fascinated by this Virgin of the Forest as she entered the meadow which contained a pool fed by a clear-running spring. She walked to the pool, holding out her hands. Two men appeared among the trees; by their look and manner I understood that they were dying of thirst. The dying men saw the water and rushed to the pool.

The first man fell on his knees at the spring, dipped his hand and drank, but the water turned poisonous in his mouth and he died, clutching his throat. The second man approached the Virgin of the Forest and consulted her, at which she produced a cup and offered it to him.

Taking the bowl between his hands, the man filled the cup from the spring. He drank from the cup and his life was restored; he left rejoicing in the wisdom of the maiden.

The image changed and I saw the maiden once more, but grown: she stood with one foot on high Yr Widdfa and the other on the banks of Mor Hafren; her head touched the sky and stars glinted in her tresses. In one hand she held a forest, and in the other the cup, the marvelous cup. And as she walked across the land, the spirits of the ancient Britons awakened.

And the Island of the Mighty flourished once more.

Ganieda led me from the pool. We moved farther into the cavern, descending all the while, penetrating deeper into the heart of the earth. Through cracks and crevices on either side, I glimpsed the ruddy glow of molten rock seething up from below. In the lurid light I beheld strange creatures frozen in stone—massive muscled behemoths with bony shieldplates and claws the size of scythes, their strange and ponderous bodies trapped in postures of predation or defense; menacing reptiles, their hideous flat heads bristling with spikes. I looked with dread fascination upon them, and wondered at the dire purpose of their creation.

Deeper and still deeper we went, past seams of gold spangling the walls of my Underworld palace, gleaming in the flames of subterranean fires. I beheld halls of crystal and precious stones. Turning neither right nor left, Ganieda led me through the endless halls of Annwn until at last we came to a rock ledge, where she halted.

The place proved a shore of stone, rimming a limitless underground sea which I viewed by virtue of seething patches of burning oil afloat on the surface of this Underworld ocean. We stood together overlooking the dreadful deep, where no breath of wind ever stirred, nor sea-swell billowed, nor ebb-tide flowed. It was a vast, dark water grave under a stony sky, an iron-hued firmament, solid, unchanging, inviolable.

"I must leave you now, Merlin, my heart," she said, turning to me, her eyes full of sorrow at our parting. "Where you are going I cannot return, and where I am going you cannot enter."

"No, Ganieda—not yet." I reached out for her, but she stepped away.

"Even so," my beautiful one replied, "we must part. There is nothing more I can do. If you are to live, you must go back the way you came."

She took two steps backwards, placed her fingertips to her lips, kissed them, and raised her slender white hand to me.

"Fare well, best beloved," she said. "Remember, I will come for you one day."

"Please, Ganieda," I cried, grief surging up like a wave within me, "do not leave me! Please!"

"God be with you always, Merlin."

With that she disappeared, leaving me to stand alone on the stone ridge above the underground sea. But not for long, for I began to run to the place where I had last seen Ganieda. My foot slipped on a bit of broken rock and I fell, striking my knee on the ledge with a tremendous crack.

I squeezed my eyes shut against the pain and when I opened them again, the darkness was gone. The luminous sky had likewise vanished, and I stood at a ship's solid prow once more.

5

 BARINTHUS BELLOWED OUT A
warning, and the ship shuddered to a
stop in the silt of a nearby bank. Aedd
and Gwenhwyvar disembarked at
once, sliding easily over the rail and wading the few paces to
shore to wait while the other ships landed and the horses were
brought. I watched them as if still in a dream, and then moved
to join them.

As I stepped towards the rail, Llenlleawg stooped where I
had been standing and retrieved a cloth-wrapped object. "Emrys,"
he called after me. "Will you leave your harp behind?"

My harp? I stared at the bundle in his hands. How had that
come to be there? I returned to where he stood and lifted the
cloth to reveal the harp I knew full well I had left behind in
Arthur's camp.

You must go back the way you came.

Knowledge came to me in a rush like a gust of wind, and
with it came certainty. Yes!

I raised my head and lifted my voice in song:

> I am old;
> I am forever young.
> I am the True Emrys, Immortal,
> Gifted of the Giving Giver
> With a perceiving spirit.
> I am a bard,
> A Battlechief of Knowledge;

339

> *I do not vouchsafe the secrets of my craft*
> *To unenlightened creatures.*
> *I am a wise guide;*
> *I am a righteous judge.*
> *I am a king whose kingdom is unseen.*
> *I am the servant of the Great Light;*
> *Though blind, I will continue to see God.*
> *All saints and angels,*
> *All things in heaven and earth bear witness:*
> *Word Singer, World-Singer,*
> *Myrddin ap Taliesin am I.*

Llenlleawg stared at me. "This," I told him, raising the harp, "is the Heart of Oak. In the hands of a True Bard it burns with life-giving song, but is not consumed. This is the way I must go."

So saying, I struck the harp with the palm of my hand and the strings gave forth a sound like a chorused shout. Sweet the sound! My heart thrilled to hear it.

May the Gifting Giver be good to you, Taliesin! May you enjoy peace and plenty in the Great King's heavenly hall, and may you sing heartfelt praise to the Lord of Life for ever!

"Come!" I shouted. "We must hurry. Arthur is waiting and I have been away far too long."

"But it is only a day since we left," Llenlleawg reminded me.

"No, my friend," I replied. "I have been away far, far longer than that. But I have returned now. Pray, Llenlleawg! Pray I am not too late!"

Impatient to be away, I mounted my horse as soon as it came ashore. "Await the other ships and follow us when all the warbands are assembled," I instructed Aedd. "We ride before you to the British camp to tell Arthur to ready your welcome."

We three—Llenlleawg, Gwenhwyvar, and I—rode as fast as we could, through the day and night, pausing only for water—only to find the camp all but deserted. A scant handful of warriors remained behind to guard the servants, women, and wounded. "They left before dawn," one of them told us. "The Vandali have gathered in Glen Arwe. Five warbands—almost the entire war host." He raised a hand to point the direction; the effort brought a wince of pain, and I noticed the arm was swollen and discolored.

"Glen Arwe?" Llenlleawg asked.

"Aye—a half day's ride to the north," the wounded warrior confirmed. "Just follow the sound—you cannot go wrong."

"Aedd and the Irish lords ride behind us," Llenlleawg told the warrior. "Send them on as soon as they arrive."

With a snap of the reins we were off again. Tired as we were we made what speed we could, encountering no one on the way. But, as the warrior had promised, we heard the battleclash long before we came upon the conflict itself. The sound echoed along the river course—raw voices shouting, the crash and clatter of weapons, the rumbling thunder of horses' hooves and Vandali drums—as if the massed war hosts of all the world lay just before us. Llenlleawg halted as we entered the glen. A haze of smoke and dust obscured the way ahead.

"I want to see how the battle stands," Gwenhwyvar stated.

"We may get a better view from there." Llenlleawg indicated a place high on the ridge overlooking the glen.

We turned aside, forded the river—now just a scant trickle along the damp earth—and climbed the hillside to the ridge-top. When we stopped again the glen lay far below us in a pall of dust. Then, as we strained to see, the dry breeze gusted and the clouds parted. The battleground was revealed: a vicious swirling tangled mass of men and horses.

The British lords had joined combat with the Black Boar's forces, and had succeeded in dividing the enemy host into three enclaves. The usual tactic would have been to continue harassing each division, cutting into smaller and smaller sections. The Vandali, however, were standing their ground and refused to be further divided.

Llenlleawg took one look. "It is not good," he said, shaking his head slowly. "Unless the enemy can be moved, and soon,

Arthur might as well call off the attack; he can do nothing."

It did appear that the assault had foundered and was, if not yet in danger of collapsing, then very close to it.

"I do not see him," Gwenhwyvar said, scanning the churning mass below. "Do you?"

Llenlleawg looked, too, his lower lip between his teeth. "Strange," he replied at last. "Where is Arthur?"

I gazed into the chaos, searching where the battle raged hottest, looking for the familiar sight: the whirling blur of Caledvwlch and the reckless, headlong lunging that marked Britain's impetuous War Leader. But I could not find him.

Fear stole over me. I imagined Arthur's body lying broken on the blood-soaked earth, life seeping from a dozen wounds as the battle surged around him. I imagined his head struck from his shoulders to adorn a Vandal spear. I imagined him hacked to pieces . . .

"There!"

"Arthur? Where?"

"No—not Arthur. Someone else." Llenlleawg's gaze narrowed as he leaned forward in the saddle. He stabbed a finger at the maelstrom below. "Cai, I think. Yes—and he is in trouble!" The Irish champion drew his spear from its place behind his saddle and prepared to join the fight. To Gwenhwyvar, he said, "Stay here—if Arthur is down there, I will find him."

His mount leapt forward and Llenlleawg disappeared over the edge of the ridge. When I saw him again, he had reached the glen and was hurtling across the valley floor towards a place where a knot of Cymbrogi had become surrounded and separated by the main body and were in imminent danger of being overwhelmed.

I watched Llenlleawg flying into battle, scattering the foe before him, driving headlong into the fight. Some there are, no doubt, who would question the ability of a single warrior to redeem such a desperate plight. But there is no one I would rather have fly to my defense, whatever the odds. And any inclined to doubt that one sword more or less could make much difference can never have seen the Irish champion with the battle frenzy on him. I tell you the truth, no foe confronting the spectacle of Llenlleawg gripped in the *awen* of battle remained unpersuaded for long.

But where was Arthur?

I dismounted and crept to the edge of the overlook to better search the heaving mass below. The battlesound rose up like the roar of an ocean gale, the men rushing, hurling themselves into the clash like seawaves breaking against one another. Most of the Britons were mounted, but the superior numbers of Vandali and the closeness of the glen had lessened any advantage the horses provided. This, perhaps, was why the attack had been repulsed and was now in danger of disintegrating altogether.

Gazing down into the melée, I picked out Cai, at the forefront of his warband, sword whirling, trying to hack a way through the mass before him. He was attempting to reunite his force with the one nearest to him, but the enemy so securely choked the gap that far from cutting a path through, it was all he could do to keep from being swept farther away.

Bedwyr, I think, led those nearest Cai, but he was hard-pressed to prevent his warband from becoming surrounded. Cador—or Cadwallo, perhaps, I could not be certain—was being forced, step-by-grudging-step, farther from the other two. In this way, the Vandal, moving fluid-like in and around the mounted Cymbrogi, surging into the empty places, filling them, surrounding, inundating, flowing on, were slowly reversing the tide of battle.

Where was Arthur?

"Look!" shouted Gwenhwyvar behind me. "Cador is in trouble!" Following Llenlleawg's lead, she spurred her horse forward, plunging down the hillside to join the battle. There was no stopping her; I did not even try.

The Vandali made best use of their numbers and the pinched confines of the glen to blunt the attack of the Britons, halt it, and turn it back. It now appeared Britain's battlechiefs had a rout on their hands. Something would have to be done, and soon, if the Britons were to escape a cruel beating.

Where was Arthur?

I gazed from one end of the plain to the other, but could see no sign of him. Where could he be? What if he had fallen in battle? I dismissed the idea at once—if he had been cut down I would have seen some sign of it by now. Indeed, the British attack doubtless would have collapsed around him. No, I consoled myself, I did not see him because he was not there.

Llenlleawg had reached the beleaguered Cai and took his place in the forerank of the fight. His sudden, almost miraculous, appearance greatly encouraged the flagging Cymbrogi and they fought with renewed vigor to extricate themselves from their dire predicament.

Following Llenlleawg's lead they succeeded in cutting through the enemy wall between them and Bedwyr's warband, and wasted no time in reuniting the two forces. This tactic proved of only limited value, however, for as the two warbands merged, the barbarians swarmed into the gap, surrounding them both. Now, instead of two half-enclosed warbands, there was one fully encircled.

Arthur! Where are you? The battle is lost and the Bear of Britain is nowhere to be found. What has happened to him?

The Black Boar, no doubt astonished at finding himself within a spear-throw of an assured victory, cast off all restraint. I saw the Boar standard waving in a frenzy, and the drums quickened, booming like angry, insistent thunder. At once the mass of Vandali foot men thickened, drew together, then hurled itself against the British host.

Gwenhwyvar had reached the fight and quickly gathered a force around her. Despite her best efforts, they were kept on the outside; try as they might, they could not find a way to break through, and were reduced to harrying the rearward ranks—which they did with great, if ineffective, zeal, while the main battle took place elsewhere.

Sensing their dilemma, the mounted British stiffened and defied the encircling pressure. Bedwyr seemed to understand what was happening and attempted a counterattack, driving into the wall of foemen, thrusting, forcing, hacking his way forward by the strength of his blade alone. A wedge of horsemen formed behind him, desperately trying to cut a swath to the surrounded Cymbrogi.

Step-by-bloody-step they advanced. Fierce the fight, savage the resistance; the enemy gave ground with life-grudging reluctance. I saw men staggering under the weight of their shields, struggling to fend off the blows of the foe with broken weapons. I saw men pulled from their mounts even as they struck down their adversaries; I saw men falling beneath the hooves of the horses, shrieking men suddenly lacking limbs.

Bedwyr was now within two spears' lengths of rescuing the surrounded Cymbrogi. They were so close! One more push, one last strike, would break the enemy line. Bedwyr saw it, too; he raised himself in the saddle, lofted his sword and exhorted his warriors to the task.

And the Cymbrogi responded. They lowered their heads and drove in over the bodies of the fallen.

Alas! The enemy also saw the line bending inward as if to break. One of Twrch Trwyth's chieftains appeared and, with breathtaking bravery, threw himself against the buckling line. Leaping, whirling, he matched Bedwyr stroke for stroke and halted him. The faltering Vandali took heart and rallied behind their wild leader. They rose up with a shout, surging like a seawave to overwhelm the British.

Bedwyr was thrown back. Within the space of three heartbeats his gallant effort was undone.

I gazed across the churning turmoil as across a bubbling caldron. Everywhere it was the same. The British were being surrounded and forced back, giving over hard-won ground . . . falling . . . failing.

The smoke and dust drifted up and up, casting a filthy veil over the sun. The cries of men and horses, the sharp crack of wood and bone, the stinging ring of metal on metal ascended to the dead white sky. My hand clenched as if holding a sword, and I felt the tug of battle in my blood.

Turning at once to my horse, I mounted, and retrieved my sword from its place behind the saddle. I made to draw the weapon, but could not pull it from the sheath. Though I drew mightily, I simply could not free it.

I sat for a moment, mystified. And then my eye fell upon my rowan staff, tucked securely in its place, under the saddle. I am the Bard of Britain, I thought. What need have I of a sword?

Drawing out the staff, I lofted the rowan and raised it over the battlefield, in the age-old motion of a bard upholding his people in the fight. And as I did so, I heard the words of Taliesin from my vision: *you must go back the way you came.*

Understanding burst within me, dazzling like the fall of lightning from a clear sky. Gripping the staff with all my strength—as if the meaning of my vision might elude me once again if I let go—I sat upon my red horse in a wonder of illumination, my thoughts reeling. Yes! Yes! This . . . this is the way I must go. Not by the sword, but by the rowan!

I dismounted and carried the staff to the cliffside and there I knelt, clutching the rowan rod to me as if it were salvation itself. Gazing down upon the battle, my spirit writhed within me. I saw death as a gray vapor stealing over the plain, and a putrid, sickening smell rose up to sting my nostrils. The vapors mingled with the stench and spread out over the plain and beyond, to poison all Britain. It was the plague and war combined with the fear and ignorance of terrified men. It was the stink of corruption hovering over Britain.

And then, ringing high and strong, cutting like a sword-stroke through the tumult: the strident sharp blast of Rhys' battlehorn. Its ringing call sliced the air like a spearhead flung into the heart of the enemy. The horn sounded again—a piercing, insistent shriek, keen and angry.

Behind the ringing call came Arthur and the Dragon Flight, sweeping down the hillside and into the tumult. They appeared so suddenly, their flight so swift, the Black Boar had no time to order his forces to meet this new attack. The Vandal host, chagrined by this unexpected event, melted before Arthur's fresh onslaught.

The impetus of the attack carried the Dragon Flight deep

into the enemy host, scattering foemen in all directions. By the time the Black Boar had regained control of his warriors, Arthur had succeeded in breaking the line in several places. The Britons were not slow to seize their freedom. Within moments the essential shape of the battle was transformed and the enemy wall began to crumble in disarray.

Seeing their advantage dwindling before their eyes, the Vandali lashed themselves to a frenzy. Screaming, wailing, shaking with fury, they threw themselves against the mounted Cymbrogi. They fought with hopeless courage, hurling themselves into the breach, trying to halt the British with their own corpses.

Even Arthur could not stand against such desperate determination. Rather than risk becoming encircled again and hopelessly enmired in a fight he could not win, Arthur chose flight; he quit the field.

Thus, when the Vandal host rose once more to the counterattack, they found the Bear of Britain in full retreat. Many another battlechief, encouraged by the fleeting success of his unexpected appearance, would have misjudged the moment—thinking his surprise maneuver had won the day. Arthur knew better. So, before the enemy had a chance to rally, the Cymbrogi were already riding away.

The High King turned from uncertain victory, choosing instead the sure saving of his men, using the momentary advantage gained by surprise to secure a safe corridor for their escape. It was, as I say, a circumstance decreed by dire necessity. Oh, but it exacted a terrible price.

I stared down into the bloody glen, horrified. Where the fight had been most fierce, I could not see the ground for the dead; they lay atop one another, toppled and stacked like felled wood. Limbs were strewn here and there; entrails coiled like bright-colored snakes; heads also, salted among the bodies, gape-mouthed and empty-eyed. And the earth, Dear God in Heaven, the earth was stained deep, deep crimson-black with the gore.

The futility! The waste!

Sickened by the loathsome extravagance of death, I felt my stomach heave. I gagged, but could not keep it down. I vomited bile on the ground at my feet, then fell sobbing with the humiliation of having witnessed—nay, encouraged, aided, promoted!—such an evil. I wept, and cursed the blindness of my soul.

Great Light, how long must hate and bloodshed reign in this worlds-realm?

I closed my eyes and raised my voice in keening lament for the dead on both sides. When I finished, I saw that the last Briton had fled the field. The Vandali had withdrawn farther up the glen, and the battlefield lay very still and terribly silent.

The only movement was that of carrion crows, hopping obscenely from corpse to corpse; the only sound their rasping croak as they gathered to their grisly feast. I felt the stain of death in my soul and in my heart. Aching with shame and grief, my hands shaking, I remounted my horse and made my way back to camp.

6

 WARRIORS LAY ON THE GROUND where they had collapsed. Exhausted, too tired to move, they lay gasping, hardly more alive than the dead we left in the glen. Some men sat slumped over wounds, contemplating the extent of their injuries as if they revealed the source of the world's sorrow. Women and boys hurried among the scattered warriors with jars of water to help revive the beaten war host.

Dull eyes watched me pass with little recognition. I did not pause, but made my way to Arthur's tent. The Bear of Britain was holding council with his battlechiefs outside the tent.

"We have fared poorly today," Arthur announced. "It was only by God's grace that we escaped."

"It is true," Cador conceded. "The Vandali were ready for us today—"

"More than ready," observed Bedwyr sourly. "It was as if they knew each move we would make before we made it."

This brought a chorus of agreement from the gathered chieftains. "Aye," said Cai, speaking up, "the Boar is showing himself a fighter at last. The farther inland they run, the more fierce they become." He ended, shaking his head wearily. "I do not understand it."

"We are losing this war," I declared, taking my place before them. "And if we persist on this course, we *will* lose it, and all Britain as well."

Arthur drew a deep breath. "We are tired," he said, "and

349

we all have duties elsewhere. We will talk again when we have seen to our men and taken some rest." He dismissed them then and, as they departed, he said, "Attend me in my tent, Myrddin. We must speak."

As soon as we were alone, he turned on me. "I cannot believe you would speak like that in front of the men, Myrddin! Are you trying to discourage them?"

"I spoke the truth."

"You spoke of losing and defeat. I do not find that helpful—especially after such a battle as we fought today."

"It was not a battle," I replied. "It was a disaster."

"I was ambushed!" he declared. "The sneaking barbarian had a warband lying in wait in the gully. It was a trap! God love you, man, it was a trap. I was anticipated and taken by surprise. It was unfortunate—a disaster, yes. But I cannot see what good it does to wallow in it."

"I do not say this to grieve you, O king. I say this to open your eyes to the truth."

"But it *does* grieve me, Myrddin. I am aggrieved! You speak of disasters and loss—as if I did not already know it. Well I know it! I am the War Leader, I own the fault."

"No," I replied, "if fault is to be apportioned, I am mostly to blame. I have not served you as I should. I have failed you, Arthur."

"You?" he wondered, surprised by this unwarranted admission. "You have ever stood by me. You have been my wise counselor and my best advisor."

"You did not need another advisor," I told him flatly. "You needed a bard. Britain needed a True Bard—and was made to suffer a blind meddler instead. That is my fault and I own the blame."

Arthur drew his hand through his sweaty hair. "I do not understand you, Myrddin. I led good men into the most simple trap of all. I have chased Twrch Trwyth all summer, I should have known. I should have seen it straightaway. But why sit here moaning about the blame? Where is the virtue in that?"

"Great the virtue if it leads to salvation."

"Our salvation is as close as the next battle," Arthur contended. "The Black Boar's ambush held me too long from the fight, or you would have seen a different ending to this day's battle. I will not make the same mistake again, believe me. And now that the Irish lords are soon with us—"

"You have not heard a word that I have said," I snapped. "This is not about a single battle, or even a war. This is about the failure of a *vision*! Are we better men simply because we have better warriors, or better weapons?"

"With the Irish here," Arthur maintained, "we will yet drive the barbarian from this land."

"Hear me, O king: the realm is dying. Plague and war are bleeding us to death. If we persist, we will die."

"It is not so bad," Arthur said lamely.

"It is the ruin of the world!"

Arthur glared at me, sullen and annoyed. "We will yet drive the invader from this land. That is the truth, I say."

"And those dead on the battleground—what do they say?"

"Agh! There is no talking to you."

Arthur turned away and flung himself into Uther's camp chair. He put his head in his hands and rubbed his face. I moved to stand over him.

"We must change, or we will surely die. We must go back the way we came," I declared. "Think on that," I challenged. "Think long and hard, Arthur. For until you begin to understand what I am telling you, Britain is lost."

The tent felt suffocatingly close; I could not breathe. Leaving the High King to his thoughts, I went in search of a place where I could be alone. I moved through a camp sunk in the gloom of defeat: silent, unmoving, awaiting the night's shadows to cover and claim it.

Warriors, spent and forlorn, sat or lay before unlit fires, speaking in hushed tones if they spoke at all. Boys were leading horses to the pickets, and women were working to bind the wounds of the injured. A pall hung over the camp, a lethargy deeper than simple fatigue—as if all understood the futility of effort alone to win any lasting gain.

I saw men sleeping, and knew that some of these would not rise in the morning. Jesu, have mercy! I saw several of the lords, heads together, holding close council; they stopped talking as I approached, watching me darkly. I ignored them and moved on.

My feet found the path leading to the stream; moving among the slumbering bodies of those who had come to drink and dropped there, I descended the bank, crossed the water and continued on. The path began to climb, ascending the hillside, and I followed where it led—up through pungent bracken and prickly gorse. Eventually, I found myself in a grassy hollow scooped out of the hillside. Smooth, lichen-covered rock formed a wall at the rear, fringed by elderberry and blackthorn shrubs; beech trees stood on either side of the hollow, leaving the front open to a good view of the British camp below.

I sat down cross-legged on the soft turf between the two trees and watched twilight gradually enfold the glen in deep blue shadow. The sky held a pale lingering light for a long time, at last giving way before oncoming night. From my lofty perch I watched and listened, attending to the slow descent of the world into darkness.

My heart moved within me, for it seemed that as night stretched its dark hand over the glen, a weight of sorrow settled in my soul. Death had taken many good men this day, their sacrifice all but forgotten. As chief bard it was my duty to lead the people in laments of mourning for their fallen kinsmen. Yet here was I, sitting aloof from the concerns of my brothers. Once again, here was Myrddin, this day and always, a man apart, bearing all things, whether in triumph or tragedy, alone.

You must go back the way you came! Thus spoke the truth of my vision, and thus I did believe. But how? Alas, I had no idea how such a thing might be accomplished, nor where I might begin.

I sat looking out over the glen in the steadily deepening twilight. Lost in thought, I did not hear the footsteps approaching from behind. Then, hearing them, I turned, supposing Arthur had sent Rhys to find me . . . I turned and strange faces rushed at me out of the shadowed darkness. Before I could lift a hand, I was taken.

Four immense Vandali, armed with stout spears, surrounded me. I made no move to resist; that would, I was instantly persuaded, have been futile. So I simply remained seated and forced myself to appear calm and unafraid.

It was a small thing, but great events often swing on such modest hinges. The Vandali, confronted by an unarmed enemy who appeared neither frightened nor in the least disturbed, hesitated. This emboldened me. I regarded them impassively and raised my hands in welcome—as if I had been expecting them.

"I recognize you," I said, knowing full well they would not understand me. That was not important, however; I merely wanted to be the first to speak, thinking to keep them off their mettle. "Put up your weapons and let us speak together as reasonable men."

My ruse did not work. One of the Vandali raised his lance and made to strike. The narrow blade hovered, poised in the air, but the hand was stayed by a quick shout from the shadows. A voice barked a harsh order and the warrior froze.

I waited, my heart thumping violently in my chest. The spear still hesitated over me. I was less than a hair's breadth from death.

Then the voice spoke again. This time, to my complete surprise, it said, "Stand easy. You are in great danger."

With these words, a figure emerged from the gloom and came to stand before me. Though large and fully as powerful as those with him, he was younger than any of the others. I recognized him at once as one of the Black Boar's piglets: the young chieftain they called Mercia.

"I am well aware of my danger," I replied easily. "You need have no fear of me, Mercia. I am unarmed."

He started at my use of his name. "How do you know me?"

I remembered him as the one who had remarked on Arthur's

youth at that first meeting. "You speak forthrightly," I told him. "Hergest has taught you well."

He stared. "You know this, too?"

Well, it could be no other way. But I did not let on. Instead I touched my forehead meaningfully and said, "I am a bard; I know a great many things."

His eyes narrowed shrewdly. "Then tell me why I have come here."

Without hesitation, I said, "You have come to spy upon the British camp as you have done many nights before. Amilcar depends on the information you bring to order the battle. This is how Amilcar was able to defeat Arthur today."

His eyes grew wide. "Hergest said you were a mighty man of wisdom. The priest ever speaks true—even to his hurt." Clearly, this high regard for truth impressed him.

"Will you sit with me, Mercia?" I said, indicating a place on the ground beside me. "There is something I would tell you."

"You have been waiting for me?"

I let him think this. "Sit. Let us talk." I had no idea what I would say to him. My only plan was to win his confidence and find some way to persuade him to let me go. Even so, as he stood over me, quivering with indecision, a plan formed in my mind.

"Please," I said, smiling in what I hoped was a confident and persuasive manner, "we have little time. They will come looking for me soon."

Signaling to his men, he growled a quick command; they raised their spears and backed away. Mercia sat down on the ground opposite, cross-legged, lance in his lap. We regarded one another in the fading light. "What have you to say?" he asked at last.

"It is in my mind that Amilcar does not hold the trust of all his battlechiefs," I said slowly, watching him to make certain that he followed my meaning. It was a crude but effective guess; I have never known a war leader yet who enjoyed the entire and utter confidence of all his lords. God knows, even Arthur, fighting for Britain's survival, battled his own lords.

He studied me a long time, as if making up his mind. Finally he said, "It is true, there have been many disputes since coming here." He paused. I nodded, understanding only too well—drawing the young man further into his confession. He obliged me by continuing with quiet defiance, "Our renowned War Leader holds not the favor of all."

"I believe your War Leader often goes against those who counsel wisdom—" I suggested, watching Mercia's face for nuances of expression to guide me. I saw what I expected to see and thrust home, saying, "All the more when those chieftains are held in low esteem because of their youth."

The young battlechief's eyes flashed quick fire, and I knew I had struck the raw wound of his complaint. "He is a most stubborn lord," Mercia allowed cautiously. "Once he has set his hand to a thing, he will never yield—though it were wiser by far to do so."

His use of the words "by far" expressed worlds of meaning to me. And I began to discern the slenderest golden glimmer of hope.

"Listen to me, Mercia," I said. "You are closer to your desire than you know. Trust and believe."

He regarded me suspiciously, and I feared I had pressed him too far. Mercia threw a quick sideways glance at his men, who were watching us closely. He uttered a low, growling command, but they made no move or response.

Turning back to me he said, "Do you know my thought, truly?"

"It is as I have told you," I replied. "I know a great many things."

"I will never betray my lord," he said, and I sensed the shape of his fear.

"I seek an honorable settlement," I assured him. "Treachery will have no part in it, neither betrayal." I held him with the uncompromising certainty of my voice. "But I demand honor for honor; loyalty must be repaid with loyalty. Do you understand?"

He nodded. There was nothing sly about his acceptance but I wanted assurance.

"Hear me, Mercia, the honor I demand is costly indeed. I will be bought with blood."

"I understand," he muttered impatiently. He glanced sideways again, then said, "What must I do?"

"Only this," I spoke in an ominous tone, raising my hand in the gesture of command, "when the time comes to add your voice to the support of peace you must not be silent."

He did not expect that. I could see him struggling to find a hidden meaning in my words. "Is there nothing else?"

"That is enough. Truly, it is more than many brave men will dare."

He drew himself up. "My courage has never been doubted."

"I believe you."

"When will this take place?"

"Soon."

He rose abruptly, and stood over me, at once menacing and wary. "I could kill you now and no one would know."

"Yes. That is true."

"You said I must trust you, yet you offer no token of trust." His hand tightened on his spear.

"Then accept this as a sign," I replied, rising slowly to my feet to face him. "There will be no attack against you tomorrow. The British will remain in camp, nursing their wounds. Tell this to Amilcar."

He turned on his heel and, snapping a quick order to his men, disappeared into the shadows. The men stood watching me, and I feared Mercia had indeed ordered my death. I remained motionless—resistance was impossible, and flight would do no good. The spears swung up with a decisive motion. With an effort I held myself steady.

Within the space of three heartbeats, the warriors were gone, melting quietly back into the darkness.

I listened for them, but heard only the faint murmur of

voices rising from the camp below. I turned to see the camp-fires shining bright as earthbound stars, and sweet relief gave way to sudden apprehension.

Great Light, what have I done?

7

 I MAINTAINED MY VIGIL THROUGH the night, heart and mind clutching tight to the slender hope that had been granted me: the saving of Brit- ain and the Kingdom of Summer. Since even the most com- pelling dreams can dissipate into the empty air when touched by the sun's hard light, I waited for what the day would bring—hope refreshed, or despair confirmed.

Certainty of purpose came with the dawn. Up I rose, thank- ing the High King of Heaven and all his saints and angels for the weapon delivered into my hand. As the sun rose blood- red over the eastern ridge, I returned to camp to find the war host already stirring, readying themselves for the day's battle.

I went directly to Arthur's tent and he admitted me, yawn- ing and scratching himself. Following him into the tent, I could not help noticing that Gwenhwyvar was nowhere in sight. "She prefers to bathe early," Arthur said.

"I would speak to you alone first," I replied, and told him about my chance encounter with Mercia, and what the young battlechief had told me of dissention among the Vandali. The king sat in his chair before me, shaking his head. "Do you understand what I am telling you?"

Arthur frowned. No, he did not understand at all. "Why must we stay in camp?"

"Because," I explained, "I promised it to Mercia. I gave this in pledge for my life."

Before Arthur could make further objection, Bedwyr came

o the tent and called for the king. "I am here, brother," Arthur
answered. "I will join you in a moment."

"Well?" I demanded. "What is it to be?"

Arthur hesitated; he frowned at me and rubbed his hands
over his face. "Oh, very well," he said at last. "I will not make
a liar of you. There are many among us who would welcome
a day's rest in any event."

We stepped from the tent to greet Bedwyr. "The war host
is ready," he said. "The chieftains await your command."

"There will be no battle today," Arthur told him bluntly.

Bedwyr glanced at me in surprise. "Why, Bear? What has
happened?"

"I have changed my mind. I have decided to give the men
a day's rest."

"But everyone is ready! We have full assembly of the greatest
warband since—"

"Tell them, Bedwyr. Tell them all we will not fight today."

"I will tell them," he growled. Turning on his heel, he
hastened away.

No sooner had Bedwyr departed than we heard shouts from
the far perimeter of the camp where a commotion had broken
out. "Now what?" Arthur muttered, glaring at me as if it were
my doing. Bedwyr, hearing the uproar, came running back to
the king.

Rhys appeared on the run. "Vandali!" he shouted.

"So much for your day of rest, Bear," Bedwyr grumbled.
"Will you give the order?"

"Wait!" I said. "Not yet."

Rhys ran to where we stood. "Vandali," he said breathlessly.
"Five of them. They advance with willow branches. The slave
is with them. I think they want to parlay."

Bedwyr and Rhys looked to Arthur, waiting what he would
say. Arthur looked to me. "I know nothing of this," I told
him.

"Very well," said Arthur, "let them come to me and we
will hear what they have to say."

We waited before the tent while Rhys conducted the enemy envoy to us. As he said, there were five: the four warlords we had met before, including Mercia, and the captured priest, Hergest. All the British lords came running to see what was to take place, so the emissaries arrived amidst a great crowd of onlookers. Gwenhwyvar, Cai, and Cador pushed through to stand beside Arthur and me.

"Greetings, Lord Arthur," Hergest began. "We beg pardon to speak with you and to return to our camp unharmed."

"Speak freely, priest," Arthur said. "I give you my word that no hurt shall come to you while you are under my protection. Why have you come?"

Before the priest could reply, one of the barbarian chieftains—the one called Ida, I think—pointed to all the men pressing close, and uttered a long complaint in their rough tongue. "He says that your word is worthless," Hergest informed us. "Merlin vowed you would not ride today and yet we see that you ready yourselves for battle."

Bedwyr threw me a questioning glance, which I ignored. Arthur replied, "I was not informed of Myrddin's pledge until a moment ago, and have only just given the order to stand down. Even so, we are ready to fight if pressed to it."

While the slave repeated Arthur's words, I sought Mercia's eye. He saw me watching him and, with a slight but deliberate downward jerk of his chin, gave me to know that he accepted this explanation.

"We, too, are ready to fight," Hergest said, resuming his communication. "However, it is in Amilcar's mind that the War Leader Arthur has remained shielded behind his warriors long enough. The Black Boar's is minded that the two kings meet and prove before both nations which of them is the greater battlechief."

"Indeed," remarked Arthur. "And does Amilcar say how he proposes to make this proof?"

The slave relayed Arthur's reply to Ida, who responded with a sneer and another long utterance. "Ida says that Amilcar will meet Arthur alone on the plain beside the river which lies between our two camps, bringing whatever weapons the British warrior favors. When the sun passes midday, the two will fight. The combat will continue until one or the other is killed." Hergest paused, and Ida spoke again. "Amilcar makes this challenge, though he does not expect Arthur to accept it," the slave added.

"Tell Amilcar that I will consider his challenge," Arthur replied evenly. "I will bring my answer to the plain at midday."

Hergest repeated Arthur's words, whereupon the enemy battlechiefs, satisfied that they had delivered their message, turned to go. "Owain! Vrandub!" Arthur called, choosing two from among the assembled noblemen. "See that they leave the camp the way they came, unmolested." To the others he said, "Go back to your men and explain the challenge. We will assemble at midday and ride to the plain."

As the lords hurried away, Arthur bade his advisors attend him in the council tent. Gwenhwyvar, Cai, Bedwyr, Cador, Llenlleawg and I joined the High King to decide what to do.

"It is a very good sign," Bedwyr said as we seated ourselves at the board. "It means the Black Boar knows we have increased the strength of the war host, and he is afraid."

"What of this pledge not to fight today?" asked Gwenhwyvar sharply; the question was for me.

I quickly explained how I had been surprised and taken by Mercia. Cador professed himself amazed by this and said, "He let you go if you promised not to fight today?"

"No," I said, "it was not like that. We talked first. He gave me to know that there is dissension in the Vandali camp. Amilcar has lost the confidence of some of his lords, and—"

"See!" cried Bedwyr. "I am right! The Black Boar is running scared. The Vandali cannot withstand the might of Britain any longer."

"Single combat is the only fight he can win," Cai put in. "Attack with all our might, I say. This is the chance we have been waiting for."

"Perhaps," replied Arthur, "it is a chance to end the war without further bloodshed."

"Perhaps it is a trap!" pointed out Gwenhwyvar sharply.

"The barbarians cannot be trusted," said Cador quickly. "Even if Amilcar was defeated, what makes you think they would honor any vow of peace they made?"

It was a good question—one that would be uppermost in every British warrior's mind. I was ready with the answer. "It makes no difference," I answered.

Their silence contradicted me. "Truly, it makes no difference," I persisted, "for without Amilcar, the war will simply collapse. Can you not see that now?" The disbelieving stares of Cador and the others told me that they could not.

"See here!" I said. "Whether it is a trap"—I inclined my head towards Gwenhwyvar as I said this—"or whether Amilcar proves false, or anything else—makes not the slightest difference to us. For the selfsame moment he dies on the battlefield before his watching host, the invasion ceases and the war ends."

"How do you know this?" demanded Cador.

"Mercia told me," I answered.

"And you believed him?"

"I did indeed," I replied. "He held my life in his hands. Let there be no doubt: a word from him and my death was assured. But he let me live that I might know he spoke the truth."

"He is a barbarian!" Cador charged. "He would tell you anything to make you believe this lie. But I am not so easily persuaded."

"It may be a lie," I answered, "or it may not. I say we put it to the test and find out. If I am right, the war will end."

"But what if you are wrong?" Cai asked. "What then, eh?"

"Then the war will continue," I replied solemnly, "and Britain will become the grave of champions."

They grew silent, thinking this over. Before they could renew their objections, Rhys ducked into the tent just then to say that the priest Paulinus had returned to camp. "Let him come in," Arthur said.

The monk, gaunt and frayed about the edges like a bone gnawed to gristle, entered and all but collapsed at Arthur's feet.

Without a thought, the king raised him and sat him in his chair. "A drink, Rhys," called Arthur. "Hurry!"

"Forgive me, lord," Paulinus said. He saw the others looking on and struggled to his feet.

Arthur pressed him back into the chair with his hand. "Sit, man. Rest yourself. You have ridden hard, as we can see. Gather your strength and tell us what word you have brought."

Rhys appeared with a cup and pressed it into the monk's hands. Paulinus drank thirstily and dried his mouth with his sleeve. "I wish I had a better word, lord," the monk said.

"How bad is it?" asked Gwenhwyvar, stepping close.

"It is not good," Paulinus replied. "The fever spreads despite our best efforts. The roads from Londinium are secured, but people still persist in traveling on the river; it seems we can do nothing to stop them. Thus, the plague follows the waterways." He paused, gulped from the cup, and concluded, "We have succeeded in rescuing a few settlements where the disease has not yet gained a foothold, but much of the land south of Londinium has succumbed."

Paulinus drank again, and returned the cup to Rhys. "Three of our own have taken ill, and one has died. Nor do I expect the others to live."

Arthur stood over the priest, hands at his sides, fists balled, but there was nothing to strike. Paulinus, seeing his king's frustration, rose slowly. "I am sorry, lord. I wish I had better tidings. I had hoped—we had all hoped . . . "

"You are doing all you can, we know," Gwenhwyvar said. "Go now, we will speak again when you are rested."

Beckoning his steward, Arthur said, "Rhys, see that our friend has something to eat and a place to lay his head." Paulinus took his leave and, when he had gone, Arthur turned to the others. "I cannot stop the plague," he said softly. "But if I can end the war with the Black Boar, I deem it a risk worth taking. I will fight Amilcar."

A little while before midday, the Lords of Britain and their battlechiefs were assembled once more and brought to stand before the High King's tent. Arthur acknowledged them one by one and lauded their loyalty. Then he said, "Sword brothers all, you have heard the Black Boar's challenge. I have given the matter careful thought, and I have decided that if there is a chance to end the war by defeating Amilcar in single combat, then I must take that chance. Therefore, I will accept the barbarian's challenge and meet him on the plain."

The decision provoked a general uproar.

"Is this wise, Arthur?" wondered Ector aloud. "Certainly, we all stand ready to ride beside you." A score of voices added their agreement.

"Of that I have no doubt," Arthur replied, holding up his hands for silence. "Indeed, many good men have stood beside me already, and, alas! too many have died. Truly, if not for the loyalty of all noble Britons, we could not have driven the enemy to this desperate cast. I am persuaded that the will to continue this war rests with Amilcar. Thus, when he is dead, the war will end."

"But what if you are killed instead?" shouted Cunomor, his voice rising above the din. "What then?"

"If I am killed," Arthur replied, "it will be left to those who remain to carry on however they choose. The death of one man matters little, weighed against the death and destruction which has gone before and all that will certainly follow."

"We came to fight for you!" shouted Meurig, "not to stand by and watch you fight alone."

Ogryvan added, "We fight for Arthur! He does not fight for us!"

This produced a clamor which continued for some time. When it began to die away another cried out. "Lord Arthur!" The voice was strange to many ears. The British lords turned as Aedd stepped forward. "The man who wins this fight will gain everlasting glory and his name will be sung in the halls of kings for ever. Therefore, though I am least among your lords, I beg the boon of serving you. Let me face this barbarian Amilcar in your place. Great King, let me be your champion in this fight."

Aedd, God bless him, was in earnest; he would readily trade life for life with Arthur, but the High King could not allow it. "I thank you, Lord Aedd," he said, "and I will not forget your offer. But it seems that Amilcar believes me a tyrant like himself—in that if I am defeated, Britain's defense will crumble away. We must encourage him in this belief. My life must be the prize."

The petty kings were not at all happy with this decision. But though many argued against it, none could suggest a better plan. Thus Arthur won his way at length.

"So! It is settled," the High King concluded. "Gather your warbands. We will meet Amilcar now."

8

 I HAVE THOUGHT MANY TIMES what I could have done—perhaps should have done?—differently in those fearful days. Yet events swiftly outstripped my small ability to guide them. As is ever the way of things, those circumstances we would most gladly shape ever remain beyond our grasp, while we are made to bear unexpected burdens to unsuspected destinations. All stand helpless before a power too potent to contain, too immense to comprehend. So be it!

Thus I, who would have formed the days to my design, was made to stand with all the rest of the British war host ranged in ranks upon the plain, looking on in apprehension.

I see it now as then, always before me, the same stark image: Arthur standing alone under a blistering sun with neither shield nor helm, only Caledvwlch at his side. The sky is leached white with the searing heat; the grass is brittle underfoot and brown.

Arthur stands waiting, his shadow shriveled small beneath him, as if it dare not stretch its full length in such heat. Across the plain the Vandal host appears—warriors, women, children. All advance slowly to the place of meeting: the broad plain of Lyit Coed, where the rivers Tamu and Ancer come together. A fortress once stood nearby, but the Vandali have burned it and the settlements round about have been destroyed, the people killed or forced to run.

I watch the enemy host advance, a crabbed and clotted line of black, the dust from their feet rising up in thick white columns behind them. They move slowly and we wait. We might still attack them, or they might attack us. There is nothing to prevent it, save Britain's High King standing alone on the cracked and burning plain, waiting in all good faith for the Black Boar of the Vandali to honor his word and meet him face-to-face.

There is but one question in the mind of every man looking on: Will the hosts fight, or will Amilcar treat with Arthur as he has promised?

The advance halts abruptly and dull silence descends over the heat-oppressed plain. Then the thunder begins. The plain echoes to the rumbling roar of the Vandali war drums, and for one terrible moment I think they will attack.

"Steady!" Bedwyr calls out, and his words are repeated down the line. "Stand your ground, men."

The drums are meant to frighten, to unnerve us. But Arthur stands, and so we stand—grim-faced, sweating, our stomachs knotted in anticipation and dread as the drums boom in our ears. The sound, once heard, is not easily forgotten. I hear it now.

When the invader had drawn up in striking distance of us, the beat of the drums abruptly ceased and the long triple line halted. The Vandali stood staring at us in a silence as terrible as the bone-rattling thunder of their drums. They remained motionless, not a muscle twitching, weapons gleaming dully, rank on rank, their grotesque boar's head standards rising above them, confronting us with the dread spectacle of their military might.

Arthur stood easy, patient, regarding the fearsome battle host with an unflinching gaze. After a time, one of the standard-bearers moved from his place in the forerank, advanced a few places and stopped. He was joined by a group of Vandali chieftains, Mercia and the slave Hergest foremost among them. Then, all together, they moved out to meet Britain's High King in the center of the plain. After a few brief words—spoken in voices too low to hear—the standard-bearer returned to his place in the line.

"I cannot endure this," muttered Gwenhwyvar crossly. "I will stand with him."

Bedwyr made bold to stay her, but she shook off his hand, slipped from the saddle, and stepped quickly out from the rank to reach Arthur's side before anyone could prevent her. The king welcomed her with a curt nod and the two stood side-by-side as the black boar's head on its skull-and-scalp-bedecked pole proceeded once more. This time it heralded the arrival of Amilcar himself.

The two lords eyed one another across a gap of but three paces. I saw Arthur's hand rise in the sign of peace. Amilcar made no gesture. Arthur said something, to which the Black Boar replied through Hergest. When the priest stopped speaking, Arthur turned to Gwenhwyvar, who made a reply while staring straight ahead at Amilcar.

As her words were repeated by Hergest, I saw the Black Boar's lip curl in a savage sneer. He growled a reply of low disdain, threw his head back haughtily and spat. Perhaps this is what she intended, for in the blink of an eye her slender sword was in her hand and she lunged at the Vandal king. She was quick—quicker than Arthur's restraining hand—and Amilcar was saved a grave, if not fatal, stroke only by the swift reaction of one of his chieftains, who knocked the sword aside with the shaft of his spear as the blade sliced the air a whisker's breadth from Amilcar's throat.

Amilcar recoiled, raising his spear in the same motion. Arthur shouted, seized Gwenhwyvar's arm and pulled her bodily away from her attack. The Black Boar, still wielding his spear, made a short, angry speech, to which Arthur made a solemn reply.

In all, the exchange was brief. A few more words passed between them, and then Arthur and Gwenhwyvar turned abruptly and walked back to the British line.

"We meet tomorrow at dawn," said Arthur, with never a word of what had passed on the plain.

So began the long wait, and the British host bore the waiting hard. The warriors rested through the heat of the day while the sun made slow, slow sailing into the west, but as the white-hot disk disappeared behind the hills they began to stir and to talk, and to worry.

It was, I thought, time to remind them of the prize awaiting us, and the lord who held our trust. After a brief word with Arthur, the battlechiefs were summoned and instructed to assemble the men on the hillside above the council tent.

With the gathered host of Britain ranged before me as pale twilight crept over the vale, I advanced to my place. The stifling heat had begun to loose its grip on the land, and a light breeze stirred the wispy grass. A great beacon of a fire had been lit, a Beltane blaze to rekindle the past in their memories. A rising moon cast hard shadows on the ground and the sky above gleamed with stars from one horizon to the other.

The crowd surged; restless, anxious, wary, the warrior throngs waited, the very air tense with their uncertainty and apprehension. All knew of Arthur's ordeal and it troubled them. What if Arthur was killed? they thought. Who would lead them against the Vandali then? Thousands owed their lives to Arthur's skill as a War Leader; how would they fare without him? They watched me suspiciously; I could almost hear their muttered whispers: A song? Far better to sharpen blades this night.

I shouldered the harp, plucking notes at random and flinging them out as pebbles pitched into a seething sea. At first no one heard me—but I kept playing—and then they did not *want* to hear me. They kept murmuring, but their eyes strayed time and again to where I stood strumming the harp as if oblivious to their muttering.

Then, as the harpsong struck the fear-fretted air my vision ignited within me once more and glowed with the intensity of the sun itself. I saw again the half-burning, half-living tree and my spirit soared with the meaning of the riddle. For the first time in a very long while I felt like a bard again.

Giving the harp its voice, I played through their apprehension and unease until all eyes were on me, and I occupied every thought. Gradually, the music took hold as little by little the murmuring ceased. When all was quiet on the hillside, I called out in a loud voice, "Hear me! I am a bard and the son of a bard; my true home is the Region of the Summer Stars.

"From the earliest days of our race, the Guardians of the Spirit taught that wisdom resides in the heart of oak." I raised my harp above my head and held it high for all to see. "I hold in my hands this heart of oak. By virtue of his craft, the bard releases the soul of wisdom to work its will in the world of men.

"Hear, then, and heed all I shall tell you—that you may remember all that you are and may become!"

So saying, I cradled the harp and began to play again. Like a weaver spinning threads of silver and gold, my fingers worked the intricately patterned melody, establishing a gleaming ground for the words I would recite. I played, gazing out upon the faces of all those people—men from every part of Britain, from Prydein, Celyddon and Lloegres, and from Ierne also. They seemed to me hollow people, gaunt-eyed and empty; like their lords, they were starving for the True Word. I realized this and my heart went out to them.

Great Light, I stand humble before your loving power. Move in me, my lord, that I may move the hearts of men!

In the same instant, I felt the upwelling of the *awen*—like a long-captive bird released to the sky. The melody came first, trailing words in its glittering wake, taking shape as it touched my tongue. I gave myself up to the song; there was no longer Myrddin: only the song existed and I was but a vessel, hollow, empty of myself, but filled with the exquisite wine of the *Oran Mor*.

I sang and the Great Music poured forth unstinting in its blessing. A new song took life that night, and men were amazed to hear it. This is what I sang:

"In the Elder Age, when the dew of creation was still fresh on the ground, there arose a mighty king and Manawyddan was his name. All the world was his realm, and every tribe and clan owed him tribute. Everything he put his hand to prospered; and wherever he looked, something good and worthy favored his gaze.

"One day, evil tidings reached Lord Manawyddan and caused him sore distress. The Otherworld, it was said, had fallen beneath the shadow of a usurper who treated the people most cruelly. The Great King decided then and there to give the sovereignty of his realm to the best man he could find so that he might go and free the Otherworld Folk from the sly oppressor. And this is the way of it:

"The Great King summoned his noblemen to attend him and laid the matter before them. 'I am going away for a time,' Manawyddan told them. 'Whether short or long, I do not know, but I shall not return until I have vanquished the Usurper, who even now plunders the Otherworld and lays waste to that fairest of realms.'

"His lords and noblemen answered him. 'Full sorrowful we are to hear your purpose,' they confessed. 'It may be well for the folk of the Otherworld, but it is nothing less than a calamity for us.'

"To this the king replied: 'Nevertheless, this is what I have decided. I will place the kingship in the hands of the man I shall choose, and he shall serve in my place until I return.' And he began to assay among them who was worthy to take up the sovereignty. No easy decision that, for each man among them was as worthy as the next, and no less worthy than his brother.

"In the end, however, he devised a means to put the issue to the test. He caused his Chief Bard to make an ornament of gold shaped like a ball. And then Manawyddan brought forth this ball and held it before his lords. 'This has been made for me,' he told them. 'What think you of it?'

"And they answered, 'It is very beautiful, lord.'

"The king agreed. 'It is beautiful indeed. And more beautiful than you know, for it is the symbol of my reign.' He lifted the golden sphere before them. 'Here!' he called. 'Take it!'

"With that, the Great King threw the golden ball to his lords. The first one reached out and caught it, easily clasping it to his chest. The king said, 'Thank you, noble friend. You may go.'

"The lord turned to go, but the king prevented him until the golden ornament was retrieved. No sooner had the ball been returned to him, however, than he threw it again to another, who caught it in his fist. 'Thank you, noble friend. You may go,' the Great King told him.

"The chieftain turned to go, but the king prevented him until his precious sphere should be returned. And this is how it was with each man in turn. Each time the king threw the golden ball, it was caught and returned to him—until he threw it to Lludd.

"Up the ball flew and down it came. But the nobleman could not bring himself to grasp it. Seeing the priceless ornament fall from his open hand, Lludd sank to his knees. 'Forgive me, my king,' he cried. 'I am not worthy to touch such a valuable object.'

"But the king raised him up. 'Not so, Lludd,' he told him. 'You alone are worthy to hold my kingship until I return.' So saying, the Great King took up the ball and placed it firmly in Lludd's hand and charged him thus: 'Such authority as I enjoy, I give also to you. Hold it until I come again to my kingdom.'

"No one saw King Manawyddan after that, though they often heard tidings of his marvelous deeds in the Otherworldly realms. Lludd, meanwhile, ruled well and wisely. And the realms under his care flourished and grew great. So that none would lack the benefit of his wisdom, Lludd established lords in each realm to serve him and bring before him the needs of the people there.

"One of these lords was a brother named Mab Rígh, who watched over his island realm with dedication and devotion. Day or night, whatever trouble the people brought to him, that was all his care.

"Now, it happened that the realm of Mab Rígh was attacked by a strange and formidable enemy in the form of three plagues—each more peculiar than the one before.

"The first plague was the arrival of an enemy host called

Coranyid, whose knowledge was derived from the fact that they could hear any word spoken anywhere. No matter how hushed the speech, the wind carried the words to them. Thus, no one could say anything against them, and it was impossible to move against them for they always learned the plan and evaded it. The Coranyid laid waste to everything; nothing remained where they passed.

"The second plague was a terrible cry that arose at Beltain on every hilltop, over every hearth, and under every roof in the realm. This cry was of such tormented misery that it pierced the hearts of all who heard it, and there was no living thing anywhere that did not hear it. Men lost their strength, and women their vigor; children swooned, and animals lost their senses. If any female creature was pregnant, a miscarriage resulted. Trees and fields became barren; the water sickened and soured.

"The third plague was the inexplicable theft of food from the houses of chieftains and nobles. No matter how much food was prepared, none remained the next morning: if meat, not so much as a greasy bone was left; if bread, not so much as a grainy crumb; if stew, not so much as a drop of broth. Though they prepared enough food to last a year, by dawn the board was bare.

"These plagues so distressed the people that they raised a piteous lament. Mab Rígh was moved to gather all the tribes together to determine what should be done. Everyone was baffled by the plagues; no one knew what had brought them about, nor could anyone say how the island could be rid of them. Three days and nights they bethought themselves what they might do, and in the end Mab Rígh summoned his chieftains and, placing the care of the people in their hands, left his island realm to seek the counsel of his wise brother lord.

"A ship was fitted out in secret, and sail was raised in the dark of night so that none should learn of Mab Rígh's errand. The ship soared like a gull across the waves, and Lludd, looking out across the sea one day, saw his brother's sails coming towards him. He commanded a boat to be readied, and he set off at once to meet him. Lludd received Mab Rígh gladly, embraced him warmly, and gave him gifts of welcome.

"Yet, despite his good greeting, Mab Rígh's smile soon faded, and his brow assumed its furrow of worry. 'What has happened to produce this face of woe?' asked Lludd when they had returned to his handsome hall.

"Mab Rígh replied, 'Woe heaped on woe, and misery on misery.' He shook his head sorrowfully. 'You know I am not a melancholy man by nature.'

"Lludd agreed wholeheartedly, 'It is true. But tell me please, if you can bear it. I would hear what has brought you to this lowly state.'

" 'Most mournful of men am I, brother,' Mab Rígh answered. 'My island is beset by three plagues, each one worse than the other. In short, we are harried, aggrieved, and tormented at every turn. I have come to you for help and advice, for I am stretched full length wondering what to do.'

" 'You have done well coming to me,' Lludd told him. 'Together we will discover the cure for the ills which have befallen you. Speak, brother, and let the healing begin.'

"Mab Rígh took heart at these kindly words and roused his courage. 'I will speak,' he said, 'but first we must devise a means of guarding our words." And he explained about the plague of Coranyid, and how any word spoken would reach them on the wind.

"Lludd smiled and answered him, 'Not difficult, that.' And he ordered his smith to make a silver horn of his devising, and they spoke to one another through it. The wind could not carry the words to the evil Coranyid, but the silver horn produced an adverse result: whatever good word was spoken into one end came out the other as hateful and contrary.

"This perplexed Lludd greatly, until he discerned that a demon had established itself inside the horn, and this wicked demon was twisting all their words in order to sow discord between them. 'You see how it is,' Lludd declared. 'This is the very tribulation you face. But fret not. I know full well how to help you.'

"Priests had come from a far country and the king sent to them for wine, and when it was brought to him, he poured the wine into the silver horn. The power of the wine drove the demon out straightaway. Thereafter, Lludd and Mab Rígh were able to speak without hindrance. And Mab Rígh told his brother all about the three devastating plagues, and Lludd listened, his countenance grave and solemn.

"When Mab Rígh finished, Lludd took himself away for three days and nights to think within himself what should be done. He called his priests and wise bards to him and held council with such learned men as were close to hand. After three days, he returned to his hall and summoned his brother to attend him.

"Lludd hailed his brother, saying, 'Rejoice, brother! Your troubles are soon ended.'

"Mab Rígh asked, 'Have you succeeded where others have failed?'

" 'That I have,' Lludd answered. 'Here is the remedy for your woes.' So saying, he brought forth a bag of grain.

"Mab Rígh looked at the bag and happiness died in his breast. 'Forgive me for doubting, brother,' he said glumly, 'but I seem to see a grain bag in your hand. If grain alone could avail, I need never have troubled you.'

"Lludd smiled the wider. 'Oh, that merely shows how far from the true path you have strayed. For this is no ordinary grain. Indeed, not! It is a wondrously potent grain whose properties avail against every ill. Now listen carefully. Here is what you must do.' And he began to instruct him in how best to rid his island of the three devastating plagues.

"Holding up his finger, Lludd said, 'The plague of Coranyid, distressing and dangerous though it be, is most easily remedied. Take a third portion of the grain and immerse it in clean vats filled with water drawn from a clear-running spring; cover the vats and let them stand for three days and three nights. Meanwhile, send word throughout your realm that you have discovered a drink more wholesome than fine ale, and more life-giving than water. Invite your people to attend you to sample this wonderful drink. Naturally, the Coranyid will swarm and swell your ranks. You have only to take the grain-infused water and sprinkle it over their heads and the cure is assured. Your own people will live, but the evil Coranyid will die.'

"Lludd's words restored Mab Rígh's confidence. His heart swelled with joy to hear how his people could be delivered. However, Lludd's next words cast him into despair once more. 'Curing the second plague,' the king told him, 'will be as difficult as the cure of the first was easy. I perceive that the terrible cry which desolates the land is caused by a wicked serpent who crawls from his den on the eve of each Beltain searching for food. So great is his hunger that he screams aloud, and this is the cry you hear.'

"Mab Rígh shook his head in dismay. 'How can we rid ourselves of such a creature?'

"Lludd answered, 'What is impossible for ordinary men to destroy, is possible with this wondrous grain. Here is what you must do: measure the length and breadth of the island and quarter it to find the exact center. Where the center is found, dig a deep pit and cover it with a strong cloth made of virgin wool. Then, take a third portion of the grain and place it in a vat and fill the vat with the blood of nine lambs. Place this vat in the center of the cloth. When the snake comes searching for something to devour, he will smell the blood of the lambs and slither onto the cloth to get at the vat. The weight of the snake will cause the cloth to sink into the pit. Then you must quickly seize the corners of the cloth and tie them tightly together. Pull up the cloth and cast it into the sea, snake and all.'

"Mab Rígh was overjoyed. He clapped his hands and acclaimed Lludd's wisdom loudly. But his lord's next words cast him into a despair so black that it seemed as if he had never known happiness for so much as a day in his life. 'The third plague is the most difficult of all,' he said. 'And if it were not for the power of this grain, there would be no hope for you.'

" 'Woe! And woe again,' cried Mab Ráigh. 'I feared this all along!'

"Lludd took his brother by the shoulders and spoke to him sternly. 'Have you not heard a word I have said? The grain I give you is cure for any ill that should befall you. But listen carefully. The third plague is caused by a mighty giant who has come to your realm and taken shelter there. This giant is cunning as a sorcerer, and when you prepare a feast his spells and enchantments cause everyone to fall asleep. While the realm sleeps, the giant comes and steals away the feast. Therefore, you must stand watch for your people if you hope to catch this giant. Keep a vat of cold water nearby; when you feel sleepy, step into the water and revive yourself. Yet that is only the beginning; there is more.' And he told his brother what else he must do to rid the island of the wicked giant.

"When he had finished, Mab Rígh bade his brother farewell, took up the bag of grain and sailed back to his realm as fast as sails and sea would allow. When he reached home, he sprang ashore and went straight to his hall and prepared the libation exactly as he had been instructed, measuring out the grain and water into clean vessels. He then called his people together to try the wondrous drink, and of course the evil Coranyid heard about it and swarmed the gathering, intending harm.

"Seeing all assembled, Mab Rígh plunged a bowl into the water and dashed it over the unsuspecting crowd. The people stared at one another, dripping, and the Coranyid howled with anger. Ignoring the outcry, Mab Rígh quickly filled his bowl again and flung the contents over the gathering. The people laughed, and the demons screamed, assuming their normal grotesque shapes. They pleaded with Mab Rígh to abandon his plan, but the lord turned a deaf ear to their cries and, filling his bowl once more, sprinkled the contents over the crowd.

"The vile Coranyid shriveled and died, releasing the people at once. And everyone acclaimed the king and his wisdom, and celebrated the virtue of the healing water. Wasting not a moment, Mab Rígh set about measuring the length and breadth of the island. When he had done this, he quartered the land and thus divined the center. He ordered a deep pit to be dug at the center; and he ordered a great cloth to be made from the first shearing of all the lambs in the island.

"The cloth of undyed lambs' wool was brought to the place and spread over the huge pit. A third portion of the grain was put into a vat with the blood of nine lambs, and that vat set in the center of the cloth. It happened that the next night was the eve of Beltain, and the serpent emerged from its underground den and quickly scented the blood of the lambs. The wicked beast, drawn to the vat, slithered onto the cloth and coiled itself around the vat, preparing to feast. But before it could so much as dip its tongue into the vat, the cloth sank into the pit.

"Mab Rígh, who had been hiding nearby, ran out and grabbed the loose ends of the cloth before they fell, tied them together and bound the knot with strong ropes. He and his men pulled the bundle from the pit and dragged it to a high promontory, the snake screaming all the while. They hauled the bundle to the cliffs and cast it into the sea. The snake thrashed and screamed and thrashed as it went down. This ended the terrible scream and it was never heard in the realm again.

"And the people, who had gathered along the clifftop, sang a song of liberation as the snake sank out of sight. They lifted Mab Rígh onto their shoulders and carried him back to his hall to celebrate his victory. They prepared a great and wonderful feast, using the last portion of the grain which they made into dough and baked. The dough produced enough bread to feed the whole of the realm for thirty-three days.

"When the feast was served, everyone sat down to eat. But before even the smallest morsel could be touched by the smallest finger, the assembly grew sleepy. Yawning widely, they all put their heads down upon the board and fell fast asleep. Mab Rígh also found himself yawning and rubbing his eyes. He longed to sleep, but remembered his king's words. As his eyes closed and his head sank towards his chest, he stepped into the vat of cold water by his side. The cold water shocked him awake once more.

"As he shivered in the vat of cold water, there came the sound of a heavy footstep on the hearthstones. A heartbeat later, a shadow passed over the hall and a giant man appeared at the banqueting board. This huge fellow was dressed in leather clothes head to heel, and carried an enormous hammer made of stone. A long shield of oak bound with iron bands was slung on his back, and in his wide belt he carried an axe with an iron head. He also had a basket made of wicker, which he proceeded to fill with food: bread and meat and victuals of all kinds tumbled into this basket without end. Mab Rígh watched with amazement, wondering how any vessel could hold so much without ever growing full.

"Finally, the giant had cleaned the board to the last crumb; only then did he stop—and then merely to see if he had neglected anything—and seeing the board swept clean, the immense man turned and started off into the darkness once more. Up charged Mab Rígh, leaping from the water and splashing after the giant. 'Stop! In the name of the one who is lord over us, I command you to stop!'

"This is what Lludd had told him to say, and the giant stopped, turned, and raised his stone hammer. 'Unless you are better skilled with your weapons than you are at guarding your feast,' the giant replied in a voice to tremble the hills round about, 'I will soon add your pitiful carcass to my wicker tub.'

"Mab Rígh was ready with his reply. 'Though you have wrought endless crimes and turned the joy of many into laments of sorrow,' he said, 'I say that you shall not take one step more.'

"The giant mocked him, saying, 'Will you not defend your feast, Little Man? For I tell you, I am not easily persuaded against my will.' He swung the hammer high over his head and down with a savage sweep.

"Mab Rígh leapt deftly aside, and the hammer fell without harm. The giant turned and began walking away. He took one step, and then another, and on the third step was staggered backwards by the weight of the wicker basket. He struggled ahead another step, but the basket had suddenly become so heavy that he could no longer hold it. 'What manner of bread is this?' he wailed. 'It grows heavier with every step!'

"With that, the basket slipped from his hands and smashed to pieces on the ground. The giant saw the loaves of bread and joints of meat roll upon the earth and fell on hands and knees to retrieve his feast. He seized a round loaf in his hands and lifted it; but the bread was too heavy for him and, despite his enormous strength, the uncanny weight bettered him and he fell beneath the bread as beneath the heaviest millstone that ever ground a grain.

"Casting off his amazement, Mab Rígh strode to the nearest loaf and picked it up with one hand, raised it, and held it over the giant's head. 'I have another loaf for you,' the lord of the isle said. 'As you are a greedy giant, I shall give it to you. Add this to the one you clasp upon your chest.'

"The giant saw the bread poised over his head and cried, 'Please, lord, I yield. Do not hurt me further, for though you may not know it, I am weakened even unto death by the very loaf I clutch.'

"Suspecting a trick, Mab Rígh said, 'How can I believe you, who have stolen the life from the mouths of my people?'

"The giant wept and cried that the loaf was crushing him. 'Lord, I cannot endure the weight any longer,' he said. 'Unless you free me, I am dead. If it is my life you desire, then you have it, lord, and my word with it. Free me and I will never again trouble any who have tasted the bread by which you have conquered me.'

"Holding the loaf, Mab Rígh said, 'Your life is small enough payment for the wrongs you have done to my people, but for the good of all I will free you.' With that he lifted the bread loaf which had conquered the giant. 'Go you hence,' the lord told the giant. 'You will have neither morsel nor crumb from us for ever more.'

"The giant rose and shook himself all around. Then, honoring the oath by which he had bound himself, he took his leave of Mab Rígh and walked away to the east and was never seen in the island again. And thus the island was rid of the three plagues, and the people were released from their long ordeal. As sore had been their affliction, so great was their happiness. They delighted in their deliverance, and reveled in their release.

"For thirty days and three, the people of the island realm feasted on the bread of their liberation, and as much as they ate, there was three times that much left when they were finished. Indeed, they will feast on it for ever!

"Here ends the song of Mab Rígh and the Grain of Rescue. Let him hear it who will."

9

 AS THE LAST GLITTERING NOTES
went spinning into the night like the
flaming sparks from the fire behind
me, I gazed upon the hillside. The
people sat rapt, unwilling to break the spell that held them.
They had tasted—had feasted!—on the food of life and were
loath to leave the table.

Oh, but it was not my voice that stirred those starving souls
to their feeding; it was the Great Light, rising like the morning
sun within them, bidding them break their long fast.

I became aware of a movement nearby and Arthur was there
beside me, tall and strong, his face lit by golden firelight, a field
of stars behind him. He lifted Caledvwlch, brandishing the
naked blade as if he would drive away all dissent. I stepped
aside and Arthur took my place.

"Cymbrogi!" he cried, lofting the sword, "you have heard
the song of a True Bard, and if you are like me your heart
aches with the beauty of things we cannot name. And yet . . .
and yet, I tell you that it has a name. Truly, it is the Summer
Kingdom."

The High King spoke simply, but with the zeal of a man
who knows his greatest hope is within his grasp. Vitality shone
from him, brightening his countenance with holy fire. He was
the Summer Lord and he had glimpsed his kingdom, still far
off, but nearer now than it had ever been.

"The Summer Kingdom," he said again, his voice almost
reverential in its awe. "Myrddin Emrys says this wonderful

kingdom is near. It is close at hand, my friends, awaiting our good pleasure to establish it. Who among you would shrink from such a glorious undertaking? If we hold it in our power to establish the Kingdom of Summer, how can we turn aside?

"I do not know whether we shall succeed or fail," he continued. "The task may be more difficult than any alive can know. We may give all we have and still we may fail, but who in the ages to come would forgive us if we did not try? Let us therefore pledge our hearts and hands to something that is worthy—nay, more than worthy—of our best efforts. Who will make this pledge with me?"

At this the warrior host roared out a shout to tremble heaven and earth. My song had filled them with a yearning for the Summer Realm, and the sight of their High King bold and bright before them had given them a glimpse of its lord. They pledged themselves freely and with all their hearts.

But Arthur was not finished. When the shouts had died away, he looked at Caledvwlch in his hand. "This blade is mighty; my arm is strong," he told them.

"Cymbrogi, you know that I love Britain better than my life. Had I ten lives I would hold them worthless if I could not spend them in the Island of the Mighty."

This brought whole-hearted approval, which Arthur humbly accepted. "Believe me when I tell you that I would never do anything to defile this land, nor less yet bring it to harm. Believe me also when I tell you that this ruinous war must cease." He paused, gathering all eyes to himself. "Therefore, I will meet the Black Boar on the plain tomorrow and I will fight him." The High King, still grasping the sword, threw his hands wide. "Cymbrogi!" he cried, "I ask you to uphold me in the day of trial. Uphold me, my brothers! Tomorrow when I walk out onto that plain, I want your hearts and prayers united with mine in the battle. Cast off doubt, brothers. Cast off fear. Pray, my friends! Pray with me to the God who made us all to grant me the victory—not for my sake alone, but for the sake of the Summer Kingdom."

He paused, looking out across the silent sea of faces. "Go

now," he said, "go to your prayers and to your dreams. Let us all rise tomorrow in the strength that comes from hearts and souls joined in true accord."

Thus did we sleep. And when night faded in the east and the High King and Queen emerged from their night's rest, Gwenhwyvar stood resolutely beside Arthur, her face impassive against the day.

Arthur broke fast and held council with his chieftains. "You have pledged to uphold me through all things," he said, reminding them of their vows of fealty. "I commend your readiness for war, but now ask your willingness for peace. Today I will fight Amilcar and I demand your sufferance. Hear me: no one shall give the Vandali cause to doubt that I shall hold to the terms of the ordeal in good faith.

"If any man among you cannot agree this course, let him depart now, for he is no longer friend to Arthur. But if you stay, then you will honor me in this."

Many among them still distrusted the barbarian's intent. I do not blame them for feeling uncertain. A man can doubt, can nurse great misgivings, and yet uphold his vow though his heart is no longer in it.

This, I believe, is the spirit's highest consummation—holding fast to faith by dint of will alone when the fire of certainty has grown cold. For when the fire-wind of ardor gusts high, even the weakest soul can fly. But when the fire dies and the wind fails, the real test of a soul's worth begins. Those who persevere through all things gain strength and find great favor with God.

Arthur did not cozen them, but let the lords of Britain know what he demanded and what their support would cost. To their credit, the nobles remained staunch; none, despite their misgivings, deserted the High King, or muttered against him.

Accordingly, as the sun began to break the far horizon, the High King armed himself, donning his good mail shirt and his war helm, and slinging his iron-rimmed shield over his shoulder; with Cut Steel on his hip, he tucked a dagger into his belt, and selected a new spear. Cai and Bedwyr did what little they

ould to help him, inspecting his weapons, tightening straps
and laces, offering small advice and encouragement. When he
was ready, he mounted his horse and rode out to the arranged
meeting place on the plain, the amassed war host of Britain at
his back.

The place was not far, and when we halted a short time later
Arthur ordered the battlechiefs to take their places, bidding
Rhys to remain alert to his signal, and his chieftains to maintain
keen vigilance and order among the men, come what may.

He leaned from the saddle across to Gwenhwyvar, stoic and
steely at his side, cupped a hand to the back of her head and
drew her face near. "You have ridden at my side in battle,"
Arthur said gently. "Each time I have taken up the sword I
might have been slain. Truly, I might have been slain a thousand times over. This day is no different, so why do you fear?"

"A wife is ever happy to share her husband's lot," Gwenhwyvar replied, tears suddenly welling in her eyes. "I have
fought at your side, yes, chancing death gladly with you. But
I have no portion now in what you propose, and that is more
bitter to me than anything I know."

"I care nothing for myself," Arthur told her. "What I do
this day, I do for Britain. In this battle, I *am* Britain. No one
can take my place or share my portion, for this combat belongs
to the king alone."

He stated the matter succinctly. If peace was to obtain to all
Britain, it must be won by him who held all Britain in his
hand. Thus, Arthur and no one else. The sacrifice would be
his, or the glory. But whether sacrifice or glory, it was a sovereign act, and his alone to make.

Noble Gwenhwyvar understood this and, though she did
not like it, she accepted it for his sake. "I will abide," she
whispered. "Only, I wish I could bring myself to believe this
barbarian would honor his word."

"My heart," Arthur said, taking her hand in his and gripping
it hard. "We are not in Amilcar's hands. Truly, we are in God's
hands. And if the High King of Heaven upholds us, who can
stand against us?"

Gwenhwyvar offered a thin smile; she lifted her head and squared her shoulders, the warrior queen once more. In all that followed, she remained steadfast. Though many brave men quailed, Gwenhwyvar breathed no word of doubt or fear. Whatever qualms she might still have harbored in the matter she spoke never a word more. Nor did she ever so much as hint—whether in mood or gesture—that she distrusted the undertaking. When she at last understood that Arthur would not be moved, Gwenhwyvar took her place beside him as square and true as any of his chieftains. And, if Arthur had so desired, she would have taken the king's place on the plain without a murmur—such was her true nobility.

Arthur kissed his wife, then climbed down from the saddle and, squaring his shoulders, walked alone onto the battlefield. The Britons stood in ranks behind their battlechiefs, ardent prayers on every tongue.

Great Light, preserve our king! Surround Arthur with defending angels! Shield him with your Swift Sure Hand!

Away across the plain, the Vandali host advanced, nor did they show any sign of halting until they were close enough for us to see their dark eyes gleaming in the merciless light. Their expressions were grave, giving away nothing. They came on—nearer, nearer still—and I thought they would yet overrun us while we stood watching. But, when no more distance than the length of two spear-throws separated the two war hosts, the Vandali halted. Amilcar, with two chieftains and Hergest, advanced.

Seeing that Amilcar arrived with bearers, I called to Cai and Bedwyr to follow me, and we ran to join Arthur on the plain. He cast a quick glance over his shoulder as we came running. "It may be true that you must fight Amilcar alone," I told him, "but you need not trust blindly to his barbarian sense of honor. Cai, Bedwyr, and I will attend you and see that the Black Boar keeps his word."

Arthur glanced at the resolute expressions on the faces of his friends. "Very well. Let it be so. We will go out together."

The three of us walked with Arthur to meet the Black Boar

and I determined to do what I could to ensure the fairness of the contest. We met the Vandal War Leader in the center of the plain and halted a few paces away.

The Black Boar was even bigger and more heavily muscled than I remembered him. Stripped for battle, he presented a fierce and wildly savage aspect. He had smeared his face and limbs with lard, blackened with soot. Naked to the waist, his torso was a mass of scars from old wounds; stout thighs bulged below his leather loincloth. He was barefoot, and carried the heavy shield, short wide-bladed sword, and thick-hafted spear, or lance, favored by his kind. Around his thick neck he wore a triple-stranded band strung with human teeth and knuckle bones. His hair, too, had been greased, and hung in thick, heavy black ropes from his head.

There was indeed something of the wild boar in his aspect. He stood easily, regarding Arthur with mild contempt, no fear at all in his fathomless dark eyes. Amilcar seemed eager to meet Arthur face-to-face at last. In all, he appeared a supremely confident warrior, profoundly secure in his prowess.

The Vandal chief grunted a stream of words in his guttural tongue, which his captive priest rendered intelligible to us. "Amilcar says he is well pleased that Arthur has not run away from this fight. He would have you know that he considers it the utmost honor to kill the British king. The head of such a great lord will bring him much renown."

Arthur laughed. "Tell Twrch I may not be parted from my head so easily as he thinks. Many have tried but all have failed."

Hergest enjoyed repeating Arthur's words to Amilcar, who made a quick reply, lifting his necklace as he spoke, and rattling the bones. "Twrch Trwyth says it is the same with him. Nevertheless, he will be most happy to add the teeth and toe bones of a Briton king to his battledress."

Amilcar spoke again. "Twrch is ready," Hergest repeated. "There has been talk enough. It is time to fight."

"Not yet," I said, holding up my hand. "Before the combat begins, I would hear the warrior's vows."

"What vows are these?" asked Amilcar through his learned slave.

"That you will observe the threefold law."

Hergest relayed the reply, and the Vandali warlord asked, "What is this law?"

"The law is this: that no man from either camp shall intervene, or impede the contest; that the appeal for mercy shall be granted; that combat shall continue only so long as a man has breath to lift his weapon."

Amilcar glared at me as Hergest interpreted my words for him, and delivered himself of a mocking reply. "Twrch says your laws are the bleating of sheep in his ears. He will have nothing to do with them."

"Then neither will this combat take place," I replied firmly; Cai and Bedwyr squared themselves, hands on sword hilts, unafraid. "For unless you agree to honor this law," I continued, "the war will continue and the British lords will hound you from one end of this island to the other. You will be hunted down and ground into the dust."

Amilcar heard this with a scowl on his face. He spat a word of reply. "It is agreed," Hergest told me. "Amilcar makes this vow."

I turned to Arthur. "Agreed," he said, giving a sharp downward jerk of his chin. "I will be bound."

"So be it!" I stepped away from the two combatants. "Let the battle begin!"

10

  CAI AND BEDWYR, STEELY AND DE-
termined, took their places at my
side. "Keep your hands on your
sword, brother, and watch his every
move," Bedwyr hissed to Cai. "Amilcar is a liar and cannot be
trusted."

Twrch Trwyth, grinning savagely, raised his sturdy lance and
placed the short blade against his naked chest, drawing the
finely honed weapon across his flesh. A thin trickle of blood
dripped from the shallow wound down his black-greased torso.

This I had seen before. The barbarians believe that drawing
first blood ensures victory through the spirit of the weapon
thus awakened. While the Vandal thus occupied himself, Arthur drew Caledvwlch and dropped to one knee. Gripping the
blade in both hands, he raised the hilt before him to form the
sign of the cross, whereupon he offered up a prayer to the
Savior Lord.

Amilcar watched him narrowly. As Arthur knelt to pray, the
barbarian king moved to stand over him, gazing down with an
expression of deepest loathing. He drew a deep breath and spat
in Arthur's upturned face.

"The animal!" growled Cai. "I will—"

"Steady," warned Bedwyr, putting his hand on Cai's sword
arm.

Arthur opened his eyes and regarded Amilcar with icy indifference. Not so much as a muscle twitched. Closing his eyes
once more, he finished his prayer, then stood slowly. Nose to

nose, not a hand's breadth between them, they confronted one another. I could almost feel the heat of their anger.

"Tell Twrch Trwyth I forgive the insult to me," Arthur told the priest softly. "And when he is dead, I will pray that Jesu will forgive the insult to God, and have mercy on his soul."

Hergest repeated Arthur's words, whereupon the barbarian turned and swung out, catching the slave priest with the back of his hand. The monk's head snapped back and a livid hand-mark appeared on the side of face.

"The barbarian will regret that most bitterly," Cai muttered beside me.

As Amilcar strode to his position a few paces away, Arthur gestured behind him. Rhys, alert to the signal, blew a long, shimmering blast on the horn. The sound startled the waiting Vandali host. Twrch glanced towards the British line.

Seizing the moment, Arthur darted forth: "Die, Twrch Trwyth!"

Bedwyr, Cai, and I retreated a few paces; Mercia, Hergest and the barbarian lords removed themselves to a position opposite, which placed the combatants between us. Arthur and Amilcar began circling one another warily. It is the way of men who would learn the measure of one another. Both used the spear, grasping the weapon easily mid-shaft. Amilcar probed with his spear, swinging the blade restlessly back and forth, searching for an opening, a momentary lapse to exploit. Arthur, however, held the weapon still, poised for either thrust or throw.

I watched them edging around one another and weighed them both in my mind: neither man gave away anything in height. Arthur was more broad in the shoulder, but Amilcar was thicker through the torso. Where Arthur was surefooted and steady, the Black Boar was agile. Arthur, big-boned, strong and sturdy, possessed a strength born of the wild northern hills; the Vandal chieftain possessed the considerable stature and hardiness of his race. Both men, I concluded, were roughly equal in strength and stamina, though Amilcar, used to fighting on foot, might have held a slight edge over Arthur, who waged combat from the back of a horse.

But a warrior is not proved on the strength of his sword arm alone. If raw power were all that mattered, a warrior queen like Boudicca or Gwenhwyvar would never have stood a chance. Women are not gifted with heft of shoulder and arm of the average man; but they are clever, and craftier by far. As warriors their brains are quicker, more nimble and more shrewd. In battle, cunning easily outreaches the strongest arm. Truly, a warrior's brain is first among all attributes; the heart is second.

And here, Arthur had no equal. Although he may not have enjoyed Llenlleawg's rare gift of the battle *awen*, he owned a distinct advantage: he was fearless. Nothing daunted Arthur. Whether he faced a single spear or a thousand, it made no difference to him. Whether Amilcar fought alone or with the entire Vandal war host at his side, I do not believe it would have dismayed the Bear of Britain in the least. He might not have survived the encounter, but fear would have had no part in his death.

When men think of Arthur, they imagine him all thick-sinewed brawn, carrying all before him by sheer dint of physical prowess. In truth, no more courageous or canny warrior ever lofted spear or strapped steel to hip. He was strong, of course, but he was also wise—a very druid of battle.

So the Black Boar of the Vandali and the Bear of Britain circled one another, eyes keen, hands ready to seize upon the slightest lapse. It came almost at once. As the two moved, side-step by careful side-step, Amilcar stumbled—a small slip on uneven ground, but Arthur was on it in an instant. He lunged forward, spear stabbing up under the inside edge of Amilcar's shield.

Everyone saw the misstep and gasped at Arthur's speed in pursuing it. But Amilcar twisted away from the quick spear thrust, sweeping his lance before him. The cheers of the British died before they could be given voice, for had Arthur stepped in behind his stroke to force it home—as a warrior often does—his throat would have been sliced open.

Amilcar recovered with such aplomb, I wondered whether the misstep had not been a ruse—a subtle feint designed to catch a greedy opponent unaware. However effective in the past, Arthur was not overeager for an instant victory; he was content to allow his spear to probe a little without committing himself to the first opportunity that came his way.

The white sun blazed along the keen-edged blades, and in the narrowed eyes of the combatants. Slowly, slowly, edging sideways, the two warriors circled, searching for an opportunity to strike. Arthur seemed prepared to allow this exercise to continue as long as it may; he would not be rushed into error. Nor did the Black Boar seem anxious to grant Arthur another opening, false or otherwise.

So we stood in the hot sun—the barbarian war host, silent, rank on rank, facing the mounted might of Britain with little more than a spear-cast's distance between us—every eye watching the dread dance unfold, step by wary step. Around and around they went, never putting a foot wrong. Circling, circling, ever watchful, scarcely blinking, they moved, their feet making a large ring in the dust. The first to lose patience would make a strike, and the other would be waiting. But nerve held for both men; neither man lost his concentration.

But someone lost patience, for across the battleground a shout went up from the Vandal ranks—whether of coarse encouragement for Amilcar or derision for Arthur, I could not tell. The cry cracked sharp in the silence, and Amilcar's head turned towards the sound. Arthur saw his opponent look away and leaped forward in the same instant, his spear level, the blade slashing.

The sunlight flared on the blade; I blinked. When I looked again, Amilcar's shield had knocked Arthur's spear wide as his own lance jutted forth. It happened so fast that I thought Arthur had surely caught the spearpoint in the ribs. He threw his shield into Amilcar's face, forcing him back a step. I looked for blood, but saw none; Arthur's mail shirt had saved him a brutal cut.

The Black Boar permitted himself a sly, wicked smile, giving me to know that the shout and his apparent lapse had been another ruse. Clearly, the man was shrewdly deceptive and had taken care to arm himself with many such deceits. Arthur had avoided the first of them, and narrowly escaped the second; I wondered what Amilcar would try next—and whether Arthur would see it in time to save himself.

The cautious circling resumed, and appeared likely to continue for some time; indeed, it had settled into a dull, even rhythm, when Arthur suddenly stumbled. He went down on one knee, his spear slapping flat to the ground.

Amilcar leaped on him in the same instant. The stout black lance darted forth. Arthur stretched forward, grabbed the oncoming spear with his free hand, and pulled it towards him. Amilcar, unbalanced by the unexpected tug on the end of his lance, fell forward with a surprised grunt.

Arthur leaped to his feet, snatching up his spear once more in the same swift motion. Amilcar, regaining his balance, spun away, swinging his heavy shield before him. But Arthur's spearpoint had grazed his side and blood now trickled down the Black Boar's gleaming flank. The Cymbrogi raised a tremendous cry, signaling their approval of the daring maneuver.

Britain's king had drawn first blood, and—perhaps more importantly—served the barbarian warlord fair warning that the Bear of Britain was not without a few tricks of his own. I had never seen this stumbling feint of Arthur's and surmised that he had made it up by way of retaliation to temper Amilcar's deceptions. The enemy war host did not care for the feat and they howled their disapproval from across the plain.

The merciless sun mounted higher. The combat settled into a wary contest of stamina and will. Now and then one of the warriors would venture a stroke, which was answered in kind; but neither man was so hasty or inexperienced as to allow himself to be drawn into an impulsive exchange of blows.

Around and around they went, neither warrior presenting a weakness, nor finding any in his opponent. They circled, and the burning sun peaked, hovered, and began to lower in its long slow plunge to the western horizon. The Britons shielded their eyes with their hands and watched the contest, senses numbed by the heat and light. On and on, the ceaseless circling went, and the day crept away.

Eventually, the light failed before either man gave in to fatigue or error. I took it upon myself to halt the combat as the sun set and shadows began to claim the battleground. Signaling to Hergest, I indicated my wish to confer, and he brought Mercia to me.

"It is soon dark," I said. "We can let this go on through the night, or we can agree to stop it and meet again tomorrow."

The captive priest delivered my words to Mercia, who hesitated, regarding the fight thoughtfully. I sensed in him a reluctance to interfere, so I added, "It will be no hurt to either man to rest the night and begin again at midday tomorrow."

"It shall be done," the barbarian replied through the priest, and the two approached the combatants, calling for them to put up their weapons and withdraw for the night. This they did, though not without some reluctance.

Thus the day ended without victory.

11

THE CYMBROGI WERE RELIEVED
to welcome their king's safe return,
but disappointed that the day's fight
should leave the issue unsettled. For
his part, Arthur was tired, of course, hungry and desperately
thirsty. He desired nothing so much as a moment's peace to
recover himself. The Cymbrogi, however, having suffered the
day's endless and relentless uncertainty, now required solid reassurance that their king remained strong and keen for the
fight.

Arthur understood their need. "Tell them I will speak to
them after I have eaten," he instructed me as we entered his
tent. He removed his helm with a sigh, and lowered himself
wearily into his camp chair. "Rhys! Where is that cup?"

"Tell them to leave him in peace," Gwenhwyvar commanded sharply. She knelt beside her husband and began pulling at the leather laces of his mail shirt. "He has endured
enough for one day."

"Leave it with me," I replied. "Rest while you may."

Stepping from the tent, I addressed the gathered throng.
"Your lord is well, but he is tired and hungry. Allow him a
space to recover his strength, and he will hold council when
he has eaten and rested." I raised my hands to them. "Go now;
return to your duties and allow your king a space of peace."

"Is there anything we can do?" asked Bedwyr, stepping
near. "Say the word and it is done."

"See that no one disturbs him," I answered. "That will be no less a boon to him than food and rest."

"Done," Bedwyr replied, contemplating the crowd. A moment later, after enlisting Cador, Fergus, and Llenlleawg, he began moving the warriors along to their camps, reminding them that vigilance was still necessary for the Vandali were yet near.

I called Rhys to me and set him the task of bringing food and drink. "I have already seen to it," he said, slightly annoyed that I should have thought to command him in such an obvious duty. "The food is soon ready and I will bring it, Lord Emrys, never fear."

Arthur passed a restful night. He ate well and slept soundly, rising with strength and spirit renewed—no less eager to continue the fight than on the previous day. He greeted his lords and warriors with good humor, and spent the morning tending to his weapons, choosing a new spear from among the many presented to him by eager Cymbrogi. Just before midday, he broke fast on hard bread and water. Then, donning his mail shirt and helm, he took up his weapons and went out to do battle once more.

As before, they met on the plain, the war hosts arrayed in long ranks behind them. The Black Boar took his place, his battlechiefs by his side, looking smugly impassive. Indeed, it seemed to me as I gazed at his cold-eyed expression that Amilcar appeared even more confident than before. Perhaps their previous encounter had answered any anxiety he may have had in confronting Arthur. Or, more likely, he had armed himself with additional tricks and feints which he hoped would turn the fight his way.

Arthur did not care to allow Amilcar the first word. "Hail, Twrch Trwyth!" he called across the distance between them. "You appear most eager to die. Come then, I will give you your heart's desire!"

Through Hergest the priest, the Vandal chieftain received Arthur's taunt. By way of reply, he spat.

Arthur replied acidly, "As always, your wit is charming."

The fight began as before—both warriors circling and circling, searching for an opportunity to strike the first, perhaps decisive, blow. I took my place with Cai and Bedwyr beside me, and the Vandali chieftains took theirs; we stood opposite one another, watching the efforts of our champions.

As expected, the Black Boar had armed himself with further deceptions. These might have beguiled a less wary and experienced warrior, but Arthur handled them easily. So the day passed to the sound of spear on shield. The two warriors strained to their work, hewing at one another, each trying to beat down the resistance of the other, but neither forcing a decisive advantage. I watched the day stretch long, a feeling of frustration and helplessness growing in me.

Once, during the heat of the day, Hergest approached to offer the warriors a drink of water. I saw him standing between the two combatants and came to myself with a start; I had been drifting in reverie, oblivious to the battle before me. But I saw the priest holding out the water jar—offering a healing drink to the two combatants—and the words came again into my mind: *You must go back the way you came!*

I have done that, I thought. What more can I do?

But the words became a voice—my own, yet not my own—and the voice grew insistent; stern, accusing, it persisted, drowning out all other thought until I heard nothing else. *Go back! Go back the way you came! If you would conquer, you must go back the way you came!*

I stood squinting in the sun, staring at Arthur as he leaned against his spear and drank. When he finished, he raised the bowl and poured water over his head. I saw the High King of Britain, head back, the harsh light full on his sweating face, holding the bowl above him as the water splashed down.

It was a vision old as Britain: a weary warrior refreshing himself before returning to the fight.

The voice in my head stopped its insistent refrain, as if silenced by the sight. But it was not silent long. For, as I beheld the vision of Arthur dousing himself with water, another voice stirred to life: *This day I am Britain.*

They were Arthur's words, the words of the king to his queen, spoken to remind her of his rank and responsibility. True words, certainly, but as the cooling water bathed his face, I heard in them the echo of a truth long forgotten—too long forgotten, or overlooked in our headlong drive for victory.

Great Light, forgive me! I am a slow-witted and ignorant man. Kill me, lord; it would be a mercy.

The fight resumed and continued until pale twilight descended over the battleground. The day was spent and neither warrior had succeeded in gaining any advantage over the other. As before, I signaled Mercia and we approached the combatants with the offer of breaking off the battle and resuming the next day. Both men, weary beyond endurance, readily agreed; lowering their weapons, they stepped away from one another.

I turned to summon Cai and Bedwyr to help Arthur, and Amilcar's chieftains advanced to aid their king. The instant my head was turned, the Black Boar's lance flashed out. I saw the swift movement of his arm and shouted: "Arthur!"

The spearpoint caught Arthur in the upper shoulder. He fell forward with the force of the throw, his shield slamming to the ground. The spear glanced and dropped into the dust. Cai leaped forward, snatched up the shield, and placed himself between Arthur and Amilcar.

Mercia, shouting wildly, rushed forward and took hold of Amilcar, pulling him away before he could strike again. Bedwyr and I, having reached Arthur, stooped to examine his wound. "It is nothing," Arthur said, his teeth clenched. "Help me stand. It is nothing. Here, do not let the Cymbrogi see me so."

"Yes, yes, in a moment. I want to see the injury." I reached a hand to the wound, but he shrugged away.

"Myrddin! Help me stand! I will not be seen to lie here!"

Bedwyr, white-faced with shock and rage, took Arthur by the uninjured arm and helped him to his feet. "The brute," he growled. "Give me your sword, Artos; I will gut him like a hog."

"Stay, brother," Arthur said, his voice calm and even. "It is nothing. I would not like him to think he has gained any advantage in this. Let him think I but stumbled at the spear-cast."

I looked across to the waiting Cymbrogi. Every eye was on their king; more than a few had drawn weapons and were prepared to attack. Gwenhwyvar was running to meet us, her expression caught between concern and fury. Arthur raised a hand to halt her, and waved her back.

"Cai, Bedwyr—do not look back," Arthur commanded. "Walk away."

"May his barbarian soul for ever burn in Hell," muttered Cai. "Take my arm, Bear; let us go from here."

We made our way from the field with exaggerated dignity. Gwenhwyvar, Llenlleawg, and Cador brought the horses and helped Arthur to mount. "Cymbrogi!" he called aloud. "Have no fear for me. I am tired from the fight and Twrch's spear-cast caught me unawares. My good mail shirt has done me a service, however, and I am unharmed."

With that, he raised his hand to them—showing that his arm was not injured—jerked the reins and rode back to camp with Gwenhwyvar beside him. Cai, Bedwyr and I followed, while the British battlehost watched the barbarians and waited for them to depart.

It was as Arthur had said, his mail shirt had done him admirable service and the wound was not serious. "Well?" he asked, after I had examined it properly.

"It is not, as you say, nothing," I answered. "The lance was well thrown, if not well aimed. The blade cut through your shirt and you have an ugly gash."

"But it could have been worse," Gwenhwyvar added. "Much worse."

"Even so, I do not like the look of it," I told them both bluntly. "I think it best to let the cut bleed as much as it will, and then to bathe it with warm water. Put a little salt in the water to help cleanse the wound, and then bind it. Keep your shoulder warm through the night and I will examine it again in the morning."

Both of them caught the implication of my instructions. "Why, Myrddin? Will you not be here?"

"No. There is something I must do. Gwenhwyvar, tend to this," I replied. "I will return before morning."

Gwenhwyvar rolled her eyes in exasperation, but asked no further questions. "Go then," she said, and bent her attention to her husband.

I left Arthur to Gwenhwyvar's able care and stepped from the tent. Already my mind was running ahead to all I must do before the sun rose again on the next day. Cai and Bedwyr, looking anxious, were waiting just outside.

"The wound is not serious," I told them. "I want you to aid Gwenhwyvar and guard the king's rest. I am going away, but I will return before morning—Gwalchavad will accompany me, Llenlleawg also."

I could see the questions already forming on their lips, and waved them aside, saying, "Fret not. Trust me."

"And what shall we tell the lords when they ask after the king?" Bedwyr called after me.

"Tell them to honor the king's peace and all shall yet be well!" I turned and hurried away. "Cador! Fergus!" I called, summoning them out from among the warriors gathered helplessly before the tent. They came to me at once and I instructed them to gather the tools I needed for my night's work. The two hurried away, commanding other warriors to help. "Gwalchavad!" I called. "Llenlleawg, come here!"

The two were beside me in an instant. "Ready your horses, and get something to eat if you are hungry. We are leaving camp and we will not return before morning."

"Where are we going?" asked Gwalchavad.

"Back the way we came; back to the beginning," I told him.

He thought it a jest. "As far as that?" he inquired lightly. "And in only one night?"

"God willing," I replied, "it may not be as far away as we think."

12

 THE SKY WAS NEARLY DARK WHEN we rode from the camp. We did not go far—a few hills away—but well out of sight of any curious onlookers. I halted my small company beside a dry streambed and, while Gwalchavad tethered the horses, Llenlleawg helped me unload the wagon Cador had found.

"Why have you brought all this?" wondered Llenlleawg, hefting a hammer. "Shovels, picks, augers, saws—why do you need all these tools?"

"You will see," I told him. "Gwalchavad, hurry. Listen," I said, as he rejoined us, "there is not much time. Before sunrise tomorrow we must accomplish two tasks: we must make a quantity of lime—"

"Not difficult, that," Gwalchavad said. "There is limestone enough along the riverbank, and dry wood for burning."

"Yes," I told him, "I hoped one of you would notice. That shall be your task."

"And the other?" inquired Llenlleawg.

"We are going to make a chariot."

"A chariot!" exclaimed the Irishman mildly. "In one night?"

"In one night, yes."

Gwalchavad laughed, but Llenlleawg merely nodded thoughtfully—as if it were the most ordinary of chores, making a chariot by dark of night. "When you said we were going back to the beginning, I did not realize it would be so far," he replied. "Still, you can depend on me, Myrddin Emrys. I will aid you every way I can."

"That is why I chose you," I explained. "And for another reason: you two are unique among the Cymbrogi, and tonight I need your singular attributes."

They regarded one another curiously, trying to decide what I saw in them that set them apart. "You will not see it in your faces," I said. "The difference is this: you are islanders."

"Wise Emrys"—Gwalchavad laughed again—"is it tetched you are? Perhaps standing all day in the hot sun has poached the brain in your head."

"Perhaps," I allowed, "but it seems to me that you have lived more closely to the ancient ways than most men in the south."

"True," remarked the son of Orcady proudly. "The Eagles could not subdue the wild islands. The Lords of the North never suffered the taint of Rome."

"Nor did Ireland," put in Llenlleawg quickly.

"Precisely. I knew you would understand. Now"—I clapped my hands—"to work!"

They fell to the task with a will and never asked the reason why. Like Celts of old they simply labored for their bard at his behest; if the Chief Bard wanted a chariot, that is what he would have. My heart swelled with pride to see their simple trust. Does this, from the exalted height of your enlightened age, seem to you an insignificant thing?

I tell you it is not! Belief is *everything*.

These trusting men would labor day or night willingly because they believed—in me, in the old ways, in the loyalty which bound them to their king. They lived their belief, and if asked they would gladly die for it. Tell me now, who in your glorious age holds a belief so strong?

Well, we went about our tasks, as I say. The moonlight was more than adequate for Gwalchavad, who set about digging a shallow bowl in the riverbank—this would become the kiln he would fill with firewood and chunks of limestone dug from the cliffside. I kindled a fire for myself and Llenlleawg, as he began removing the wagon's front wheels and axle.

While the others were busy at these chores, I sought the woad. The plants were stunted and withered, owing to the long dry season, but as I had only a solitary torso to daub and not a whole warband, I soon gathered all I needed. I chopped the leaves and upper stalks into a small caldron which I filled with water and set beside the flames to boil. Then I turned my attention to helping Llenlleawg.

It is not so very difficult to make a chariot from a wagon— something that *resembles* one, at least. Once the smaller front wheels, axle, and sides were removed, we detached the pole and fixed it to the back, mounting the high frontpiece to what had been the rear to give the driver something to hold to. We then concerned ourselves with adding another harness to the pole and chain for a second horse. It is possible to pull a chariot with one horse, but much easier with two.

We worked amiably, talking quietly, the smoke from Gwal-chavad's kiln fire drifting over and around us. Once or twice I observed the young warrior leaning on the stick he used to poke the fire, his face ruddy in the glow of the fire. And I watched Llenlleawg, stripped to the waist, the firelight glimmering on his back as he worked with the wood and iron fittings.

A Celt of elder days coming upon us now would have greeted the sight with recognition and hailed us as brothers. If there is any enchantment in good men toiling together in hardy companionship, we made powerful magic that night.

The moon slid farther towards the horizon before disappearing in a white haze at last. After the moon set, I built up the fire and stoked it more often to keep the light steady. The night passed to the cold ring of the hammer and the hot crack of flame. Daylight was graying the eastern sky before we finished.

Gwalchavad unblocked his kiln and scooped the soft white powdery lime onto flat rocks to cool, then came to view the result of our night's labor. "Bring on the Vandal hordes!" he cried, leaping onto the platform. "I will vanquish them all from here. It is a beautiful thing."

"Do you think so?" wondered Llenlleawg, regarding the vehicle doubtfully. "It still looks more wagon than war cart to me."

A genuine war chariot would have been much lighter, the wheels larger, and the frontpiece made of stout wickerwork. The pole would have been longer as well—to prevent the horses' hooves from crashing against the platform as they careened in full flight over the battleground. Nevertheless, our crude imitation would more than satisfy my purpose.

"If I had such a chariot," Gwalchavad replied happily, "the enemy would soon learn to fear the thunder of my wheels."

"Fortunately," I replied, "a little thunder is all that is required. I do not think Arthur even knows how to fight from a chariot. I only hope he can manage to steer it."

"Never fear, Wise Emrys," Llenlleawg replied. "I will control this chariot for him. That is how the ancient kings entered battle. I would not see Arthur settle for less."

"You have done well," I commended them, and glanced to the rising sun. "And now we must hurry back. The camp will be stirring soon, and I want to be there when Arthur wakes."

While Llenlleawg and Gwalchavad harnessed the horse to the chariot, I packed the lime into a bag and retrieved the woad caldron. "Leave the tools," I told them, mounting to the saddle. To Llenlleawg, I said, "Remember what I told you."

"To hear is to obey, Emrys," the Irish champion replied.

"So be it." Snapping the reins, I wheeled the horse and raced back to camp.

As I expected, the warriors had begun to rouse themselves. A few cooking fires were already sending slender plumes of smoke into the clear, cloudless sky. The first rays of sunlight broke above the hill-line and I could feel the heat on my back as Gwalchavad and I entered the encampment. Not wishing to see or speak to anyone, I rode directly to Arthur's tent.

"Find Bedwyr, Cai, and Cador," I commanded as we dismounted. "Give them my instructions."

Gwalchavad gave me the bag of lime and hurried away. Glancing quickly around, I drew aside the flap and stepped into the king's tent. The sight I encountered made my heart move within me: Gwenhwyvar, her arms around Arthur, holding him, his head on her shoulder, sound asleep. Save for his mail shirt, he was still wearing his clothes of the day before.

She looked up as I came to stand before her. "He was too tired to undress," she whispered, brushing his forehead with her lips.

"Have you held him like this all night?" I asked, kneeling before her.

"He fell asleep in my arms," she replied. "I did not like to disturb him."

"But you have had no sleep for yourself."

"Arthur is to fight again today," she replied, lifting a hand to stroke his hair. "I wanted to spend the night with him just like this." She did not say that she feared it might be their last night, but that is what she meant.

Although we spoke in whispers, the sound of our voices roused Arthur and he wakened. He sat up, drawing away from his wife. She released him, but kept an arm on his shoulders.

"Oh, lady, I . . . " he began. "I fell asleep. I am sorry, I—"

"Hush," she said, laying a fingertip to his lips. "I am content. You were exhausted; you needed sleep." She put her mouth to his and kissed him. He pulled her to him in a tight, almost crushing embrace, then noticed me.

"Myrddin," he said, "is the whole camp risen so early?"

"Not the whole camp, perhaps," I replied. "But I wanted to see you both before anyone else. Let me look at your shoulder, Arthur."

Gwenhwyvar carefully peeled away the dressing and I saw an ugly red gash, swollen, and hot to the touch. The cut was not long—a thumb's length only—but when I pressed the edges of the puncture, a clear fluid oozed from it.

"How does it feel?" I asked him.

"Good," Arthur lied. "A bee sting is worse by far."

"Move your arm for me."

Arthur grudgingly moved his arm and rolled his shoulder. "Satisfied?" he asked impatiently. "I told you it is nothing. A night's sleep has done me a world of good."

"Possibly," I allowed. "But I think it would be better to give your shoulder another day's rest."

"What? And let the barbarian think that he has gained the advantage of me? I will not!"

"Let Amilcar think what he likes. You must consider your shoulder. What will it avail Britain if you get yourself killed today for the sake of your pride?"

"Twrch Trwyth and the Vandali will soon assemble on the plain. What will they do if I am not there?"

"Amilcar violated the law he agreed to honor," I pointed out. "I do not believe he will press the matter further. Let him wait, I say—until tomorrow if need be."

"Do you forbid me, bard?" he demanded, growing cross.

I hesitated, then shook my head, saying, "I do not say you cannot; I say you should not. I leave it to you. Do what you will."

"Then I will fight him today," Arthur declared. "And, with God's help, I will defeat him."

"Perhaps God has already sent his aid," I suggested.

"Why?" Arthur asked, looking from me to Gwenhwyvar and back again. "What have you done?"

"I have contrived a surprise for Amilcar," I said.

"A deception," Gwenhwyvar chided in mock disapproval. "And from you, Myrddin Emrys. I am alarmed."

"No deception," I answered, and quickly explained how Llenlleawg, Gwalchavad and I had spent the night.

"What," said Arthur when I finished, "has no one slept the night but me?"

"A chariot?" wondered Gwenhwyvar. "But that is wonderful."

"I must see this marvel at once," said Arthur, rising to his feet.

"Soon, but not yet," I said. "I would rather no one see you before the fight."

"Am I to be made prisoner in my own tent?"

"Only until all the others have gone out to the battlefield." I told them both what I intended. They listened to all, with bemused, slightly astonished expressions on their faces.

"No king has ever had a better bard," said Gwenhwyvar when I finished; rising, she smiled and kissed me on the cheek. "It is splendid, Wise Emrys. I commend your scheme, and will pray for its success."

Arthur stretched and yawned, and sat down again on the bed, rubbing his well-stubbled jaw thoughtfully. "Well, the shave will be agreeable at least."

"I will bring a basin and a razor," Gwenhwyvar said, stepping to the tent flap. It pleased me that she welcomed my plan so eagerly.

"And something to eat," added Arthur, yawning. "I am starving." He lay back on the bed and was soon sleeping soundly once more.

13

  THE OPPOSING WAR HOSTS WERE arrayed on the field of battle as before—rank on rank behind their chieftains, staring fiercely across the plain at each other. It was nearing midday and they were looking for Arthur to arrive, but he was nowhere to be seen.

A premature shout went up as I appeared, but died abruptly when they saw I was alone. They looked at one another with puzzled expressions and returned uneasily to their waiting.

The Britons were not the only ones anxious for Arthur's arrival. The Vandali also stretched their necks for a sign of him, and with even greater anticipation. For if the British king failed to appear, then Amilcar would be judged the victor; each moment that Arthur delayed, the expectation of triumph grew.

I did not know how long the Vandal king would content himself to stand aside while Arthur tarried. I hoped he might use the opportunity to belittle his opponent, but he seemed content to bide his time, and the longer he waited, the lower ebbed my hope and I began to fear that all my work would come to nothing. Had the wily Black Boar guessed what Arthur was planning?

No. Impossible.

Then why did Amilcar stand so amiably by? Why did he not denounce Arthur and call for the Britons to produce their king, or declare himself the victor?

The sun mounted higher in a formless sky, blazing hot, pooling inky shadows on the dry ground. I looked along the ranks of men, standing uneasily, sweating, their eyes narrowed slits against the hard, hard light. Across the plain, the barbarians shifted restlessly. The expectation was growing too great to contain any longer. Yet Amilcar waited.

When the Vandali war drums finally sounded, I thought: *At last! The moment we have been waiting for, Arthur. Take it!*

Amilcar advanced with his bodyguard and priest to his accustomed place. He stood for a moment scanning the ranks, then drew himself up and called out in a loud voice, which Hergest repeated: "Where is your champion? Where is your great king? Is he hiding? Is he afraid to face me?"

The words met stony silence. "Why does no one answer me? Has fear taken your tongues? Come out and fight! Show me you are not afraid!"

When he received no answer, his shouts became taunts. "Dogs! Cowards! Now you show your true nature! Kings of cowards, where is your coward of a king?"

This went on for a time. The Britons grew sullen and restive under this abuse. I could see the seeds of doubt and worry taking root. This was all to the good—my plan would better succeed if even Arthur's own Cymbrogi were taken by surprise. And Amilcar's abuse was beginning to worry our men.

Bedwyr hurried to my side, a frown of deepest concern creasing his brows. "I thought you said you would bring him."

"I did, and I have."

"Then where is he? Amilcar will not wait for ever. Whatever you are planning—"

"Peace, Bedwyr," I soothed. "Return to your place. All is as it should be."

"With you, Myrddin, *nothing* is ever as it should be." He retreated a few steps behind me, telling Cai: "It is no use, brother. He will tell us nothing."

"Where *is* Arthur?" demanded Cai.

"Peace," I replied. "He is near."

"Well, if Arthur does not come soon," Cai called to me. "Tell Twrch that *I* will fight him. That will stop him raving."

Amilcar drew encouragement from the refusal of the Britons

to meet his taunts. He preened and posed, strutting back and forth, crying his insults to the cowed and increasingly uncertain Britons. I saw in his swagger the confidence of a man who believes himself a conqueror and his adversary already vanquished.

Yes, I thought, *he is ready. Come, Arthur, it is time.*

But Arthur did not come. And then it was my turn to worry. Where was he? Why did he wait? What if something had happened to him?

I endured this uncertainty for a time, wondering what to do, and was on the point of sending Cai and Bedwyr to find him, when I heard it: a low rumble, like distant thunder. The sound grew rapidly louder, mounting steadily like the wind of an approaching storm.

The Britons heard it and looked to the west. The Vandali heard it too, and turned towards the sound. Because of his shouting, the Black Boar was the last to hear the strange thunder. His voice faltered and he turned his gaze to the west where a pillar of dust had appeared.

The sound became a steady drumming rumble and Arthur appeared, as if out of a tempest. But it was Arthur as no one had ever seen him: standing upright on the platform of a speeding chariot, brandishing a spear. Llenlleawg, also painted with blue woad, held the traces, driving two of Fergus' swift Irish stallions. The chariot—for it did look very like a war chariot—was hung with a bearskin and there were spears lashed to the uprights, giving it an even more menacing appearance. This Llenlleawg had done on his own; so pressed for time to complete the vehicle, I had not thought of it.

As remarkable as the sudden and unexpected appearance of the chariot might be, however, I think it was scarcely noticed at all. For every eye was on Arthur alone, and he held them rapt. His hair was a wild, spiky mass, white and stiff with lime. Most startling of all, he was wearing neither leather nor mail. In truth, he wore nothing save his golden torc of kingship; the champions of an elder time often fought naked, disdaining armor, trusting only their own prowess for protection. His face and body were freshly shaved, and his skin daubed blue with woad—spirals, hands, stripes, jagged lightning patterns—all over his arms and chest, and down his thighs and legs—symbols and signs now forgotten, but once possessing great power.

The impact of his unexpected appearance could not have been greater. It was as if a hero of old had taken flesh anew— Morvran Iron Fist himself, rising bodily from the dust at their feet, would not have astonished them more. Some did not recognize Arthur at first, and even those who did know him stared in amazement.

"Behold!" I cried. "The Pendragon of Ynys Prydein, riding to the defence of his realm."

"How long has it been since a British king has appeared so before his people?" I felt a touch on my arm as Gwenhwyvar came to stand beside me. Her face was alight with pleasure at the effect of the surprise. "Oh, he is a splendid man."

"Truly."

"And do not think to send me back to the line," she said. "After what happened yesterday, I will not go."

"Very well," I replied. "Stay." We stood together, the queen and I, reveling in a sight that had not been witnessed in the Island of the Mighty for ten generations or more. Such a spectacle! So bold and proud, standing in the chariot, torc glinting in the sun, adazzle with the blue of an elder age—they were heroes indeed.

Arthur and Llenlleawg raced up and down the length of the British line, encouraging wild whoops and cheers from the gathered Cymbrogi—a sound to assault the heavens! When they had whipped the Britons into an ecstatic frenzy, Llenlleawg turned the horses and drove the chariot to the center of the battlefield, where he stopped. Arthur lofted his spear and hurled it into the ground a few paces away, then stepped down. Llenlleawg turned the horses and drove the chariot from the field.

Taking up his shield and sword—both washed white with lime—the High King of Britain called out to the Vandal warlord. "Twrch Trwyth, I have heard your empty boasts! Take up your weapons and let us make an end of this battle. I tell you the truth, the world is weary of your presence, and I grow tired of you myself. Come, death awaits you!"

Amilcar, much impressed by Arthur's appearance, was slow to answer. "Indeed, one of us will leave the field, the other will stay." The barbarian king spoke much less confidently now.

"So be it. Let whatever gods you pray to receive your soul."

Thus the deadly dance began once more: around and around the warriors moved, circling, circling, edging, probing for an opening. Gwenhwyvar chewed her lip, never taking her eyes from the contest. I noticed that one hand found the hilt of her sword, the other her dagger. She stood there, at the ready, willing Arthur to make a beginning. "Take him, Bear," she murmured. "You can do it. Strike!"

And, as if in answer to her prompting, Arthur took a quick backward step, and Amilcar, suspecting a trick, hesitated. That momentary lapse was all Arthur needed; indeed, I saw now that he had cultivated it, using the Vandal's devious nature against him. A man who employs deception always looks for it in others, and Amilcar thought he saw it now.

But Arthur used no trick. His quick step backward was but preparation for an honest and open attack and, like Arthur's altered appearance, it caught Amilcar unaware.

Arthur stepped back, releasing his sword and letting it fall to the ground. His arm swung out and his hand closed on the spear he had planted. He whipped his arm forward. The Black Boar, flat-footed in hesitation, made to dodge aside. But too late. The spear struck Amilcar's shield square in the center.

It was a supremely well-executed throw, but I wondered at its prudence—it had done no hurt to the Black Boar and now Arthur lacked a spear. "No, no, no," Gwenhwyvar groaned.

But we were wrong. Arthur's ploy was genius itself: the spearhead was deeply embedded in the center of Amilcar's shield where he could not easily reach it. To rid himself of the nuisance, Twrch must either lower the shield or somehow swipe at the spear with his own and try to knock it off. He could not leave the spear where it was—an unbalanced shield was too awkward and his arm would soon grow tired just trying to steady the unwieldy thing.

The Black Boar was in trouble, and the look of incredulous anger creasing his face said that he knew it. He made an ineffectual swipe at the infuriating spear with the butt of his own weapon. Arthur was ready; he scooped up Caledvwlch and darted forward, swinging the great blade through a tight arc as if to sever Amilcar's spear hand.

This brought a howl of exasperation from the Chief Boar, a roar of approval from the Britons, and a yelp of delight from Gwenhwyvar. "Good!" she cried. "Well done, Bear!"

Amilcar evaded the stroke with a quick side-step, but Arthur pressed his slight advantage. Moving closer, sword slicing the air above the upper rim of his adversary's shield, he weighed in against the Black Boar, forcing him back and back.

Amilcar, desperate, his face fixed in a snarl of rage, thought to use the bothersome spear against Arthur. He threw his shield before him, heaving the protruding spearshaft into Arthur's face.

Arthur, unencumbered by the weight of leather and mail, ducked easily under the shaft and charged headlong into Amilcar as the shield swung wide. The Black Boar's chest and stomach were momentarily exposed and Arthur's swordpoint found its mark.

Amilcar made a futile chop with his spear as he fell, rolling onto his back. Arthur lunged at him to deliver the killing blow.

But Amilcar released his useless shield and hurled it up into Arthur's face. The protruding spear deflected Arthur's strike, allowing Amilcar to squirm away as the blade bit into his hip. He regained his feet in an instant and backed away. He had saved himself a terrible gash, but now faced Arthur without a shield, and bleeding from two wounds. Neither injury was mortal, but the steady loss of blood would fatigue and weaken him.

The balance of battle had tipped towards Arthur; he had placed his opponent in a critical, if not grievous, position. What would Amilcar do? The next move would likely augur the end.

Gwenhwyvar realized this, too. I suddenly felt her hand on my arm, fingernails digging into my flesh. "Take him, Arthur," she urged, eyes bright, her brows lowered against the sunlight. "Oh, take him quickly!"

Knowing himself in dire distress, Amilcar's reaction was immediate and decisive. He attacked.

Like the boar cornered by the pursuing hound, he gave an ear-splitting shout, lowered his head and charged. I could but marvel at the daring. "Truly," I murmured, "he is a very boar of battle. I see that his name is well earned."

Gwenhwyvar did not care for my approval. Her mouth bent down; she gave a derisory snarl and removed her hand from my arm.

The Black Boar's attack on Arthur lacked nothing: an act of concentrated fury, its ferocity was breathtaking. A stone hurled from a sling is not more relentless or unswerving. Nor less swift.

Amilcar drove in behind his lance, broad back and shoulders hunched for a mighty thrust. Straight and true, he charged, risking all on this one feat.

Arthur caught the blow square on the shield. I heard a loud crack as the thick Vandal lance shattered. Arthur staggered, and almost went down. Amilcar threw the splintered shaft into Arthur's face, drew his short sword, and, before Arthur could move, charged again, hurling himself forward with an ear-splitting scream of rage and desperation.

But Arthur did not meet this attack; at the last moment, he stepped aside and allowed the Black Boar to pass unscathed. I wondered at this. It is not like Arthur to permit even the slightest opportunity to slip by . . . but . . .

He seemed to be having difficulty with his shield . . . his arm hung down . . .

"No!" groaned Gwenhwyvar suddenly. "Please, God, no!"

Then I saw it, too. And my heart clenched like a fist in my chest.

14

  AMILCAR'S LANCE HAD PENE-
trated the stout oak of the High
King's shield and embedded itself in
Arthur's arm. Blood cascaded freely
down the inside of the king's shield. Skewered, his forearm
pierced, Arthur could not free himself.

Desperate to make the most of this unexpected advantage,
Amilcar seized his sword hilt and leaped at Arthur, loosing a
furious rain of double-handed blows upon the wounded arm
beneath the shield. Again and again, the blade rose and fell,
each stroke hammering at the broken spearpoint, forcing it
deeper into the wound.

Arthur reeled, his body convulsing in agony each time Amilcar struck the point. He tried to fend off the blows, swinging
Caledvwlch in powerless, futile strokes. The Black Boar swung
hard and struck the sword from Arthur's hand. The blade spun
from his grasp and landed in the blood-spattered dust at his
feet.

Gwenhwyvar groaned, but did not look away.

Staggering back and back, no longer able to respond to the
Black Boar's assault, Arthur swayed under the blows. Glimps-
ing his chance at victory, Amilcar lifted his voice in a growling
shout of triumph.

Leaping, driving, striking again and again . . . again . . .
again . . . again—wild, savage, ruthless blows, each one falling
with bone-shattering impact.

Dearest God in heaven, what keeps Arthur on his feet?

Chips of wood from Arthur's shield flew into the air. Blood splashed from the split shield-rim in a steady rain, pelting into dust.

My throat seized. I could not swallow. I could neither watch nor look away.

Crack! Crack! The great shield began to break under the shattering attack. Chunks of splintered oak dropped to the ground.

I saw the point of Amilcar's lance protruding from the inside of Arthur's arm. The blunt blade had passed between the bones, making any movement of the arm impossible. Arthur was fixed to the shield.

Amilcar, terrible in his fury, raised his heavy blade over his head and brought it down on the rim of the broken shield. Arthur's head jerked back, his features twisted in agony.

Shoulders heaving, the Black Boar threw the blade high and brought it down with all his strength. *Crack!* The shield rim burst and the oak split top to bottom.

Another such stroke and the shield would break completely.

"Arthur!" Gwenhwyvar screamed. "Arthur!"

Twrch Trwyth bore down mercilessly. The Vandali filled the air with a clamor of encouragement for their king—a sound to strike terror into the stricken British.

Again the short black sword rose and again it fell.

Arthur collapsed.

His legs had given way beneath him and he went down heavily, landing on his hip. He rolled, as if trying to crawl away. But Amilcar was on him instantly, striking furiously. Another massive chunk of Arthur's shield came away.

Amilcar howled. He hacked at Arthur with a savage, demented glee. Arthur, struggling to rise, kept the broken shield over him. Every warrior who saw it knew he was only delaying the terrible, inevitable, final fatal thrust.

The High King heaved himself up. The Black Boar raised his foot and kicked Arthur back. Arthur rolled on the ground again.

"God help him!" cried Gwenhwyvar. "Holy Jesu, save

him!'' I echoed her prayer with one of my own, no less blun
or heartfelt.

Still the Black Boar struck, his iron blade cracking loud o
the shattered remnant of the High King's shield. Arthur rolled
his good arm flung wide. He seemed confused, his hand fum
bled uselessly in the dust.

Great Light, save your servant!

Arthur squirmed on his back as the Black Boar's swor
smashed the broken shield. The battered wood parted, falling
away completely. His last defense abandoned him.

"Caledvwlch!" cried Gwenhwyvar. "Arthur! Caledvwlch!"

In the same instant Arthur's hand found his fallen sword.
saw his fingers tighten on the blade and pull it to him.

"He has it!" I shouted.

"Rise, Bear!" cried Gwenhwyvar. "Stand!"

Arthur gathered his legs beneath him and pushed himself up
on one knee. Twrch lashed out with his foot, striking Arthu
on his injured shoulder. Arthur fell.

"Arthur!" cried Gwenhwyvar. Her sword was in her hand
and she made to dash forth.

Amilcar, exultant, bellowing his conquest, raised his weapon
one last time.

Grasping Caledvwlch's naked blade in his bare hand, Arthu
made his final stand.

And I remembered that time long ago when a young boy
stood alone on a mountainside against a charging stag. Now
as then, Arthur made no attempt to strike; he merely lifted the
blade against Amilcar's double-handed assault.

Amilcar's sword swung down as Arthur's rose to meet it
There was a peal of ringing metal, a flash of spark, and the
Black Boar's blade fractured, sheared neatly in two.

The wild-eyed triumph in the Vandal chieftain's face melted
into disbelief as he stared at the swordblade lying at his feet
Cut Steel had served its master well.

With a heroic effort, Arthur gathered his legs beneath him
and raised himself up. He stood, swaying, his wounded arm
hanging uselessly at his side, the lancehead still firmly stuck

The bright blue woad on his body was now mixed with sweat and deep red blood. Head bowed, he stared unblinking at his adversary.

The Vandali, stricken by the swift turnabout, fell silent, the shouts of triumph dying in their throats. Silence claimed the plain. Arthur steadied himself and squared his shoulders.

The Black Boar, clutching the useless hilt with its stub of broken blade, glowered at the High King. With a shout of defiance, he flung himself at Arthur, slashing fiercely with the broken shard of his blade.

Unable to fend off the blows, Arthur stepped aside and lowered Caledvwlch. But his courage had not deserted him; even as he evaded Amilcar he prepared his last defense. As Amilcar leapt, Arthur's hand—steady, calm, unhurried—snaked out, swinging the sword level. The Black Boar's charge carried him onto the blade. Amilcar threw back his head and roared—a cry of shock and sharp defiance—then lowered his eyes to view the sword driven up under his rib cage. He had impaled himself on Arthur's sword.

The Black Boar raised his head and smiled—his eyes glazed and his grin icy. He lurched towards Arthur, forcing the blade still deeper into himself. Blood bubbled out of the wound in a sudden crimson rush. He opened his mouth to speak; his tongue strained at the words, but his legs gave way and he fell to the ground, where he lay twitching and convulsing.

Stepping to Amilcar's body, Arthur extracted Caledvwlch from his enemy's chest. Clenching his jaw against the pain, he raised the blade to shoulder height and let it drop swiftly down, severing the Black Boar's neck with a stroke. Amilcar's head rolled free and the dreadful quivering ceased.

Arthur stood for a moment, then turned and staggered towards us. In the same instant, a scream tore the stillness of the battleground. One of the Vandal warlords—Ida, it was—rushed out onto the battlefield, readying his spear as he ran.

"Arthur!" Gwenhwyvar shouted. "Behind you!"

Arthur turned his head, not yet apprehending the danger closing on him from behind.

"Arthur!" she screamed, already racing to his side. Llen-lleawg was instantly at her back.

Britain's king half turned to meet his new assailant and his legs buckled under him. He crashed to his knees. Arthur made to rise, but his attacker was closing fast. One quick spear thrust and Britain's High King would be dead.

Gwenhwyvar's knife glinted like a fiery disk in the sun as it spun in the air. It did not stop the barbarian; he ran on a few steps before his hand lost strength and the lance slipped from his fingers. He glanced down to see the queen's dagger buried up to the hilt in his upper arm.

He stooped to retrieve the lance, and Gwenhwyvar's sword sang through a tight arc and caught him at the base of the neck. The barbarian pitched onto his face, dead.

"Here I am!" cried Gwenhwyvar, her voice towering with defiance. "Who is next?" She stood over the corpse, her sword red with the blood of Arthur's false assailant, shouting, daring the Vandali to attack. Llenlleawg, bristling with menace, took his place beside the queen.

Another of the barbarian chieftains appeared eager to take Gwenhwyvar at her word: he drew his sword and started forth. Mercia seized him and threw him back. The battlechief staggered up, thrusting the head of his lance in Mercia's face. Mercia grabbed the shaft of the lance and lashed out with a cruel kick, catching his bellicose comrade on the point of the chin. The chieftain subsided in a heap.

Cai and Bedwyr dashed to Gwenhwyvar's side. The four stood over Arthur, weapons drawn, daring the enemy to attack. Meanwhile, I ran to Arthur's side.

Mercia stepped boldly out from among the others. He called in a loud voice, and summoned Hergest to him. Together they advanced to where the three Britons stood.

"Help me stand!" groaned Arthur through clenched teeth.

"In a moment," I told him gently. "First I must look at your wound." There was blood everywhere, and sweat, and dust, and woad.

"Help me stand, Myrddin." He shrugged away and, using

Caledvwlch, raised himself up on his knees; his injured arm hung down limp and useless. Blood seeped from the wound in a steady dark flow. I helped him regain his feet and he turned to meet the advancing Vandali.

Mercia, with Hergest beside him, presented himself to the High King. "Lord Mercia says that he recognizes Arthur to be victor," Hergest explained. "He will abide the terms of peace. Do with us what you will."

With that, Mercia threw the disarmed chieftain's lance to the ground at Cai's feet. He then drew the short sword from his belt, laid the blade across his palms, and offered it to Arthur, bowing his head in submission. "I am slave to you, Lord King," he said.

The High King motioned to Gwenhwyvar, who took the sword.

"I accept your surrender," Arthur said through clenched teeth, his voice hollow. To Cai and Bedwyr, he muttered, "See to it."

He made to turn away, stumbled, and would have fallen if not for Llenlleawg's quick reaction. The Irish champion threw an arm around the king's shoulders and held him up. "For the love of Jesu, Arthur, sit down and let me tend you."

But Arthur would not hear it. "Walk with me to the chariot," he said to Gwenhwyvar.

"Let me bind your arm at least," I objected.

"I will leave the field as I came," he growled. His skin was ashen and waxy; he was on the point of fainting. "Join me when matters are concluded here." He gripped my arm. "Not before."

Arthur walked with slow, painful dignity to the waiting chariot, Llenlleawg on one side and Gwenhwyvar on the other. Upon reaching the chariot, Llenlleawg all but lifted his wounded king onto the platform, and the queen took her place beside him to steady him and keep him upright. They drove from the battleground to the ecstatic cheers of the British. The Cymbrogi hailed him loudly as he passed, but Arthur kept his eyes on the far horizon.

I bade Mercia summon the remaining Vandali battlechiefs and there, over the corpse of their dead leader, I received their surrender.

Mercia, assuming command, made bold to answer for all. Through the captive priest, he said, "The battle was fought fairly. Our king is dead. We accept your terms and stand ready to give whatever spoils you ask, whether hostages or victims for sacrifice."

Cai did not like this. "Do not trust them, Myrddin. They are all lying barbarians."

"You will be disarmed," I told Mercia. "Your people will be taken from here and returned to your camp to await the Pendragon's pleasure."

Hergest repeated my words in their tongue, whereupon, under Mercia's commanding glare, the Vandali battlechiefs threw their weapons upon the ground. When they were disarmed, the young chieftain spoke once more, and Hergest said, "You called the king of Britain a strange name: Pendragon. Did you not?"

"I did," I replied.

Mercia spoke up, addressing me directly. "What means this word?"

"Pendragon—the word means Chief Dragon," I explained. "It is the title the Cymry use for the supreme ruler and defender of the Island of the Mighty."

Hergest translated my words, and Mercia placed his hand on his heart and then touched his head. It was a sign of submission and honor. "I place my life in the hands of the Pendragon of Britain."

Leaving Bedwyr, Cai, Cador, and the rest of the lords to deal with the Vandali, I returned to the line, mounted the nearest horse, and raced back to camp as fast as the beast could fly.

I pressed through the worried throng gathered before Arthur's tent. The few women and invalid warriors who had not attended the battle—but had witnessed their wounded king's return—swarmed the entrance to his tent, anxious and worried. Pushing my way through, I entered the tent to find Gwenhwyvar cradling Arthur against her as she held him, half-sitting, half-lying on his pallet. Her clothing was smeared and stained with blue woad and red blood. "It is over, my soul," she soothed, dabbing at his arm with a cloth. "It is finished."

"Gwenhwyvar, I—it is—" Arthur began, then winced, pain twisting his features. He bit back the words and his eyelids fluttered and closed.

"Be easy, Bear," she said, kissing his brow, then raised her head and looked around furiously. "Llenlleawg!" she cried, saw me, and said, "Myrddin, help me. He keeps fainting."

"I am here." Keeling beside her, I took the cloth and, gently, gently, oh so carefully, I lifted Arthur's arm; he groaned. Gwenhwyvar gasped at what she saw.

The point of the lance had been driven through the arm, passing between the two arm bones. The broken shaft protruded from one side—a mass of splinters where Amilcar had hacked at it—the thick iron tip poked through the other. But there was more. The force of the thrust had driven the spearhead through the arm and into the soft crease above his thigh, where the veins gathered thick. One of these had been severed. He was bleeding into his abdomen. I pressed the cloth to the gash, and sat back to think.

"Where is Llenlleawg?"

"I sent him for water to bathe the wound."

"Hold tight," I told her, indicating Arthur's arm.

"What are you going to do?" Gwenhwyvar asked.

Easing the arm upright, I took hold of the Black Boar's broken spear. Grasping the splintered stump, I gave a quick, firm pull.

"Aghh!" Arthur gasped in agony.

"Stop it!" shouted Gwenhwyvar. "Myrddin! Stop!"

"It must be done," I told her. "Again."

I tightened my grip on the stub end, greasy with blood. Gwenhwyvar, her lips a tight line, held Arthur's arm in both her own, clutching it to her breast. Blood welled from the wound, spilling over her hands.

"Now!" I shouted, and yanked with all my might.

Arthur gave a strangled cry, his head lolled on his shoulders. The shaft broke away from the head, but the blade did not come free. I had succeeded only in making the wound bleed more freely.

Llenlleawg entered the tent with a basin of water. He brought it to me and knelt down, holding it. I took the bit of cloth he offered, dipped it into the water and began to bathe the wound, washing away the blood and dirt.

"Is the arm broken?" asked Llenlleawg.

"No," I replied, probing the injury with my fingertips, "but this is not the worst." I told them about the groin wound. "Truly, that alarms me far more than the arm."

I rose, making up my mind at once. I turned to Llenlleawg. "There is room in the chariot for three. You will drive; Arthur and Gwenhwyvar will go with you. I will ride ahead to alert Barinthus and ready a boat." I turned, starting away. "Make him as comfortable as possible, and come at once."

"Where are we going?" demanded Gwenhwyvar.

"To Ynys Avallach," I called over my shoulder.

CHARIS, GRAVE WITH CONCERN, emerged from the room where Arthur lay. "I think the bleeding has stopped at last," she said solemnly.

"Thank God," Gwenhwyvar breathed, her relief almost tangible.

"But," Charis continued—there was no comfort in her voice—"he is very weak." She paused, looking from Gwenhwyvar to me. "Truly, I fear for him."

Gwenhwyvar shook her head, denying what Charis was saying. "The wound is not so bad," Gwenhwyvar insisted, her voice growing uncertain. "Once the blade was removed, I thought . . . I thought he would . . . " Her voice cracked, very close to tears.

"Arthur has lost much blood," Charis said, putting her arm around the queen's shoulders. "It often happens that loss of blood is more harmful than the injury itself. We must pray he awakens soon."

"And if he does not?" asked the queen, horrified by the thought, but asking nonetheless.

"It is in God's hands, Gwenhwyvar," Charis said. "We can do no more."

After a breathless chase through the vale and Barinthus' swift boat across Mor Hafren, we had reached the Fisher King's palace. Charis and Elfodd had taken over Arthur's care. With skills honed by long experience, the point of the broken lance had been carefully removed from the High King's arm, and he had been given healing draughts to drink.

Arthur had seemed to revive at first; he sat up and talked to us. Then he slept, and we thought the rest a benefit to him. The thigh wound had opened again in the night, however, and by morning, he had lapsed into a dull, insensate sleep. He slept all through the day; and now, as evening stole across the quiet hills, Arthur could not be roused.

Charis was clearly worried. She squeezed the queen's shoulder. "It is in God's hands," she whispered. "Hope and pray."

Gwenhwyvar clutched my arm, her fingers digging into my flesh. "Do something, Myrddin," she urged. "Please! Save him. Save my husband."

I took her hand and clasped it tightly. "Go with Charis and rest a little. I will stay with him now, and send for you if there is any change."

Charis led Gwenhwyvar away, and I entered the chamber where Arthur lay on the litter the Fisher King used when his old affliction came upon him. Abbot Elfodd raised his head as I came to stand beside him. He saw the question in my eyes and shook his head.

"I will watch with him now," I whispered.

The good abbot declined to go, saying, "We will watch together."

We stood a long time in silence listening to Arthur's slow, shallow breathing. "God will not let him die," I said, willing it to be so.

Elfodd looked at me curiously. "I remember another time when I stood here like this and another spoke those selfsame words." He paused and indicated Arthur's sleeping form. "But it was you, Myrddin, lying there in the sleep of death, and it was Pelleas standing over you, refusing to let you go that way."

My mind flooded with the memory: we had been in Armorica, Pelleas and I, where Morgian thought to slay me with a wicked enchantment. Pelleas had brought me to Ynys Avallach for healing, much as I had brought Arthur.

"I remember," I said, thinking of that strange, unhappy time. "With all thanks to you, I was saved."

"With no thanks to me," the abbot objected. "It was Avallach's doing, not mine."

"Avallach?" I had never heard that part of the tale before. "What do you mean?"

Elfodd regarded me with an expression close to suspicion. "No?" he turned away. "Perhaps I have said too much. I have spoken above myself."

"What is it, Elfodd? Tell me, I charge you. There is a mystery here and I would know it." He made no answer. "Elfodd! Tell me, what is it?"

"I cannot," he said. "It is not my place."

"Then tell me who may speak?"

"Ask Avallach himself," the abbot said. "Ask your grandfather. He knows."

My heart quickened within me. Leaving Arthur to the abbot's care, I fled the chamber and went in search of Avallach. It did not take long. I found him at prayer in the small chapel he had made in one of the rooms in the west wing of the palace. I entered the chapel and went to kneel beside him. He finished his prayer and raised his head.

"Ah, Merlin, it is you," he said, his voice a soft rumble of thunder. "I thought you might come here. How is Arthur?"

"Weak and growing weaker," I replied, speaking the full force of my fear. "He may not live through the night."

Avallach's generous features assumed an expression of heartsick grief. "I am sorry," he said.

"The Bear of Britain is not dead yet," I replied, and told him what Elfodd had brought to mind.

"I remember it well," Avallach agreed. "Oh, we were worried for you, Merlin. We almost lost you."

"Elfodd said that but for you I *would* have died. Is that true?"

"It was a miracle of God's blessing," the Fisher King replied.

"And when I asked him what he meant, Elfodd would only say that he had spoken above himself. He would tell me nothing more about it. He said I must ask you." I stared at him hard. "Well, Grandfather, I am asking you: what did he mean?"

Avallach regarded me for a long time in silence, then lowered his curly, dark head. "It is the Grail," he answered at last, his voice still and low. "He is talking about the Grail."

I remembered: the holy cup of the Christ. It had come to Britain with the man who had paid for that last meal in the upper room, the tin merchant, Joseph of Arimathea. I had seen it once, years ago, while praying in the shrine.

"I have always thought it was a vision," I said.

"It is more than that," Avallach answered. "Very much more."

My heart leapt with sudden joy. "Then you must use it to heal Arthur, as you used it to heal me." I jumped to my feet and made to hasten away.

"No!"

Avallach's stern refusal halted me before I had taken two paces.

"Why? What do you mean? Arthur is dying. The Grail can save him. If you have it, you must use it to heal him."

The Fisher King rose slowly; I could see sorrow like an immense weight upon his shoulders. "It cannot be," he said softly. "It is not my place to decide such things. It is God's place; He must decide."

"It is ever God's good pleasure to heal the sick," I insisted. "How can you withhold that healing if it is within your power?"

He merely shook his head. "The Grail," he said gently, "the Grail, Merlin, is not like that. It is not to be used so. You must understand."

"I do not understand," I declared flatly. "I only know that Arthur is dying, and if he dies the Kingdom of Summer dies with him. If that should happen, Britain will fall, and the West will die. The light of hope will fail and darkness will overtake us at last."

"I am sorry, Merlin," Avallach said again. "I would it were otherwise." He made to return to his prayers.

Now it was my turn to challenge and refuse. "No!" I shouted. "Do not think to pray for Arthur's healing when you hold that healing in your hands yet refuse to give it."

"Death," replied the Fisher King sadly, "is also God's good pleasure. Do you think this easy for me? I sit here every day and watch people die. They come to the shrine—this plague has oppressed us sorely!—and we do what we can for them. A few live, but most die. As I said, it is for God to decide. He alone holds power over life and death."

"He has given you the Grail!" I argued. "Why has he done that if he did not intend you to use it?"

"It is a burden more terrible than any I know," moaned Avallach.

"Yet you used it once to heal me," I persisted. "You took it upon yourself to decide then. You saved my life. Where is the harm?"

"That was different."

"How so?" I demanded. "I see none at all."

He looked away, sighing heavily. "You are my daughter's only child; the only son of your father. You are my flesh and blood, Merlin, and I am weak. I could not help myself. I did it to save you."

"Indeed!" I cried, my voice ringing in the rock cell. "My life was saved so that the Kingdom of Summer would not die. Perhaps I was saved so that I could stand here before you this night and argue for Arthur's life."

The Fisher King observed me thoughtfully. "Who is to say?"

"You preserved me, and so preserved the vision of the Summer Realm. Hear me, Avallach, the Kingdom of Summer is near—closer now than it has ever been. How can we let the Summer Lord die?"

He said nothing, though I could see that he was wavering.

"If you are the keeper of this Grail," I said solemnly, "then it is for you to exercise the power of your position for the good of all. I tell you the truth, there is not another life the worth of Arthur's, and even now it is slipping away from us. Saving that life will lead to the salvation of generations yet unborn."

Avallach pressed a hand to his head wearily. "Do you not know I have been entreating the Throne of Heaven on his behalf? I have not left off one moment since he arrived."

"God will welcome Arthur in his time," I affirmed. "But that time is not yet. This I know. If a life is required, I stand ready to give mine." I raised my hands to Avallach in supplication. "Save him. Please, save him."

"Very well," Avallach relented. "I will do what I can. Though I do not command the Grail, as you seem to think. I can only ask. The Grail answers how it will."

I did not know what form the Fisher King's ministrations would take; but, as we hurried back across the yard to Arthur's chamber, I offered to help in any way I could. "Tell me what is to be done, Grandfather, and it will be done."

Avallach stopped beneath the gallery roof. "No one can aid me, Merlin. What I do, I must do alone."

"As you will."

"Every mortal creature must be removed from this place," Avallach continued. "Every male and female, all mortal flesh, whether human or animal, must be removed beyond the walls of the palace. Arthur only may remain."

I wondered at this, but accepted his instructions. "It shall be as you say."

While Elfodd and I ran through the Fisher King's palace, rousing everyone from bed, Llenlleawg awakened the stable hands and began moving the livestock from the barns and pens. By torchlight we made our way down the narrow twisting path to the lake. Some led dogs on leashes, others horses; several drove cattle: sheep, kine, and goats; two or three carried bird cages, and one child held an armful of kittens. In a little while, all who lived in the palace—mortal, Fair Folk, birds, and beasts—were gathered at the lakeside below the abbey. The horses and cattle grazed quietly in the long grass.

Charis and Gwenhwyvar were the last to leave Arthur's side. "Come, lady, we can do nothing more for him," Charis said, taking Gwenhwyvar by the hand. "It is time to give him up to the care of another."

"I am loath to leave him, Lady Charis," Gwenhwyvar said, tears swelling in her eyes. She lowered her face to Arthur's and kissed him. A tear splashed on the king's cheek; she kissed it away.

"Come," I said gently, "for unless you leave, he cannot be healed."

Charis and I led the queen from Arthur's deathbed. At the doorway, I paused and looked back at his body sunken in the cushions of the litter, so still, so silent, as if already sinking into dissolution and decay. Gwenhwyvar hesitated and turned; she ran back to the litter and, unfastening the brooch at her shoulder, removed her cloak and spread it over him.

As Gwenhwyvar covered Arthur with a cloak, I covered him with a prayer: *Great Light, banish the shade of death from the face of your servant, Arthur. Shield him this night from hate, from harm, from all ill whatever shall befall him. So be it!*

She kissed him again and murmured something in his ear, then rejoined us, dry-eyed now and resolute. We hastened through the all-but-deserted palace. I looked for Avallach, but saw no sign of him as we passed quickly through the empty hall and gallery, and then flitted across the vacant yard and out through the open gates.

In darkness, we made our way down the narrow path to join the others waiting at the lake. Elfodd and Llenlleawg were there, holding torches; the rest of the palace-dwellers were scattered along the shore, sitting in small clumps, or standing, some on the hillside, some by the lake. We appeared an exile band, cast out from our homeland in the dead of night. The air was warm and calm. Though the moon had already set, the sky overhead blazed with stars, casting a pale silvery light over all below.

"Are you certain all the animals have been removed?" I asked.

"Every dog to the smallest pup," Llenlleawg answered.

"Every horse and colt, sheep, lamb, and cow. Nothing on four feet, or two, remains behind."

Elfodd scanned the small gathering around us, his finger wagging in the air as if counting motes. "I think—yes," he said when he finished, "everyone is here."

"Good," I said, and we talked a moment, but our eyes kept stealing to the Fisher King's palace above; soon our talk ceased and we stood silent and expectant, waiting, wondering what, if anything, we might see. A group of the brothers from the abbey came down to see what was happening. They stood with us, gazing up at the dark edifice on the tor.

A young woman—one of Charis' serving girls, I think—began to sing a hymn in a voice as soft and sweet as a nightingale's. The words were unfamiliar, but the melody I knew. One by one, others joined in and soon the song filled the night—hope made audible in the heart of darkness.

When the first song was finished, another began at once, and another when that was done. In this way we passed the night: singing, every eye on the Fisher King's palace, waiting for a miracle. I felt Gwenhwyvar's hand slip into mine. She clasped it tightly and I pressed hers, whereupon she raised my hand to her lips and kissed it.

There were no words for what we felt, so we simply stood, clutching one another's hands and listening to the voices in the night. The songs continued and the stars drifted, wheeling across the skybowl. It seemed to me that the songs became a prayer, rising up to heaven. *Let it be so,* I thought. *May Heaven's High King honor his High King on earth as we honor him with our sacrifice of song.*

This thought had no sooner gone than a voice called out. "Listen!" A young monk who had been sitting on the hillside a few paces away, jumped to his feet. Waving his arm and pointing into the eastern sky, he said, "Look! They come!"

I looked where he was pointing, but saw nothing save the bright stars shining. Silence claimed the hill and lakeside. We all stared into the shimmering sky.

"They come!" another cried, and I heard a sound like that

of the harp when it sings of itself in the wind—a music at once moving and mysterious. It might have been the wind, but it was deeper and more resonant: the sky itself was breaking forth in song.

The air stirred softly, as with the light flutter of feathered wings. I felt a silken touch like a cool breath on my face, and tasted honey on my tongue. I inhaled a fragrance surpassing in sweetness any I have ever known: blossoms of apple and honeysuckle and other blooms combined.

An unseen presence had passed through our midst, trailing perfumed music in its wake. My spirit quickened in response. My skin tingled all over and my heart beat fast.

I saw, as out of the corner of my eye, a faint, phantom image, pale, half-veiled shapes falling out of the sky and swirling around the Fisher King's palace. Strange lights began to play in the darkened windows above.

Turning to Gwenhwyvar, I saw her face bathed in golden light. Her hands were clasped beneath her chin, her face upturned in the starlight, her lips trembling. "Blessed Jesu," I heard her say. "Blessed Jesu."

The golden light gleamed forth from every window of the Fisher King's palace. The holy music swelled, resounding through heaven's vast halls. The swirling, fluttering, shifting, seen-yet-unseen shapes seemed to have multiplied until the sky could not contain them. They were everywhere!

"Angels . . . " breathed Abbot Elfodd in an awed whisper. "Heaven's champions have come for Arthur."

I gazed into the golden light now boldly blazing from the palace atop the tor, casting all below in sharp relief, the shadows of men and animals thrown hard upon the ground. The light was a living thing; dazzling, brilliant, it pulsed with ardent power, brighter and more potent than lightning.

And then, as swiftly as it had begun, it ended.

The light dwindled and the music hushed to a swiftly fading resonance—disappearing so fast, I wondered if I had heard or seen anything at all. Perhaps I had only imagined it. Perhaps it was a dream.

But the unseen presence returned, moving back through the waiting throng the same way it had come. I felt my soul rise up within me, and my heart moved in response; my skin tingled. And then this too was gone, leaving only a lingering fragrance and a sweet taste in the air.

We were alone in the night once more, and the night was dark indeed.

There was no more music; there were no more lights. All was still and quiet, as if nothing—from one eon to the next—ever happened. But we still looked above, at the palace and the sky full of stars beyond, searching for the wonders we had known.

That is how we saw him: Arthur, bold in the gateway of the Fisher King's palace, alive and hale, dressed in his finest clothes, kingly torc gleaming gold at his throat. The Summer Lord raised a hand to us—a signal that he was healed and he was well. Then he started down the trail.

I saw Gwenhwyvar running, swiftly mounting the path. I saw Arthur descend to seize her, catch her up and lift her off the ground. I saw their fervent embrace. . . . But then I saw no more through the tears that filled my eyes.

Epilogue

 HOW NOW, GERONTIUS! RICH
the life of an exile! Do you not savor
it? And you, Brastias, ever and always
turning your eyes toward the home
you left behind. Does your well-earned shame keep you warm
at night?

Ulfias, weak-willed and easily led; if you must follow a king,
why not the one you were sworn to honor? Is your great regret
a comfort to you? And Urien, young schemer, is your foreign
bed made more luxurious with the knowledge of your treachery?

False lords! The dogs begging scraps under your table know
more of fealty than you. Did you really think the Cymbrogi
would follow you? Did you believe you could take Arthur's
place? Or was this hope, like the vows you so quickly abandoned, merely empty air as well?

Faithless Ones, hear me now: the Kingdom of Summer was
more than a dream! More than a tale to beguile children. Brave
men died to secure it—pledging life to faith. Any realm
founded on the rock of such faith cannot fail.

Do you wonder that the lords of Vandalia, Rögat, and Hussa
received mercy from Arthur's hand? I tell you that they did.
For in victory, Arthur's full grandeur became apparent. He
took pity on his enemies, fed them, and offered them peace.
The Pendragon of Britain, having shown heroism in adversity,
in triumph practiced Christian mercy. Arthur befriended his
enemies, and thus made cruel foes—the very same who had

come to respect his valor—realize his nobility. The Vandal lord, Mercia, was baptized at Arthur's invitation, and the High King welcomed him as brother.

And if these former enemies gained a boon by virtue of Arthur's generosity, how much more did the Irish lords benefit? Those who forfeited home and lands to aid Arthur obtained all and more in return. Thus is faith rewarded.

Say what you will, Britain was exalted then. No, we did not escape the further torments of plague and drought. The Yellow Ravager gnawed deep, and dry winds carried our harvest away on the dust. But to those who knew where to look, the Summer Realm was even then sending forth its first faint rays.

For the High King of Heaven had blessed us with the holiest object in this worlds-realm: the cup of Christ—that Grail which would become the bright Sun of the Kingdom of Summer. Arthur declared that this most sacred object should become the symbol of his reign, to be established in the church that he would build. In truth, all Britain trembled when it learned of that most Holy Grail. . . .

Ah, but that is another tale.

THE PENDRAGON CYCLE
STEPHEN R. LAWHEAD

𝔐ERLIN

70889-2/$5.99 US/$7.99 Can

He was born to greatness, the son of a druid bard and a princess of lost Atlantis, a trained warrior blessed with the gifts of prophecy and song. Respected, feared, and hated by many, he was to have a higher destiny.

"Entertains and tantalizes...Fascinating...
An exciting and thoughtful addition to the
ranks of Arthurian fantasy"
Locus

Read all of the
PENDRAGON CYCLE

TALIESIN   70613-X/$5.99 US/$7.99 Can
ARTHUR   70890-6/$5.99 US/$7.99 Can
PENDRAGON   71757-3/$5.99 US/$7.99 Can

THE PENDRAGON CYCLE
STEPHEN R. LAWHEAD

ARTHUR

❦

70890-6/$5.99 US/$7.99 Can

They called him unfit to rule—a lowborn, callow boy, Uther's bastard. But his coming had been foretold in the songs of the bard Taliesin. He was Arthur, Pendragon of the Island of the Mighty—who would rise to legendary greatness.

"Evocative...Intriguing...
Enthralling"
Locus

Read all of the
PENDRAGON CYCLE

TALIESIN	70613-X/$5.99 US/$7.99 Can
MERLIN	70889-2/$5.99 US/$7.99 Can
PENDRAGON	71757-3/$5.99 US/$7.99 Can

Buy these books at your local bookstore or use this coupon for ordering:

Mail to: Avon Books, Dept BP, Box 767, Rte 2, Dresden, TN 38225   D
Please send me the book(s) I have checked above.
❑ My check or money order—no cash or CODs please—for $_____is enclosed (please add $1.50 to cover postage and handling for each book ordered—Canadian residents add 7% GST).
❑ Charge my VISA/MC Acct#_____Exp Date_____
Minimum credit card order is two books or $7.50 (please add postage and handling charge of $1.50 per book—Canadian residents add 7% GST). For faster service, call 1-800-762-0779. Residents of Tennessee, please call 1-800-633-1607. Prices and numbers are subject to change without notice. Please allow six to eight weeks for delivery.

Name_____
Address_____
City_____State/Zip_____
Telephone No._____   PCC 0995

BESTSELLING AUTHOR OF
THE PENDRAGON CYCLE

STEPHEN R.
LAWHEAD

In a dark and ancient world,
a hero will be born to fulfill
the lost and magnificent promise of . . .

THE DRAGON KING

Book One
IN THE HALL OF THE DRAGON KING
71629-1/ $4.99 US/ $5.99 Can

Book Two
THE WARLORDS OF NIN
71630-5/ $4.99 US/ $5.99 Can

Book Three
THE SWORD AND THE FLAME
71631-3/ $4.99 US/ $5.99 Can